Circus

of the

Queens

The Fortune-Teller's Fate

Audrey Berger Welz

A Vireo Book | Rare Bird Books
Los Angeles, Calif.

T0161104

THIS IS A GENUINE VIREO BOOK

A Vireo Book | Rare Bird Books
453 South Spring Street, Suite 302
Los Angeles, CA 90013
rarebirdbooks.com

FIRST TRADE PAPERBACK ORIGINAL EDITION

Set in Minion
Printed in the United States.

10 9 8 7 6 5 4 3 2 1

Publisher's Cataloging-in-Publication data
Names: Welz, Audrey Berger, author.
Title: Circus of the queens : the fortune-teller's fate / Audrey Berger Welz.
Description: First Trade Paperback Edition | A Genuine Vireo Book | New York, NY;
Los Angeles, CA: Rare Bird Books, 2017.
Identifiers: ISBN 9781945572968
Subjects: LCSH Circus—Fiction. | Fortune-tellers—Fiction. | Acrobats—Fiction. |
Ballerinas—Fiction. | Soviet Union—History—Revolution, 1917–1921—Fiction. |
Russians—Fiction. | United States—History—1919–1933—Fiction. | Historical fiction. |
BISAC FICTION / Historical.
Classification: LCC PS3623 .E51 C57 2017 | DDC 813.6—dc23

To my loved ones, especially Gary
past, present, and future

It is said that the elephant is a cousin to the clouds
and has the ability to cause lightning.

—South Asian folklore

PROLOGUE

HE SAT ON TOP of the same horse in the exact same spot they had been standing the day he saw her for the very first time. He knew he was in the right place by the sound of the creek nearby and the way the tree next to him was split in two by lightning in a big storm that had hit the area the week before they met. The red-and-white wild roses mixed with dandelions and weeds covered the brush, overriding the smell of anything else, and over the years his feeling of aliveness depended upon the strength of that scent. It represented the memory of what he thought he was to her and who he thought they would become. It was the last time he felt really alive or would think of her that way.

The day before she left, they had taken vows, which he had thought were sacred. They had sworn their undying love, and he had expected it would last a lifetime. She had worn garlands in her hair and kissed him sweetly after expressing what she thought he would want to hear. It was a dream for her, a young girl's fantasy. However, in his mind's eye he had proposed and she had said, *Yes*.

When he had woken up the next morning, he had decided it was time for him to talk to her father and tell him their intentions. Yes, she was young, but he would wait. He knew he wasn't of their class, but he could offer her a place of honor and respect in society and he would worship her and take care of her for the rest of his life.

He tossed and turned that night and barely got a wink of sleep. An hour before sunrise, he put on his cavalry uniform, brushed his hair, and ran his hands over his cheeks as if to freshen them. He then looked at himself in his mirror with great approval, gathered his horse, and left.

The sun was shining brightly. The brisk morning air helped him wake up as he practiced the words he wanted to say. When he arrived at the house her father had rented, he noticed much of the furniture was out on the front lawn where the help was beating and airing it. A strange feeling started to grow in his stomach as if a serpent had found its way inside and was slowly nibbling away at his passion and joy. Wanting to hold onto hope and promise, he dismounted his horse and walked through the front door that was swung open wide. A maid was standing close by. Not wanting to accept the implication that this most likely had, he asked, "Where has the family gone?"

"They left early this morning to return home," she said.

Then the serpent swallowed his heart whole and that was the last he saw of it.

He wrote letters. All came back unopened. Not wanting to face the truth, he returned to their meeting place every day, and each day he waited in anticipation, holding his breath, believing and desiring more than any man should that his love would be there. She and her father would find they had made a terrible mistake, and that the only man for her was him.

His horse grew tired and bored of this ritual. He would pace, grunt, and snort as he was forced to stay with his master and appear to be as foolish as he.

The young man heard rumors from time to time from the lady maids of the house where she had stayed. And each story he heard seemed to add fuel to the fire and feed the serpent inside.

Wanting to stay close by in case she returned, the young man turned down positions that could have made him rich. Unlike him, she moved on with life and became a sensation. Granted, she was immediately sensational with or without him; he would never have waited for someone just ordinary. Nevertheless, over time he came to resent her finding happiness while he suffered and began to lose stature. It was whispered she was given gifts, sharing what she had learned from him, while he had been given not a thing. And all that he had thought and hoped would be his had gone to another man; even the son he had dreamed about who would so proudly carry his name.

Anger started to fester and boil over where there had once been love, and one day when he returned to their special spot, he realized even he couldn't bear his own foolishness any longer.

His horse started to snort as he normally did. Then he began to pace. Before he knew it, his master had torn a switch from a tree, and in one sweeping move of his hand, he removed the leaves. He slapped the right rear of the horse with the twig. The horse started to gallop, but that wasn't fast enough for the master. Not knowing where this would lead, the horse and the master continued until neither could take another step.

Both were drenched in sweat and delirious, so much so it took him several minutes to hear the woman who was speaking to him and for him to see where he was.

When he opened his eyes, it was as if he were in a dream. There was a small, colorful tent with a pig tied up outside and a woman with dark hair down to her waist with streaks of gray greeting him.

"You have traveled a long, hard path to find me," she said.

"I didn't know I was looking," he replied, uncertain if he was truly awake.

"Oh yes, you have been circling me for several years. I have been right in front of you, but you haven't seen me. I know why you are here. The serpent has told me everything."

Just then, the young man dismounted his horse and went to the woman and collapsed in her arms. Laying his head on her lap, he broke out in tears.

"There, my boy," the woman said, for he was still a boy to her. "Do not worry, you will get what is due you, for together we will put a curse on this one who has taken so much and this curse will extend to her loved ones."

The man and his horse were barely coherent and in that moment would have agreed to just about anything to ease the pain.

"Your curse will suffocate the serpent, but I have spoken to the serpent and he says he is full and is willing to die for you; however, only if you eat him after he is dead. He has asked to be made into a stew so that you can eat what he has taken from you. Now nod your head yes or no and we will make your decision so."

The young man and his horse were then fed the stew and they fell into a deep sleep. When they awoke, the woman was gone and the serpent's skin was lying next to him. The young man knew he would never return. He would live with the curse he had made in his sorrow, get back on his horse, and start riding north.

CHAPTER 1

Macon, Georgia, 1917

I COULD HEAR OUR tigers, Midnight and Satin, being loaded onto the train as I pulled my old purple shawl tighter around my shoulders and stretched my hands out toward the fire. Lately, Vladimir and I had been staying up into the small hours most nights. We'd take folding chairs over to the fire outside our carriages and watch the glow of the embers, tell stories, and play cards. We'd say it was the creaking of the big top in the wind that kept us awake, but it wasn't—it was our need to talk about our childhoods, our Russia, and remind ourselves that the memories we shared had once been our reality.

"Your mother was a great dancer, Donatella," Vladimir said that night when we'd turned over the last card and fallen silent. But then he frowned, as if he hadn't said enough.

"'Every move you make tells a story,' my mother would say. Then she would glide like a seagull through our front door to show me. All I ever wanted was to be her." I stretched my arms and sighed.

The circus had been in Macon the last few days and soon we'd be pulling out. Exhausted, I start to drift, as if I were floating on a raft through the evening sky. I take a deep breath and close my eyes. Memories surround me like fireflies and stars on a hot, moonless night. And through the sea of flickering lights I find myself seated on an overstuffed velvet chair in the parlor of my family's home in St. Petersburg, on an avenue lined with elegant houses, just like ours.

If I listen carefully, I can hear the *clop, clop* of steel on stone and the sound of squeaking wheels of late-night carriages going up and down our street. I can see the heavy gold-embroidered crimson curtain rise at the Mariinsky Theater, and feel the weight of my mother's soft hand, squeezing mine. It's spring and I'm wearing a silky dress dyed to match the rich violet-purple tulips blooming in our garden.

The orchestra is playing like it's dizzy, until each instrument finds its place and settles in. The theater is still, but not for long. The conductor walks out to a roar of applause, nods, and signals the musicians with a wave of his baton. Perfect notes surround me—Tchaikovsky's *The Queen of Spades*. What an odd coincidence, I think now.

"Take off my shoes; they're too big for you," my mother teased when we came home that night. The shoes she wore were sparkly, and I couldn't resist trying them on. How I loved the way she tickled my belly until I giggled so hard I threw them on the floor. "You could trip and fall," she said, laughing, "and then what kind of dancer would you be?"

She took out the hammered silver box that held her prized abalone hairbrush. Its swirls of iridescent blue brought out the color of my eyes, she said. Unwrapping it lovingly from its silk coverlet, she stroked my long, dark, wavy hair, one, two, three, a hundred times. As a child, that's how I learned to count.

❋ ❋ ❋

My name is Donatella Petrovskaya. I wasn't always with the circus. Born in St. Petersburg, I was christened Donatalia, and I attended the Imperial Theatrical School. I even studied under the great Cecchetti and performed at the Winter Palace while Grand Duke Sergei Alexandrovich played the flute. But that was before he went into hiding.

Chapter 2

Macon, Georgia, March 1917

"DO YOU REMEMBER WHEN you came to our house for New Year's dinner?" Vladimir asked, pulling me out of my dreamlike state. He liked to reminisce. Of course, I did, too. It was that pivotal moment in time that connected me to him. "Even then," Vladimir continued, "it was understood. You would become a dancer, a very good dancer, and I would walk in my father's footsteps and take over the most famous Russian circus. It was so clear back then."

I took pleasure in his words. They almost woke me up. Vladimir's family had owned the circus that was located near the Bolshoi and everyone in St. Petersburg wanted to be friends with them.

"I was so young, and your family seemed so grand," I said, thinking back. "After dinner, you showed me an album of circus pictures bound in a red leather cover. I was completely mesmerized. At the time, they seemed so exotic."

Vladimir was refilling his glass. My eyes wandered into the fire. Flames were leaping as were visions from the past. Vladimir had that effect on me. I was a young girl again, hearing the clink of glasses, my father's laugh, and my mother's sweet voice.

St. Petersburg, January, 1897

IT WAS NEW YEAR'S Eve, in the old czarist calendar. We were going to celebrate with the Vronskys. I'd been beside myself with excitement for a week. My mother had known Anton Vronsky since the time when, as a young ballerina, she'd spent a summer dancing in his circus's pantomime ballets—she told me how she'd paraded around the ring in a little cart pulled by four dogs. When he married, she became good friends with his wife, Lillya, a talented equestrian. Their son, Vladimir, was several years older than me. I didn't know him well, but I idolized him.

Papa had Alexi, our gardener and driver, hitch our Orlov Trotter, Chayka, to the sleigh and bring him around to the front of the house in the early afternoon. "We'll go out on the Neva while there's still light," he said. In the winter, the sun hardly rose above St. Petersburg's rooftops before it began to sink again. Already, the shadows were long and the snow on the street had taken on a violet tinge.

My father spent a lot of time tending to business, so it was a treat to have him around for a whole afternoon. It felt like a real holiday!

He lifted me up onto the carriage bench, and then handed my mother up beside me. Alexi, in the driver's seat in front, clucked to Chayka, and he trotted out briskly, his ears pricked forward as if he too were enjoying this outing in the snow.

St. Petersburg's social season was in full swing, and the streets were crowded with elegant sleighs like ours and long, flat drays pulled by shaggy carthorses, stacked with cut blocks of river ice destined to keep the caviar cold at hundreds of New Year's meals. We crossed the two canals before we finally reached the wide Neva. Trotters flashed past each other in front of the Winter Palace, pulling long, narrow sledges, their fur-hatted drivers perched on little coach boxes in front. Dashing young officers and the occasional adventurous young lady crouched forward on the narrow seat behind, lap rugs tucked around their legs.

"They call those sleds 'egotists,'" my father told us.

My mother laughed. "It seems to fit." She looked happy and very beautiful, her cheeks flushed in the cold, wrapped in her favorite flame-red cloak that matched the scarlet lipstick she always wore, a strand of dark hair blowing across her face.

Chayka danced and snorted at the sound of hooves behind him. My father had to grip the reins tightly to hold him as a troika flew past. A sharply dressed young officer urging his horses on had his arm around the waist of a slim girl beside him, the harness bells jangling furiously, their steel shoes throwing up a cloud of ice chips as they took great leaps. "The young fools," my father muttered under his breath, but I could tell he was more admiring than annoyed.

At the side of the Neva, some men were stacking and carving ice: a little ice cottage and a swan whose glassy wings were spread as if to take flight.

"Look at the skaters!" my mother said, leaning forward. Families glided sedately past, hands linked to form chains. A few young couples waltzed together as if on a ballroom floor, and a little apart from the rest, cutting graceful arcs into the smooth ice like a gull swooping over the sea, was a girl whose pale gray cape swirled around her like a cold flame. I turned back to watch her until she was only a faint blur in the blue twilight.

The double front doors and high-ceilinged, tiled foyer of the Vronskys' town house made me feel small. Everything seemed larger than life. The carved lion's paws on the old oak dining table's legs were gigantic and looked as if they were crouching, ready to spring. I couldn't stop staring.

The food—there was so much: bilinis and caviar, slices of radish, little plates of pickled herring, then came the rabbit and pheasant—but what I remembered most was the champagne glittering in the adults' glasses. The bubbles looked like grains of sand basking in the sunlight, almost too pretty to drink.

"To Nicholas and Alexandra, long may they rule!" They toasted.

I anxiously counted the forks, spoons, and knives by my place—*so many!* The plates were decorated with a mesh of raised rose-pink lines and little flowers where they crossed. Vladimir's mother, Lillya, smiled when she saw me run my fingers over the delicate glaze. "Those are made at the Imperial Porcelain Factory here in St. Petersburg," she told me. "Empress Elizabeth once ate on plates very much like these."

Lillya was slender and tall, with red-gold curls and the grace of a natural athlete. She seemed younger and more carefree than her husband, a man whose family tradition was to walk the high wire. He was kind with a somewhat sardonic air and a dry sense of humor.

My mother had told me stories of the Vronskys. "They are favorites of Empress Alexandra. Sometimes in the summer the empress invites Lillya to the Winter Palace, just to watch her white Lipizzaner stallion dance in the czarina's private garden. Then they sit under big umbrellas with iced drinks and play cards."

The light from the chandelier overhead sparkled in my crystal glass, but the sparkle that captured me the most was the glint in Vladimir's eyes when he smiled at me.

Our parents gossiped about dancers, circus people, even the royal family. I hardly heard most of it. I was trying too hard to keep track of the bewildering number of forks and spoons. But when I heard my mother telling the Vronskys about the ice carvers we'd seen, I looked up.

"A long tradition in our St. Petersburg, sculpting with ice on the Neva," Anton Vronsky said, turning toward my mother. "Surely you've heard of the accidental empress and the ice palace on the Neva?"

My father frowned a little—he never liked to hear the royal family criticized—but my mother ignored him, holding up her champagne glass and gazing at the little strings of bubbles rising in it instead.

Lillya, her eyes gleaming, began. "It was a very hard winter—seventeen forty, wasn't it? I suppose she wanted to distract her people from the cold. She certainly put on a grand show. Elephants and camels—"

Vronsky guffawed. "You're too sweet-minded, darling. It was a monstrous joke, plain and simple. She was angry with her Prince Michael for marrying an Italian Catholic. She'd already made him a jester, but that wasn't enough. She had a taste for matchmaking, and she got the idea into her head to marry him to her own servant, a Kalmyk hunchback."

"Good thing attitudes have changed," Lillya stated, her eyes flashing. "Your own mother is a Catholic Italian, isn't she?"

"Please tell me about the ice palace and the elephants!" I cried, forgetting my shyness, and Vronsky turned to me in some relief.

"The wedding was set for February, which happened to be the tenth anniversary of Anna's coronation. She had an architect supervise the construction—all made out of ice blocks, three stories tall, with ice statues decorating every room. Even the bed was carved of ice.

"The bride and groom were carried all around the city in an iron cage on the back of an elephant, in a parade of farmyard beasts as well as exotic animals. When they got to the ice palace, a guard was posted to make sure they spent the whole night inside. There was a stove, but I don't think it could have helped much. They both nearly died from the cold."

I shivered, thinking of that poor couple. Vladimir, sensing my distress, smiled at me and began talking about his favorite clown at the circus and the tricks they played on each other, and I soon forgot about everything else, basking in his attention.

After dinner, our parents sat down to play cards.

Vladimir and I sat on a small velvet settee in the corner and looked through an album of circus pictures. Then he showed me a small watercolor a patron had painted of his mother, dressed in a dark green riding costume and standing gracefully upright on her stallion's snowy back. "He's called Pluto Gaetana," Vladimir said. "The czar bought him from Emperor Franz Joseph especially for my mother. She says Pluto Gaetana is horse royalty."

I knew Vladimir was showing off. Still, I wished the evening would never end and I wondered when I'd see him again.

Outside the front door, Chayka was stamping his hooves on the snow, plumes of white streaming from his nose into the sharp night air. Some of the neighbors had stacked snowballs into pyramids in front of their houses, with candles flickering inside them. They gave the street an enchanted look.

My father wrapped my mother and me up in an enormous bearskin to keep us warm. Secure in my mother's arms, breathing in her soft fragrance, I tilted my head back to look up at the stars while she told me the names of the constellations and pointed out the planet Venus.

CHAPTER 3

St. Petersburg

THE DAY BEFORE MY universe split in two, my mother decided we'd take the carriage to Nevsky Prospekt. It had been a lazy, golden morning. Like most within our social class, my mother hid her jewels, but every once in a while when she got bored, to my father's great dismay, she would spread them all over her bed and rummage through them as though they were trinkets. At least, that's how I remember those bright hours as a child. The brooches, rings, and bracelets, and the little cameos on chains looked so delicious I wanted to eat them, but she dressed me in a beautiful gown and draped me in her jewels instead. If someone had told me I was a member of the imperial family, just then, I would have believed them.

There was one small, simple brooch the shape of a circle that had a little emerald in the middle. I told her it reminded me of the color of Vladimir's mother's eyes. "Funny," she said. "Lillya gave this to me. The circle represents love eternal. I don't think she'd mind if you had it. She said someone special gave it to her when she was a girl and it was best she pass it on. We'll leave it here for now." Then she scooped my necklace along with the rest of the jewels back into their wooden box and asked my father to have our carriage brought around.

When she told Mme Strachkov, my rather harsh governess, that I'd be excused from French and piano for the day, Madame opened her mouth to protest. But after one look at my mother's face, flushed with pleasure, she closed it again without a word. My mother had been pale and quiet for the last few days, quite unlike herself, and as gruff as Madame was, I could tell it worried her.

"We'll have tea, just like they do in England!" my mother said. "Then we can look at books at Schmitzdorf's. And you can help me choose flowers for the house."

My mother loved flowers more than anything, other than dancing and music. We spent hours together in the little garden she'd set aside for herself behind the house. Alexi kept a bigger vegetable garden—I loved to help him pick early peas, though he complained that not too many I picked ever made it into the house— but my mother's garden was only for beauty. She delighted in having the latest plants from all over Europe. Her English friend Winifred, whenever she went back to England, would bring seeds or cuttings for my mother: lupines, cottage pinks, shy violets, and the primroses. I was told a famous English gardener had bred them herself.

But my mother also adored Dutch bulbs and was always begging my father to ask his European business contacts to bring them over. "'Greuze,' they're called," she told me as she cut the deep-violet tulips in the little garden behind the house. "They're named after a French painter. Do you remember the painting we saw in the Hermitage—the one with the young girl in a lilac tunic? Well, when I saw the painting for the first time, I came home and ordered these bulbs from Holland immediately. Dutch tulips were the very latest thing then. When I saw them bloom, I knew you would have a dress of that color one day, too."

She laid the tulips in the wooden trug I held for her and then reached for some others with deepest purple streaks. "These are called 'Gloria Nigrorum'— 'Black Glory.' People thought they were 'broken,' because of the way the colors separate. It's a weakness, really, a virus that makes the streaks, but at one time they were rare and valuable." She laughed. "One rare tulip bulb was once worth nearly as much as a house. I read a story that a sailor ate a rare bulb thinking it was an onion—he could have sold it and fed the ship crew for a year." She stroked the petals with a little frown. "Funny to think it was really just a disease. Anyway, now they're only beautiful, but isn't that enough?"

In the house, she let me put the flowers in silver pitchers, dropping them in and letting them arrange themselves as they fell. I stroked the silky petals and buried my face in one to breathe in the faint scent. My mother laughed as she dusted the pollen off my nose. I cherished moments like this, when I had her to myself. She made me feel as if I were the only one in the world.

But on that June day we needed more flowers than my mother's little garden could ever hold. My father was a partner in a textile factory in St. Petersburg, the Petrovsky & Sutton Spinnery, and the next day he would be entertaining very important guests.

"Of course, Archie and Winnie will be here," my mother told me. Archie Sutton was my father's partner, a short, rather chubby English gentleman who wore spectacles as round as he was; his wife Winifred, my mother's best friend other than Lillya, was half his size with dirty blonde hair and always seemed to be somewhere else. Sometimes I played with their daughter Rosie, who was around my age. "There'll be another couple—the Bradleys, I think they're called. Imagine, they've come from right across the ocean! Your father hopes he can convince them to sell him their cotton exclusively."

My father, who'd just walked into the room, smiled at my mother. "I have high hopes for this meeting, it's true. George Bradley's said to grow the best cotton in Georgia. It will make our fabrics the envy of St. Petersburg. But no need to get worked up, Katya. I imagine this Bradley is a simple kind of man."

My mother leaned over toward me and spoke in a stage whisper, "Your father's idea of entertaining is a game of cards and a bottle of vodka, but *I* hear that Georgia planters are very genteel. And there's Mr. Bradley's wife to consider. We have to show them we're not all big, rough Russian bears like your papa."

My father laughed. "I don't think they'll mind if I'm a big Russian bear, my dear, as long as I'm a big Russian bear who will buy all their cotton. But you two go bring home all the flowers in Hertzner's, if you think it will help, and get yourselves something sweet. Archie says there's a new English confectionary just a few doors down—maybe you'll see Winnie there." Then he went off, whistling, to ask Alexi to harness Chayka and bring him round.

CHAPTER 4

I FELT SO ELEGANT, riding through the streets to Nevsky Prospect with the roof on the barouche pushed back. It was unusually sunny. I wore a hat to shade my face; I remember that it itched when I put it on. But I wanted to please my mother, and I was happy to see her feeling better.

We went to Schmitzdorf's first. My mother found a copy of Chekhov's new play, *The Seagull*, and some sheet music for piano from *Swan Lake*, and then she bought me a special collection of my favorite Russian fairy tales. We carried our presents to the tea shop next door where we sat at a little table. I turned over the pages of my new book, looking at the beautiful illustrations, wondering which story I would read first.

"Just think, we're drinking the exact same tea that Pavel, the proprietor, invented for the czar," my mother told me. "It's made with a fragrant citrus called bergamot and flower petals, and it came all the way from China on a caravan. These men take a very dangerous route by land and therefore tea of this quality is very scarce, so we must savor every sip."

The hot tea felt tickly going down my throat. Fascinated by the sensation, I didn't notice anyone approaching until a shadow crossed the illustration I had turned to.

My mother coughed to get my attention, as lightly as a butterfly flapping her wings. "Donatalia, let me introduce you to Mademoiselle Pavlova."

"Anna," the girl said, holding out her hand. I couldn't help gaping at her. Tall and thin, almost angular, her short dark hair held off her forehead with a deep red satin band, she seemed another breed from the neat, compact ballerinas I'd seen with my mother. This girl seemed so frail, yet I knew she was special.

Anna chatted politely with us for a few minutes, then left—she had to go buy some thread to mend her toe shoes, she said.

My mother watched her walk away. "Anna's been attending the Imperial Theatrical School since she was ten. You'll go there too. She's the one you'll study and watch." There was such certainty in my mother's voice. There was no maybe in her tone. Suddenly I saw my destiny laid out before me like a straight, clear, shining road.

When our teacups were empty and our pastries had been reduced to crumbs, we walked to Hertzner & Co., the best flower shop in all of St. Petersburg. The shopkeeper knew our family, and he bowed to my mother and shouted to his assistants, who brought out the freshest, most beautiful bouquets—lupines, lilies, roses, snapdragons—too many to fit in our little carriage. The owner clapped his hands and shouted to a man at the back of the store. Soon a cart was brought around, pulled by a donkey, ready to carry flowers to our house.

When we returned home, my mother and I filled the parlor and music room with blossoms of every hue. I lay on the floor, turning over the pages of my new book, and listening to my mother play a piece from *Swan Lake*.

I could not have been happier. But I was still a child, too young to see what awaited me.

❈ ❈ ❈

I'D ALWAYS LOVED IT when my mother tucked me in at night. "Are you in bed yet?" she'd call from the upstairs hallway. Each night, when I said yes, she'd come in to say good night as a different character. I don't think she even knew who or what she would be until she stepped through my door. One night she might lift her arms as if she were an animal standing on its hind legs. Or she'd open her mouth wide and blow as hard as she could. "I'm coming for you," she'd say and snort through her nose. Then, somehow, she'd shape her body until she looked like a dragon, or a dog, or a horse.

I'd hide under the covers, but I couldn't resist peeking, just as she made one last giant leap and bent down to kiss me.

"You were a dragon tonight," I might say. "I liked the way you spit out fire."

I was beginning to get too old for this, but neither of us were ready to let go of our nightly ritual.

"It's cold outside," she'd say. "I wanted to keep you warm. Now scoot on over." Then we'd say our prayers together and she'd make up stories or read one to me. Safe in the soft cloud of the rose scent she wore, I'd close my eyes and fall asleep.

On that night, my mother brought in the biggest bouquet of the flowers we'd bought and set it next to my bed. Then together we read from my new book, the story of the Frog-Tsarevna.

"During the long white days," she repeated to me, "they flew about on their fiery, beautiful horses…" My eyes heavy from all the excitement of the day, I closed them; then I jumped on one of their horses and rode it into my sleep.

When I looked to the left, Lillya was riding beside me, her red-gold hair flying behind her like a flame against the dark trees. Then the horses disappeared, and so did Lillya, and I was alone, surrounded by the scent of lilacs and orchids, lilies and roses. Suddenly a big wind howled, as if the man in the moon had exhaled all the breath he held in his cheeks, and he wasn't the same man I had known him to be. He blew the color right off the flowers until all that was left were the stems.

I screamed! My parents tried to comfort me, but I knew my world had shifted.

The following morning I was anxious. My head couldn't hold all my thoughts; so some just slipped out. "Papa, I think you're going to have learn how to make me breakfast."

"What a funny thing to say," he said.

"I need to meet Archie and prepare some papers for the Bradleys to look over," he told my mother. "I'll be back in good time—they'll be coming over at six." Then he grabbed his coat and hat and left.

Later that day, my mother went out for an afternoon game of cards with her friends. When my father returned, she still wasn't back. He paced back and forth in the drawing room, looking at his pocket watch. Despite his teasing earlier, he knew my mother's charm would do more than any number of flowers to win the Bradleys over.

It was nearly six when there was a knock at our front door. "There, it's the Suttons already," my father muttered. "Where on earth is Katya?"

Mme Strachkov went to answer the door, but instead of welcoming the visitors in, she called for my father to join her. Curious, I hid behind the banister and saw that the newcomers were two police officers.

"We're very sorry—there was nothing we could do," I heard them tell my father. I didn't understand, but by the look on my father's face and the tone of the officer's voice, I knew something was wrong. When my father shut the door, I ran to him. His face was white as paper.

"Your mama's appendix burst," he said.

"What is an appendix?" I asked, but he was too distraught to answer. It was Mme Strachkov who finally made me understand that my mother would never come home again. And it was Mme Strachkov who answered the door later, first to Archie and Winifred Sutton and then to the Bradleys, and quietly told them the news and sent them away. My father sat in a daze all evening, unable to answer the simplest questions.

That night, instead of going to bed with flowers and fantasies filling my head, I tried to imagine a world in which my mother wasn't there to brush my hair, teach me French, or make me laugh. That's how my father explained her death to me: "You'll have to live without your mother doing those things for you." It was a concept I couldn't grasp.

The next morning, I awoke thinking it had been a bad dream. I ran downstairs, hoping to see my mother in the kitchen. But instead there was my father, pouring me a bowl of Kasha for breakfast.

CHAPTER 5

St. Petersburg

OVER THE NEXT FEW days, all the flowers we'd filled the house with wilted and fell off their stems, just as they had in my dream. Sunk into his own misery, my father didn't seem to notice. Finally, Madame emptied all the vases and Alexi threw the flowers onto the compost pile. I asked my father where my mother had gone. "How could she disappear? And who is bathing and feeding her now that she is locked in a box covered in earth?"

My mother's death changed everything for me, but in some ways it changed nothing. She had long before decided how I would be raised: she would show me how to hold myself and move and would tutor me in French; Mme Strachkov would teach me to play the piano; and Papa would spoil me, as she expected him to. After she was gone, Madame and Papa carried out her wishes faithfully. Within several weeks, Madame was helping me with my French as well as teaching me piano.

Madame was a sturdy, squarish woman with a no-nonsense manner and a wooden leg. "Papa," I'd ask, "what happened to Mme Strachkov's leg?" He never told me, and I never found out.

Madame could be harsh, even while giving a compliment. When she first met me, she'd said, "I saw your mother perform before your father stole her from the world of dance." I'd thrown a fit. My father was not a robber. He was a respected man—I knew this by the way men tipped their hats when we met them on the streets. Only years later, when I was old enough to start my own career as a dancer, would I understand what Madame had meant.

Every day I conversed with Madame in French and practiced conjugating my verbs. Subjunctive was the hardest. Either way, my French lessons always segued to the piano. By the time I was nine, I had played Chopin for so many hours I thought he lived with us. Placing her hand on the small of my back, she'd beat out the time—*a one and two and three and four and one and two*—until I developed an internal clock. I don't remember which I disliked more, playing the piano with her pounding on my back or learning to speak formal French correctly.

I wasn't always kind to Madame. Curious to see if she would react, occasionally I'd kick her wooden leg. She'd pretend not to notice and continue our lesson as always. "Slowly, Donatalia," she would say. "You must feel Chopin run through your veins, and then, maybe, you'll be able to dance half as well as your mother did." But sometimes a shadow would cross her face.

Recently a memory came back to me. My mother and Madame were sitting at our kitchen table together. My mother was talking quietly to Madame, who was sobbing, her head buried in her hands. Madame, who hadn't seen me, cried, "It was only for some sausage and gingerbread, and a little enamel cup!"

I asked my mother later why Madame had been so upset. There'd been a grand banquet at Khodynka Field outside Moscow, she explained, to celebrate the coronation of Nicholas II. The people were promised gifts of food and commemorative cups. When rumors spread that the food might run out, and that each cup held a gold coin, there was a stampede. A cousin of Madame's was one of those who were trampled and died.

It was hard for me to imagine Madame having a cousin, or a mother or father for that matter. To me, she was just my Madame, always the same. For a few weeks I felt sad for her and did my best not to try her patience. But soon thereafter, I lost my mother, and all thoughts of other losses were swept away.

My father spent weeks sitting in his study, unable to face the world. But, finally, he began to think about his business again. The Bradleys were still in St. Petersburg exploring the culture of a city that must have seemed very exotic to them. Finally, in July, my father and Archie Sutton arranged to meet them at our house again, though this time the only flowers were a few I picked in my mother's garden. The tulips were long gone by then, but my eyes filled with tears as I remembered them. Madame wiped my face, made sure the samovar was filled, and sent Alexi out to buy French pastries for our guests.

George Bradley was a tall man with sandy hair, bright blue eyes, and a long, distinguished nose. His wife, Mary, had soft dark curls and a sweet smile and was very kind. "You poor thing," she said in her soft Southern voice, scooping me up in her arms.

The meeting went well, and an arrangement was soon reached: George Bradley would ship his cotton only to the Petrovsky & Sutton Spinnery. But as my mother had predicted, he was not very fond of the vodka my father proffered. Nonetheless, both men were happy that an alliance had been made between their two companies and the two men developed a genuine fondness for each other.

"A little strong for me," I could hear Mr. Bradley in the other room. "Give me a nice Sazerac any day, the way they make them in New Orleans."

"Now that's a lively place." Soon my father was being regaled with stories of that city—"my favorite, only after Savannah," George Bradley said. "Many's the friendly game of poker I've had there."

At that, Archie perked. "All the rage in England, these days, poker is. Why don't we have a hand? I'm sure Pelle will pick it up quick enough." Pelle was my father's first name in honor of his grandfather, Peter.

So while I took Mary Bradley out to the garden and showed her my mother's favorite flowers, my bear of a father got his game of cards in after all.

The Bradleys stayed in St. Petersburg into September and visited us quite often. I grew very fond of Mary Bradley, who always brought me a little gift. But more than that, she worked with me in my mother's garden and listened to me talk about her nonstop. And having a direct supplier of quality cotton, as my father had predicted, was a great boon to the factory, which prospered.

Actually, industry was booming all across Russia at the time, my father said, though these glory days were not without their shadows. The memory of the textile workers' strikes still troubled my father, and now workers were demanding shorter hours and higher wages. Of course, I was too young to understand this, but I overheard and listened to my father talking about the factory's troubles with Archie and George over cards.

At times, their conversation got a bit heated. "Well, it's easy to see that it can't go on the way it is," I heard Archie say at one point, after he'd had a little more vodka than he was accustomed to. "The spinners here work much longer hours than anywhere else in Europe and for wages that hardly keep them fed. What do you expect?"

My father bristled and spoke somewhat shortly to Archie. I wasn't used to hearing that tone of voice coming from my father, but I could tell that what they were discussing was on his mind and troubled him. It appeared that Archie was right; however, my father was not in a position to admit it and he was irritated. I could tell because he took out his pipe. This was the method he used to calm himself down. It was his coping mechanism.

* * *

FOR MY BIRTHDAY THAT year, my father bought me a pony. His name was Sasha, and he had belonged to our gardener, Alexi, who used to bring him to the house and keep him with our horses while he did his work. Sasha pulled a little cart carrying shovels and mulch and other garden materials for Alexi. When I overheard Alexi talking to my father about selling him—he wanted to get married and needed the money—I was heartbroken. Madame must have told my father about it, because in the middle of November he called me to his office.

He smiled at me. "I can buy you any pony you want for your birthday, my dear." He'd spoiled me even more ever since my mother's death, and he could afford it in those days. "Lillya Vronsky was talking about a pretty little gray mare one of Vladimir's friends has grown out of, much better bred than that shaggy little beast of Alexi's. Wouldn't you like to see her?"

But Sasha was the pony I had fallen in love with, I told him. I didn't care what kind of pony he was or what family he came from. I knew what I needed to know.

Sasha's eyes were so big and dark that I could see my reflection in them. The first time we met, I knew I could trust him. While Alexi turned the soil and planted our garden, Rosie and I would braid Sasha's black shaggy mane and tie ribbons into it. I don't think he liked it very much, but he tolerated it all the same.

Most Sunday afternoons, Archie and my father liked to kick a ball around in our garden.

Rosie, feeling a little left out, suggested we teach Sasha to play soccer, a big English sport that had made its way to Russia.

My father, of course, gave in and spent hours patiently schooling my pony. By the next weekend, Sasha knew how to bend his head down and butt the ball with his nose. He was a clever boy, that Sasha. I'm sure he was the first and maybe only pony in Russia to learn this new game.

* * *

St. Petersburg

IT WAS MY TENTH birthday—today was the day, if I showed promise and talent, that I would begin to fulfill my destiny. Finally, I was old enough to apply to St. Petersburg's famous Imperial Theatrical School. My father and I walked briskly through the busy streets, trying to stay warm, though that seemed impossible. The chill from the cold burned my face, and my nose was dripping little ice sculptures. We'd have been a little warmer in the buggy, but the streets were so congested and the buggy moved so slowly that I'd been afraid we'd be late. My father, worn down by my fretting, asked Alexi to stop and let us go on foot the rest of the way.

Even the sidewalks were crowded with pedestrians. Horses snorted and shied as a little horseless carriage rolled by slowly and fitfully, trailing popping sounds and a cloud of smoke. "A Benz Velo," my father told me. "Our old friend Vitaly was one of the first in St. Petersburg to have one."

An angry band of protestors was marching down the street, bringing the already slow traffic to a halt, carrying banners and shouting slogans about workers' rights. My father reached for my hand; I could tell they worried him, but I had decided the night before that I was too old for that. So instead I distracted him with nervous conversation about the sun and clouds. I was the sun in my father's life, and he had become my moon—not the scary moon, but the one that would safely cradle me through the world.

"Hurry, Papa. We're going to be late!" Forgetting about being too old, I grabbed his hand and dragged him forward through Ostrovsky Square. Pigeons wheeled around the figure of Catherine the Great towering at the center of the square. I tugged again toward the gold-and-white facade of the Alexandrinsky Theater, with the four bronze horses on its roof. Beyond it lay the calm, elegant symmetry of Rossi Street. The Imperial Theatrical School stretched along its entire left side.

"Calm down," said my father. "They're not expecting you until nine."

Inside, we stood in the high-ceilinged lobby, unsure what to do. Other children and their parents stood in line, waiting for their auditions; a girl about my age came out of the room they were waiting to go into in tears. I guessed that she'd been turned away. I thought we should join the line, but just then an elegant lady approached us.

"Are you Pelle Petrovsky?" she asked my father.

He nodded, at a loss for words.

"Follow me," she said. "Maestro Enrico Cecchetti would like to interview your daughter himself."

We followed her down a hall to an office, where an elegant balding man with a long, expressive mouth stood up and held out his hand to me. "So, you're my little Katya's daughter," he said. "I hope I'll teach you here one day, as I once taught her." He turned to my father. "I'm sorry for your loss. Your wife was a lovely dancer, and a favorite student of mine. I'm happy to see her daughter following in her footsteps."

He asked me to point my feet and do some stretches. I showed him some positions, the way my mother had taught them to me. Then he sent us along to the doctor's office, where my measurements were taken. I also had to write a few pages and do some mathematical exercises; the Imperial School taught all the academic subjects as well as dance. Finally, we were told I'd been accepted. My father filled out some paperwork.

As we walked back along the hall toward the lobby, I saw a flicker of flame red disappearing through a doorway. I imagined a faint whiff of roses in the air. Surely my mother was near, watching as I embarked on the life we had chosen for me.

CHAPTER 6

Imperial Theatrical School

I CLIMBED OUT OF bed slowly, every muscle complaining. I was stiffest in the cold early morning, feeling every set of port de bras exercises and every battement tendu I'd done the day before. I'd stay under the covers until the last possible minute, then rush to throw on my school uniform, scrub my face, and pull my hair back neatly before I heard the jingle of harness bells and impatient hooves outside. Every morning, Alexi harnessed Chayka to the little buggy and drove me to Rossi Street through the dark, icy streets.

How my life had changed! No more idle hours reading fairy tales. My days revolved around the Imperial Theatrical School and the endless work of becoming a dancer. In the evening, I'd eat dinner and fall gratefully into bed.

Each morning, I thanked Alexi, patted Chayka, and turned toward the doors of the school. Coincidentally, Bronislava Nijinska and her elder brother Vaslav seemed to arrive at the same time and were already pulling them open.

Bronia would smile when she saw me. We were both in Stanislav Gillert's beginning dance class and immediately felt a connection. She was a year younger and looked small next to the other girls, but she had already been studying for a year with Enrico Cecchetti before she entered the Imperial Theatrical School. I found that a little intimidating, but after our first lesson she'd confided that it was hard for her to follow the French terminology. That made me grateful for all the grueling French sessions I had had with Mme Strachkov. It made me feel more like her equal.

We climbed the marble staircase together, Bronia and I, to the second floor while Vaslav headed up one more flight to the boys' floor. Boys and girls were kept strictly apart except in school performances.

In the cloakroom, Bronia and I changed into the gray dance dresses all the students wore. Some of the girls complained about their color, finding them drab. But when I put mine on, I thought of that New Year's at the Vronskys' when we passed the young girl gliding and leaping on the frozen Neva, and I thought of how her gray cloak looked pale against the deep violet of the January dusk. Remembering how I'd ached to jump out of our carriage to join her that day, I spun around the dressing room. My dress flared out like hers did. And similar to the mysterious girl, the studio floor being my ice, I would glide and leap.

Later Bronia and I changed into the ankle-length brown skirt and long-sleeved blouse that was our school uniform. We'd eat in the lunchroom together and wash down our buns with hot tea and plenty of sugar.

We were very strictly supervised, and our manners had to be impeccable. Our forks and knives were lined up absolutely straight; later in life I could never get used to seeing forks and knives laid on a table any which way. At least, I thought, remembering that New Year's dinner with the Vronskys, there were many less knives and forks to worry about. We bowed to our teachers when we were approached and were told we looked like peasants if we used our arms when we spoke.

After lunch—before we began our afternoon classes: writing, history, mathematics, and science—we were allowed to walk around for a while in the school's small inner courtyard. This was when Bronia and I found time to talk. Walking side by side, we would go over our morning lessons and the exercises we had trouble with—Bronia was a great perfectionist and often worried when her leg or foot refused to behave exactly as she wished. At first, we didn't speak much about our life outside the school, though she talked about her brother Vaslav occasionally. He was high-spirited and mischievous at home, chasing a wooden block around with a broom—a game that had resulted in more than one broken window. Bronia adored and fretted about her brother in equal parts. Although he was stronger and more talented than most, the other boys often teased him about his strong Polish accent and his Tartar features—high cheekbones and slanted eyes. Some of the boys called him "the little Japanese" and made his life difficult.

Bronia and I would gossip about our teachers or the older students. It was Bronia who told me that the great Cecchetti's mother had given birth to him in a dressing room in Rome. I felt sorry for his mother, but it was hard not to giggle at the idea, too. Still, Bronia had the deepest respect, almost awe, for Cecchetti.

At the end of each day, Alexi came and fetched me and brought me home. I'd hardly have energy for dinner before I fell into bed, exhausted, and each new morning I'd enter the studio wondering what the day would bring. I worked hard, and eventually I too graduated to Maestro Enrico Cecchetti's class. Cecchetti was not only passionate about dance, but he knew how to pass that passion on to his students. When he guided me with his hands to show me a step, I could feel the electricity of his fervor running through my body, and I'd find myself breaking out in a sweat.

Cecchetti was a brilliant dancer himself with his leaps and multiple pirouettes. I remembered my mother telling me about the day she saw him dance as the Bluebird in *Sleeping Beauty* at the Mariinsky. "Oh, my little Donatalia, what a sensation he was! The crowd had never seen anything like it." At that time, the men in dance had really just been props for the ballerinas. Enrico changed all that. How proud I was to be taught by such a man. "It was the hardest decision I ever made, to give my dancing up." Looking at me, she seemed to recollect herself. "Oh, but then you came along. The moment I first saw you, I could never wish for anything else." When it came to ballet, my mother and I had some very grown-up conversations.

Now, under the spell of Cecchetti's teaching myself, I wondered if my mother had really been telling the truth. I dreamt of the day that he would teach only me, as he had my mother. Surely, she had sometimes mourned her dancing days, no matter how much she loved my father and me.

Cecchetti's method was grueling, designed to work every muscle. He had a set of exercises for each day of the week so that every part of the body would be strengthened but not stressed by too much repetition. But even this system could not always prevent the cramps in my legs. At times, I felt like an old woman, barely able to climb the stairs, but then I would hear Enrico's voice whispering in my ear, "Let none of the effort of your labor be visible," and I would straighten myself up and move as if I had just started my day.

I was learning that there were no shortcuts in becoming a dancer. When I felt sorry for myself, I'd think of Anna Pavlova to whom classical ballet did not come easily. She was turned down the first time she applied to the Imperial Theatrical School. Her high arches and thin ankles made the work harder for her, and the other students teased her and called her "the Broom" and "little savage." I'm certain, though, she had the last laugh when she was promoted to prima ballerina.

At home, I'd ask Madame to make me bergamot and citrus tea. Inhaling its fragrance, I'd remember the first day that I met Anna and the next morning, I'd get up and start all over again.

The classes continued and I improved, and over the years I found my place.

❋ ❋ ❋

"IT'S AS IF SHE'S inhabited her mother's body and made the dance steps her own." Mme Strachkov spoke to my father as if I weren't there, though I was standing right next to her in the lobby of my school. But still, there was truth in her words. Despite the changes in my body, I was developing an aesthetic and ease.

I had counted every step it took, every position, leap and spin that got me to this place. I'd finally been chosen as prima ballerina in a recital at the Imperial School of Ballet. How I wished my mother could have been there to see me!

It was spring, the air fresh and invigorating. Snow was dripping off the roofs of the buildings, forming puddles that my friends and I had leaped over, competing to see who could jump farthest without getting her feet wet. But now, here I was flanked by Mme Strachkov and my father, greeting a line of well-wishers, acting grown up.

I hardly heard Madame's words—I'd just noticed Vladimir and some of his friends standing in line to pay their respects. He had grown into a young man: slim, with a decisive square chin, steel-blue eyes, and the same grin, only wider, that could make you think you were the only one in the world.

Vladimir was the boy every girl wanted as her boyfriend. His family was famous, and he was already becoming a bit of a celebrity himself. But I was too young for him to take seriously—he thought of me as the young daughter of his parents' friends. Still, he had a kind, playful way of talking to me that made me feel special. We had something in common, too: both of our mothers had been celebrated in their own way, mine as a dancer and his as an equestrian.

"Congratulations," he said when he reached me. "Now you're in company with the best." He was right. Russian ballet had finally surpassed the French. It was an exciting time. Prince Sergei had taken over as the director of the imperial theaters, and Anna Pavlova and Michel Fokine were international stars. Russia was training the best dancers in the world. Many of them came from our ballet academy. I was considered one of those dancers now, and the doors of the world were about to swing open for me.

❄ ❄ ❄

DURING THOSE SCHOOL YEARS it seemed as if I was losing my father through no fault of his own. My thoughts revolved entirely around dance and dancers. And with the egotism of youth, I spent my time chattering about nothing else. It pains me now to think how little I noticed the slump in his shoulders and the shadows under his eyes.

As constant as the sun rotating the earth, I spent my days practicing perfect pliés while political unrest was lengthening across my country. Times were growing harder, and strikes among the factory's workers became more frequent and strident.

❄ ❄ ❄

THE NEW YEAR OF 1905 brought with it a revolution. On January 22, the czar's army shot and killed five hundred protesters who were taking their grievances to the Winter Palace. In February, the grand duke was assassinated. By May, as the flowers in my mother's little garden began to unfurl their silky petals, the gravity of the situation couldn't be denied any longer.

My father was afraid for me. "Innocent people are getting hurt, even killed," he argued. "I lost your mother. I have no intention of losing you to violence." Then he reminded me of Grand Duke Sergei, who had recently been blown to bits by an assassin. I didn't want to hear it; I was happy where I was. I would become a prima ballerina. My father listened patiently to me. I could stay through the summer, he said. But if things hadn't settled down by then, I wouldn't be going back to the Imperial Ballet School that fall. To protect me, he'd have to send me away. I'd be on an ocean liner instead, headed for the New World.

CHAPTER 7

En route to Hamburg

WHEN I THINK BACK to those first days on the ship, I can still feel the rolling of the sea. I could barely keep food down, and the stale air in my cabin made me dizzy.

My father traveled with me on the first leg of the journey on a small passenger ship from St. Petersburg to Hamburg, where the great ocean liners set off for the New World. He said he had a supplier to meet there, but I think he just couldn't bear to let go of me until the last possible moment.

I stayed in my cabin with a washcloth over my eyes for most of that first day, until my father came and knocked on the door. "Come walk on the deck, Donatalia," he said. "The sea air will do you good." I was an obedient daughter, so I went with him, but I stubbornly kept my eyes on the sea, refusing to look at him as he tried to tell me about the wonders of the SS *Amerika*. I knew he must have been working on this plan for months behind my back, and that sharpened my indignation. I couldn't forgive him for tearing me away from my life in St. Petersburg, my friends, my dreams as a dancer.

"She's a queen of the seas—a floating palace." His voice sounded distant through the fog of nausea and resentment that clouded my mind. "There's an à-la-carte restaurant made to look just like the Carlton, in Pall Mall—on a smaller scale, of course. From morning to midnight, you can order anything that takes your fancy. There's even an electric passenger elevator—the first ever on a ship."

I couldn't think of anything to say. The way I felt then, nothing a restaurant afloat could offer would ever tempt me. And what would I, a dancer in the prime of youth, want with an elevator?

I stopped and turned toward the railing, and for a while we both looked silently out over the leaden sea. Finally, he cleared his throat. "Catherine lives in a very good neighborhood. I think you'll be happy there." Catherine was the sister of an old family friend, and she'd invited me to stay with her in New York. She'd always been kind enough, but my image of her was hazy; she was a colorless woman, the kind who fades into the background.

"She's looking forward to seeing you—I think she's a little lonely. You can continue your studies there. I'll wrap up my business affairs in St. Petersburg as soon as I can, and perhaps I'll join you there next year." He smiled tentatively, his eyes pleading for me to understand, to believe him. "We'll find a place in the neighborhood and make a happy life for ourselves. There are plenty of business opportunities in New York. I've arranged for you to study with Olga Preobrajenska."

Olga had trained under Marius Petipa before he retired—or was forced out for political reasons, as rumor had it in the halls of the Imperial School.

"I'm afraid, the way things are going, it's too risky for you to return to Russia until things settle down." *Settle down?* Despite my resentment, I almost smiled at that; my father was an incurable optimist. "But she spends time in Paris every summer. If you do well in your lessons, we'll travel to Paris together next summer. You'd like that, wouldn't you?"

I nodded. Although I was heartbroken to leave St. Petersburg—never again to visit my mother's grave—and the Imperial Theatrical School, the idea that I might someday dance in Paris felt like a patch of blue sky among gray clouds.

I knew I wasn't the only one leaving. Many other artists and aristocrats were leaving Russia at this time. There was a rumor that some of the dancers at the Imperial Ballet—Anna Pavlova, Vaslav Nijinsky, Michel Fokine, and Tamara Karsavina among them—were thinking about striking. They were angry at the way Petipa had been treated; they wanted higher salaries, a five-day workweek, and the right to choose their own company directors. Within the next few years, Anna, among others, would abandon the International Russian Ballet entirely.

I couldn't admit it to myself, much less to my father, but I knew he was right to send me away. My beloved St. Petersburg had become a scary place. The anger and desperation of the farmers and factory workers had reached a boiling point. The strikes at my father's textile factory were becoming more bitter and frequent. Poor Mme Strachkov, who had already lost her beloved cousin and was torn between our world and her family's, was now too frightened to leave the house at all. Her wooden leg made her vulnerable, and she was afraid because she could not run.

But I didn't want to hear the rumors of change. I could see nothing beyond my dreams, the dreams my mother had left and given me.

❋ ❋ ❋

THE NEXT MORNING, A knock on my cabin door woke me. "Come out, Donatalia! We're steaming into Hamburg."

The sun was just emerging from behind the clouds, casting light on the port's warehouses and cranes. There were ships of all sizes and kinds.

"The third largest port in the world," said a man with ginger sideburns, leaning on the rail next to us. "All of Europe comes here, to trade or to travel." He pointed out what he called a "windjammer," a tall ship with big square sails on its five masts, sailing out the harbor. "It's on the way to Australia. In the spring it will circle back, all the way around Cape Horn."

As we walked down the gangplank, I could feel the energy of this crossroads of Europe, with its throngs of merchants, seamen, poor immigrants, and wealthy travelers. We made our way out, crossing a little arched bridge over a canal, through the cobbled streets to the inn where we'd stay the night. There, we dined on minced steak and potatoes. A boisterous group of Swedish travelers lined the benches at the one next to ours. Well lubricated with good German beer, they began singing drinking songs. Their joyful spirit made our table seem even quieter. I simply listened silently to my father but had nothing to say.

As we climbed the worn wooden stairs to our rooms, I suddenly had an impulse to throw my arms around his neck, as I had as a child. But my resentment was still too strong. In the end, I only said, "Good night, Papa," and closed the door behind me.

❋ ❋ ❋

IN THE MORNING, THE innkeeper's wife served us a hearty German breakfast before we made our way back to the port. I glanced over at my father, who looked tired and worried. I remembered that freezing spring day when I'd dragged him through Ostrovsky Square, heedless of the demonstrators. So much had changed. Suddenly, I had an impulse to reach for his hand. But then he looked up, his face cleared, and he pointed to a ship in the harbor. "Isn't she amazing," he said.

The *Amerika* was vast—more than an eighth of a mile long—a city on the water, with her four masts and two huge funnels, and her white decks stacked like a layer cake. The pier was abuzz with activities and family members embracing each other in teary or jovial goodbyes.

My father wanted to escort me to my cabin, but I wouldn't let him. I knew I was being cruel, but I couldn't help myself. "If I'm grown up enough to make this trip on my own, I might as well start practicing now," I said. Then I looked up into his sad eyes and I let him hug me. I buried my face in his fine wool overcoat, which smelled of the sweet pipe tobacco he loved, and washed my face with tears.

A steward took my trunk for me, and I followed him up the gangplank. At the top, I asked him to take the trunk to my stateroom. I found an empty spot along the crowded railing of the passenger deck and looked for my father. He was easy to find in his formal black coat, white waistcoat, and dapper top hat, his face lifted toward me and his hand raised. I leaned over the railing as far as I could and waved at him.

The whistle blew, steam billowed from the funnels, water churned white behind the ship, and the pier began to slide away. My father grew smaller and smaller. Suddenly I felt a stab of regret. All those hours walking on the ship, our dinner in Hamburg—I'd wasted the last time I had with him, trapped in my own resentment. Now he was only a speck on the pier, lost in the crowd, and we were both all alone in the world.

❋ ❋ ❋

When finally I turned away from the rail, my eyes were watering once more; I told myself it was the sting of the salt spray. A ship steward approached me and asked for my name. He ran his finger down a long list of names on the sheaf of paper he held. "We're carrying over four hundred passengers in first class, miss," he said, "not to speak of tourist class and steerage. Ah, here we are…on the bridge deck, miss. A very nice cabin."

I followed him up a sweeping flight of steps, along a corridor, up some narrower stairs, and along a broad deck. At last he opened a door. "Here you are; that's your trunk, right, miss? There's a bell on the wall here—ring it anytime, for anything you need."

I nodded and walked past him through the door. It *was* a lovely cabin. The bed was tucked into a little curtained alcove and made up with soft snowy sheets. There was a mahogany fold-up washstand with a mirror above it and a desk with stationery laid out and ready to use. A ship employee had already shaken out my clothes and hung them up.

As soon as I was alone, I sat down, dipped the pen on the desk in the inkwell, and pulled a piece of *Amerika* stationery toward me. "Cher Papa," I wrote. It took me twice as long to write in French as it did in Russian, but I had nothing else to do. Father had warned me not to speak to strangers, so I didn't intend to make any new friends. I'd study old French textbooks on the ship to pass the time and to prepare myself for this new destiny.

"I will do what you told me to do," I wrote, "but I am already sad and lonely. There is no room to dance and move, and your laughter is already beginning to sound like a faint echo. I'd rather be home with you, practicing my routine and playing soccer with my poor dear Sasha. Please give him an apple and tell him I miss him!" These words passed a little time, but they didn't nearly express the depth of my feelings. My Russia was fading away, more unreachable with each passing wave.

I wondered what Catherine might look like now. Certainly, she wouldn't recognize me; I had been a little girl the last time she had seen me. I tried to think about my destiny and everything new that my father had arranged, but instead of looking forward, all I could do was look back.

✻ ✻ ✻

THE LIGHT THROUGH MY stateroom window was growing dim. For a moment, I thought about trying to find the dining room, or at least a saloon where I could ask for a cup of tea, but the vastness of the ship intimidated me, and I didn't want to ask anyone for directions.

I rummaged through my trunk for my book of Russian fairy tales, the book my mother had bought me on the Nevsky Prospekt. Then I changed into a nightdress, curled up on my bed, pulled the cord to light the electric sconce on the alcove wall, and drew the curtains. I let the book fall open to the story of the Sea King and Vasilisa the Wise.

I read a few pages and fell asleep. In my dreams, I was alone in our sleigh, trotting along the Neva, past the skaters and the ice carvers, then up onto a soaring bridge of ice, just like the crystal bridge Vasilisa built for the Sea King in a single night.

CHAPTER 8

The Voyage

THE SUN WAS ALREADY high when I woke the next morning. My seasickness had passed; the *Amerika* was so huge that the ocean's movement could hardly be felt. My appetite back, I rang the bell the steward had shown me, and within minutes a neatly dressed young lady knocked on the door. Of course she could bring me breakfast in my room, she said, handing me a menu printed in English and German. I knew just enough of both languages to get by, but the choices were bewildering: fried bananas, "Beefsteak à la Tatar," calf's liver with bacon and onions… In the end, I ordered potato pancakes with cranberries and Russian sardines. There'd be plenty of time to try American food later.

The day stretched before me like a featureless desert. I wandered around the halls and decks aimlessly. On the ship's main deck there was a giant grandfather clock. I spent hours staring at it. The pendulum had a hypnotic effect on me. Its monotonous swing back and forth seemed to outweigh my own impulses and thoughts; minutes were passing, it reminded me, and eventually my life would go someplace.

Finally, I made my way to an elegant ladies' salon where everything was upholstered in pink. I ordered a hot tea to pass the time and warm me up, and perhaps take a bite out of my own attitude. Still, the minutes went slower than I ever expected they could. An hour felt like ten. I could see that the ship was beautiful, and I tried to admire it. But my eyes were not ready to open and my heart was not ready to take it all in.

❊ ❊ ❊

FOR THE NEXT FEW days I followed the same routine. When the ship stopped at Dover, I went on deck to get a glimpse of the famous white cliffs, but at Cherbourg I only looked out my window as the new passengers boarded. I had breakfast in my cabin every morning, then read or worked on my French exercises. When I tired of my room, I ventured out to the ladies' saloon for a cup of tea or a sandwich, then walked the decks for exercise. I avoided the eyes of the other passengers strolling past me or lounging on deck chairs. I didn't want to speak to anyone.

In the evenings, I ate a sandwich in my room and played solitaire. My father had given me a deck of cards printed in St. Petersburg as a parting gift. The famous Russian officer, author, and artist Nikolay Karazin designed them. I knew his name because my mother used to read his children's book *Cranes Flying South* to me. I spent more time looking at the cards than playing. When I picked up the king of hearts, with his gentle face and royal scepter, I bit my lower lip and thought of my father.

❋ ❋ ❋

ON THE FOURTH MORNING, the sun sparkled through the sheer net over my cabin windows. I spent a little more time on my morning toilette and realized I was growing tired of my self-imposed exile. By lunchtime, the rumble in my stomach convinced me to look for the à-la-carte restaurant my father had boasted of. I'd never been to the Ritz Carlton in Pall Mall, but I could believe that the dining room the steward led me to was just like it. A huge rose-colored Art Nouveau skylight flooded the room with light. The fresh-cut flowers on the tables with bright snapdragons reminded me of our garden.

I ordered a chicken salad sandwich with melon and trimmed off the crust of my bread with my knife, as Madame always did for me. A sharp-faced Russian woman at the next table asked me how I could be so wasteful. "Think of all the starving people in our country," she said. "For some of those poor wretches in steerage, that would be a meal."

When I returned to my cabin, I crawled under the covers and wished all my misfortune away. But I kept hearing the voice of the woman I sat next to at lunch. *Think of the people below.* Wanting to block her out, I got up and opened the stateroom window and I listened to the wind whistling lonely Russian folk songs while blowing across miles of empty ocean.

I began to count. It was something I did whenever I was unhappy or had a thought I wanted to push out of my head. I had reached 8,003 when I was startled by a knock at the door. I opened it to find a young man dressed in a stiff cabin boy's uniform, and looking decidedly awkward, he handed me an envelope. I opened it and drew out a thick cream-colored card; on it, in peacock-green ink, an elegant scrawl: *Would Madame Petrovska do Captain Knuth the inestimable favor of being his guest at his table in the main dining salon that night?*

"Tell Captain Knuth I'd be delighted," I told the cabin boy and looked through my purse for a coin to press into his hand. As soon as he'd gone, I splashed my face with rosewater, as my mother always had. It made me feel close to her. Today I felt she was smiling down on me. I changed the ribbon in my hair several times before I finally settled on the royal-blue satin that reminded me of the sea at Odessa.

I had been prepared to sulk the entire trip, maybe even the entire year; yet despite myself, I found the corners of my lips turning up. How exciting it would be to sit in the grand dining salon at the captain's table!

I imagined the clinking of glasses, the hum of conversations, elegant ladies whispering intriguing secrets. There'd be an orchestra melting into the floorboards, and maybe even a mysterious boy staring at me from across the room. I gave myself a mischievous grin. My father would be shocked to hear my thoughts. But I was alone, and I believed I deserved a little indulgence.

❋ ❋ ❋

THERE WERE HOURS TO pass before dinner, so I decided to take a walk. On deck, I saw a family playing charades. We used to play that game at home and at parties, so I stood off to the side where I could watch them without being noticed and began to play along, too. They were trying to act out the story of the Firebird. Without thinking, I began to dance. When I glanced up, I felt my cheeks turn bright red. I'd caught the eyes of a handsome gentleman, who was smiling directly at me. I quickly straightened my dress and hair, nodded, and walked briskly back to my room with as much dignity as I could muster.

He must be at least twenty years older than you! I scolded myself, but I was already taken by his bright hazel eyes, and his challenging smile. I might have been a sulky, unhappy girl, but I was a teenager nonetheless, and I couldn't help but act like one. I didn't expect to see the man again; however, the encounter had put a smile on my face and shaken me out of my gloom.

Without my knowing, my father had taken several of my garments to one of the best dressmakers on Nevsky Prospekt before we left and had them outfit me with everything I'd need for an elegant ocean crossing. "Make sure she'll look the part in New York City, too. We want everyone to see that we know how to dress in St. Petersburg," he told the dressmaker.

Madame, a more practical kind of lady, warned me to dress conservatively on the crossing and save my finery for New York. "A real lady doesn't draw attention to herself on board. One modest dinner gown, a walking skirt, and two or three shirtwaists are all you should need. Oh, and some sensible shoes for walking on deck—I know it's a big ship, but it's still a ship on the ocean, and you don't want to risk a fall. Oh, and pack plenty of wraps, the sea breeze gets chilly, especially after the sun goes down."

I just nodded. Finery was the last thing on my mind. I was still in shock and miserable at the thought of leaving and hardly noticed the clothes my father was so proud of. But now, as I was about to step out, I was glad for my father's forethought and pushed Madame's voice out of my mind.

I pulled out a long velvet dress in a pale yellowish green. It had a wide square neckline and was trimmed with gold brocade and abalone buttons. Over it, I wore a short satin cape the color of heavy cream, edged with fur dyed to match the color of Siberian pine needles. I fastened a simple strand of pearls around my neck, and at the last minute I pinned the simple circle brooch with the small emerald to the dress's bodice. It once belonged to Lillya, Vladimir's mother, who then gave it to Katya, my mother. How I hoped some of their charm and charisma would be channeled through the stone and cast an aura around me. I glanced in the mirror. Feeling satisfied, I took a deep breath, opened the door, and waited to see what the evening would bring.

CHAPTER 9

WHEN I CLOSED THE cabin door behind me, it was as if I were seeing the ship for the first time. How could I not have noticed the paintings in their gilded frames, the soft green walls, the leather club chairs, the skylights in the high ceilings, and the beautifully painted filigree mirrors? I looked at my reflection and was surprised to see a young woman staring back at me. Had this happened in these few short weeks?

My heart started to pound when I entered the dining room. At the head of a long central table stood a distinguished gray-haired man with a friendly, weathered face waiting to greet me. Introducing himself as Captain Knuth, he gallantly gestured to the chair beside him. All around the table, other passengers were taking their seats, the men in formal suits and the women in simple but elegant evening gowns. I silently thanked my father for insisting that he buy me new clothes for the journey.

With its high ceiling, crystal chandeliers, and decorative balcony, the room looked like a grand ballroom. Candles flickered softly down the center of long tables, making the crystal sparkle.

An orchestra was playing, and waiters in white uniforms were running about carrying silver trays. The captain introduced me to the table. Every seat had been taken except for one—the chair next to me. The captain glanced at it, then caught my eye and shrugged. I leaned over to read the card: "M. Hervé Fleury." I hoped my neighbor would show up; perhaps I could practice my French.

We'd just been served beet soup with parsley and sour cream when a voice begged my pardon, and someone pulled out the empty chair next to me. Turning, I found myself looking into the same hazel eyes I'd seen that afternoon. I could feel my cheeks getting hot. Seeing the mischievous gleam in his eyes, I couldn't help but wonder if M. Fleury had arranged to be seated next to me.

He glanced at the music program on the back of the menu and smiled. "It looks as if I may be just in time," he observed. "They're playing a French waltz, *Toujours ou jamais*, always or never." Leaning toward me flirtatiously, he murmured, "I'll hope for *toujours...*"

I knew he was being very forward, but his playfulness set me at ease, and soon we were chattering away in a mixture of English and French, hardly paying attention to the courses being placed before us one after another. M. Fleury lived in the countryside near Paris, he told me, where he bred, trained, and sold horses. He was on his way to America on a buying trip, looking for new stock. "They're breeding some very good Thoroughbreds in Virginia," he said.

I told him about my pony Sasha and our dapple-gray Orlov Trotter in St. Petersburg, and his eyes lit up. "Oh, you're from St. Petersburg? There's no more beautiful city, no? At one time I had hoped to live there myself." He paused and gazed out into the distance, as if he were seeing some faraway place. Then he seemed to recollect his manners and began asking about my life in St. Petersburg. I told him I was a dancer and that my father was sending me away because of the political unrest at home.

"He promises me he will take me to study in Paris in a few years," I said. M. Fleury seemed to know all about the Imperial Ballet, and his interest was so flattering I found myself telling him about my recital at the Winter Palace where I danced with my friend, Vladimir Vronsky. I realized at once that the subject was a mistake. As soon as I said Vladimir's name, my stomach started doing flips just as it did whenever he was near. I looked down at my plate, hoping M. Fleury wouldn't notice.

Wanting to change the subject without being too abrupt, I began telling him about Vladimir's mother instead. "Lillya Vronsky, Vladimir's mother, is a celebrated horsewoman—you might have heard of her. Her husband is a tightrope walker, and together they own the most famous circus in all of Russia, the Vronsky Family Circus."

M. Fleury was silent for a moment, apparently concentrating on removing a tiny bone from his fillet of sole. "I think I've heard that name before," he said finally, "though I can't recall exactly where." I suspected he was just being polite, but nevertheless he listened attentively and asked in detail more than I could answer. He asked about Lillya's riding, the breeding of her horse, about her husband, and how the circus was doing in these changing times. *He has very good manners*, I thought, *showing such an interest in me and my friends.*

I didn't need a lot of encouragement to talk. I hadn't had a real conversation with anyone in days, and since the captain had invited me to his table, I could tell my father I was only being polite. Sooner than I wished, coffee and after-dinner drinks were being served.

M. Fleury asked if he might have the privilege of being seated next to me again the following evening, I quickly said yes. I didn't want to think about it too much. Besides, he had charm, and when he spoke I got goosebumps on my arms.

※ ※ ※

THE NEXT MORNING, I woke up, threw some water on my face, brushed my hair, and pinned it up in a twist. I practiced my French and studied my books, looking for phrases I could use that evening in conversation. I knew M. Fleury was too old for me and I too young for him, but that fact didn't stop the butterflies I got thinking about the dashing figure he cut in a morning coat. He was entertaining, yes, and when I spoke with him I could almost pretend I wasn't as miserable and upset as I had convinced myself.

Before going to lunch, I went through my wardrobe, thinking of what I might wear to dinner. I settled on a soft lavender dress, remembering how M. Fleury had talked about the lavender fields in the South of France.

The sharp-faced Russian woman chose to sit next to me again. I'd wished she was anywhere else, but I could hardly say so. Almost immediately she started talking again about "the people below."

"Do you mean in the third class?" I asked. "They have more modest accommodations…"

She started to laugh sarcastically. "Modest! They're packed in like sardines—and are mostly peasants, Jews, poor Europeans. Many are just trying to escape conscription into the czar's army. Others are looking for a better life because the work conditions in the factories are so bad. Textile mills are the worst."

I opened my mouth about to argue; surely my father cared about the people who worked for him. But I realized I had little real knowledge of his factory—I'd never really thought much about my father's business. And I couldn't help remembering some of the things I'd heard Archie say. *And for wages that hardly keep them fed…* Besides, admitting that I was a daughter of a factory manager would hardly improve her opinion of me.

Wanting to prove her wrong, I asked the waiter for two more sandwiches and an apple. "If you would, please wrap them in a cloth for me," I said. "I'd like to eat in my cabin."

He looked at me oddly. He must have thought I was really hungry. I didn't usually lie, but somehow in this situation it seemed all right.

For several hours, I paced along the promenade deck, carrying the little bundle of sandwiches, trying to work up my nerve. I stopped to watch other passengers playing shuffleboard and children skipping, and I visited the grandfather clock to make certain time continued to move forward. I approached the stairs straight ahead and looked left and right before quickly taking two flights down to the second-class deck; then, collecting my courage, I inched my way slowly down another flight.

It was the chill from the ice-cold rail that woke me up and pulled me out of the dream I had been living in. I looked down and saw a mass of people huddled together, trying to stay warm. Some were lined up on benches by a long table, eating bowls of something, perhaps cabbage soup. The smell rising from their quarters was mixed with a faint odor of urine and vomit.

I realized how absurd it was for me to offer them two sandwiches and an apple. What had I been thinking? And how would I choose which of these hungry people to give them to? By now dozens of faces were turned upward, staring at me. Alarmed, I began to step back up the stairs and ran right into a middle-aged man who tried to take my arm. I didn't know if his intentions were good or evil, but I kicked out at him, my foot easily reaching his jaw. The bundle of food fell out of my hand and bounced down the stairs. I didn't stay to see who caught it. I ran back to my cabin as fast as I could.

In the genteel comfort of my room, the door locked behind me, I realized that the man had probably just been trying to help me. I felt ashamed.

※ ※ ※

I SAT NEXT TO M. Fleury—or Hervé, as he insisted I call him now—at dinner that evening and the next, though after the first time I retrieved my manners and spent time talking to my other tablemates as well. Many were leaving Russia, like me, and we all lied as to the reason we were going; to visit long-lost relatives, help a sick brother or sister, do some business, or see the sights. It was clear none of us were telling the truth, but we didn't know where any of the others stood politically. As a result, we kept the dinner conversations resolutely light, strangely so, considering the temperature of our country. None of us would admit we were fleeing in fear, nor did we mention the name Lenin.

Having been miserable for what seemed like months, I was happy to play my part in keeping the dinner conversation frivolous. By now I was becoming a real chatterbox. I could see the hard lines of Hervé's lean face soften when I laughed at his jokes, making him look younger. The minute he sat down next to me, a girlish whimsy shone through my unhappiness, though while alone in my cabin, I still pined for St. Petersburg.

I spent the days quietly, reading and sleeping and writing in my journal. I ventured out for a brisk walk along the promenade deck and up and down the staircases at least once every day—if I hoped to dance in New York, I had to stay strong. I avoided the Carlton, not wanting to run into that woman again, but her words kept intruding. Why did she think it was her duty to educate me in the miseries of the world?

I thought about the little stone church my father and I attended and how at the end of each service a basket was passed for donations. My father had always been so generous; I'd assumed that since I was his daughter, his good graces covered me, too. With all I'd lost and left behind, wasn't that enough?

CHAPTER 10

AFTER MY ILL-FATED TRIP to steerage, I felt edgy and rebellious. I was sick and tired of the endless cycle of guilt and self-justification. I had told Hervé how my father loved to play poker with his friends and business partners, and his eyes had lit up. "Did you play this game also?"

I'd laughed. "Not a chance! In St. Petersburg proper ladies play vint—what you'd call Russian whist—and drink lemonade."

With an exaggerated Gallic gesture, Hervé had swept the idea of whist away. "Bah! That's old-lady cards. I will teach you to play the *vrai* poker, like a modern girl, *non*?"

At the time, I'd blushed and changed the subject. But now, when Hervé sent a message to my room, inviting me to be his guest in the first-class smoking lounge at two that afternoon for a game of cards, I didn't hesitate to say yes. It was time I joined the modern world, I told myself. Surely the liberated women of New York wouldn't think it wrong!

✳ ✳ ✳

THE LOUNGE WAS QUIET and intimate, furnished in leather club chairs and dark wood. The windows were covered with deep red velvet drapes, but the skylight on the ceiling let in plenty of light. At this time of day, the room was almost empty. Hervé nodded to a gentleman in a corner booth, smoking a pipe and reading a German newspaper. The sweet smell of the tobacco made me think of my father. Why hadn't I learned to play poker with him? Despite what I'd told Hervé about ladies playing vint, I wasn't so sure my father would approve of what I was doing now.

The combination of regret and guilt clouded my mood for a while, but Hervé was a good teacher, and it wasn't long before I was enjoying myself.

Two German men Hervé knew came and joined us. They complimented me on how quickly I'd learned, though the younger one said, laughing, that I'd have to work on my poker face.

Time passed quickly; I was surprised when the clock on the wall chimed five. I wanted to write a letter home before dinner, so I excused myself. Assuring Hervé that I could make my way back to my cabin on my own, I left him starting up another round with the two German men, who were ordering whiskey and ale as I left.

In my cabin, I tried to write to my father, but nothing I wrote sounded right. I crumpled sheet after sheet of stationery. Finally, I gave up and started dressing for dinner. I had just finished when I heard a knock on my cabin door. I opened it to find the shy cabin boy outside, holding a small parcel and an envelope. "M. Fleury asked me to bring you these," he said.

I opened the envelope and pulled out a thick sheet of folded stationery, with a tiny rearing horse next to Hervé's name. He'd written in a vigorous scrawl in bold black ink:

My dear Mme Petrovskaya,

I regret that I won't be able to see you at dinner tonight. Some urgent business has come up, which I can't avoid attending to. Will you do me the honor of allowing me to escort you to the grand ball tomorrow night?

Please also accept this small gift. These were given to me when I was just a lad, and at one time they brought me great luck. But I believe the greatest luck wears out in time if it's not passed on. I hope they will be your companions on many a brilliant evening.

Your admiring friend,

Hervé

AT DINNER THAT EVENING, I was vague and distracted; the gentleman seated next to me must have thought me a half-wit. The table was abuzz with anticipation of the grand ball the next evening. I eavesdropped on a mother and daughter across the table, deep in discussion of Empire gowns, corselet skirts, the exact length and shape of a modern train, and the merits of pale blue satin or banana-colored taffeta. I couldn't decide whether I was more anxious to look through my own wardrobe or open the little parcel from Hervé. As soon as it was reasonably polite to do so, I excused myself from the table, saying I had a bit of a headache and didn't want dessert.

In my cabin, I decided my own choice of a gown would have to wait. The little parcel was too intriguing. I tore off the simple brown paper wrapping to find a box of playing cards, marked: "F. d'Alphonse Arnoult (Paris)."

I drew the cards out and turned them over one by one, setting them down in rows on the bed. On their backs were a pastoral scene, with several horses standing in the shade of a small cluster of trees, others grazing in the distance. The aces were scenic, showing the stables or *ménages* of the great centers of classical equitation. I recognized the names from overhearing Lillya tell my mother. The ace of spades showed a grand white facade and was captioned "Cadre Noir, Saumur." The king of hearts walked beside a dapple-gray mare teaching her to dance in place. The queen of diamonds wore a harlequin circus costume, doing a somersault on the back of a cantering horse. Then I turned over the queen of hearts, and I felt as if my own heart was going to jump out of my skin. On a snowy stallion balanced on his hind legs, his front feet in the air, sat a familiar figure in a tailored riding costume. *The costume is deep red, not green; and the lady is sitting sidesaddle, rather than standing upright,* I told myself. *It's clearly different.* But still it took me back to that long-ago winter evening when I sat with Vladimir looking through a leather-bound album.

※ ※ ※

I DIDN'T DECIDE WHAT to wear to the ball until the next afternoon. Finally, I settled on a very simply cut gown of dark blue voile, its hemline long enough to pool on the ground behind me. Over it I wore an opera cloak of a deep peacock-green lace, hemmed with deep blue velvet. And last I pinned the small circle brooch with the emerald to the cloak. My mind had been on Lillya ever since seeing the ace of hearts.

I rummaged through my trunk until I found a small square box wrapped in gold tissue paper. Lillya had pressed it into my hand the last time I saw her. "Open it when you go out on the town or do something special," she'd said. A grand ball on an ocean liner crossing the Atlantic had to qualify as special.

I delicately tore off the tissue to reveal a box printed with a pattern of green fern leaves. Inside was a heavy cut-glass flask. On it, a small silver label was printed, "Parfum Fougère Royale, Houbigant." I twisted the glass stopper, rubbed it against my wrist, and breathed in the heavy scent of sweet hay mixed with lavender and sage. I imagined myself in a sun-drenched meadow in Provence. Then I dabbed a bit on my finger and put the scent on the backs of my ears.

Hervé came exactly on time. "You look lovely, Donatalia," he said gravely when I opened the door. "I hope you'll consent to dance with me." Tonight, he seemed to have set his usual teasing, sardonic manner aside. "I'm certain you dance better than anyone else on the floor." Suddenly I found a true smile upon my face. I couldn't decide if by wearing it I was betraying myself.

He took my arm and led me toward the staircase. I could already feel the warmth of the ballroom rising toward us. I paused to pull off my cloak with the brooch attached to it and I laid it over my arm.

Hervé touched the brooch and commented on the beauty of its simplicity. We were standing at the top of the grand, curving staircase that led to the ship's ballroom, designed to make every entrance a grand one, so I merely smiled and thanked him.

The merriment of the music could be heard where we stood, as could the rustle of the women's satin gowns as they swirled with the beat. My feet were getting itchy, ready to move. Hervé leaned in closer and smelled the perfume on my neck. Then he drew back and gazed at me for a moment. If I hadn't spent the last days with him, I would have thought it was a look of disgust. His face so intense, at first I thought he was in pain. Then, as if transfixed by reflex alone, surprising even himself, he took me by the waist and pulled me toward him, his mouth seeking mine.

Suddenly everything was a blur. It seemed that he pushed me away, but perhaps it was I trying to free myself. Either way, I took a step back, but there was no floor, only space. The next thing I knew, I was tumbling down the stairs, my legs tangled in the train of my gown. I tried to curl into a ball to protect them. I was almost at the bottom when I heard a snap. My world went white with pain just as the grandfather clock chimed out the time.

❋ ❋ ❋

FOR ANYONE ELSE, IT would have been a horrible inconvenience to break a leg, but for me, it was the end of my life as I knew it.

"You'll be fine in five months' time," the doctor said. "Your limp will be almost unnoticeable." Then he set my leg on a board and strapped it in place. He brought me a used pair of crutches and told me the captain would make sure someone brought me my meals. "I'll check in with you, but when we land, go to a bone doctor. I'm better with colds and fevers and upset stomachs." And then he walked out.

❋ ❋ ❋

A LIMP! HE HAD no idea what those words meant. I would never dance again, at least not seriously. My career was finished before it had begun. I wept all night, hearing my mother's voice: "You'll trip and fall, and then what kind of dancer will you be?"

I knew the answer. That small difference between my legs would change what I would do, who I would become, how I would look at myself. I wanted to jump off the deck, swim back to the start, and do it over again. But the ship just steamed on, and the clock kept ticking.

Hervé seemed truly contrite, and guilty at the same time. It was a bit confusing. I wasn't certain what to believe. He did all he could to help, constantly asking what he could fetch me and offering to escort me onto the promenade deck, where he'd arranged to have a deck chair reserved for me. Seeing how much he blamed himself, I tried not to blame him. In fact, it was myself I berated more bitterly. I knew I had gotten carried away in a fantasy I had created and I had acted like a foolish girl. But still I couldn't help feeling a bit humiliated and angry. Why did he push me away?

At times, I accepted his help—in fact, I needed it—and I held up my end of our stilted conversations at dinner, not wanting to make a fuss about changing our seating arrangement. But other than meals, I avoided him as much as I could while still being civilized.

Sometimes I'd call the steward instead and he'd help me limp on my crutches to the deck, where I'd lean over the rail, watching the gulls gliding over the ship's wake. They made me think of Chekhov's play *The Seagull*. I remembered the night the play opened. I'd heard my parents coming in. "What a disaster!" My mother said to my father. "The audience didn't understand Chekhov's art. The way they booed Vera. They were so loud, she lost her voice!" But my mother did not follow the crowd, she loved the play, and she returned to see it again and again.

A young girl lives all her life on the shore of a lake, she'd recite dreamily. She loves the lake as the gulls do, and is as happy and free as they. But like the seagull in the play, my mother had been broken, and now, so had I.

CHAPTER 11

New York Harbor

WHEN WE PASSED THE Statue of Liberty, everyone cheered. Propped up on my crutches, my leg throbbing, I turned my face away from Hervé so he wouldn't see the tears welling up in my eyes.

A steward had come to fetch my trunk earlier. When we reached the entrance to the New York Harbor, Hervé came to help me onto the main deck. He'd insisted on seeing me off the ship and making sure I met Catherine safely. Although I still felt awkward and uneasy in his presence, I had to admit I was glad for some support; I'd been anxious about getting off the ship on my crutches, even with a steward to carry my trunk. It had been some time since my feet had stepped foot on land.

When we arrived on the main deck, the engines had fallen silent, and a cutter was approaching across the harbor. Ladders were lowered, and a number of officials climbed up onto the main deck. Hervé explained that they were medical examiners, to make sure we were healthy and didn't have to be quarantined or, in the worst case, deported. He laughed at the look of panic that crossed my face.

"Donatalia, don't worry," he said. "For first-class passengers, it's the merest formality." If he'd dared, he would have patted my back.

"But what about my leg?" I asked, my voice shaking.

"A lame steerage passenger is one thing—a young lady of good birth traveling first class is another entirely." He spoke as if that should make me feel special, but it only made me feel bad. I'd heard stories of families being separated, sick children or lame old women deported back to their home countries alone. For the first time, I wondered if the student protestors in Ostrovsky Square and the strikers at my father's factory might have been right. If this was how it was in

America, where everyone spoke of equality, how bad had it been in my Russia? But I didn't say anything. I knew Hervé would find the idea absurd.

The ship picked up steam and started toward Manhattan again. Beside us, a family leaned over the railing their eyes wide as they watched the blocky skyline behind Battery Park draw nearer. I wished I could share their excitement. But although I was young, I felt old and misplaced.

✻ ✻ ✻

AT THE PIER, HERVÉ courteously escorted me off the ship, along with all the other first- and second-class passengers. When we reached solid ground, it seemed to sway under me. My crutch slid away uselessly, and only Hervé's hand under my elbow stopped me from falling. "We'll stand here awhile, Donatalia, until you get your land legs back again," said Hervé. After the steward brought over my trunk, and a customs officer asked me a few questions about what was in it, Hervé helped me sit down on it.

The steerage passengers were staggering off the ship now, carrying their own baggage and wearing tags with large numbers written on them. They were herded over to a separate waiting area. A big red-faced man with an eagle insignia called out numbers and loaded them onto a waiting barge in groups of thirty or so to be taken to Ellis Island. Watching a sweet-faced young boy clinging to his parents, his pretty older sister rubbing his head, I hoped that they would all have an easy journey through immigration and find a good life in this strange new land.

✻ ✻ ✻

I BARELY REMEMBERED CATHERINE—SHE'D left Russia when I was a young girl— but still, from my father's description, I picked her out easily enough, waving enthusiastically from the waiting crowd. She had kind, rather faded blue eyes and wiry, sandy hair under her broad-brimmed gray hat. I turned to introduce Hervé to her, but he'd melted away, and only my trunk was there, the smaller bag he'd been carrying for me sitting on top of it. I was surprised; he didn't seem like the shy type. I opened my mouth to say something, but then closed it again. It seemed she hadn't noticed him, and I didn't feel like explaining who he was.

I was surprised to hear that Catherine's Russian accent was thicker than my own, since I had just left Russia. It seemed a little affected, as if she wanted everyone to know her origin. But I pushed this thought down. She was doing a kind deed, taking on an angry and hurt teenage girl. I was even more of a liability now, only able to walk on crutches—I wouldn't even be able to run errands for her. Besides, she was the closest thing I had to a relative or friend in this country.

She'd received a telegram from the ship telling her about my broken leg; I'd deliberately avoided any specifics about Hervé, and the telegram implied it was an innocent accident. "I've arranged for a bone specialist to meet us at the hospital, dear," she said breathlessly. "Oh, and"—she produced a crumpled sheet of paper from somewhere in her voluminous blue-gray skirts—"here's a telegram from your father."

I glanced at it:

The world is big. There is much to explore. Remember you come from good blood.
Stay strong!
Your loving father

I wanted to throw it away, I was still so angry with him for forcing me to leave. But seeing Catherine's anxious glance, I murmured a few words of thanks and tried to look pleased.

❋ ❋ ❋

CATHERINE OWNED A HOUSE she called a brownstone. Although it was four stories tall, because of my leg she made up a room for me on the ground floor at the back of the house, overlooking a shady little garden. Every afternoon at five o'clock, just like the czar and her friends in Russia, Catherine served tea scented with bergamot, citrus, and flowers. She insisted that I join her, and at least once a week she invited another misplaced person like herself to eat biscuits and sip this delicacy with us.

My favorite friend of Catherine's was named Alexandra Katrina Teresa Borkavic. A tall, thin middle-aged woman who always wore a tweed suit with a high collar, she never went anywhere without a little dog she called Woof-Woof. I asked her one day how she came up with the name. Smiling at me, she pulled out a treat from her pocket and put it on his nose. He flipped it in the air and then let it fall on the floor. I thought he had made a mistake, but the second it landed he barked twice. After he had properly pronounced his name, he gobbled his treat down. "It was very easy. I just had to listen," Alexandra said. I grew quite fond of this little dog.

* * *

WINTER TURNED TO SPRING, and spring became summer. Slowly my leg healed, and I was able to get around by myself. Still, I was sad and lonely.

My only solace was the time I spent in a little trattoria a few blocks from Catherine's house. The floor there was covered with little hexagonal tiles in an enchanting geometric pattern of diamonds, and dark-green stamped tin covered the high ceiling. It felt cool and tranquil inside, and the big fans spinning slowly overhead helped to wash away any unwanted thoughts. I liked listening to the animated babble of the family who ran the place, even though I couldn't understand them. I knew the place was Italian, but to me it represented New York City and America. I would sit at a table at the front by a big window and wonder about the history of the people passing by. What had they been through to get here? Did they miss their families, too?

Through the sweltering days and nights of a New York summer, I limped my way through Greenwich Village, first on crutches but eventually without, though I never seemed to gain my footing. The atmosphere on the Village streets was lively, almost like a carnival. The storefronts were small and quaint, and they seemed to go on forever. New York was so different from St. Petersburg. On every street corner, I could hear different accents and languages, people from all nations gathered here to pursue their dreams. But they only served to remind me that I'd never achieve mine.

My leg was beginning to heal, but New York held no meaning for me now. I pushed thoughts of ballet out of my head; they only represented all that I would never do.

Catherine tried to pull me out of the mourning I'd fallen into. She took me to the Metropolitan Museum for beauty and culture. But still I felt trapped in a life I hadn't chosen.

Chapter 12

August 1906

O NE SATURDAY IN AUGUST, Catherine interrupted my endless games of solitaire. "Put away those old cards, Donatalia," she said brightly. "I've planned an expedition! After all, this week was your father's fortieth birthday and he wouldn't want to see you moping around the house on such a beautiful day."

"Wear your seersucker suit," was all she said; she herself had dressed in a white shirtwaist with a long beige linen skirt and insisted we take parasols. We set out toward the subway station at Bleecker and Elm Street, much to my surprise; Catherine never took the subway herself and had advised me to avoid it. "It's so crowded," she said. "Men stand too close, and some of them might not be as respectful as I'd wish to a lady." But apparently today she would make an exception.

We took the train going south. I have to admit I felt a twinge of excitement, looking at all the different kinds of people on the train around us: Jewish men in dark suits and beards, stout German women, and wiry Italian teenagers. At the Canal Street stop, a Chinese couple got on, the woman carrying a bag full of strange-looking vegetables, along with a crowd of laughing, chattering girls. Catherine looked more and more anxious as the car filled up, and as we went through the long dark tunnel under the East River, she gripped my arm tightly.

From Atlantic Avenue in Brooklyn we took an elevated tram, and Catherine started to look as if she were enjoying herself. Finally, the tram pulled up at the end of the line. "Here we are—Coney Island!" she said and climbed down out of the tram.

Catherine was looking around to get her bearings when an open car with rows of bench seats pulled up. The driver hopped out to pull down a ladder from the side, and more than a dozen teenage girls climbed down to the sidewalk. Their frazzled chaperone followed, herding them with motions of her parasol.

We both watched the group head down the broad avenue, giggling. Catherine smiled as if remembering her own youth, but I felt a small stab of wistfulness wishing I were here with a group of my own friends.

We followed the girls toward Steeplechase Park where, at its entrance, an enormous face grinned at us with its bizarrely wide red mouth. Catherine winced at the sight, but she bravely marched under it into the park, past the tall spiral of the Dew Drop. Ahead of us, the school girls were already scrambling onto the mechanical horses of the Steeplechase ride, and soon we heard their shrieks of delight as their mechanical steeds raced neck and neck along curving steel tracks. I tugged at Catherine's hand, but she merely shook her head. "I think that's for younger folk than me," she said. "Why don't we walk around a little and see the sights?"

A little downcast, I agreed. We spent a pleasant afternoon wandering around, stopping every now and then for a lemonade in the shade of a pagoda or to watch children riding the brightly painted horses on the merry-go-round. I wanted to walk out onto the beach, but Catherine soon said the bright sun gave her a headache. I think the bathers made her nervous, though their costumes seemed quite modest to me.

Catherine was hungry, so we ate hot dogs and clams in Feltman's Bavarian Beer Garden under the shade of a big maple tree. Catherine even allowed the waiter to talk her into a beer. Though she insisted on lemonade for me. I saved a napkin as a souvenir.

By the time we left, the sun was beginning to drop toward the horizon. I pleaded once again for Catherine to go on just one ride with me.

"How about the Ferris wheel?" she said finally, and I nodded eagerly. We joined the line and soon were climbing into a brightly painted cage that rose jerkily higher and higher as others climbed into the cars below us. From the top of the wheel, I could look down at the Steeplechase and a big swimming pool. Across Surf Avenue, a tower soared up from the center of Luna Park, like a pink and green confection. "That's called the Electric Tower," said Catherine. I wondered why, but I'd soon find out: as we walked along Surf Avenue after getting off the Ferris wheel, it suddenly flickered to life with thousands of lights glowing in circles.

The lights drew me in. It was as if I were hypnotized, but soon that spell broke and another was born. Coming slowly toward us was an enormous elephant led by a small man wearing a purple turban and robes. Catherine shrieked and stepped back, but I was transfixed. The great creature passed so close to me that I swore I could see the fine hairs around its eye. They were bright brown against the elephant's wrinkled gray skin. For a moment, I felt it looking into my own eyes, as if it knew something about me that I myself didn't know. When it finally passed, I was in such a trance that Catherine felt the need to ask if I was all right.

"Oh, perfectly." I smiled, pulling myself together. I knew how kind Catherine had been to bring me here. It was clear that she found this city of sand alien and a little frightening, though she did her best to cover it up. Across the promenade, a calliope was playing circus music. Above the sound of this giant air organ, I could hear a woman scream. We were told a man had just stuck his head inside the mouth of the tiger. I wanted to see this for myself. I loved cats, but Catherine said she preferred them much smaller.

Looking around for something less scary, I saw a booth decorated with tarot symbols. "Fortunes Read," the sign said. A woman with a dark gypsy face and long, thick hair with streaks of gray stood in the doorway, smiling at us. "Good evening, ladies. Shall I look into your future?" she said in a husky accented voice. Catherine nodded and pulled out some coins. She went into the booth first. I asked her in a soft voice what the fortune-teller had said when she came out, but she just smiled mysteriously and shook her head.

The fortune-teller gestured to me just as a man with a giant serpent wrapped around his neck approached her and whispered something in her ear. I could see Catherine wanted to leave but didn't know how to maneuver our exit without causing a scene. In Catherine's brief moment of indecision, I quickly ducked my head and peeped it through the low entrance of the booth. Inside I found myself in a dim candlelit room, draped with colorful fabrics like a tent. From behind a narrow table, the woman gestured to a stool across from her. I sat down, and she took my hand. But when she looked at it, she frowned and shivered and then said nothing for what seemed a very long time. Finally, she dropped my hand and stood up. From a mirror on the opposite wall, I could see the beady eyes of the serpent peaking its head in. It was as if he had come to eavesdrop on our conversation.

"There is nothing *I* can tell *you*," she said. "You belong on the other side." Then she turned her head in the opposite direction as if I should understand the meaning and walked away.

More puzzled than annoyed, I reemerged into the dazzling lights of Luna Park. I stood still for a moment, listening to the music, the lion's roar, the voices of barkers. A strange elation seized me, a feeling as if I were on the edge of something momentous.

"Come this way, little lady," a voice rasped, startling me; I turned to find a weasel-faced man standing only inches away from me. "Come see the woman with no head."

Catherine turned pale and grabbed my hand, and I followed her meekly back toward the tram. We said little on the journey back home. Catherine seemed tired and withdrawn. I shut my eyes, and images from the evening flickered in front of me as the tram rattled through the dark streets.

From that night on, I felt a growing restlessness, a hum in my whole being that seemed almost audible. I sipped tea with Catherine and her friends, and I watched the people passing on the streets outside the trattoria's front window, but still, I felt very far away. I didn't know where I belonged, but I knew that it was not here.

It was on a chilly November Sunday, that I finally made up my mind. Catherine had gone out that evening. "I've been invited to play bridge with the Ostrovs," she'd said, standing in the doorway, already in her fur-collared winter coat. "Would you like to come?"

I remembered the Ostrovs vaguely. They'd come for a dinner at Catherine's brownstone in the spring. He did something in shipping. His wife was a small dark-haired woman. I felt rather certain that they'd talk all evening about the old country, and for some reason this subject, usually so dear to me, left me feeling restless and bored.

"No, thank you," I said now, a little too quickly. "I…I think I tired myself with too much walking this afternoon. I thought I'd stay in, and write a letter home."

Catherine brightened. "Your father would so appreciate that, and I know the Ostrovs would like you to send their regards as well."

With a gesture rare for her, Catherine embraced me briefly. I closed my eyes, feeling the soft fur of her collar against my cheek, inhaling the familiar jasmine and lemon of her scent. Suddenly I knew I would never see her again.

The sound of the front door opening and closing had been like a signal. Late fall chill and evening blues seemed to unexpectedly flood the room. I felt restless and moody. On an impulse I didn't quite understand, I started up the stairs.

Gripping the banister, I limped slowly to the top floor, to Catherine's bedroom, which I'd never entered before. I hesitated a moment, then pushed the door open.

A heavily carved sleigh bed dominated the room. The walls were covered with gilt-framed photographs of stiffly posed, richly dressed women, children wearing wide-brimmed straw hats, and sharp-eyed men in military uniforms. In the back was a photo of four men in dark fur hats. They stood holding rifles behind the body of an enormous bear that lay as if sleeping on the snow. "Royal Hunting Party, 1884" was written in faded ink in the margin below.

Though the daylight was still stronger here, shadows were forming in the corners of the room. I found a box of matches on the dressing table, struck one, and lit the gas wall sconce above it. The clutter of carved boxes, enameled tins, and jars of face cream suddenly became too much for me. Like ghosts, the stiff ladies, the hunters, the fallen bear, all came alive, and in their shadows all I could see was decay. I took a deep breath.

There was a little writing table by the window, where there was still a little light. I sat down in the chair, took a sheet of Catherine's stationery, and dipped her fountain pen into ink.

I'm sorry, Catherine. I need to find my own life, and I can't see it here.
Don't worry, I'll be careful.
—Donatalia

I went to my bedroom, hid the note inside my book of fairytales, and quickly prepared my belongings.

And before the sun had a chance to find its way through the blinds and into Catherine's bedroom, early the next morning I put the note on her dining room table. Then like a seagull I spread my wings, flew down the hall like my mother had taught me, and gently opened and closed the door behind me.

CHAPTER 13

Goodbye Again

I LOOKED UP AT the brownstone. I remembered with a pang of guilt that Catherine had already ordered a turkey—a twenty-seven-pounder, she'd said proudly—for November 27, my birthday.

I hoped Catherine would have other friends to celebrate it with. I didn't expect her or my father to understand. Was I a bad person for leaving? It didn't really matter; I knew I couldn't stay another hour. Ever since that evening when I had looked into the elephant's tawny eye and heard the fortune-teller's words, I'd felt trapped in Catherine's brownstone. I felt as if I were holding my breath, as if my lungs would burst.

There were other reasons to go, more rational ones. Catherine had carelessly left a letter from her sister in Russia lying on the table in the front hall. My father and Archie had been forced out of their own company, she wrote, and Catherine would have to make do with the money he'd sent with me. I knew it wouldn't be enough to keep me fed much longer, and I didn't want to be a burden. All our futures looked grim.

I was angry at the world for stealing my dreams, but anger was no longer enough. To build new dreams, I'd have to become someone new, and I couldn't do that here, where every ornament on the shelf, every picture on the wall, pulled me back toward Russia and the life I'd lost. Now that I could walk again, I wanted to run.

❋ ❋ ❋

IT WAS COLD THAT gray November morning. Milkmen in their horse-drawn carriages were clanging their way up and down the streets as I walked to the landing where I could take the ferry to New Jersey to Exchange Place in Jersey City.

The wind off the river sent chills through me, making me glad I was wearing my babushka, like any good daughter of Russia.

I was afraid but determined. I had never traveled such a far distance here by myself, but I reminded myself I had made it across an ocean and I was Katya's daughter.

At the train station on the other side, I handed some money to the man behind the counter. "How far south can I go?" I asked, using my dictionary. Seeing as winter was near, I thought my decision to go to a warmer climate made sense. It would be something new after the harsh winters of St. Petersburg. I surprised myself, for I had been a directionless compass several hours prior when I'd closed the door to Catherine's brownstone.

Knowing I had made a decision gave me a slight boost of confidence.

"Savannah," he answered, "but you'll need another nickel."

"Why of course," I thought. "George and Mary Bradley live in Savannah." So, I slipped my hand into my bag, and I bought the ticket.

The Bradleys had spoken so fondly of Savannah and if that didn't work out, there was always Archie's New Orleans to explore. And then I realized I didn't even have the Suttons' address. I had always contacted them through my father and Archie's factory in St. Petersburg, and that had been taken over and we had received not a word from either of them recently, only the letter from Catherine's sister. That was worrisome and I hoped temporary, but for now I had to think about what was best for me and accept that I was alone.

All I knew of Savannah were stories from my childhood, that it was south of New York City, there probably wouldn't be ballet in Savannah, and the Bradleys had made their home there. "If Mary Bradley liked it, that was good enough for me," I mumbled to myself. Then I realized other people behind me were getting impatient and they too had someplace to go and were anxious, so I stuck my change quickly in my bag and stepped aside.

I wandered the station. The train would leave in ninety minutes. I kept glancing over my shoulder for anyone trying to find me, but I was just one more head in the mass of people. Thirsty, I found a water fountain next to a store with souvenirs and maps of the United States. I asked the clerk if he would point out Savannah, and I counted the states between New York and Georgia.

I walked toward the waiting room. I sat in a hard chair, my head in my hands. A drunk next to me threw a bag under my seat. The empty bottle of beer inside made a clinking sound against the floor. "*All aboard the train for...*" was all I could hear over the loudspeakers; the announcer seemed to be mumbling from some underground cave.

I thought about the ship and crossing the ocean. How I felt lying on the cold marble floor, my leg throbbing, listening to the faint sound of the grandfather clock passing out time. I wondered about the emerald brooch Lillya gave my mother. It had vanished. And where might Hervé be? Sunk in my own grief, I couldn't see that what was happening might have been God's plan from the start; that an entirely different life was meant to grow out of the one I'd thought would be mine.

I was awakened from my daydreams by the sound of the announcer calling the passengers going to Savannah to board the train. People came scurrying from all directions in the station toward Track 11. A heavyset woman stepped on my foot and I wanted to cry, but I realized crying was now a luxury I couldn't afford. I had to stay focused. My life depended on it.

Some persons in the crowd looked as if they knew what they were doing and where they were going. Others like me were a bit more tentative, unsure they had heard the announcer correctly. Assessing the situation, I decided to rely on the seemingly kind gentleman I noticed at the top of the steps who was examining each person's ticket before letting them pass. "He'll let me know if I am in the wrong place," I said to myself, quite proud that my instincts seemed to be in prime condition even if I was not.

CHAPTER 14

I SAT BY THE window and stared out, hoping to avoid conversation. I was fidgeting with my clothes trying to get comfortable and needed a tissue to wipe the few beads of sweat that had formed at the top of my brow when I realized I had packed my handkerchief in my bag that was above my seat.

"I'm Mrs. Butler," said an attractive woman with gray hair and bright blue eyes who had taken the aisle seat next to mine. In her hand was a delicately stitched lace hankie. "I always pack two or three for trips just as these. It's impossible not to get flustered. Don't worry, I have more," she said with a big smile.

I was surprised to hear a Russian accent. Still, I just nodded a thank you, took the kerchief from her extended hand, wiped my brow and cheek, and didn't speak.

Looking out the window, we passed one factory after another and more run-down apartment buildings than I knew existed. Clothes were hanging off of staircases blowing in the wind. I saw some dogs fighting. They seemed so viscious, but perhaps they were fighting for their lives? Who was I to judge?

We passed fields of corn that had already been harvested and structures that my dictionary called a "silo." It was the first time I had seen the American countryside. The leaves were either crisp or a deep red-brown and had mostly fallen off the branches. The landscape was rather barren. Still, I had the urge to stick my head out a window and breath in what I suspected would be the smell of sharp country air.

I pretended to be asleep. I didn't want anyone to find out that I knew only the Bradleys in Savannah, and I didn't know where to find them or if they'd even be there. I had no clue where I was going or what I'd do when we arrived. In a sense, I was like a runaway, though that seemed funny—for all I really wanted was to run home into my father's arms, feel Mme Strachkov's hand on the small of my back, and hear her correct my French.

After sitting silently for several hours, listening to the squeaky wheels of the train pushing us forward, Mrs. Butler politely offered me a lemon drop. It was the type of candy older American women seemed always to have little containers of in their purses. In New York City, when I rode the motorbus, I'd see grandmothers pulling lemon drops out of their purses, offering them to their grandchildren. I believe they were hoping the taste of lemon mixed with sugar might sweeten the children's sour dispositions.

I was extremely hungry, and out of reflex I put out my hand imagining its sweet and sour taste in my mouth. "My name is Donatalia Petrovskaya," I said cautiously. "My family is from St. Petersburg, and I'm on my way to see some friends."

"Ah, St. Petersburg"—Mrs. Butler drew out the last word—"my favorite city. "Much livelier than Odessa," she continued in Russian, "which is where I come from. I was born Irina Anjelika Rusakova, but 'Mrs. Butler' is much simpler in the South. Oh, but how I remember those carefree summer days playing in the Black Sea." She paused for a second as if to smell the fresh sea air even though we were on a train passing through a drought-ridden countryside. After she seemed certain she had gotten a proper whiff, she continued with her question.

"Have you ever been to Odessa, Donatalia?"

"My family used to go there when I was young," I told her, but what I omitted was that we quit going after my mother passed away. I suspected it was too painful for my father. Still, I think Mrs. Butler could read my body language and she changed the subject.

"Southern society in the United States has its own rules and ways of doing things and it's lovely," she went on. "But it's young in comparison to our country. Very few do anything on the scale of us Russians. Why, the czar's ball at the Winter Palace several years back...that's a good example, people spoke of that event around the world. Mrs. Butler could see that I didn't much want to talk about the aristocrats of St. Petersburg, so she changed the subject back to the present, another subject I had hoped to avoid. "Where do your friends in Savannah live, and what do they do?"

"She's a ballerina, and her father a prominent businessman," I said, deciding to stick to the story I knew best. "Her mother died several years ago." Deciding I had said enough, I pretended to be absorbed in my French book that was resting on my lap.

I remember to this day how Irina Anjelika Rusakova Butler looked that first moment I saw her on the train. She'd have made a fine Southern belle if it weren't for the scarf around her neck, which was very Russian. Going back in time, I don't think I fooled her for one second. With her sharp intuition, she probably knew from the start that I was talking about myself.

I sat quietly thumbing through my books, truly paying little attention to any of them. Curiosity had gotten the best of me, and I asked Mrs. Butler a question about herself. I had meant to stop at just the one, but she turned out to be so entertaining and full of *joie de vivre* that I became a captive audience. Her tone reminded me of my mother and the way she used to tell me stories. I could almost imagine Mrs. Butler reciting the story of the Firebird or that of Ivanushka and Alanushka. Her voice became so hypnotic, I didn't want to miss one word.

✳ ✳ ✳

THE SECOND WIFE OF a Confederate colonel, Mrs. Butler was a widow when I met her. Sparkly and warm in her gestures and speech, she chatted as if we were old friends.

"I came to Savannah in eighteen seventy with my father and his caviar. And I met my Colonel Butler at a party when I caught him spitting our delicacy into his napkin. What a guilty look he had!

You should have seen the colonel, Donatalia," she continued, "still very handsome and distinguished-looking. He had all sorts of medals for bravery and a charm about him that made my heart sing." The colonel had treated her to the world while he was alive, she told me. "I suppose all that fighting made him really appreciate life. He was dazzled by my cold-water Russian skin and loved my happy spirit. I think that after the Civil War, he preferred a belle less wounded than the Confederate girls who'd lost their homes and families.

"When he got down on one knee to propose, everyone in his circle was on pins and needles, waiting to see what my answer would be. We were the gossip of Savannah.

"One night," she continued, "the colonel took me to a huge country affair. All of high society was in attendance; it was called the Grand Indigo Ball. I remember the ballroom had the most beautiful crystal chandeliers that were made by a craftsman in England. I was told they were the only ones he ever shipped across the ocean.

"Large paintings hung like murals on the walls of the Savannah low country painted in silver and gold. I felt like royalty on my colonel's arm.

"We arrived a little late—on purpose, I might add. As we entered, I stopped the gentleman from announcing us, and I looked at my loving colonel and then at the crowd below and declared, 'Y'all, it's a yes!'"

I laughed at how she'd said *y'all* with her beautiful Russian accent.

"After that, we didn't need to be announced," she went on. "Everyone cheered, first for the colonel, and then even for me. I was different, which was generally not looked on kindly in Savannah society, but over time everyone came to love and accept me. Sometimes our friends even said I was more Southern than them. The colonel had that effect on people. He brought out the best in everyone."

She looked at me. "Never apologize for who you are, Donatalia."

For a moment, she was quiet—thinking of her husband, I thought. Then she brightened. "Have you ever ventured this far south? Savannah is one of the most glorious places in the world. I swear! We have magnificent ancient spreading trees called Live Oak that are covered in what they call Spanish moss. The funny thing is Spanish moss is neither Spanish nor moss. I'm told it has more in common with a pineapple of all things." And we both laughed.

"Some people think it looks like an old gray beard, but it reminds me of a delicately wrapped present covered in angel hair.

"And the architecture—it's grand in its own way. Why, it stopped the northern general Sherman in his tracks during this nation's Civil War. When he entered Savannah, he was so moved by its beauty that he didn't have the heart to destroy it. Instead he wrote a letter to President Lincoln and gave it to him as a Christmas present."

Mrs. Butler smiled. "Savannah has charm. You'll see."

❈ ❈ ❈

THOUGH I'D BEEN MISERABLE and frightened when I got on the train, now, as I listened to Mrs. Butler, my flight started to seem more like an adventure. I began to get curious, even excited. Fear of the unknown could wait until I arrived. For now, I only wanted to lose myself in the comfort of Mrs. Butler's voice. I could almost dance atop the lilt and cadence of her speech.

After talking for several hours, Mrs. Butler seemed to come to a decision and asked who would be picking me up at the station. Unable to lie to her, but not wanting to tell the truth, I paused. I could feel my eyes getting teary and I was about to speak when, very diplomatically, Mrs. Butler extended her hospitality. "My house is much too big for one person, and sometimes it gets lonely. I wonder if your friend would mind if you spent a few days with me?"

I'd always been cared for, and I didn't know how to start living on my own. Profoundly relieved, I accepted with gratitude.

※ ※ ※

WHEN WE ARRIVED IN Savannah, the doors opened, and a warm, soft breeze carried the smell of fresh tobacco into the train. I stuffed my babushka in my traveling case, took off my jacket, and unbuttoned my sweater. The slow, soft sounds of the people chattering around me seemed reassuring. The horns of the ships in the distance made me feel as if I'd landed in some exotic place. It felt good to stretch my arms and legs and know they had some place to go.

I helped Mrs. Butler down the steps as the porter gathered her bags and my leather case. Her driver greeted us with a big, warm smile, and Mrs. Butler told him I'd be staying with them for a while. Then he opened the door of her spacious Ford Model B.

I pressed my nose to the window, the landscape so different from anything that I'd ever seen. We rolled past fields of cotton and the big, soft green leaves of tobacco and what Mrs. Butler referred to as Chinese vetch, though later people would call it soybeans. I wanted to tell the world that I, Donatalia Petrovskaya, from St. Petersburg, Russia, was in Savannah and the state of Georgia.

We passed a few dilapidated shacks with laundry drying out front on lines strung between trees. It reminded me of the scenery I had seen from the train window. In the back of a truck going the other way, I saw black men in chains and a white man carrying a rifle. Mrs. Butler explained that the men had committed crimes and picked cotton to help pay for them. On our twenty-minute journey, we honked hello to several other automobiles that looked like hers. Finally, we pulled onto a long driveway that would take us to Colonel Butler's farm. At the end of the drive was a mansion draped in what Mrs. Butler had described as Spanish moss. It was flanked by weeping willow trees so lovely I could barely speak.

An elegant porch wrapped around the house, its roof supported by the grand white pillars so typical of the South. On it hung two swings, one facing east toward the Butlers' tobacco, the other facing the cotton fields to the west. After the Civil War, Mrs. Butler told me, the colonel had been so sick of the division between North and South that he'd moved his porch swings so they faced east and west. The eastern swing, he said, represented prosperity; the western swing, opportunity; and the north and south—well, they weren't going to get any more of his attention.

There I planted myself, surrounded by cotton, tobacco, and soft Southern voices.

CHAPTER 15

Ｈ
OW INTERESTING IT WAS to learn that the crop my father and Archie used to spin their garments originated in India, had been known to grow wild in Egypt and Peru, and was growing in a field next to me while I sat on Colonel Butler's porch swing in Georgia conversing with his widow. "It's been documented in the journals of Spanish explorers," Mrs. Butler said, "American Indians were growing cotton in Florida as early as the fifteen hundreds."

I told her about my father and Archie's business and I could see that she was stitching together the bits and pieces of my story as if she were a quilter. It was clear to her that I was loved and therefore she assumed there were people worrying about me.

I had been in Savannah for three days. Tomorrow would be Thanksgiving. I would give myself until Saturday and then I would begin my search to find the Bradleys. All this talk about cotton made me long to see them. The thought of how Mary Bradley's arms wrapped around me would be so reassuring. I found I could not stop myself and I asked Mrs. Butler, who now insisted that I call her by first name, Irina, if she happened to know a nice lady named Mary Bradley.

"Not George's wife? Sweet Mary Bradley of the cotton Bradleys?" Irina asked.

"Why I suppose so," I answered back, and I went into great depth about my father, Archie and Winnie, Rosie, and my pony Sasha who learned to play soccer. We talked and talked throughout Thanksgiving Day and stopped only to say grace before we sat down to eat. Irina insisted that the help have the day off, as she believed the holiday had more of a symbolic importance to them than a Russian widow. She mentioned Polly. Anything having to do with food and the kitchen supposedly fell into Polly's jurisdiction.

"She went to visit her ailing father on some island off of South Carolina. Polly comes from a special breed of people," but Irina didn't say anything more.

Neither of us were very handy in the kitchen, so my most vivid memory of my first Thanksgiving was the conversation, the company, and Irina's generosity.

"The Bradleys sold their farm about six months ago," Irina saind, breaking the news to me.

"Where are they?" I asked in a panic trying not to convey how much I had depended upon their being in Savannah, knowing the kindness Mary Bradley had shown me the first summer after my mother died.

"I was told Mary wanted to travel the world, and on a trip they took to Africa, they stumbled upon an orphanage that needed help. Mary just could not leave the children that would have suffered had she gone. George, who had always been so devoted to his business, understood Mary's true nature and decided to take a sabbatical. Unable to live without her, he sold the farm and joined her. She had always gone wherever he asked her to go, I guess he felt that it was his turn to support Mary."

I was happy for Mary, but I couldn't hide my own sadness. I started sobbing uncontrollably. Irina didn't quite know what to do, so she just let me sit with my tears until they stopped.

"Now tell me what has happened," Irina commanded in a voice that would only listen to truth. Once I got started I couldn't stop, and I talked about my dreams of being a prima ballerina, all my teachers and friends, my accident, my mother, Catherine, Mme Strachkov, my father, in no particular order. When I was through, she simply looked at me and said, "Tomorrow we will write a letter to Catherine, she must be worried sick!"

Irina never judged my actions of the past nor did we discuss the future. I continued to stay and Irina never asked me to leave.

After years of conversing in English with her funny Southern accent, I think Irina enjoyed being able to speak with someone in Russian again.

The house was large but simple; nonetheless, Irina kept a staff to cook, clean, and garden. Still, there was always plenty to do to help, and there were ways to keep busy. Irina loved animals and all things natural. Why, just the day after Thanksgiving, Ben—her driver, handyman, and sometimes butler—knocked on the door. Ben had a quiet way about him. He was a tall, thin man with big hands that appeared to be quite capable of fixing a large piece of farm equipment or making the tiniest lure to bait a fish. He also proved he knew how to keep calm during excitable situations.

When he left, Irina told me her favorite animal was about to give birth, then asked if I would assist her with the delivery of her prize pig's offspring.

"All you have to do is change your clothes and follow my instructions, and don't be surprised if they keep on coming," she said. Irina was like that: one minute, a very proper lady, and the next, if you didn't know she was the lady of the house, you would have thought she had been hired to tend the animals. After changing my clothes, I followed her to the barn.

I'm not sure who squealed louder that day, Daffodil after giving birth to twenty-one piglets or me! "You just might have some promise, Donatalia," Irina said when we were through. We walked back to the house to clean ourselves up and get something to eat.

Just as she had with the many emotionally scarred Confederate soldiers she'd met through Colonel Butler, Irina helped take the pieces of my shattered life and reassemble them into something I could believe in, but it wasn't easy.

She created an exercise routine to help me build back the muscles in my legs that I had lost. "The Colonel fell off his horse and his doctor gave these to him." She verbalized the truth: "You are no longer destined to become a prima ballerina, but that does not mean you cannot dance at all. Donatalia, there is something else out there for you to love." Her optimism was infectious. Occasionally I'd catch myself smiling and I'd forgot my slight limp.

Irina wrote Catherine a letter, but no one had heard from my father in months, so I began a campaign. I wrote to family friends —anyone I could think of who might tell me news of "my" Russia—but received not one reply. My anger toward my father for having sent me away changed to worry.

Days turned into weeks, and Irina became not only my friend but my family. She introduced me to Savannah society, telling people that I was a younger cousin of her favorite cousin Katya who had died; and she had sworn to look out for me if ever it were needed, and so it was she began to wear some of my family history, and I began to wear hers.

Although we often conversed in Russian, Irina insisted we also speak in English. Every night she tutored me, and when we'd had enough, she'd say, "Donatalia, will you dance for me?" Then I would leap and spin for my amusement and hers, using every inch of her spacious parlor. Sometimes, when Irina's mood and spirit were aligned just right, she'd sing Russian folk songs or put a record on her phonograph and sway to the music as if she were seventeen.

Irina had a young woman who worked for her. Her name was Polly. And as Irina described it, Polly owned the kitchen. "I own the house and the land, but the kitchen is Polly's. In the kitchen, I ask Polly for permission. When she speaks, she repeats herself like a parrot: 'My name is Polly, that's Polly. It's like holly. You know, Christmas holly, only with a P. P for Polly.' She's as colorful as a parrot, too. She always dresses in bright colors, never pastels. But don't let the way she speaks fool you, she's sharp as a whip!"

When I first met Polly, I was a bit apprehensive. I knew that Irina depended upon her and if one of us were to go, it would be me. Determined to get Polly's approval and to be on her good side, I came up with a scheme that I hoped would win her over.

In the middle of the night, I tiptoed down the stairs. Using my hands to guide me, I found the kitchen. I had memorized where Polly kept her favorite spice, cinnamon, in the front row of her spice drawer, the third from the right in between the nutmeg and cloves. I smelled the container to make sure I had the right spice then gently slipped it into my pocket.

When I woke up the next morning, I could hear Polly cursing in the kitchen. "How can I make my apple pie without my favorite spice? Who's going to want my oatmeal?"

Polly pulled out every spice from her drawer. She banged pots and pans so loudly looking for it everywhere that, of course, I had to come down and see if I could help. Actually, my plan wouldn't work unless I convinced Polly to let me help her.

I emptied cupboards looking for the cinnamon, trying to be as loud as she to demonstrate how hard and far I would go to be helpful. Finally, when she was on the opposite side of the kitchen, I pulled the cinnamon from my pocket and carefully tucked it behind the coffee grinder. But several minutes later when I circled back, it wasn't there. When Polly saw the look of horror cross my face and saw that I had been sufficiently shocked, she opened the spice drawer and surprise of all surprises it was there, exactly where it belonged.

When I realized Polly had played the joke on me, I looked at her expecting to see malice, but instead she smiled, and we both burst out in laughter and we laughed until tears fell down our cheeks.

At dinner that night, Polly awarded me the first slice of her pie. Irina could tell something unwritten had passed between us. She didn't know what it was, but she knew she would not have to choose.

To this day, I cannot smell cinnamon without thinking of Polly.

My suitcase had laid next to the bed unopened all of these days. When I got back to my room that night, I instinctively began to unpack.

I set the playing cards Hervé had given me on the walnut table, next to my mother's abalone hairbrush, in its silver case, and the perfume Lillya gave me. On the small table next to the bed, I laid my book of Russian fairy tales and in its top drawer I placed a small carved wooden box that held my few remaining pieces of jewelry. Finally, I pulled out my sensible walking shoes, a dainty pair of button-up ankle boots, and an old, worn pair of toe shoes, and lined them up on the floor under the left-hand window.

I sat down on the braided rug and looked around the room, *My room.* All my life I'd lived in luxury, created for me by someone else. In this clean, simple, bare place, I could begin to find out who I was as a woman, no longer a child.

CHAPTER 16

POLLY WAS FAMOUS ON the farm for baking bread that surpassed any we'd ever tasted, but her true love was desserts. For my birthday that next year, she made me a combination of the two, a creation she called bread pudding, soaked with real bourbon. She ringed the edge of the platter with orange and yellow dahlias and topped it with a candle. I couldn't believe I was having bourbon for breakfast.

I came to love being around Polly. I put up with her repeating herself and she put up with my difficult to understand English until it improved.

I was trying to absorb the customs, but I could not bite my tongue any longer and ignore the obvious question: "How come there are two lines and two entrances for everything? And why wasn't Polly allowed to eat with us? Didn't the Yankees win?"

There weren't many negroes in Russia, but the ones who were there were educated and valued. "Why, Peter the Great emancipated then adopted an African slave. The gentleman was given a superb education, served in the Russian military, and became a member of the noble class," I told Polly one evening when we were in the privacy of our own home and could more freely interact.

Irina opened up the dialogue by reminding me that this man I was speaking of was also the great grandfather of Russia's heralded poet, Alexander Pushkin. Irina followed certain Southern traditions out of her love and respect of the colonel and she had no desire to bring trouble down on herself or his good name, but at home, that was private and where one should be able to relax. Besides no one was going to keep Polly down!

"Well, my grandfather was emancipated in eighteen sixty-one," Polly quickly retorted. Polly came from an island off the Carolinas that did things a little differently. "He served in the Union's first South Carolina volunteer army. And his daughter, my mother, was an educated woman. Some teachers came to our island with their church. They called themselves Unitarians."

I had never heard of this church, but they gave Polly a louder, more confident mouth from which to speak. And late at night I'd see her turning the pages of the books Irina bought for her but having to do so without drawing attention to herself or anyone else. One night, I remember passing her room only to see her reading *Great Expectations*. Polly smiled at me and asked, "Do you like Dickens?" Embarrassingly I had to admit that I had never read Dickens.

The following week, I found her book next to my bed on my nightstand.

❋ ❋ ❋

IRINA COUNSELED ME ON the things she thought young girls needed to know, like distilling wildflowers and herbs to make natural remedies and reading tea leaves and palms. "How else will you know which way to go in life," she'd say, "or if your suitor has good intentions?"

Sometimes she'd say, "Did you notice that you told me exactly what I was thinking before I could form the words? My darling, you have a gift, one that's much greater even than the gift of your legs." Then, to close our lesson, she'd repeat one of three old Russian proverbs: "Without rest, even the horse can't gallop"; "Without effort, you can't even pull a fish from a pond"; and, most importantly, "Be swift to hear and slow to speak."

We took walks every day. Irina would pick a flower or herb, tell me to close my eyes, then she'd ask, "What is this, Donatalia? Keep your eyes closed." If I wasn't able to name it by scent, Irina would put the flower in the palm of my hand and direct my fingertips to identify it through touch.

My senses heightened, and my world blossomed beyond anything I could have imagined. Irina was captivating almost as much so as my mother or Maestro Cecchetti; nonetheless, I found it strange that after all my years of dance, it was Irina who truly awakened my senses and introduced me to the mysteries of life.

Being the owner of a grand estate brought Irina into contact with businessmen from around the globe, which set her apart from most women of that day. With her lively spirit of inquiry, Irina absorbed knowledge from these men, knowledge she now passed on to me.

She had me practice the "breath of fire," which she'd learned from an old Indian businessman, who swore he'd learned it from a yogi. She showed me the power of crystals and amethysts, explaining, "This is what my mother taught me, just as your mother taught you French and how to dance ballet. This is what I have to pass on. Mothers teach their daughters what they know."

After spending a day learning the magical arts of nature from Irina, at night, when I closed my eyes, I was free of my limp. In my dreams, I was healed, and I danced for our czar, for kings and queens. I was content. My life, it seemed, was beginning to have purpose again.

CHAPTER 17

ALL THE WOMEN IN my life had left their mark. Irina acquainted me with many abilities that up to that point I had been unaware of. She said, "You've always been spinning too fast and only focused on one thing: dance. Your accident," she continued, "allowed you, no, forced you, to discover your truest nature. Someday you might even be thankful that a situation arose that made you examine the deepest part of yourself."

With Irina's guidance, I learned midwifery—how to predict if someone would live a long life, have children, find love. Explore and have adventures, be rich or be poor. "But remember," she added at the closing of each lesson, "read not only their palms but their eyes, too. It's the little crease in the hand, the sparkle or a shadow in the eye, that makes the difference. Truth is in the nuances."

And every night when I said my prayers, I silently thanked Mary Bradley because I felt quite certain that my family's association with her good name helped to solidify Irina's decision to have me stay. She once said to me that if "Mary can look after all the children in an orphanage in Africa, why surely I can take care of one wayward misplaced girl from Russia whose dreams got lost in a revolution."

"You have a gift," Irina told me. "You can see things others cannot," she went on. "Don't be frightened. It's just that your senses are more highly developed." Strangely, I understood what she was trying to say. I suddenly remembered the night before my mother passed away and I had the dream of the moon and how it blew my mother's flower petals right off their stems. The next morning, I recalled telling my father he would have to learn to make me breakfast. I couldn't tell you why I said what I did, only that somehow I knew it was true. That same afternoon it went from premonition to truth.

There was something about the way my mother, Irina, and Lillya, the three most influential women to me, were determined to grab every ounce of life. They could make a simple tea party feel like the grandest affair. They were radiant because of the way they chose to walk through the world. Instead of seeing ugliness and despair, they gravitated toward beauty whether it were a deep-violet tulip, a new dress, a special exhibit at an art museum, or architecture old or new.

Irina loved to make up excuses to go into town, look at the buildings, and watch the townsfolk walk by. Her latest obsession was Savannah's newly completed city hall with its distinctive copper dome. She acted as if her father or Colonel Butler had built it especially for her.

"It's Italian Renaissance," she told me. "Oh, how I admire its architect for creating a building so exquisite and functional at the same time. And the flowers, look how beautiful!" She swept her hand grandly so that I not only noticed the flower beds but all the magnificent live oak trees and their Spanish moss. "Forgive me"—Irina laughed—"I get carried away."

We spread out a brightly colored Mexican shawl that Polly had packed along with the desserts and spent the afternoon on the lawn talking and eating.

"By the time I leave this earth, Donatalia," Irina said as I took the last bite of Polly's banana cake, "you will understand your talents and know how to best use them." I brushed the crumbs off my lap, folded Polly's shawl, and silently contemplated the weight of Irina's words.

✻ ✻ ✻

IN 1908, GEORGIA PROHIBITED alcohol, ten years before Prohibition, starting up a booming bootlegger business. Ford came out with the new Model T, and Irina was first in line to buy one. In 1909, the Great White Fleet returned to Hampton Roads, in Virginia; William Howard Taft was elected president, and Robert Peary claimed to have reached the North Pole. We read about these things in the paper, sitting on the porch swing, but they came from a world that seemed very far away.

Living with Irina, like living in the South, was slow and easy. Time passed and I hardly knew where it went. I thought about what my life might have been but quickly buried those dreams. I was happy and it didn't do any good to obsess on what wouldn't occur. Irina knew the time was coming for me to step out into the world and perhaps meet a boy. I had carried a joyful spirit through much adversity for several years, but underneath it all, there was still fear. And if I left behind what I no longer needed, how would that feel?

My slight limp, a remnant of my past life, continued to be a reminder when the weather got cold and damp. I tried not to focus on it. But sometimes I couldn't help myself and my thoughts would wander to the mysterious Frenchman, Hervé, and just how different my life would have been if we hadn't met. How strange he didn't say goodbye and disappeared. Then I would turn my thoughts back to my family and Russia, the Imperial School, and sometimes even Vladimir.

❄ ❄ ❄

A FROST HAD HIT Savannah the night before. Earlier Polly had brought in some fresh bread pudding for us to share. Her favorite spice, cinnamon, with its distinctive scent, drifted from room to room. Irina, with a bit of a chill, was wrapped in a brightly colored woolen scarf I had given to her. We had just finished celebrating the twelfth day of Christmas the night before and now Irina and I were taking the Christmas ornaments down from the tree and neatly packing them in their boxes. The fireplace was crackling and the sweet smell of burning pine needles filled the room. The moon was high in the sky, shining in through the windows. Only the angel at the top of her tree remained to be taken down when suddenly Irina started speaking in Russian, as if some ghostly spirit had inhabited her and a deep voice inside me told me it had. So I climbed a ladder and carefully lifted the angel and put it in Irina's hands.

"The colonel gave me this," she smiled. Then she got serious. "I'm happy you came here, Donatalia," she said. "Us Russian girls were meant to be together."

Then Irina—usually so independent—let me help her up the stairs. She pulled her nightgown from her drawer, and I turned down her bedcovers. She told me she loved me, and that the angel that had always watched over her would now watch over me. "My angel is strong," she whispered, "stronger than the serpent and the one who poses as a witch." I felt Irina's forehead, certain she was running a fever, for her words made little sense.

Then she kissed me on both cheeks, closed her eyes, and never opened them again. Sometime between her good night kiss and the morning light, she died in her sleep.

❄ ❄ ❄

I'D LIVED WITH IRINA four years before I buried her in the colonel's mausoleum, amid winter honeysuckle and golden winter jasmine. Apart from the money she bequeathed to her favorite charities, she willed all her worldly possessions to me. Unlike most young women, I was now self-sufficient. I could take my time deciding which road in life I would follow.

Uncertain what to do next, I spent the rest of the winter and most of the spring swinging on the porch swings, one day swinging east toward prosperity and the next west, thinking about opportunities. I planted herbs, mostly for cooking—oregano, rosemary, thyme—relaxed in the sun, and became very good at putting off the big decisions. There'd be plenty of time for those later.

❋ ❋ ❋

June 1911

I STEPPED OUT FROM the fabric store's dimness into the bright early June sun of Habersham Street, clutching a little tissue-wrapped bundle of fabric and lace that I was sure Polly would find good use for. Ben had driven me into Savannah to shop; I'd left him reading a newspaper on a bench in Oglethorpe Square. Irina had always admired Savannah's many little grass-covered squares, always so beautifully planted. "We can thank Mr. Oglethorpe for making Savannah such a convivial place. All those benches where neighbors can sit and talk—a brilliant touch!" she'd say.

Lately I'd been feeling a new impatience. I'd barely been off the farm since Irina passed. There was a big world out there. Surely it had a place for me, and I knew I would find it. Yet I hadn't. Months had passed without a sign, a clue, a dream. Nothing. I was beginning to doubt myself.

I'd begun to cross Columbia Square, headed back toward Ben and the car, when suddenly I stopped. Struck with a craving for some fresh bread and honey, I turned and went the other way.

At the general store on East President, its wide-plank floors worn smooth by countless feet, I bought bread and honey and a few other things, set them on the counter in front of a pale young man, and signed the account ledger. I was about to turn and walk out when I froze. My childhood friend Vladimir was staring back at me from a colorful poster on the wall behind the clerk. I immediately recognized the smile in his eyes. He had gotten older, but he hadn't changed. The years and miles that separated us felt both long and short.

Memories began to wash over me. "I know that man!" I finally told the shopkeeper, who looked as if he was wondering what had come over me. "He and I studied together at the Imperial Ballet School in St. Petersburg when we were young. The Vronskys were circus royalty there. Probably every child in Russia knows who Vladimir is."

The clerk murmured something politely and turned to the next customer, but I didn't pick up my parcel. I stood reading words on the poster over and over:

Come One! Come All!
The Vronsky Family Circus
welcomes Children of All Ages
for an Unforgettable Experience!

And, in smaller letters below the decorative headlines and sublines:

Savannah at sunset on Tuesday, June 8, 1911
Performances the following five nights
Admission only five cents, children free

I could hardly believe my luck. June 8 was this very day.

CHAPTER 18

W HEN I CAME HOME from the store, I looked in the mirror thinking of all that had happened since I last saw Vladimir. It had been a world away and I wondered if he would recognize the girl who was once me, and I the man he'd become.

How could it already be 1911? I asked myself. The image of planting New Year's wishes in Russian soil with my father, greeting the twentieth century, seemed so fresh and recent.

❋ ❋ ❋

IT WAS THE KIND of late spring day that seemed to stretch into two, making one feel like August had come early. The kind of day when even the most Yankee-hating Southerner would have welcomed a cool northern breeze. The night before, I'd felt as if I were living in a swamp, the air so heavy with moisture that I felt I was inhaling mosquitoes with every breath. So many, I could picture them dancing around in my lungs.

I didn't have a lot of time to prepare. I pulled out a light blue party dress that I liked and asked Polly if she would cut some flowers from the garden. Then I dusted myself off.

"I brought you some mock orange for your hair," Polly said, marching back into the room.

Together we carefully set a few midnight blue combs with freshwater pearls in my hair to hold the fragrant white flowers in place. Polly looked at me with questioning eyes, but she knew not to ask. I took a deep breath, thanked her, and left.

❋ ❋ ❋

THE HUM OF ACTIVITY at the circus grounds was overwhelming. Men were putting up the tents, the dull ring of hammers filling the air. Brightly dressed, exotic-looking women bustled about, preparing for the show. I felt lost. I asked several men who looked as if they could have been Russian lumberjacks if they knew where I could find Vladimir. "Bella," every one of them replied.

Who is Bella? I wanted to ask.

I walked around in circles until finally, dizzy, I found myself headed for home. The poster said he would be staying five days so I allowed myself to give in to my nerves. I passed a field spangled with meadow flowers and stopped to pick a white daisy. One by one I plucked the white petals. Should I try again, or just leave well enough alone? Surely, he knew my heart. The last petal I plucked directed me to try again. I promised myself I would return the next night.

The hours passed slowly the next day. I felt like a child waiting for the last snowflake to fall in a Russian winter. Oh, how anxious I was to talk to someone from my past—how anxious I was to talk to him, but I was also afraid that Vladimir's memories might be very different from mine. But then I told myself it was just a schoolgirl crush and I made up my mind to go see my friend.

Polly gave me a knowing look as I left: for the second night in a row, wearing a dress and flowers in my hair.

The circus grounds that had been skeletal before were now full of life. Something about the gaudy confusion drew me in. Actually, it reminded me a bit of Coney Island. My senses awakened. My nose and ears felt bigger. Touched with the salty tang of popcorn and sweat, the air tasted sweet. Children were laughing, parents were scolding, and lions were roaring. It was magnificent! I was already happy I had come.

Before going to my seat, I explored the midway. Along the way, I stumbled across a frightening fortune-telling machine but was momentarily distracted by a woman charming a snake. For a penny, the animated metal automaton with a wild, curly dark wig, brown eyes almost popping out of their sockets, and bright red lips smiled mechanically as it handed you your fortune. This one looked especially sinister, as someone—no doubt unhappy with what she'd foretold—had painted one of her teeth black.

How worthless, I thought. A machine can't read a palm or look into eyes for clues to a life. I could do a much better job, and I'd certainly be more entertaining. I found myself looking around as I walked the grounds, searching for a live fortune-teller of any sort. I can't tell you why I wanted to know. I just did.

The midway was quite a parade. I passed big people, little people, a bearded woman, lions, and bears; parents, husbands, and boyfriends trying to win prizes for girls, wives, and little ones—but not a fortune-teller anywhere.

I turned to leave, I headed back toward the big top, musing about the creepy fortune-telling machine. Then I heard myself listing my qualifications. Surely the Vronsky Family Circus would never find anyone more qualified to interpret tea leaves at the bottom of a cup or see a person's true nature in the lines of his palm better than me. I tried to put this thought out of my head. I was getting ahead of myself.

But without Irina, I suddenly realized, I'd become lonely. Perhaps I could use the arts Irina had taught me.

I'd changed since I first set foot on Ellis Island. Who was this adventurous person who'd come to inhabit me? I was so much freer and more daring than the curious disciplined dancer who'd left Russia.

I was even more anxious now for the circus to begin, and to see my old friend. Memories of Vladimir and my past had occupied my every waking moment since I saw his face on the poster. But although I was impatient, I took into consideration what I had learned many years ago. "It is always better to visit a performer after the show."

Stuffing down my eagerness, I found my way to the bleachers of the big top. The crowd's excitement was contagious. The elephants entered, followed by the horses. One equestrian rider left everyone spellbound as she stood upright on the rosined back of a cantering horse, playing the flute. She wore a bright red plume on her head. It made me think of the stories I had heard of Lillya in her free-spirited youth.

The clowns riding unicycles were funny and made me laugh. Watching the trapeze artists, I imagined what it would be like to fly through the air.

Then Vladimir entered the ring, shining like the star he'd always been. Charismatic and handsome as ever, he climbed the ladder to the high wire. The blood in my veins felt like a river overflowing with thoughts from our past. Stepping onto the taut line, he waved to the crowd. The hair on my arms stood straight up. "The Vronsky Family Circus has saved the best for last," the man sitting next to me told his children. I had to agree.

In this carnival kingdom, Vladimir was the emperor and he held the audience in his palm. Children squeezed their parents' hands until he arrived safely to the other side. Women were afraid their leading man might fall; men admired his strength and presence, the attention he commanded. Everyone was brought to their knees, then they stood and shouted for more. I had never heard so many encores.

But as I sat on the hard bleachers, as transported as any child, a truth struck me that I had never seen before. The circus was a traveling home for individuals with unusual talents and quirks. In this context, society deemed them delightful in small doses, but the same people who applauded them at the circus would likely reject them outside. Here, they found the place where they belonged, just as they were, protected by the big top's magic circle.

And I realized I wanted to be in that magic circle with Vladimir more than anything else. If the Vronsky Family Circus would have me, I'd happily join them.

❀ ❀ ❀

I WALKED OUT OF the big top in a trance, though the heat and humidity outside hit me like a slap to the face, bringing me back to earth. When I asked several workers where I might find Vladimir, the men smiled and pointed, and the women said, "Bella," as they had the previous day. Later I discovered that many women, with not the purest of intentions, often sought out Vladimir.

I was really no different. Secretly, I had to admit, my head had been full of fantasies ever since I saw his steel-blue eyes staring back at me from a poster.

CHAPTER 19

VLADIMIR DROPPED HIS GLASS of champagne when I entered the tent. "I thought I saw a ghost, so I closed my eyes," he said. "But look…you're still here." He was a little cloudy from drink and utterly bewildered. How had I made my way from St. Petersburg to Savannah and then to his circus and become a young woman along the way?

He embraced me and kissed my cheeks, and then we found a table where we could talk. My stomach was turning cartwheels, like the clowns I had just seen. I played with the flowers in my hair to calm myself.

Neither of us knew where to start. He asked about my father, and I asked about his parents, and several other friends we once had in common. The shadow of loss lay over our words, however light we tried to make them. I asked how Vladimir had come to be in Georgia.

"The circus was becoming a burden to my father," he said. "It's young men's work. And he was worried about Russia's future. He told me it was time to pass the circus on to me, but with one provision: I leave St. Petersburg."

"My father, too, made me leave." I told him briefly about my voyage and Catherine, leaving out the accident that broke my leg. "I know he was right, but I still find it hard to accept."

"Isn't it strange, the way our stories are a bit like mirrors?" Vladimir reflected.

"And that we never knew we were following a similar path," I responded. "Only I crossed the ocean alone, with just a trunk and leather case, and you brought an entire circus!"

"I think we both mourn our St. Petersburg," he said solemnly. We were silent for a moment. Vladimir shook himself. "But enough of this dismal talk. Do you remember my younger cousin, Viktor?"

"Yes, of course—we rode ponies together as children. Why?"

"He left Russia with me and the circus. I tried watching over him, but when we were in France, an older gypsy woman cast a spell on him, and he ran off with her in the middle of the night. I guess I should be grateful they only took a horse! But still, it caused quite a scandal—I don't think his parents will ever forgive me. They blame me, as his elder. What could I do? I couldn't lock him in a cage like a bird."

"These are such different times, Vladimir. So many of us have found ourselves following paths our parents can never understand. Who's to say which paths are wrong?" I smiled, keeping my voice light, though for some reason my heart had begun to race.

Vladimir opened his mouth to answer, but just then there was a stir in the room, everyone turning toward the doorway. He swung around too. A petite brunette, the rider with the bright red plume, had entered the room. Vladimir's cloudy eyes began to sparkle. She had a presence that made her look much taller.

"Bella!" Vladimir called out, then turned back to me. "She's my everything."

The way the workers had said Bella's name every time I asked where I might find Vladimir, I expected her to be cold and jealous. I was quite wrong. They'd simply been acknowledging that wherever Bella went, Vladimir would be close by. As for my own reaction to this unexpected turn, I would berate myself later, and more than once. For now, though, I would have to bury my disappointment.

Bella brought an air of festivity into the room, though behind the warmth in her eyes flickered a shadow of concern. Of course, she would be on guard whenever a young woman came around, what with Vladimir's looks. It didn't stop her though from smiling widely; she remained genial and cordial as our conversation lengthened and I began to see how truly remarkable Bella, in this confident grace, could be.

"Do tell us where you've been," she said in her lyrical Italian accent.

"Yes, of course!" Vladimir shouted.

I glanced sideways at him, bemused. You'd think, to hear him now, we had barely exchanged a few words. But who could blame him for his caution? He had a beautiful young wife he was clearly deeply in love with. And no one really knew what to make of this young woman who moved like a ballerina, had white flowers and freshwater pearls in her dark, wavy hair, and spoke in English, Russian, and French.

"They knew each other in Russia," I overheard a man standing behind Vladimir whisper to the woman beside him. "She appeared out of nowhere tonight."

The woman glanced at me and then at Bella, then smiled and murmured something to a friend at her other side. A low hum and stir through the room made me think that she wasn't alone in anticipating a little gossip. I shifted uneasily. Why had I come at all? Vladimir and I weren't schoolchildren anymore, and my interest hadn't been strictly platonic.

But Bella handled the situation masterfully. She swept over with a plate of food and handed it to me, introducing herself in a way that put everybody at ease making it clear that I was welcome.

They'd married earlier that spring, Vladimir told me. My heart sank despite myself as I watched the small movements of Vladimir and Bella's hands, the way their bodies talked to each other. This would take some getting used to. Yet slowly, as I watched and listened, I became aware of my own breath becoming more even. It had been a long time since I had socialized with people close to my age.

Bella had grown up in an equestrian setting. Her father bought and sold fine-blooded horses in Italy. She was one year older than myself, and her mother, like Vladimir's, had once been a well-known equestrian. I wondered whether that was part of what had drawn Bella and Vladimir to each other. Obviously, the men in both families had a weak spot for beautiful women who rode well.

"I first saw Bella performing in Florence—it was love at first sight." Vladimir grew warmer and more animated as he talked about his wife. She blushed, but the flicker of wariness evaporated from her eyes.

She turned to me, her graciousness relaxing into genuine ease and warmth. "Oh, he was such a pest. He sat under my window and sang to me. I could never get any sleep—eventually I just had to give in."

He grinned. "Well, I never had any illusions, did I? I know it was Senofonte who really won her over, not me."

"That's true enough." Bella laughed. "Vladimir bought Senofonte, the best horse my father had, and then presented him to me. Quite a trick."

Vladimir put on an injured face. "You wrong me, darling. I promised to take the stallion to America, just because I knew it would make you happy. But it didn't hurt to make your father happy, too."

"You were certainly determined." Bella turned to me, smiling. "He might have gotten some of that from his mother. You knew Lillya, didn't you, Donatalia?"

"Yes," said Vladimir, "Donatalia knew my mother. But she was probably too young to have heard my favorite story about her."

"Oh, tell it now!" I said. It was true that Lillya had always fascinated me, ever since that New Year's dinner when she'd seemed as sparkling as the champagne she held. But it was also a relief to hear about something other than Vladimir and Bella's courtship. I leaned toward Vladimir and lost myself in his story.

"When Lillya was only fifteen," Vladimir began, "and already a daring rider, her father, my grandfather, took the family to the Loire Valley where she could improve her French, and he could stock his wine cellar. Every morning she borrowed a horse from a nearby stable and rode through the woods.

"A young officer at the famous Cadre Noir riding academy saw Lillya galloping through the trees, floating along on her saddle effortlessly her red-gold hair trailing like fire behind her. The young man was dazzled by her grace and fearlessness.

"The next week her father was invited for a tour of the famous riding academy. Lillya, who dreamed of learning the secrets of the Cadre Noir, begged him to let her come with him. In the end, not surprisingly, she got her way.

"And as fate would have it, the same young officer who had seen her in the forest was asked to give the visitors a tour. Recognizing her as the rider he'd seen, this courtly young man in his impeccable black uniform bowed and asked if she would like to go riding with him.

"Almost every day for the next month, Lillya and Laurent rode together through the Loire's meadows and wooded hillsides. But first, every day, Lillya watched as her suitor schooled his horse in the Cadre Noir's manège. With intense focus, she noticed every shift of his weight in the stirrups, every subtle movement of his fingers on the reins." Unaware of mine or Bella's feelings, Vladimir poured us each another drink and continued talking.

"The sultry nights became cooler," Vladimir explained, "the golden summer dimmer, but this young man's affection for my mother grew brighter and brighter. Business back in Russia was beginning to demand my grandfather's attention. My mother's suitor realized his time to express himself was becoming as short as each passing day. My mother, an eager student, went along with the young man. This was more of an adventure for her, I believe.

"Knowing my father would never let her stay, when things began to get too serious, she let her father overhear a conversation with a chambermaid. Needless to say, my mother's time in France came abruptly to an end."

Back in Russia, Lillya spent her days mastering the movements she had watched Laurent perform. She'd close her eyes as her horse shifted restlessly beneath her and imagine his fine hands, his polished boots. But her heart didn't beat for her teacher; it beat for his skills. When she'd perfected the knowledge she'd taken from him, Lillya passed it on to the aristocratic ladies of St. Petersburg. Some, in turn, revealed this little-known but highly sought-after European art to their husbands.

"Though in secret, of course." Vladimir winked at me, breaking the spell. "No man wants to admit that a woman has taught him anything, especially about horses and riding. But my mother's gift raised her stature among the upper class. They flocked to see her, and everyone else followed. When she married my father, she was showered with lavish gifts."

He fell silent for a moment, his eyes unfocused. "Well, that's the true beginning of the Vronsky Circus's fame. It's my mother, in a way, who made it a success." A shadow seemed to cross the room, the shadow of time and glory faded. Then he threw back his head and raised his glass, his eyes sparkling.

"To my brilliant mother, Lillya!"

"What happened to Laurent?" I couldn't help but ask.

"From what I was told, Laurent was left heartbroken. He did not take it well."

❀ ❀ ❀

WE TALKED UNTIL THE candle had burned down to a stub, the words falling off our tongues in Russian and English; every once in a while we threw in a little French.

Vladimir's parents were still in Russia. So far, they had kept their place in St. Petersburg but were spending more and more time in the country with his grandfather on the family estate where his mother had first learned to ride. "For their safety, they need to be more anonymous. The political climate is getting hotter by the day. Their ties to the aristocrats no longer serve them well," Vladimir said. "Things at home are bad now. There have been many uprisings, police and government officials assassinated. You should be grateful your father had the foresight to take precautions for your safety."

I told my old friend how I'd ended up in the South and met Irina. He didn't ask why I wasn't dancing; to the ordinary person my slight limp might be almost unnoticeable, but he knew what it meant.

When I told Vladimir and Bella about my encounter with the scary machine that spit out fortunes, they both laughed. Bella and I spoke about babies; she was a few months pregnant. We talked about medicine, and she told me that her grandmother knew much about healing. When we went to say goodbye, my old friend and my new one kissed me on the cheek. Then Vladimir surprised me by saying, "It would be wonderful to have a fortune-teller who feels compelled to tell the truth."

Bella added, even more surprisingly, "A midwife who knows about medicine and herbs would also be very welcome here."

In the few hours I'd spent with them, they seemed to have each come to the same conclusion: not only that I could have a role in their circus but that I might play this specific role. Vladimir wanted to extend an invitation to an old friend and schoolmate, and Bella, it seemed, had decided that not only would I be a welcome addition but we might even become fast friends.

I left to find Ben, my ride home. My head was full of thoughts, each one vying for center stage. My friend Irina was in the heavens; I had no commitments that someone else couldn't handle, and Vladimir was my only connection to my past. He was the only person left in my world who had ever met my parents, the only one who could bring that faraway life back to me with words. What we shared, few understood.

At home, I said good night to Polly, who was pretending she had something to do besides wait up for me, and then climbed the stairs to my bedroom, reached into the closet, pulled out a suitcase, and started to pack. Fate had called me, and it was time to answer.

I prepared the house for my departure.

CHAPTER 20

"PEOPLE ARE MORE APT to listen to a happy man and do business with him," Joseph's father preached, and over the years, a little of that rubbed off on him. A tall, thin man in his early thirties with a skinny wisp of a mustache, he always dressed in wrinkled pants one size too big, but he had a way with numbers and was smart as a whip.

Joseph's father owned and managed the general store for as long as anyone could remember. While some kids went to school to learn about the world, Joseph's father taught him how to pick a product and negotiate. At seven years of age he was helping buy the vegetables for his father's store and negotiating with the farmers, by eleven he was ordering their fabric and lace, and by fourteen he was named the assistant manager. Although the Butler Plantation was quite a bit bigger than anything he had ever managed, Joseph knew an opportunity when one revealed itself, so when I asked if he would like to be our caretaker, he jumped at the chance.

I only had a few days to get things in order. I put Polly in charge of anything inside, and Joseph anything outside including the farmland and gardens. After all, his father had been teaching him how to turn a profit since he was five. "Use every inch of what you have, be honest, plan, and remember to smile, always remember to smile," his father repeated to him daily.

I compiled a list of all the tasks that needed to be completed before I could leave, and I worked night and day with Joseph at my side until every single one of them was crossed off. The last item on the list was of a personal nature but was none the least as important. I promised Irina that I would make it known that no one could slaughter her prize pig, Daffodil, and keep their job and home. Daffodil would be free to roam the rest of her natural life. Fulfilling my promise, I could now leave.

Ben drove me to the train station just as the circus was about to pull out. I made it in the nick of time. When we got settled in the next town, Vladimir pulled the penny fortune-telling machine out of the midway and threw it in the garbage. "You're going to put it out of business, so I might as well take it out," he smiled.

Next, he painted a gilded carriage in mysterious colors and draped it with tapestries to make it look more inviting. And inside this carriage, a once aspiring Russian ballet dancer became a fortune-teller.

❅ ❅ ❅

BELLA WAS KIND, BUT it was clear she had mixed feelings about me and was unsure of her invitation to have me join them. It wasn't with her words, but I could see it in her eyes. She questioned my intentions and wanted to know, *What does that girl want?* Truthfully, I didn't know.

I had no idea what to expect of circus life. I'd had a lot of dreams, but this had never been one of them. Vladimir and Bella's patience with me was sorely tested. It took a while before I understood the delicacies of my new profession.

"Donatalia," Vladimir remonstrated, "you can't tell someone that in two months' time, they're going to be hit on the head with a rock and die. You must remember, the circus is a place of entertainment." Though I tried to be gentle and diplomatic, I'm afraid I had a touch more of Mme Strachkov in me than Irina or my mother. More than once I packed my bags, ready to move back to Savannah. But the more I thought about leaving, the harder I worked at my job to get better.

Then one day Vladimir came to my carriage to drop off some bread Bella had made. While he was there, an old man knocked on the door.

"Pardon me," the raggedly dressed man with the kind eyes inquired. "Are you the fortune-teller?" I could see a brood of children behind him, five in all.

"Well, I guess I am," I answered back. "What can I do for you?" I asked.

"Well um, you see, miss, I'm a miner and lately there have been some accidents."

I lit several candles and squeezed all the grandkids along with their grandfather into my carriage. It was tight, but no one wanted to be left out. Vladimir stood outside, his ear up against the carriage window. He was listening as hard as he could. "You see, these young ones depend on me. The oldest is only nine.

"Well, to get right to the point, these kids, they're afraid for me! They want to know if I'm going to get trapped and die the same way their daddy, my son, did."

I looked at the old miner, then at the children he was responsible for feeding.

Finally, I had learned to phrase my predictions truthfully yet positively and for that I was grateful. I took a deep breath. The scent of Bella's bread could still be found floating in the air. Its residue lingered on my nose hairs. My senses had been awakened and now they needed somewhere to go. I had practiced finessing my predictions and hoped they'd be helpful. I repeated my answer using different tones, modulating on the select phrases I wanted to emphasize. I spoke very deliberately so that each of the grandkids and Vladimir too, could hear my words: "Spirit says you will live a long life, if," and I paused, "for the next three months you keep your attention on the sky and are always ready to run or catch what falls."

The grandkids all sighed a big sigh of relief and fought for a position on their grandfather's knee. "Calm down," the old miner said as he tried to decide if the fortune I gave him was good or bad and what he should do. Nonetheless, in this moment his grandchildren were happy so he decided he would be too. "See, you're going to have lots of time to sit on Grandpapa's knee. Bobby, it's Kevin's turn."

And I noticed, the more helpful I became, the more people lined up to hear what I had to say. My reputation grew, although I was certain my mother must have been turning over in her grave. I could hear her and Mme Strachkov speaking in Russian about how they hadn't struggled to teach me French so that I might read the palms of French immigrants residing in the southern United States. Over time, however, I realized that I truly had a gift and if I let go of the past, perhaps I could even be happy.

Then one morning it happened: I woke up content. I didn't know how long it would last, but I now knew how it felt. My life up until then had been all about drilling and training. In Russia, I'd learned the art of discipline and practice. With my mentor and friend Irina, I'd developed my senses. But now, in the circus, for the first time in my life, I was truly becoming my own person. Vladimir was like family to me and Bella and I were slowly developing a friendship. I understood all the reasons she could resent me, but then I'd think about her generosity, her fun, kind spirit, and my animosity would melt away.

"Come eat breakfast with us," she often asked, and Vladimir frequently invited me to dinner. Vladimir and Bella took to calling me Donatella. Bella liked it because it sounded Italian. I liked it because it had no history. Donatella could become whoever she wanted to be.

✳ ✳ ✳

I PRACTICED MY MIDWIFERY skills almost as much as my fortune-telling. In three months' time, Bella's belly brought her riding days to a halt, too. We had just finished our morning coffee and were sitting quietly by the fire when she felt a disturbance in her belly and asked if I would check her out. When I placed my ear to her belly, I heard a *boom, boom* echoed twice. Two hearts were beating instead of one. It was clear Bella and Vladimir were going to have twins!

I relayed the news with a pinch of sadness mixed in happiness. It was hard for me to be completely happy. My fantasy of marrying Vladimir had been rooted since childhood.

Vladimir could have jumped over his high wire, he was that excited. I knew what I was feeling was not rational. But if I was happy for them both, then why did it hurt me so?

As thrilled as Vladimir was about the upcoming birth of his babies, he was that anxious, too.

At night, when he couldn't sleep, I'd see him walking past my tent on his way to play cards with the roustabouts. In particular, he had developed an unusual fondness for a heavyset giant of a man whose name was Boris. Boris was Russian, too. He came from the city of Perm in the Ural Mountains. Perm, when translated, meant "far away land," and far away it was for on the other side of this mountain range, Siberia started, Europe ended, and Asia began.

Boris worked in construction. He had come to the United States to follow a girl, but by the time he got here, she was with someone else. A friend of his who worked for Vladimir had mentioned that he had a strong, hardworking friend looking for a job.

It was rumored Boris could carry four times his own body weight. We didn't believe it until we saw him carrying an eight-hundred-pound piano down three flights of stairs all by himself. Vladimir hired him on the spot.

Vladimir took a special liking to this big burly man. They could talk in Russian, play cards, and relax. "Boris is easy to be around," Vladimir would say to me. "I find him calming."

Somehow, this giant man that most others found frightening displayed a gentle kindness toward Vladimir and genuine affection. And it didn't hurt that Boris let him win at cards!

"Do you want to know a secret, Donatella?" Vladimir asked one night when Boris was out with friends and unable to play. Bella had gone to bed early and Vladimir was trying to convince me to join him in a hand of his favorite game, poker.

Poker reminded me of Hervé, but Vladimir promised if I played just two hands, he would share a secret; something he hadn't even told Bella. I found it impossible to turn him down.

"You can't tell a soul," he said, and he made me swear on my mother's grave. "When Boris was a child…"

"This isn't even about you?" I scolded.

"Listen carefully," he swung back at me. "You'll find this interesting!" He continued on as if there had been no objection.

"You know Boris is from Perm. Well his father mined copper in a cave all day so he spent his days in darkness. But when he came home at the end of the day, he insisted their house be filled with light until he left for the mines again the next morning. As a result, Boris and his brothers and sisters all learned to sleep in the light.

"His entire childhood lanterns were lit during the day throughout their home and that became what was normal. To this day, our big Boris must sleep with a light, for this giant of a man is afraid to sleep in the dark! Can you imagine that, Donatella?

"Boris shared with me his innermost secret and when he did I was so moved, I saw the light inside of him."

One month later, just when Vladimir and Boris usually played cards, Bella went into labor.

CHAPTER 21

December 1911

I STOOD ON THE ice-encrusted midway. Nothing was stirring—not a leaf, not a bird. The freak storm from the night before had left the circus grounds encapsulated in a thick layer of ice. The world was silent and crystalline when I heard the distinct crunch of feet walking on frozen ground. I turned to see who it was. Vladimir was walking toward me. Despite all my resolve, my heart beat faster the closer he got. "Bella needs you," he said when he was certain I could hear him.

The last few weeks, he'd been stretched between joy and fear. By the time I saw his face I forgot the foolish past. Vladimir looked like a ghost of himself, almost translucent with fatigue. Wordlessly, I followed him to their carriage. When I entered, there was Boris sitting next to Bella telling her not to worry, "Vladimir will be back soon with Donatella."

"Thank god it's you!" Bella said between the sharp pains of labor when I entered.

"You two go play a hand of cards, but stay near in case I need you," I said to Boris and Vladimir. "You did your part by fetching me." Then I turned to Bella. "You are going to be fine."

The next hours were a blur. Vladimir proved to be helpful by gathering towels and hot water for me and Boris made Bella a simple chicken broth so she'd have something warm to drink.

And as the sun crept above the horizon, early the following morning, a cry of new life could be heard over Bella's scream.

Minutes later, a second cry bouncing off the sides of the glittering tents rang clearly through the circus grounds, alerting everyone that the newest Vronskys had arrived.

I wrapped the babies in blankets and laid them on Bella's chest before fetching Vladimir who was right outside the door. Then I left to get some rest.

Vladimir swore his firstborn stole his heart the moment he saw her, so she became Ann Marie Heart. Her sister had eyes like coals, so dark they almost looked black, and so sharp and warm they melted his soul, thus they named her Spade and nothing more.

I fell instantly in love with the twins. It was a deeper love than I had felt for anyone other than my mother or father. Ann Marie had fine auburn curls similar to Lillya, and Spade's hair was dark and straight with a deep satin-like glow.

❀ ❀ ❀

BELLA SMILED, SHE HAD been sleeping, but then her face turned surprisingly grave. "Donatella, I have something to ask you. You have a great gift—I've seen it, and it will only get stronger. But I must ask you not to look into my daughters' futures, as tempting as I know that is."

I flushed, stung. "But, Bel—"

"No!" Her voice was so sharp I sat back, shocked. "Please let me explain." And she took a deep breath and continued.

"When I was a girl, I asked my grandmother, a great interpreter of tea leaves, if she would look into the future of my favorite cousin and see if she or I would win the spelling contest. My grandmother flashed her evil eye at me. 'Never read the tea leaves of someone close to you,' she said. 'It's bad luck.' Perhaps you'll say it's just foolish superstition from the old country. But I believed her then, and I believe her now."

She caught my eyes and held them. "Swear it, Donatella."

I had no choice. I promised.

❀ ❀ ❀

THE GIRLS WERE STRONG and healthy. Bella made a carrier that she could slip over her head and strap around her back. In the front she sewed two pouches, one for each baby, with holes for their tiny legs to slide through.

I bought a book filled with blank pages in which to keep a record of all those I assisted in entering the world. I had many others to fill in, but the first two names I entered there were Ann Marie Heart and Spade. I held the pen in my hand a second longer, feeling that something was missing. Then it came to me and I added "Queen" in front of both names, for if they had been born in Russia, like Vladimir, they would have been treated almost like royalty.

❋ ❋ ❋

AT CHRISTMAS, VLADIMIR DECIDED it was the perfect time to throw a party celebrating the birth of the twins. We decorated the "big top" with garlands and wreaths of Spanish moss, sumac berries, and holly and put the largest Christmas tree we could find right in the center of the tent, with presents for all the children who would attend.

Besides ourselves, several other circus owners came, along with many of the best trapeze, high-wire, and equestrian artists in America. It was an exotic group, indeed.

Vladimir proudly showed off the twins. Women cooed over Ann Marie and Spade. The babies seemed to be fascinated by the sequins on the girls' sparkling costumes.

The men convened by the fire outside the tent where they lit up their cigars, lifted snifters of old French brandy, and congratulated a beaming Vladimir.

"Yes, very well done, though next time monsieur, I will wish for you two boys," said Henri, the Frenchman. Henri owned the circus that was based down in Baton Rouge.

Vladimir stared at him, aghast. "What do you mean?"

Henri shrugged and puffed his cigar. "Girls like yours will be beautiful, but doesn't a man need a son to carry on the family name and business, or am I old-fashioned?"

"Things may be different up north, but us Southerners go by tradition," said a rival circus owner from Atlanta who went by the name Jim Baldwin. Then he slapped Vladimir's back with his big beefy hand. Jim was a huge man, but he was small compared to Boris. Vladimir filed the thought when he shared all of this with me later.

"Girls are great, but a boy inherits the keys to the kingdom," Baldwin said.

Just then, Bella and I appeared and the subject was abruptly dropped. But Vladimir would not forget the words that had been said. He was Lillya's son, after all, and his daughters would come second to no one. Later that evening, when most everyone had gone and Bella was putting the queens down, Vladimir shared with me his conversation with Jim and Henri.

"Men, men, men, men. They love their women, but they don't want them for heirs. How foolish. Look at my mother and all she contributed to our family."

I thought about her too and my own mother. *Did my father have to defend my mother when she only gave him a girl?* From that moment on, my feelings toward Vladimir became more brotherly or that of a favorite cousin.

Even when she was a child, I could see the fire in Ann Marie, and not just because she was born under the sign of Sagittarius. Red reflected who she was and how she would live her life.

She was fascinated by horses. Bella beamed with pride every time she saw her daughter stroke their soft muzzles and scramble fearlessly over their backs: Ann Marie had inherited her passion, as well as that of her mother and her other grandmother, Lillya. She was riding in front of Bella by her first birthday. "Faster!" It took a while for Bella to figure it out. "Asta," she'd cry, her little hands clutching the horse's mane, relishing its power and speed.

Quietly determined, Spade was in many ways the diametric opposite of her twin. She spent hours walking carefully along any log she found. Her favorite colors were olive and black, and all things dark intrigued her. She made an exception, though, for lightning bugs, which she never tired of chasing.

❋ ❋ ❋

It would have frightened Mme Strachkov, but I found it deeply satisfying when on New Year's Day 1914, just over two years after the first set of twins had been born, I was able to tell Bella, "You're going to have two more."

Vladimir was as nervous as he'd been before the first twins' birth, if not more. As Bella's due date approached, he paced during the day and lost himself in endless games of poker through the night. On the steamy July night when Bella went into labor, I could hear him outside the birthing car, mumbling to himself, playing solitaire. *Snap! Snap! Snap!* When he wasn't working the deck, I could hear him pacing and whispering to himself.

Bella mumbled through her pain with sentences no one understood. When the third queen appeared, with a wail like an angel, Vladimir burst into the room, then ran back out.

Ten minutes later, the fourth queen appeared, and Vladimir cradled the bundles in the soft dawn light filtering through the curtains and cooed at them as they slept.

The first had a face so bright that it sparkled. They christened her Diamond Claire. The second, it seemed, had no intention of leaving the comfort of her mother's belly without a suitable audience. She kicked and then waited, and then kicked again, until Bella howled like a siren. But not until Bella had squealed the highest note in her register did the baby girl bounce her way onto the table so we could welcome her to this world.

"No one would guess that they're twins." Vladimir gazed at them, entranced. "They're as different as night and day."

To Vladimir's chagrin, Bella insisted that this second girl be named for each of her grandmothers. Just when Vladimir couldn't hide his disappointment a minute longer, she added, "Do you like the name Lucia Akinsya Club?"

Vladimir's chest blew up with pride. "It's beautiful. Maybe we could call her Lucky for short."

"Yes, Lucky is a good family name." Bella smiled, and Vladimir passed out vintage Chas Goodall & Son playing cards instead of cigars to all his friends, in honor of his queens.

That night, after everyone else had fallen asleep, I got out my book of births and wrote in it "July 7, 1914," and then "Queen Diamond Claire" and "Queen Lucia Akinsya Club."

I paused, holding my fountain pen just above the paper. Outside, a whip-poor-will called. "Diamond Claire's cheeks sparkle, and her white-blond curls shine like the moon," I wrote.

It was true. I could have stared at Diamond for hours—she was as hypnotic as a lit candle. Vladimir had been as awestruck as I was. "Donatella, if you hadn't been the one who assisted Bella when she was born, I might think Diamond was a fairy changeling. How did two people with dark brown hair ever make a child so blond?"

There was no doubt whose daughter Lucky was—even at birth I could see Bella in her. "Determined, intelligent, and a good screamer," I wrote in my book. Already, though, I wondered if a child so insistent on attention might find life with three dazzling sisters difficult.

All of the queens of the deck were now in play. Sadly, there would be no kings. When the doctor called in the afternoon, he congratulated Bella on her healthy twins. But he frowned when he looked at Bella's white face. He took her pulse, and then pulled Vladimir aside.

"Any attempt to expand your family further is out of the question," he said sternly. "This delivery weakened Bella terribly—another would endanger her life."

Bella cried when she heard the verdict. "Vladimir, I'm sorry. I wanted to give you a son."

"Listen to me, Bella." Vladimir put his hand on her arm. The steel was back in his eyes as he looked straight into hers. No longer was he the pacing wreck he'd been the last few weeks. "Our daughters are all I could ever want. I have all my queens in one hand." Still Vladimir sometimes wondered if his cousin Viktor wasn't the only one the gypsy fortune-teller had put a curse on.

I found my jealousy of Bella was quickly replaced by the love I felt for these babies. Even my misguided feelings toward Vladimir began to wane by comparison. So I helped Bella change diapers and fix bottles and babysat, and Bella became dependent on me, and I let this attachment grow for it was the purist love I had felt since I was a child.

Every once in a while, I imagined what it would be like to have my own family, and when I did I sometimes saw the mysterious face of Hervé. But by now so much time had passed that I was not certain if the face I saw was his or my imaginations. Several circus men had vied for my attention, but they only saw the fortune-teller and never the Russian dancer. Truthfully, they didn't know what to do with me, but it's not as if I made it easy. So, I put my love instead where it was returned in kind without expectation, in the twins.

Our lives developed a happy rhythm, and time proved a balm to me, helping to bury much of what I had lost. The girls continued to grow. However, every time I heard a sigh from one of the queens, I had to stop myself from looking into their future. Now, I wonder, would it have made a difference?

✳ ✳ ✳

OVER SEVERAL YEARS, I saw Vladimir get frustrated and upset. "Don't they understand how grateful I am to have such a wonderful wife and four amazing girls?" he'd say. But he was patient and also determined to defend his family. He had plenty of time to play his hand. Occasionally he'd stop by and test the waters of my female mind by asking me questions—"What do you feel about the suffragettes?" "Should a woman have the right to inheritance?"

Then one morning he buttonholed me in my carriage. "I'm going to honor Bella and the queens," he said. "The entire world is going to know just how proud of them I am." And I knew he meant it.

I watched him stride briskly away, and I didn't hear another word until the morning Bella came to fetch me.

* * *

"He's outdone himself this time. Come!" Bella pulled off my covers, awakening me. I had no idea what she was talking about, but by the sound of her voice I knew I had to get up to see what Vladimir had concocted. Ten minutes later, I was out the door and rushing right behind her, my breath making little puffs in the crisp late-fall air.

Bella entered the girls' room like a steam train about to slip a rail. "Hurry, get dressed! We're going to the big top."

Both sets of twins were lying in their beds with their covers over their heads. When they heard Bella's high pitch, they scrambled to put on their clothes, not caring which shirt belonged to who, or if it was inside out. Bewildered, we all hurried out the door, the girls rubbing their eyes.

"What did Papa do?" Lucky asked me. "Mama's really excited." I didn't have a clue, though obviously it was big.

"Congratulations!" carnies yelled as we hurried through the midway.

"Thank you," Bella replied.

Anxious to discover what everyone else seemed to know, the girls and I increased our speed.

We arrived at the big top and stopped, looking up. High above, a new banner, much bigger than the one it replaced, gleamed in the early morning light. Where *The Vronsky Family Circus* had flown for generations, flanked by a bold heart and spade on one side, and a diamond and club on the other, a new name was painted in huge, bright letters: *The Circus of the Queens*. Ann Marie giggled and Spade started to cry. Diamond and Lucky wanted to know what it said.

Bella put her hand over her mouth, overwhelmed, and looked at me. "I swear I love my Vladimir even more than before, if that's possible." She didn't say it out of spite or to hurt me. She said it because she meant it and she knew that I would understand. Then she looked at Diamond and Lucky, Ann Marie and Spade, and a tear brought about by pure emotion was falling down her cheek. "It reads, 'The Circus of the Queens.' The queens are you four girls. Your father has dedicated our circus to you. That's how much he loves you."

Vladimir played his hand, and he held it up for the whole world to see. "It's the best play I ever made," he told me years later.

"It was a brilliant move," I agreed. "Both the girls and the circus reaped more rewards than either of us could have imagined." Yes, word of the Vronskys' Circus of the Queens traveled fast, across oceans, even to Europe, even to France, even to a man whose main ambition was revenge, and another who was jealous of their past.

The circus was a pipeline to the world, and by the time the third or fourth person told the same tale, it usually was more interesting than when it began.

Talk of Vladimir, Bella, and the queens preceded us everywhere we went. There was something in the way Vladimir chose to honor his wife and daughters that captured the imagination of women, men, and children everywhere. And as the word got out, these tales grew taller and wider, until sometimes even I didn't recognize them.

Images of the queens were woven into tapestries. Mythical adventures with just enough truth in them were shared over late-night fires, then passed from stagehand to advance man as the circus journeyed from town to town. "The Vronskys come from Russian aristocracy," I heard one stagehand tell another.

"They share the blood of the royals," the advance man replied, and I did nothing to correct him.

Ann Marie Heart, Spade, Diamond Claire, and Lucky became famous across the country. The Circus of the Queens became much more than a name, and I became the keeper of our truths.

CHAPTER 22

I N OUR PRIME, THE Circus of the Queens had twenty-four train cars, including six sleepers and several tableaux wagons of ornate design. In each town we visited, the festivities began with a parade. The windjammer band would march down Main Street with a calliope not far behind. A clown riding a brightly dressed floppy-eared donkey doubled as security.

The horses and camels had names like Nellie and Concetta. The tigers were Midnight, Satin, and Baby. Before each show, a promenade of clowns, red-nosed fun-makers, entered on unicycles while their dancing dogs did somersaults and dives. Our collection of clowns, trapeze artists, equestrians, and high-wire acts was larger than our menagerie of exotic animals. Many other circuses had more; however, we had something they didn't—our history and our myth.

Bella and I developed an unspoken understanding and my relationships with each of the queens grew deeper than I ever thought possible.

❋ ❋ ❋

"GOOD," SAID SAM, "NOW lean forward and put your hands on Napoleon's shoulders. Close your eyes, one-two-three, one-two-three. Can you tell which hind leg is pushing off, which front leg is leading?"

"Yes, Sam. Please, can I stand up now?"

"No, no, not yet. Patience, girl. Sit up straight. Now, let's see your scissors… Let your legs swing. Give yourself time to feel the rhythm."

At first I could only see dust swirling in a single bar of light, piercing the canvas overhead. As my eyes adjusted to the dim light, I could make out the massive form of a dapple-gray horse, cantering very slowly in a circle around a slender young woman: Samantha Devine, the circus's head horse trainer.

Sam's parents were circus people too, and Sam had been performing with them since she was a little girl. When her folks retired, Vladimir, who knew her family, had invited Sam to join the Vronsky Family Circus, and after the birth of the first twins, she'd stepped into Bella's place. Many had fought for the job, but Bella had been firm. "It's only fitting, given our family history, that a woman head the equestrians."

I squinted at the tiny figure on the horse's back, at the glint of red sequins... Could it be? I blinked.

Several days later, a voice called me from the wooden bleachers. "Here, Donatella. Come watch my baby girl!"

I started up toward Bella, glanced back down at the arena, and nearly fell off the step I was balanced on. Ann Marie had risen to her bare feet, standing like a living flame on the horse's broad bare back.

"Bella, are you both crazy? She'll slip and fall! And what if the horse spooks?"

"Calm down, Donatella. That's why they call Napoleon a rosinback—the rosin gives her a good grip. And he'll take care of her. Worth his weight in gold, that horse."

It was true; the triple beat of Napoleon's feet was hypnotically steady, never wavering.

＊＊＊

"HANDS IN THE AIR, Ann Marie," Sam called. "Now bend your knees...hold your balance...come down to sitting again. Good girl!" She whistled softly to the horse, and he fell smoothly into a walk and then halted.

"Okay, now we'll show your mama your new trick." Sam walked over and stood beside the horse. "One, two, three..."

Ann Marie leaned back until she was lying over the horse's rump.

"And...now!"

Curling herself over her shoulders, Ann Marie gracefully somersaulted to the ground behind Napoleon. She looked over at us, beaming from ear to ear.

"Mama, did you see?"

I glanced over at Bella. There were tears of pure joy in her eyes. "Yes, darling, I saw." And she opened her arms as Ann Marie flew up to her.

From that moment on, nothing could have stopped Ann Marie Heart. Although she had a very sweet nature, she liked to stir things up, and she could be defiant.

Her tutors loved her for her quick wit, though when one told her she was wrong, and she had decided she was right, she'd push and push until the tutor gave in.

She rarely had to push that hard, though. She was like a magnet: somehow, people almost always ended up bending to her will.

Sam was one of the rare people who could stand up to Ann Marie. I liked talking with Sam. Her parents were from New Orleans, and she spoke French. It wasn't quite the same French that Mme Strachkov had beaten into me, true, but when she sang Cajun songs and one of the men brought out an accordion, it could sound as good as the best opera, and as lively and passionate, too.

Ann Marie loved being around Sam, and Sam enjoyed baiting Ann Marie. "I'll show you a better way to do that if you practice your dismount three more times," she'd say. Then Sam would share a trick, and Ann Marie would almost always get it right. It was clear that, like her mother and grandmothers, Ann Marie was born to be on a horse.

All of us were finding our places in those early years. My own life became just one of a much larger whole. I'd become the circus: its blood my blood, its life my life, its burdens mine to shoulder as well.

It was not an easy life, but it was absorbing. It wasn't the life my parents would have chosen for me. But I was a different person, in a different world, and I knew in this time and place I was where I should be.

※ ※ ※

DIAMOND'S TRANSLUCENCE WAS MORE than skin-deep. She wore her feelings where everyone could see them, on her face. People seeing her for the first time were certain that they knew her; so much so that it became easier to go along with them and Diamond didn't care. She was a natural actress, with the ability to transform herself into any character she pleased. When she entered a room, her presence was so striking that even the most talkative person in it would stumble over their words. Her seriousness was matched only by her humor. And it soon became obvious that she had a connection with what some would call the other world.

It was good that Diamond was such a clever mimic, since she didn't speak a word until the age of three. Living with her became a nonstop guessing game, and we all learned to play. "She's so good at showing exactly what she means;

maybe there's no reason for her to speak," Bella would explain to guests. She shone in every conversation effortlessly without ever saying a word.

Still, Vladimir and Bella were concerned. They got opinions from doctors in every town we passed through, but no one had answers. "Nothing is physically wrong with your daughter," they'd say. "For now, it appears that she simply doesn't feel the need to talk."

"When Diamond is ready to say more," I'd say, trying to reassure them, "she'll let us know." But Vladimir and Bella got more and more worried.

Lucky, who was speaking at one, was afraid that somehow she had swallowed Diamond's voice. "Did I take Diamond's talk?" she asked.

Bella and I both answered, "Absolutely not!" But Lucky didn't seem to believe us. She began to compensate for Diamond Claire's lack of vocabulary, acting as Diamond's translator and never straying too far from her sister's side. Lucky could read Diamond's body language better than most people comprehend the words in a book, and when she was only two, Lucky through Diamond asked her father for a swing.

When Diamond finally did decide to speak, her first word wasn't *Mama* or *Dada*, it was *"push."* Upon hearing that, Vladimir immediately instructed his men to build Diamond a miniature trapeze and they were to hang it from a tree in every town we visited. It was soon obvious that Diamond's disinclination to talk had no effect on her ability in the air. She'd laugh as she swung, as if her legs might touch the heavens. Watching her, Vladimir's eyes would light up with fierce admiration.

Even on the ground, Diamond was full of cartwheels and games, and when we sang around the campfire, she'd happily hum along. Her second word wasn't *Mama* or *Papa*. Bella swore it was *"go."*

"We were boarding the train," Bella said, "and Lucky got distracted by a woodpecker. Diamond inpatient, gave Lucky a little push, and said, 'Go.'"

I laughed. "Perhaps our Diamond Claire has a bit of drifter in her soul."

Lucky was a bit like the last kitten in a litter, rushing for the food bowl the second it was put out. She always tried to insert herself into whatever was going on be it with her sisters, her parents, or me. She was kind and considerate and truly loved all the members of her family, but I knew that privately she was jealous of her twin, Diamond. Diamond could attract an audience simply by wearing an expression, and it was to Lucky that everyone turned for an explanation.

While Ann Marie was learning tricks on her pony, Spade was dancing across a high wire, and Diamond was flying through the air, Bella and I struggled to find a place for Lucky. Lucky was small, like a gymnast, but she tripped over twigs, ran into beams, slipped on dry floors, and didn't like speed or heights. She hated when she scraped her elbow or bruised her knees, but she was smart, and she had a natural ear for a beat.

One afternoon I took her to pay a visit to Fred, the leader of our windjammer band. He talked to Lucky about rhythm and how it keeps everyone together. "It's the most important ingredient in a band," he said. "Everyone would get lost without it." Then he handed Lucky a tambourine. Surprise of all surprises, she was good.

"The band's rehearsing this afternoon," he said. "Would you like to join us?"

She looked at me. "Can I, Donatella?"

"I don't see why not," I replied, smiling.

Lucky played with the band for an entire hour. I had never seen such a big smile on her face. Soon she was marching with them. Though she was still a bit insecure, playing with the band gave her confidence: now she had a place in the circus, too. She'd play her tambourine as loud as she could, so everyone would notice that she was keeping the band together.

Meanwhile, Spade walked in her father's footsteps across a rope tied tight. It began when Ann Marie and Bella found her balancing on a thin log over a creek in northern Atlanta, and it continued with her walking every railroad track wherever we stopped. She would balance on one foot on the great wooden stakes tying down the big top, and in a few months she'd mastered skipping from tree stump to tree stump, or walking across thin boards laid between those stumps, pinwheeling her arms and throwing her body back and forth for balance. The more she fell, the more she got back up and tried, tried again, and as spring gave way to summer, her hesitant, jerky movements became supple and rhythmic. By the age of five, she could dance across the wire as naturally as most young girls skipped rope.

So it was that the girls found their places; Ann Marie on a horse, Spade on a wire stretched tight, Diamond flying through the air, and Lucky marching with the band. I watched them with as much pride as if they were my own, four queen bees in the middle of the circus's great humming hive.

CHAPTER 23

"SHE TOOK A DEEP breath. Everything was fresh. The bark she was eating smelled sweet, almost like candy. The sun was beating down on her body, covering her like a shield with its warmth."

"That's so beautiful, Aunt Donatella," Spade would say to me each time I began the story she loved to tell with me. "Making it into a story makes it hurt less, at least if it has a happy ending—right, Emily?" She reached over and patted the elephant's leg. Emily was standing quietly beside us as we sat on a hay bale in her pen. Occasionally she stroked Spade's dark hair with her trunk.

I closed my eyes, picturing the group of elephants, imagining the way the sun felt on their backs. "All her few years before that day," I went on, "Emily had felt safe with her herd. It must have been an ordinary day. She was out walking with her mother, aunts, and sisters, who grazed peacefully near her. Maybe she saw something in the distance, and went to look."

I opened my eyes and looked into Spade's. They were almost the same color as Emily's, a luminous dark brown.

"Maybe it was a creek," she said. "And Emily thought, wouldn't it be great to jump in?"

I nodded. "So she walked to the water all by herself."

"She jumped into the creek and got so clean, she wanted to show her mother so she blew her trumpet."

I hesitated. "We don't have to tell the rest of the story now. Don't you want to get some grass for Emily?"

"No, Donatella, we have to finish. Otherwise Emily's stuck in the middle, just remembering."

"Okay, but it's hard," I sighed. "There were two men hiding in the bushes, carrying ropes and chains, staking out their claim, and this was their chance, a young elephant all alone. They knew her mother had to be close by, and she could be very dangerous to them."

"What did they do?"

"They probably surrounded Emily and dropped ropes around her ankles and legs so fast she couldn't escape. I'm sure her mother came charging toward her as she called out for help."

"Emily's mother cried when she saw her child being taken away," Spade added.

"The men used a tranquilizer dart to make her mother fall asleep. Then they put Emily in a wagon with bars and Emily watched as her mother got smaller and smaller, until she wasn't even there."

Spade jumped in again. "Her mother never got to see how clean she was from her swim." Then Spade crossed her arms. "I'll never let anything bad happen to Emily again."

"I know you won't," I said. "Let's go get an ice."

The rest of the story I kept to myself.

Two days after she was captured, the poachers wheeled Emily up the gangplank of a cargo ship called the *Pacific*, which was headed for the States. They took her below the decks, to the dark, airless space at the bottom of the ship, and there she stayed for weeks. Emily had never been alone before. She was very frightened. When she trumpeted, the men on the ship yelled and threw water on her. Once, when she tried to get loose, they'd beaten her with a stick. Her stomach became upset, and she couldn't keep her food down. I remembered my own sea voyage and thought about how much worse Emily's must have been.

By the time Emily arrived at the Circus of the Queens, she was as depressed as an elephant could be. I'd never thought I would feel such empathy for an animal. Like me, she arrived to find herself in an alien land, mourning the family she'd lost.

The men who sold Emily to Vladimir told him she'd been born into captivity, but it didn't take long to figure out that she'd been poached from the wild. Her fear of humans was obvious. But by then, it was too late. And elephants played an important part in most circuses. Dressed in embroidered silk with gold fringes and small mirrors sewn on to deflect the evil eye, trained to do endearing tricks and to show off their immense strength, these astounding exotic creatures equaled money. No one would be sending Emily home for a grand reunion. I accepted that, but that didn't mean it sat well.

The first time Spade and I visited Emily, we looked into her dark brown eyes and saw an infinite sea of sadness. She needed some kindness, and Spade had some to spare. Spade would gaze at Emily until their eyes met and speak to her from her heart. Then I'd lift Spade up onto my shoulders, where she'd try in vain to wrap her small arms around the elephant's neck, singing to her gently. Emily seemed to understand the sincerity behind the words of this small two-legged creature.

The singing helped calm Emily down. Gradually, over the months, her memories of being torn away from her mother and of the ocean crossing, things that had haunted her in her sleep, faded into peaceful dreams.

Spade and I made up our own ending to Emily's story. Spade would ask, as though she were Emily, "Will my mother and sisters save me?"

I'd answer, "Emily closed her eyes and squeezed them really tight, until she saw her mother standing right in front of her. She imagined the way she felt with her mother's trunk wrapped around her own, safe and warm."

Then together we'd say, "And she didn't feel that way again until she met Bess, who became her best friend."

If Emily was the lost soul, Bess was born the star, the prize everyone wanted. Circuses everywhere were looking for ways to attract larger audiences. Wild West shows were gaining popularity. Several years back in Kansas City, a circus had imported eight polar bears from England. Now wild animal shows were exhibiting on the pier in Venice, California. This worried Vladimir, but still he felt he held a winning hand. He had four queens and an elephant named Bess.

"Look how big she is, Spade," he'd brag. "She's more than two feet taller than me, and I'm five foot ten. Yet her trunk is so sensitive it can pick up a single blade of grass! Did you know that an elephant has over sixty thousand muscles in its trunk?"

Bess was a gentle giant with a great sense of humor. She loved sucking up water and spraying it on Vladimir. "How can I get angry?" he'd say. "Even the Hindu god Ganesha has her face, and more often than not Ganesha has multiple trunks. Can you imagine what Bess would do with that?"

Vladimir took pleasure in all Bess's antics. Anything she did entertained him. A stranger, hearing him, could be forgiven for thinking he was discussing one of his daughters. He'd waylay me and Spade, insisting that we stop to hear yet again about all of Bess's accomplishments and how she came to our circus. We'd be standing up when he started. After a while, I'd notice Spade leaning against a wall, and before he was done, we were all sitting on bales of hay.

Bess's had been a happy childhood, he'd tell us. He wanted everyone to understand that he wasn't the sort of man who went around stealing animals in the wild from their mothers.

"The broker in Thailand told me they called her Busaba—that means 'flower.'" He said our little Busaba learned to come to her name within a month after she was born. "She's not only pretty"—he'd wink—"she's smart."

Born into captivity, thousands of miles away from anywhere our circus traveled, like other elephants raised in an urban environment, Bess began her training when she was only two days old, quickly learning the meaning of yes and no.

The villagers thought Bess was the prettiest little elephant. They smothered her with love and attention. "How could they not?" Vladimir would say. "Look at her." Spade and I would just grin at each other as we slumped against the hay bales. It made us happy that Vladimir cared for her as he did. I thought that perhaps Bess was just as therapeutic for Vladimir as she was for Emily, though of course I didn't tell him that.

"They painted Bess for parades, and the women made her costumes," Vladimir would say dreamily. "The villagers wanted her to always know that she was loved." Then he'd take a tissue from his pocket and turn away, just long enough to wipe a tear from his cheek.

Every day Bess went out with her handler. They would stand on street corners like buskers in a carnival. Her broker said it was clear to everyone that Bess had charm, a natural presence, the kind you are either born with or not. She could work a crowd simply by standing. She was magic!

The broker—"really more of an animal talent scout," Vladimir said—had been scouting exotic animals for ten years. One morning, he came to Bess's village.

While taking a walk to get in some exercise—"and get things moving, you know what I mean," Vladimir would say every time, pausing to make certain we understood (every moment that led to Bess's coming to the Circus of the Queens was important to Vladimir, so we indulged him as he had so many times indulged us)—the broker noticed a sea of people crowding around something, craning their necks. He crossed the street to see what the commotion was about. Rising on tiptoe, he looked over the heads of the crowd and understood. They were all waiting to ride one pretty little elephant. Other elephants were lined up and down the street, ready to go, but only Bess had such an audience.

"He returned to watch Bess for several days." Vladimir was now sitting on the edge of his seat, as if he were hearing his own story for the first time. "Every day it was the same—lines of parents and children waiting for a moment of this one elephant's attention. The parents tried to persuade their children that the other elephants would be just as good." Vladimir grinned. "But the children knew better."

The broker was a smart man. He knew a good thing when he saw it. He found the little elephant's owners and went to talk to them. But they clearly had no intention of selling their prize. Every time they refused, he upped his offer, until he reached an amount that would last them most of their lives. Still it wasn't enough.

Finally, the sum was so elephantine that the owners couldn't refuse. However, they made him swear on the life of his mother and whatever god he prayed to that Bess would be treated like a princess—no, a queen.

And so it was settled. Vladimir had a spotless reputation for his treatment of animals, and the broker offered Bess to him first. "So she came home with me"—Vladimir's chest puffed out with pride—"and just as the villagers asked, I've always treated her like a queen."

The broker let everyone know that Bess was first class, and when they loaded her on the ship, that's exactly how she traveled—with her own enormous suite and a veterinarian to make certain she didn't get sick.

"Now she's one of the queens—well, almost." That was our cue. At this point we'd start to brush off the hay, straighten our clothes, and stand up again. "But, however, you put it, she's more than an elephant to me."

Clearly Bess is blessed, I thought to myself. Some animals, like some people, are just born lucky.

❋ ❋ ❋

DURING A SATURDAY MATINEE in September, when most children Ann Marie's age had just returned to school, as the audience began to cheer at what would have normally been the end of Sam's routine, Sam took a deep breath so she could project her voice and address the audience.

"Today, I have a special guest," she said after calming them down. "We have been working together for several years, and she asked if she might be able to give a short performance as a gift to her father for his birthday today. Yes, today is the tenth of September, which means it's Vladimir's birthday."

Suddenly the spotlight picked out Ann Marie Heart, who yelled to her father, "Happy birthday, Papa!" The spotlight moved to Vladimir, who had now entered the ring and was standing to the right, joined by Bella, Spade, Diamond, and Lucky.

Dressed in her best sequined scarlet costume, the one that sparkled more than any of the others, Ann Marie prepared herself for what was coming next. She waited for Sam's commands, and, just as she had done for me with Bella, Ann Marie displayed her talent by standing upright on the back of the Rosinback stallion, Napolean. Step by step, just a little bit at a time, Sam had taught Ann Marie what she needed to know. Anne Marie later grinned, "It was as if Sam was somehow attached to me, talking me through every step until I slid off Napolean's back and took my final bow."

Wearing a bright scarlet plume, one exactly like Bella's, no one in the audience clapped louder or longer than Vladimir for Ann Marie. I could feel Bella squeeze his hand when Ann Marie led the crowd in singing "Happy Birthday" to him.

❄ ❄ ❄

"I'M GOING TO WEAR something scarlet in every performance," Ann Marie told me. "Just like you wear purple, Aunt Donatella. It sets me apart." She smiled, thinking she had explained herself well, and in a way I guess she had. Then she giggled and blushed until her cheeks turned her favorite color.

Sometimes I felt as if the ballerina in me lived on in Ann Marie. The School of Russian Ballet had become a pleasant memory, something I was proud of. However, the pain of my lost ambitions would never be completely forgotten. At night in my dreams occasionally I'd wake up shaking, finding myself at the bottom of a ballroom staircase, Hervé's face like a cloud lingering over me.

❄ ❄ ❄

SPADE WAS IN MANY ways the diametric opposite of Ann Marie. She competed with her twin when she performed, but despite their differences they accepted each other without question. Looking back, I believe Ann Marie was born with the most natural talent and Spade with the greater determination, but their friendship and love for each other never faded.

Being the only child of a widowed successful businessman, I found that I enjoyed the commotion of family life and the unconditional love that I never had to ask for but was boundless and freely given.

❋ ❋ ❋

SPADE WAS NOT ABOUT to let Ann Marie have all the thunder.

"They stomped their feet and shouted, 'Spade! Spade! Spade!' Mama, I felt like I had been put in a cannon and shot to the moon," Spade confided to Bella the evening after her first public performance.

"At first," Bella told me, "she paused, as if to get a better understanding of her feelings. And when her thoughts were formed and the words were ready to leave her lips, she started shivering.

"She shivered from head to toe. And it wasn't because she was cold. Donatella, I believe Spade saw her soul, which had to frighten her. Then she sat up in bed, and with all her heart she said, 'This is what I was born to do! I think this is why I'm here!'"

"And I knew Spade was speaking the truth.

"When I got up to leave the room, a strange feeling came over me, as strong as the pull of a magnet to a safety pin. I couldn't deny it. I found myself turning around and going back to where Spade lay. I whispered in her ear, so no one else could hear, 'It's understood.'

"And I pulled Spade's covers around her little body once more and tucked her back in."

❋ ❋ ❋

THAT DAY WAS A place marker. I remember it vividly: the Saturday after Easter.

We were spending a few weeks in Lake Charles, a place I loved for its stately old Victorian mansions that reminded me of the elegant homes of St. Petersburg. The weekend before, I had gone to a small processional to celebrate the Easter holiday. The children had lined Main Street, as excited about the procession as they were about the upcoming circus, shouting, "Here, here!" as the elders and choirboys threw chocolates into the crowd. I was wearing a big light lavender hat I'd bought in a shop the day before, adding some fresh wildflowers so I wouldn't look out of place.

Caught up in the festivities, I wasn't looking where I was going, and I'd bumped into a boy. He happened to be a boy we'd recently hired. He was huddled with some other boys his age and an older man. When I realized who it was, I said, "Excuse me, Billy," but the boy did and said nothing. He just looked sideways at his friends. Something struck me as off, but the day was too lovely for thoughts of intrigue; still, I felt as if an unknown shadow was following me. There was something familiar about the older man, but I had barely had a second to see him. He seemed to gasp when I ran into them. I wanted to look back, but instead I just walked on—and when I turned the corner, my feet started to run. I couldn't get away fast enough and I didn't know why.

The following Saturday had been the long-awaited day, the day of Spade's debut on the high wire. I was in the main tent, drinking a cup of tea watching the carnies setting up for her act under Vladimir's watchful eye, when suddenly one of the barkers ran in and grabbed Vladimir's arm. "We've got trouble," he said.

It better be important, I thought, running outside to see what it could be. Dust was flying everywhere. One of the carnies was wrestling with a boy of maybe seventeen, who looked as if he were trying to get away.

"You owe me money from last week!" the kid was yelling. "I was just taking them for a walk. We weren't going nowhere."

Under the dirt and sweat on his face, I recognized Billy, the boy I'd bumped into the day of the parade. Hired to help groom the horses, he'd decided to walk off with them instead.

"Boy, did you think no one would notice?" said Vladimir. "To try to steal one of the stallions, that's unforgivable! You're lucky I'm not my father. If you had tried to steal one of Lillya's horses… Someone, just go get the sheriff. I've got to welcome the new lion tamer. Don't let him go while I'm gone."

This time I was the shadow who was lurking, but I felt as if another set of eyes were staring from the bushes. However, Spade was about to perform, so I left to take my seat.

Vladimir went to greet Louie, the new lion tamer, and his son, Roman. They'd arrived at the circus just in time to see Spade's first performance. But right after Vladimir left, there was another commotion by the horses: someone had set a trash can on fire. All the men who were supposed to be guarding the boy left him unattended and ran to get water, including Boris, for there was nothing scarier than a circus fire.

It later became clear that Billy—who was the distant cousin of circus owner Big Jim Baldwin—must have had an accomplice hiding in the bushes, and Billy was simply a decoy for something bigger. Someone wanted us frightened, but it was unclear other than that what they wanted. I wondered if it was Big Jim himself or maybe one of his men. Word had spread that he had recently hired a new horse trainer. But why? It made no sense, so I pushed the connecting dots out of my thoughts. By the time the men got back to where Billy had been, he'd vanished. All that was left were the ropes he had been tied up with.

What a day that was—the young horse thief, the mysterious eyes that continued to puzzle me, the arrival of Louie the lion tamer and his son Roman, and Spade's first performance.

✳ ✳ ✳

THAT DAY BURNED ITSELF into Roman's mind as well, but it wasn't because of the fire that broke out. Years later he would confess, "Spade's act was all I could think about. That night I asked God for a favor, Donatella, but even then, I knew. I asked God if he would make that girl notice me.

"At the edge of the circus grounds where we were parked that first night, there was a huge wisteria vine attached to a tree. I sat under that tree thinking of Spade. For the rest of my life, whenever I smell wisteria, I see her.

"Even then, Donatella, I knew my world would revolve around her."

However, no one could underestimate the special affinity shared between Spade and Emily.

Emily and Bess came to represent the heart of the circus. Emily's display of kindness after receiving such cruelty, and Bess's generosity of spirit and capacity for joy, made them favorites.

Sometimes, though, when I thought about life's twists and turns, Vladimir's, Emily's, and my own, a question lingered: Could we adapt? Could we come to terms with all that we had been through and lost?

✳ ✳ ✳

NEWS OF RUSSIA WAS getting uglier by the day. Which of our classmates and teachers had been blessed like Bess? Who was alive, and who might be dead?

I thought about the role I had come to play in the lives of the four queens and I prayed I was worthy and up to the challenges ahead of us all. For life, I'd learned along the way, wasn't always fair.

CHAPTER 24

ACCORDING TO CIRCUS FOLKS, there are five seasons: spring, circus, summer, fall, and winter. It was not an easy life, but it was exciting, and for a long time it helped to drive away much of my anxiety about what had happened to my father, my poor Russia, even the trauma I still carried in the difference between my legs. Polly and Joseph and his family kept up the farm in Savannah, sometimes so well that I almost forgot it was mine. I kept track of the prices of soybeans, cotton, and tobacco, and I met with a lawyer out of Atlanta to discuss the profits and how to spend them, but the Circus of the Queens was home. "Where else would my eccentric talents be so appreciated?" I laughed. Even the police had begun to seek me out for help. Me, an immigrant fortune-teller.

✻ ✻ ✻

March 1917

IT WAS MARCH 1917, and Vladimir and I had our ears glued to the radio. George, a bald handyman with a long gray beard that Ann Marie loved to braid, was thoroughly enamored by the invention of the radio. Praising the wonders of this new technology, he'd convinced Vladimir to buy the circus a boxy Clapp-Eastham Blitzen, which George kept along with his tools on his workbench in the train, lovingly maintaining it.

We visited George's car every day that month. He would pull up an old metal chair with a threadbare pillow thrown on top and serve me hot coffee he had made on the fire outside.

"Miss Petrovskaya, sit down and drink this or you'll get a chill," he'd say. "You and Mr. Vronsky might be here for a while." And we were, most days and nights, as he and Vladimir played with the signals until they found something worth listening to.

But as long as we could listen, we couldn't get enough. It just didn't stop. It started in our home city. The people were marching for bread. Mutinies and strikes followed, one after the other. In another month, Czar Nicholas would give up his throne, and no czar would ever again take his place. We knew another revolution would erupt; we just had no idea how many years it would last. Every time we spoke of Russia, our conversations came back to Lenin, Stalin, and Trotsky.

My St. Petersburg was no longer mine. It even had a different name, Petrograd, and didn't seem to belong to anyone. There had been so much fighting and so many changes in the government, but we certainly didn't think events would unfold the way they did. Vladimir had family in Russia, and I still held out hope that I did, too. The damage the revolutionaries were inflicting sickened me, but so did all the hungry people.

To my mind, nobody was entirely in the right. So much of the bloodshed seemed senseless. The revolutionaries, like their enemies, sought power, and they too used their political platforms to achieve personal successes that they said were for the betterment of the people. The madness had depleted me, but I couldn't separate myself from it.

The broadcasts stopped the first week of April, when America finally, reluctantly entered World War I, and the US government confiscated most radios. But somehow the silence then was even worse.

"There's no going back," I told Vladimir. Bella had insisted I join them for supper. She had made a thick, hearty stew with lots of potatoes, hoping to comfort us. On the side, she served us stuffed cabbage and beets, which she knew were my favorite.

Vladimir nodded. "There's nothing left." He grimaced ruefully and glanced over at Bella. "I don't know how you put up with us."

It was clear we both were suffering from our sadness, but we went through the motions that night, trying to please Bella, who had placed candles around the table and brought out the dishes her parents had sent her from Italy. The queens insisted Bella help them bake poppy seed cookies. It had been more than three years of not knowing, and although we continued our life in this new country, and many days were good, the war halfway around the world raged on in us as well. The fate of our country was strapped to our hearts, and we didn't know how to cut it loose.

I tried in vain to find any news about my father. I knew it would be futile, but what had become of him, or of Mme Strachkov? There must be some record somewhere with their name on it. I knew my father had paid Mme Strachkov a good severance and she had intended on moving in with her sister, but I was disappointed that she hadn't answered one letter I wrote to her. Then one day I received a note from an old neighbor who had heard I was still looking for news of my father, any news to give me closure.

"I want you to know that three other families and I live in what was once your home. Last I heard, your father was in the hospital, struggling with heart failure, but that was a long time ago.

"Rumor has it he made it out alive, but he never returned. Mme Strachkov visited him every day and tried to convince him to move into the house with her and her sister, but the day before he was to be released, Madame must not have been focused for she walked out in front of a horse and carriage going at a rather fast clip. It was too much sorrow for your father to take. I believe he walked out of the hospital a broken man. No one has heard from him since. However, in previous conversations, your father told me that he felt at peace, knowing you were safe.

"Your father was always very proud of you. He mentioned your broken leg. So sorry, but many of us have had to give up our dreams."

The neighbor left no return address; he didn't need to.

Finally, I knew that my father was as good as dead. I tucked the note under my pillow, lay down on my bed, and didn't get up for days. I couldn't stop thinking about my father, Mme Strachkov, about my old teachers and classmates, and about what had happened to Czar Nicolas and his family. All the visions of the past several years repeated themselves like a bad dream and wouldn't stop. I tried blocking out my memories and imagined little soldiers in my brain stomping out what remained, but some just wouldn't disappear. Like the night Vladimir and I danced at the Winter Palace, and I saw my first Fabergé egg; a once happy memory was now rooted in sadness.

In my dream, I was lifted in the air and then twirled and twirled. As I spun across the dance floor, I tried to look into my partner's eyes, but instead I saw two sapphires: the Fabergé egg had become my partner. The speed of the dance became too much for the egg, and all its perfect jewels went flying off its sides and out to the protestors, who had only been begging for bread. When the egg realized it was bare and had not a ruby or a diamond left, it ran and joined the people.

Obviously, my little trick didn't work; my brain swallowed all the soldiers like quicksand, and I thought and thought until I made myself sick.

* * *

I'd been hearing Vladimir's stealthy footsteps pacing past my tent at night, even more frequently than before Bella gave birth. Although it was getting chilly, I preferred being outdoors to staying in my stuffy sleeper car, but outside, I was more highly tuned to the sounds that surrounded me.

It was all too obvious that playing cards was no longer just a game to Vladimir but a way to relieve his pain. Worried, Boris and several of the men came to see me in my carriage. At first, they pretended to want readings, but they soon told the truth: they needed to warn Bella and me that Vladimir was gambling recklessly, but they didn't feel comfortable saying anything more.

"I don't know how to help him," Bella confided several nights later, after dinner, as we nursed cups of coffee. Earlier we had gone for a ride on two of the circus's quarter horses trying to blow off some steam.

Vladimir had gone out "to check on the elephants," he said, though we both knew he'd be gone for a while. I had never seen Bella like this. Her skin had broken out in hives, she'd become so anxious. "I'm afraid Vladimir's going to do something he'll regret."

Sadly, I had no advice to give. I could only offer her a paste of stinging nettle and coltsfoot to apply to her arms and advise her to use cold compresses. I was barely holding my own life together and certainly not in any position to pass along words of wisdom. Bella would have to deal with her husband by herself.

* * *

For the first time in years, I felt as if I'd lost my anchor again, and I was drifting out to sea. With Vladimir lost in his drinking and cards, and Bella consumed with anxiety for him, I had no one to turn to.

As March turned to May, even the sweet sound of courting robins outside my tent struck tinny and flat on my ears. I knew I couldn't stay any longer. I needed to find the earth underneath me again before I could start to help anyone else. The next morning, I packed my bags and went to say goodbye to Bella and the queens.

Bella didn't say a word, only hugged me and then turned abruptly away and started wiping down the kitchen counter as if the task were urgent. I knew she was unhappy, but I also knew she understood. The girls looked confused, but I assured them I'd not be gone long. Ann Marie told me to enjoy myself and that she would miss me. Diamond wanted to know if she could borrow a book she had seen on my shelf about Greek mythology. Lucky asked if I would bring her back a book of poetry.

Only Spade seemed really distressed. "Please let me come with you, Aunt Donatella," she said, clinging to my arm.

"Right now, I wouldn't be good company," I said. "But I'd like you to visit me in Savannah as soon as I'm ready." I embraced her tightly, and then turned and left before I could change my mind.

※ ※ ※

SAVANNAH'S SALTY SEA AIR felt like a soft slap across the face when I stepped out onto the platform. Polly was waving excitedly, and Ben, who tended the garden, when necessary was our butler, and was always our driver, stood stoically at her side. Still, I could see his mustache twitching upward as he tried to not show that he was excited, too.

I hadn't been back in over a year. Counting on Joseph's numbers and what the accountant in Atlanta had showed me, I believed rightfully so that the farm was healthy and didn't need my input. However, I soon realized I needed it. I could see that Polly and I had both aged. I was no longer the girl she'd first met, and she was no longer a young woman; streaks of gray had come to look at home on her head, while her smile was still as wide and inviting as the front gate of the Butler mansion and as easy as its porch swing.

I was glued to the window of our restored Model B Ford all the way to the plantation, just like that lost, feverish girl of more than a decade before. In front of the house, Ben helped me out and then carried my bags in. I stood beside the car, looking up. I had forgotten how big the house was, but I hadn't forgotten how much I'd loved its solid elegance, the Spanish moss in the live oaks, the rustling leaves of the willows, and the smell of rich, newly turned earth carried on the breeze.

"Ahh, I have missed the sweet smell of our fresh tobacco," I said to Polly. "Do you mind if I go for a walk on my own before I come in? I want to say hello to the land." I hardly needed to say it. Polly was almost as intuitive as Irina; she could see I had come to Savannah to be alone. But sometimes, as she used to say, alone can be the busiest place. In truth, I wanted to say hello to Irina, too. I'd always thought she belonged more to the earth than to any space with walls and a floor.

I made my way along a rutted lane that ran between fields and woods behind the house, amazed and overwhelmed. I owned all of this! It hit me in a way it never had before. In one field the ground was freshly turned over, ready for planting our cotton. The velvety leaves of young tobacco unfurled in their long rows. My body seemed to be unfurling, too. I stood in the middle of the field, my face turned up, my eyes closed, feeling the warmth of the sun and the pull of the earth working its magic on me. Then I turned back toward the house.

I looked at the counters laden with "a few things": a blackberry pie, three pecan tarts, a peach cobbler, and, of course my other favorite, bread pudding with bourbon. "Thank you, Polly. I think I'll start with a piece of the blackberry pie and save the pudding for later."

I had collected some fabric swatches in my travels and had seven of the most decorative made into aprons for Polly, remembering how she loved her aprons. As I pulled out each one and handed it to Polly, she named it with a day. "You look like a Friday—no, a Tuesday. This blue reminds me of the sea, so it has to be Sunday." By the time she'd finished naming the aprons, I'd finished the pie.

Polly had kept her bedroom downstairs, even though on many occasions I had offered her the biggest one in the house. She said she had grown up with eight brothers and sisters sleeping in one room. "All that extra space would make me uncomfortable, and I would never get to sleep. Big houses like these scare me. I guess I like to get scared, but I have my limits, I have my limits."

I'd told the Vronskys I would be gone for two weeks, but like the Russian Revolution, I stayed on. Once again, Savannah was the place where I could stop and breathe, the place where the scattered pieces of my life could be made whole again. Polly and Ben only wanted to please me. They respected my privacy and expected nothing in return. Spring turned to summer, and nothing told me to leave.

CHAPTER 25

I walked. I walked through fields, along lanes,
through piney woods and under oaks.
I walked until my head was empty and my feet were numb.
It was the only thing I knew to do.

I WALKED AND WALKED for weeks, maybe months, until the spirit of Irina appeared.

I was hiking on a slippery trail near a stream when I tripped over a root and landed on top of one lone good-luck clover. Covered in mud, I didn't feel so lucky. I started to cry, thinking about all the things that had gone wrong in my life. Then the wind started to blow. It picked up speed until the rustling of the leaves sounded like the percussion section in an orchestra. Through the steady brushing of the snare drum, I thought I heard Irina whisper to me. I couldn't make out her words, but I felt her embrace. "I'm so sorry," I found myself sobbing. "How can I be so ungrateful?" My heart seemed to split in two, all that I had been holding in for years seemed to burst out, and I poured out my troubles to the forest and the trees. When not a tear was left and I was thoroughly exhausted, I picked up the clover and asked it for help. Nothing happened. Then I asked for help again, only this time I got on one knee. Nothing again.

Desperate, I held the clover between my thumb and forefinger, and I asked God to let me witness grace in a physical form. "Give me something to believe," I said to the clover. I stood up and wiped the dirt off my face. Out of nowhere, three hummingbirds appeared. They circled above my head as if it were a pot full of honeysuckle nectar. After showing off their tricks, they flew backward as only hummingbirds can. They flitted and fluttered from one flower to another, flirting with nature all the while.

Seconds seemed like minutes; each time the hummingbirds returned, they circled my head. Through the leaves on the trees, I heard a whisper once more, reminding me that the hummingbird is a symbol of energy. Then, as if the song of their wings had transformed me into a bird, I flew home as fast as I could.

I knew exactly what I was meant to do.

I went directly to the shed, picked up a shovel, and spent the entire day and the next turning over the earth, using the energy of the hummingbirds. Ben and Polly both knew to keep their distance.

Each shovelful of loam I turned over was fresh and rich. I went out and bought pots of fuchsia, crocosmia bulbs, and dahlia tubers, as well as packets of seeds—morning glories, sunflowers, portulacas, and zinnias, purple, yellow, and orange. I soaked the morning glory seeds overnight, and the next day I scattered them next to a piece of old fence that I'd staked in the ground. I planted the dahlias near where the iris grew wild and hung up baskets of fuchsia on wrought-iron posts. I didn't stop working until I had planted everything I'd bought and given the hummingbirds a reason to return.

I'd dug the garden outside my bedroom window so I could watch the flowers grow when the sun filled the sky or by moonlight. Every morning I'd get out of bed, lift my blind, and look to see if anything had sprouted.

Ben and Polly told the workers not to touch this small piece of land. It was mine to care for, mine alone. I lovingly watered this little patch of life and pulled out any weeds that tried to pose as flowers. When the first green sprouted and then a little color showed itself, I felt a sense of happiness return. Still, I waited for the hummingbirds.

I played the phonograph and danced by myself in the living room, remembering my nights with Irina. I took long walks by the sea and thought of my mother as I watched the gulls skim over the waves. Sometimes I would have Ben take me to the Tybee Island Lighthouse, next to the Savannah River, just to watch the egrets and herons stalking near the shore on their long legs. On Sundays people came with special glasses to see the migratory birds there. Other times I'd have him drop me off at the port, and I would sit and watch the men load the big containers onto the ships, some filled with cotton, soybeans, and tobacco from Butler Farm. Then I would find a spot where I could dangle my feet in the water, later rubbing them dry with a towel that Ben kept in the car for occasions like this.

On one such afternoon, I thought I saw a silhouette of a figure from my past. I started to chase after it. But the sun was at its peak, glaring in my face, and I became temporarily blinded; I closed my eyes, but when I opened them again the figure was gone. "It must have been my imagination," I told myself. Then I blinked once more, this time to wash the image away.

It was a solitary time. I let the sea air wash over me, and though I thought about the circus and the queens and missed them all madly, I waited for the hummingbirds as I said I would.

The zinnias showed their faces first, bursting with orange, purple, and yellow. The purple-blue morning glories with their hint of yellow scrambled up the fence, and the elegant irises grew like weeds. Dahlias showed off their red, gold, and oranges. Billows of yellow-and-white marguerites flanked the entrance to the house, and pink-and-purple fuchsias hung in baskets from the rafters of the porch.

Every morning when I walked out the door, the cheerful faces of my portulacas greeted me. Ben, who had learned about them from a Mexican gardener, introduced me to these dainty succulents. They open every morning to greet the sun, and at night they close to rest. I tried to follow suit.

Then early one morning I opened my blinds, and three ruby-throated hummingbirds were circling the flowers. I threw on my robe and ran outside, but by the time I arrived, they were gone. The following morning, before the first rays of sun had touched the garden, I decided to plant myself in the middle of it. Polly and Ben watched from the kitchen. When the sun's golden arms reached out and touched me, three hummingbirds—I believe, the same ones—returned to visit the flowers. My garden was in full bloom, and my self-pity had turned to gratitude. After years of pain and sadness, my heart was full.

The time had come for me to return, but before I could go, I had a promise to fulfill.

I arranged with Bella for Spade to come to Savannah. She'd stay for several days and help me with my bags and getting on and off the train.

Spade was so excited! I gave her the tour. Ben played the role of butler and driver; Polly greeted her with a double chocolate cake. She was very impressed!

Later, as we were sipping lemonade on the porch, she said something I would never forget: "Your house and land must be what heaven looks like." I had never thought about it that way, but I realized she might be right.

We took long walks and I pointed out herbs and wildflowers she hadn't been familiar with. We went to the Butler family cemetery, and I told her all about Irina. "Irina was very generous and such fun," I said. "She had me laughing every night. She understood the importance of play and the importance of doing good. She taught me all she thought a mother should teach a daughter, and when she passed, she left me her house and farm as if I really was her daughter. I don't know who I would have become without her, or your family." There was a piece of me now that only Spade knew, and I hoped it made her feel special.

Looking at Spade I was shocked to see how much she had grown in this short period of time. I wondered if Ann Marie was as tall as her, too. Soon they would no longer be children.

Spending time with Spade, I became anxious to see the rest of my circus family. I was ready to read a stranger's future, look into a crystal ball, interpret tea leaves at the bottom of a cup, deliver precious babies, and sit around the fire. But best of all, I'd see the queens and Emily and Bess.

Yes, the time had come for me to leave. I didn't need to say a word; Polly began to pack my travel case.

※ ※ ※

ON OUR LAST AFTERNOON in Savannah, I found Spade relaxing in the middle of my garden, her head tilted up toward the sky, and I remembered thinking that she looked like an angel.

Spade asked if she could say goodbye to Irina. "I want to thank her for giving you a home and someone you could love after you lost your own family."

I thought it a beautiful gesture, so we went to the cemetery. Each of us told Irina what we'd come to say. When we returned, I noticed Polly had finished my packing and on top of my suitcase she had left a freshly baked loaf of bread wrapped in what I knew to be Polly's favorite piece of fabric.

Like I had so many years before, I left a note. I thanked Polly and Ben for their kindness and hard work and told them I'd return, but I didn't know when. I left Ben an envelope to give to Joseph, for although I had been in Savannah for months, I had only seen him once.

Spade and I said our goodbyes to the garden and the hummingbirds. Then Ben took us to the train station. We would meet up with the Circus of the Queens in Nashville. I had no idea what surprises awaited me.

CHAPTER 26

HANDED LUCKY A book of poetry by Robert Louis Stevenson, *A Child's Garden of Verses*, and a copy of his classic *Treasure Island*. "We can read these together." Lucky loved books and words, while Ann Marie loved things of beauty. Wrapped in scarlet tissue paper with a scarlet ribbon, she carefully untied the bow and lifted the paper off the box. Inside was a long hand-embroidered silk scarf and a matching beaded barrette for her hair, both scarlet of course.

"Thank you!" She hugged me, adding, "I've missed you a lot."

I wanted to encourage Diamond to find her voice so I hired a luthier to make Diamond a ukulele out of rosewood. "It comes with a book." Diamond immediately began strumming.

Spade's gift was a planter box and packets of flower seeds. "You can plant a garden and take it with you everywhere we go."

Excited to see me, the queens made a happy commotion. They wanted to hear all about Savannah, but soon they shifted to gossip.

Ann Marie spoke up first. "Did Spade tell you Papa hired a ringmaster-in-training? His name is Marvin. He's old, but he's still cute."

"That's disgusting!" Lucky butted in.

Right then Marvin walked past and tipped his hat. I could see immediately that he was tall and handsome. The creases at the corners of his eyes gave him a bit of ruggedness that contrasted with a suave tailored European style jacket.

The girls called him over. "You have to meet our Aunt Donatella," they shouted before he could get away. He walked over, and Ann Marie introduced him as the very Marvin they'd just been telling me about. I was immediately taken by the boyish grin that belied the lines on his face. He was polite but didn't try to engage in conversation. Still, the way he'd smiled at me was enough ammunition for the girls.

"I think he likes you," said Diamond. The queens were having a good laugh at my expense, and I didn't mind. "Papa said he might let some boy from India take care of Emily and Bess. He's got a name that's hard to remember—it begins with an H?" She looked at the other girls, but none could help her out.

"Mama's missed you a lot!" Ann Marie declared. "Papa hasn't been himself lately. He moped around the circus for months, but I think he might be doing a little better now." The other girls agreed.

The queens insisted that we have dinner together. Spade and I made a date to visit Emily in the morning, and she asked if Roman could join us. She and this boy had gotten close. When everything was settled, I left to go unpack my things.

I was anxious to see Vladimir and Bella. Bella had taken the time to air out my sleeping car and tent and make them more inviting. She'd put fresh-cut flowers on a table in the tent to remind me of my garden and made up my bed in the sleeper car with crisp new sheets that smelled of lavender.

I was admiring her handiwork when I heard her calling my name. "You didn't think I could wait an hour more to see you!" she exclaimed, kissing my cheeks.

Vladimir had come too, and he seemed pleased to see me as well. Nonetheless, I could tell that something was on his mind. When I leaned in to kiss his cheeks, I could see he hadn't been well.

"Bella's cooking a grand welcome-home meal," he said. "Come over with us now, and we can catch up while she finishes."

As we walked along the midway, I noticed that Vladimir was limping.

"What happened to your leg?" I asked.

"I—"

"A master tightrope walker," Bella cut in, "and he lost his balance while skipping across a log! Can you imagine that, Donatella?" We pretended to find it funny, but we both knew it was no joke.

He looked at me as if pleading for understanding. "Every morning, Donatella, I search for a way to put one foot in front of the other and make sense of my world. But there has been so much sadness and anger these last years—it makes me dizzy."

"Consider it an honor he'll tell you these things. These days it's Bess who's his greatest confidante." Bella's voice was friendly, but she looked a little hurt.

After dinner, when the girls got up to go to bed, to my dismay, Vladimir rose, saying that he needed to check in on the elephants. Clearly his old habits hadn't changed. Bella didn't look happy, but she didn't argue with him.

A gust of wind blew in when Vladimir left. I shivered and hugged myself.

Bella got up silently, made us both cups of tea, then sat down and sighed. "He finds it easier to share what's troubling him with an elephant than with me. I guess he knows she'll only share his secrets with Emily." Bella picked up her teacup and cupped it as if to warm her hands. "I've done everything I can, but I'm starting to think that only Vladimir can heal himself. But enough about us! Tell me all about the plantation!"

I told her about Polly's cooking and her aprons, about swinging on the porch, my walks, the tobacco harvest—all the little details of the plantation's daily life.

"What a time it's been!" Bella sighed. "You were like the Pied Piper when you left, it seemed—everyone else went after you."

"Oh, Bella—"

"No, don't be silly, I was just joking. You were hardly to blame for the war."

The war... How could I have been so oblivious? The war had hardly entered my mind all the time I was in Savannah. My head had been so full of Russia's troubles and my own, it hadn't truly registered with me. The plantation was a world to itself.

"I knew you had to go," Bella was saying. "How could you take care of us if you didn't take care of yourself?"

Over a quarter of the men in the country between the ages of eighteen and thirty-one had joined the military. "Should it be surprising that the circus would lose a lot of men? After all, Uncle Sam was a circus man.

"Did you see those 'I Want You' posters in Savannah? That spiffy costume, with the star on the top hat—it belonged to Dan Rice, the most famous circus clown—he was the first to sign up. And who could blame him? Uncle Sam was always there, pointing at him, in every town.

"A few men came back when the war was over. Some of them were never the same, but we tried to give them jobs any way. Some never came back at all. Our elephant trainer John fell in the battle of the Somme."

Ghosts on the midway, I thought in the silence that followed.

"But the circus doesn't look empty now," I said finally.

"I guess we can thank Lenin. Don't tell Vladimir I said that! But it's true. Earlier this year Lenin nationalized the Russian circus, and the western European performers fled, many of them to America. There's some amazing talent out there, but the competition is fierce." Bella's natural enthusiasm had returned, her troubles temporarily abandoned. I'd forgotten how much she loved the circus. "I try to keep an ear to the ground."

I laughed. "Any hot tips?"

"Well…" Bella leaned forward, her eyes sparkling. "There *is* a dark horse…" Just then Vladimir walked back in.

He sat down at the table, putting his head in his hands. "There's something I need to confess. It's important." Then he paused.

With my return, I believe Vladimir felt the need to get everything out, so we could all start fresh.

"Please sit," he said. When we did, he took a deep breath and Bella and I both knew that what he had to say wasn't good. "Big Jim's circus—you've met Big Jim Baldwin before… Well, unbeknownst to me, he's had his sights set on our circus. It seems he wants to redefine himself and his circus and wear our family history as if it were his own. There is something vengeful underlying his actions, like he's out to even a score. I don't really understand his motivation. There is nothing personal between us."

"How could he even dream he could steal who you are and what your family has built?" I asked indignantly. "Besides, everyone knows you."

"This isn't just a job," Bella added. "It's your life."

"Yes, that's all true, but what circus people know and what the public knows are two different things.

"Big Jim doesn't want the Circus of the Queens because of its size; he wants our reputation, which makes him even more frightening." Vladimir went on. "It appears that he's been plotting and scheming, and waiting for manifestations of weakness. He wants to hurt us!"

I knew that rumors had been spreading through the circus grapevine that both Vladimir and I were both unraveling at the seams.

"I think it's common knowledge that you've been gambling recklessly," I said. "If he's looking for a weakness, he'll find one there."

"That's true." Vladimir lowered his head. "As it turns out, Big Jim—over breakfast one morning—heard just that from a traveling advance man. And ever since those ham and eggs, I think his brain has been spinning. He arranged a card game in Atlanta and invited me to join the game, along with three more of the South's biggest circus owners including our friend Henri. On the surface, it appeared to be a nice gesture. We were supposed to discuss business over a friendly game of cards. Of course, I couldn't say no.

"Well, he must have been proud, for he cooked up an almost flawless cover-up. We met in Atlanta, just as Big Jim had planned, and checked into our hotel. An hour later, a mysterious man dressed in all black wearing sunglasses and a fedora hat picked us up and took us to a darkly lit backroom parlor."

"Weren't you concerned when you saw where he was taking you?" I asked.

"Maybe a little, but it's not the eighteen hundreds. We're in a modern world. And I had no reason to think adverse thoughts. When we arrived, Big Jim was there to greet us like the perfect host and gentleman. I did find it strange, though, that his driver never spoke a word.

"The atmosphere was dark and rather formal. Another man in a fancy black suit escorted us to a private room. A fifth of whiskey and vodka were waiting for us on a table. The driver stood quietly in a corner observing. He could have been a fixture or a chair. He drew no attention to himself except silence."

Vladimir barely took a breath between words, not wanting anyone to interrupt. "After a couple of drinks, everyone was feeling festive," he continued. "And we toasted Big Jim for bringing us together. I think we all appreciated an excuse to take a night off. We toasted our driver, but he simply nodded."

"What are you trying to tell us?" I asked, wanting to get to the meat of the matter. I was getting frustrated. I had looked at my own demons up close and in the face. It was up to Vladimir to look at his.

But Vladimir acted as if I hadn't said a word. "Without them knowing, Big Jim arranged for the other owners to win and lose a game or two. It's much easier to pull off a con when no one is expecting one. I underestimated the man, I never took him for being so smart. In hindsight, maybe someone else orchestrated the night."

Bella froze at the word *con*. She bit her bottom lip to force her mouth closed.

"The more we played, the more we drank," Vladimir went on. "The driver in the corner seemed to vanish into it. And before long our tongues were wagging like dogs' tails. We talked about rising costs, unexpected losses, tours, advance men, trains, and trucks. For a while I was happy I had come.

"But Big Jim was just warming us up. The driver like a shadow had the bartender bring out another fifth of whiskey and a fifth of vodka, and then later he had him top that off with a box of Cuban cigars. I had not seen that kind of finesse since leaving Russia, and I was falling for his ruse. I wondered if Big Jim had planned it all or if someone else was pulling the strings.

"I remember it getting hot. I was sweating, even though the ceiling fan was cooling my brow. The bets were getting larger. My head felt like a circus balloon, ready to burst from too much air."

Bella and I held each others' hands, afraid of what Vladimir would say next.

"My cigar in hand, I felt an inclination to became a bit of a showoff, and I told the men that I'd been playing cards and drinking vodka since I was a child. 'You have to start young,' I said to them"—Vladimir winced at his own foolishness—"'or our Russian vodka will eat you alive!'" Then he winked at me, wanting to lighten the mood.

I gave him a little difficult smile. I wasn't too anxious to humor him.

Vladimir had overestimated his tolerance, he admitted. Before long the stakes had shifted from money to horses and camels, and he was betting many of our prize animals. He could no longer look us in the eye. "I was on a lucky streak, I swear, and honestly all that mattered to me was that I was winning. The other men lost, but my winnings kept piling up. I should have known something was wrong, but that feeling of being a winner took over my good sense. This I believe was all a part of Big Jim's plan."

I could see this was painful for Vladimir, but I could also tell he was savoring his words and it angered me.

"Big Jim bet his entire circus. The other owners pulled out."

Bella not sure if she wanted to listen or leave, began cutting up lemons and juicing them. "Who would like some cold lemonade?"

"I would," I told Bella, afraid of what was going to come out next.

"It would have been bad manners to leave the game," Vladimir chimed in, determined to get out what he came here to say. "Besides, no one believed he was serious, it was so preposterous. We thought he had to be joking. So, in the spirit of good sportsmanship, I bet the Circus of the Queens." Bella was handing Vladimir his lemonade. I thought she would spill it on him. Instead she put the glass down on a table nearby and clutched her heart. As far as Vladimir was concerned, Bella's disappointment was worse than almost any reaction she could have given. He could see she was ready to pack up the girls and return to Italy.

"Honestly," Vladimir sighed, "after all the vodka Big Jim poured down our throats, I don't have a clear recollection of what happened. I do recall when I looked up, the mysterious driver had slipped out. I think he smelled trouble in the air."

Bella's Italian temper was about to explode.

"The entire parlor got very quiet. I sneezed just to hear the echo. The bartender stopped pouring drinks. Even the girls who were serving us started biting their fingernails. That's when I began to understand that I might be in bigger trouble then I realized—that Big Jim might actually be serious.

"I looked at the cards on the table, took a breath, and picked them up. The tension in the room was as thick as smoke in a burning barn. Though I was scared, I put on my best poker face. Still, all I could think of was you, Bella, and the queens. How was I going to get out of this mess?"

My fingers were in my mouth, and I was biting my nails, too.

"Big Jim thought his bet was a sure thing." Vladimir continued. "I trusted the man. I thought he was an honest fellow. Besides, I had been winning all night, and I never would have taken Big Jim for a cheat."

"A cheat?" Bella and I said in unison.

"Finally, it came time to lay my cards on the table. I laid down four tens. That's a darn good hand. But Big Jim laid down…four queens."

Bella gasped.

"I couldn't move. Big Jim slapped me on the back and said, 'Sorry, old man.'

"The other owners were horrified. They began to pressure Big Jim.

"'You have to give Vladimir another chance,' they argued when they realized he was serious. I was so stunned, I just sat there like Lot's wife, turned into a pillar of salt."

Vladimir leaned back in his chair, reflecting on the scene. He looked as if he were preparing to count the stars in the sky.

"Big Jim agreed to a rematch. The other owners gathered around the table. The dealer spoke through a big waxed mustache that curled at the ends. 'This will be the final hand,' and he dealt the cards. I tried not to show I was shaking inside for I knew this was my only chance of redemption.

"One of the owners—Henri, from Baton Rouge, he was at our Christmas party—had a cramp in his leg, so he stood up to stretch it out. He found himself directly behind Big Jim. When he noticed that Big Jim had been dealt three aces, he became suspicious. The French have a nose for cheats, just as they do for food. They can smell a rat!

"Then Henri saw that a tiny mirror had been planted in the corner behind me. And forgetting about his leg, and that the dealer was thirty-five pounds heavier than him, Henri jumped on the dealer."

Bella and I put our hands over our mouths, holding our breath.

"The next thing I knew, Henri had flipped him over and had pinned the dealer down on the floor. He must have been a champion wrestler in his youth, for while he held the dealer with one hand, he reached down his sleeve with the other. When he pulled it out, he was holding three more aces and a pair of kings!"

"My God!" we exclaimed.

"Big Jim knew his plan had been turned upside down, so he began to run. But he hadn't counted on the woman who had been serving us drinks. She stuck out her foot as he was running for the door, and Big Jim tripped and fell. Then she planted her heel on top of his chest. That girl was a hero! We all cheered!

"Big Jim, we found out, had paid the dealer a hefty sum to have him in his pocket, so to speak. He only agreed to a rematch because he knew he would win."

"That's some story," I said to Vladimir through gritted teeth. I was furious. How could he have bet all our lives and so many peoples' jobs? How could he have bet the queens' inheritance, and Emily and Bess?

Bella was relieved, but I could tell she felt the same. We were angry, and Vladimir knew it. "After things calmed down," he concluded, "I sat on a barstool, shaking from top to bottom, as if I had just been pulled out of a frozen pond. Henri slapped my face, then handed me a coffee to help bring me to my senses. Then he insisted on calling a taxi and taking me back to my hotel room.

"I almost ruined our family. I know it was just plain stupid behavior," and Vladimir started to gently weep. "I had no right to be so reckless, no right to risk our future. I owe Henri a lot." Vladimir lifted his head.

"His daughter, Juliette, is an equestrian. I know you're angry, Bella, but I'd like you to pick out one of our finest horses and arrange to send it to Henri in Baton Rouge as a token of our gratitude. He'll give the horse to Juliette." Vladimir looked Bella straight in the eyes. "It would mean a lot to her."

"What happened to Big Jim?" I asked.

"We decided it wasn't in our best interest to have him arrested—we didn't want to risk our own reputations, or those of our circuses. The dealer was sent packing—he's probably in Texas by now cheating someone else, but he won't return to these parts. The driver who was quite mysterious vanished and we didn't see him again.

"Big Jim failed to steal our circus and his reputation is in ruins, but we'll have to be on the lookout for him. He's not a happy man.

"Before I left Atlanta, I found a Russian Orthodox priest," he said, looking at Bella. "He had me repent for my transgressions and said I needed to tell you what happened. It would help to wash away my sins," he said. "Bella, I needed to hit rock bottom to see all that I could lose. You, the circus, and the queens—I couldn't bear living without you. Please forgive me...

"Such fools we can be," he said directly to me as if I should understand.

I stared right back at him and pulled from my heart the words that seemed most fitting. "It's what one does with the hand they are dealt that makes the difference." This stuck with me, like all good clichés do, because of its element of truth.

CHAPTER 27

"**R**OMAN IS SMITTEN WITH Spade," Louie the lion tamer declared of his son. Since I was a fortune-teller, all sorts of problems landed at my carriage door. In this case, Marvin had suggested that Louie discuss his worries with me.

"Ever since the day we arrived in the middle of Spade's act, he's thought of nothing and no one else. Every night before he falls asleep, he plays Spade's performance over and over in his head. He believes that if he thinks of her when he closes his eyes, he'll see her in his dreams."

"They're young, Louie," I told him.

Louie fumbled with the keys on his belt. Obviously he had something else on his mind. "Donatella, I'm afraid Roman witnessed more than he should have when his mother left us," he finally blurted out. "I'm worried we damaged him. His mother tried to ease her troubles with drink. I explained to Roman that his mother was sick, but what a young boy remembers is that the first woman he put his faith in abandoned him."

"Roman will be fine," I reassured him. "Spade feels safe with him, and she has good instincts."

❈ ❈ ❈

IT WAS TRUE—ROMAN and Spade had become inseparable. The day after he came to the circus, Roman couldn't wait to go to school, knowing that the girl on the high wire would be there, too. When he walked into the tent where their lessons were held, he told Spade she had an interesting name.

"I was named after a queen," she replied. And from that moment on, he followed her everywhere.

Eventually, the other queens had no choice but to accept Roman. Tall for his age and lean, with his shirttails always escaping from his trousers, he was like the favorite overcoat that Spade wore every day; and she wasn't going to throw him out. She often asked him to join us, and he always jumped at the chance. I wondered if she knew her power over him. I don't know how much interest he really had in the elephants, but he would do anything that pleased her.

Unlike Spade's sisters, Roman was truly interested in plants and wildflowers, so my portable classroom grew. I showed them how tea made from slippery elm bark could soothe a sore throat, and other herbal remedies. "Irina taught me these things," I told Spade. Ever since her trip to Savannah, anything to do with Irina held special meaning for her.

Roman and Spade's friendship grew deeper. It was evident even in the way they played simple games like hide-and-seek. Although they traveled throughout the South, from Baton Rouge to West Virginia, some things stayed the same. Roman would hide with the lions, a place Spade would never venture; and Spade would hike to the top of the ropes and wait for Roman to shout, "You know I'm afraid of heights!" They infuriated each other, but it was the only way they could express their feelings.

Roman tried to keep his infatuation to himself, but it was clear to all that he loved Spade in spite of the ache his father told me he felt when she was near.

❋ ❋ ❋

As MUCH TIME AS Spade spent with Roman, though, she devoted at least twice as much to her act. "Spade's determination is going to make her a star," I told Vladimir and Bella. We were playing cards by the fire. The chorus of crickets in the grass were chirping so loud they almost drowned out our voices. I had just laid down two kings, but that didn't interrupt our perennial favorite subject, the queens.

"I think it's time for the queens to greet the children after each matinee," Vladimir said. "Besides it's a tradition in my family. In Russia, the schoolchildren knew my father, and when he married my mother and they had me, children came to our circus so they could meet me, just as their parents had met my father. The people got to know us, and we got to know them. It made the circus personal, Bella. Donatella can tell you. Over the years, we watched each other's families grow and our families became like old friends. I'd like our daughters to experience this."

Bella went inside and brought out a fresh peach cobbler, surprising us with the recipe Polly had asked Ben to deliver to me—fresh Georgia peaches with a pinch of this, a handful of that, and a dollop of vanilla and sugar under a crumbly biscuit topping.

"The girls will have their cobbler in the morning," said Bella. "We can talk to them about greeting the children then."

After we'd all cleaned our plates, we got back to another game of cards.

"I'm glad you see it too, Donatella. I believe Spade has the Vronsky gift. Every night when the lights go down, she turns walking the wire into an art form. Her vision is so sharp she can see right across the big top to a little queen of spades that she cut out from my favorite deck of cards." Vladimir smiled. He was doing much better, on his way to being once more the man I'd always known him to be. She's young, but she has genius!" he bragged, his eyes shining. "She uses the card to balance and stay focused. So intuitive."

"The schoolchildren will learn much from her," I added.

"Vladimir can barely stay in his chair when he talks about Spade," Bella said, smiling at him. "He's so proud."

Everyone knew, though, that Ann Marie also filled his heart with pride. Inside the big top's magic circle with a scarlet plume tucked in her headband and her long auburn hair trailing behind her, like her mother and both her grandmothers, Ann Marie's skill and beauty became legendary. Standing upright on the back of her stallion, she waved to the audience and sometimes threw a kiss or two.

She was sassy in a polite kind of way, and passionate. I believe part of her gift was innate, and some of it came from our own Samantha Divine. The people loved her. They'd walk miles, climb hills, find their way from cities, cross lakes and oceans to see her perform. Everyone wanted to be a part of it and say they had seen the scarlet Ann Marie Heart.

I tried to teach Ann Marie how not to give too much of herself away; an audience's adoration could be enticing to a teenager and swallow her up. "There will be people who will want to take and take and take. For now, it's best you save yourself for your parents and sisters," I told her. "Someday this will change, and you'll share your deepest secrets with someone worthy of your heart."

I could tell that she'd heard what I had to say, but she cleverly diverted the conversation. "Is Marvin nice?" she asked. "You know what I mean—do you like him?"

I didn't want to answer, so I changed the subject back to her and her sisters.

* * *

THE FOUR QUEENS BECAME like daughters to me, or nieces as Bella preferred me to say. Vladimir more like a brother, and Bella like the sister I never had. My jealousy over the years melted by her generous spirit that allowed me to love her children. She believed that the love I had to offer the queens would make them better people, and I hope it did.

And as different as the suits for which the queens were named—heart, spade, diamond, and club—it became clear they could not be broken apart, for each possessed what the other one lacked. Together, they were strong; but take them apart, and the house of queens would collapse.

I believe Ann Marie's gift was her big, loving, passionate heart. It put people at ease and made them comfortable in her presence. Spade, Diamond, and Lucky depended upon it too; the warmth Ann Marie radiated softened the sharp edges of their souls and filled in the empty spaces in their own hearts.

Spade's vision was almost supernatural. She could see things invisible to the other three. "Look out for the spider web at one o'clock," I heard her warn her sisters one night. "You don't want to wear that on your head." The owl of the bunch, she liked to stay up late. She would spread her protective wings, determined to avert any harm that might sneak in. That included boys bent on seeing Ann Marie.

Diamond sang songs and inspired her sisters to paint. She captured their essence perfectly in music and art. "Our Diamond must have come from someplace mythical," I heard one of them say. "She sounds like the sirens we read about in Donatella's books."

"She'd better watch out," Spade said. "Or one day we're going to find her head carved on the front of a ship."

"Or maybe on a poster in Greenwich Village," Lucky chimed in.

Lucky's mouth was rarely closed. She read poetry and attempted to write limericks, and soon she discovered that not only could she feel a beat but she was clever, too, and when she got excited, she shrieked. "I can't help myself," she'd say. "It just slips out."

Lucky's lungs had an impressive capacity; she could scream louder and longer than a sax player could hold a high note, but late one night Lucky's shriek saved us all.

One night, when everyone was sleeping, the sound of something dropping woke Lucky up. Her nose began to twitch. By the third twitch, she recognized the smell, and with a scream that could have brought the lava out of Mount Vesuvius, she yelled, "Fire!"

Everyone in the circus heard her and woke up. The stagehands came running with buckets of water, throwing them on each of the queens to get them safely out through the flames. Thanks to Lucky's lungs, and the power and projection of her yell, everyone survived, including all the animals. Marvin created a special medal and awarded it to her for this feat, and she could not have been more proud.

✳ ✳ ✳

MARVIN CARPENTER—CHARISMATIC, WELL SPOKEN, intelligent, and known to our audiences as Marvin the Marvelous—came to play a bigger part in the life of the circus as time passed. He also began to play a leading role in mine.

I was quite an enigma to Marvin, at least early on; he felt uneasy about letting me get too close. "You see layers, Donatella, that sometimes I'd prefer you didn't," he'd say. But this didn't stop him from asking me to dine with him, spend my free time with him, or read his palm.

Marvin's favorite place to talk was while swinging in his hammock. He had procured it from a Jamaican craftsman who'd sewn two hammocks together.

The minute the circus arrived in a new town, Marvin's first thought was to find a spot to hang his hammock. Then he could commune with his deepest thoughts or, if he chose, completely forget them all. As I got to know him, I noticed that the longer he rocked, the more he revealed.

Marvin explored the valleys of my heart, and I explored his. For the first time in years, maybe even since I was a young girl with Vladimir or the mysterious Frenchman who disappeared, did a man give me goose bumps by just standing next to him. I found most everything he did and said to be charming. Marvin never lost his boyish enchantment with the circus but remained constantly amazed. When he wasn't working, or lying in his hammock, contemplating, he would stroll around the circus grounds admiring everything around him. Many times, he invited me to join him.

"Look at the gold detail on these carriages," he'd say, smiling with pride, as if he had gilded them himself. Or he'd sample the air like a chef sniffing his most renowned dish, as if he'd conjured up aromas of the circus all by himself.

"Doesn't the cotton candy make the air smell sweet?" he'd ask. And when he got truly sentimental, he'd testify like a Southern preacher. "Listen to the howls of the men when they're taking down the tents. They sound like a band of brothers, chanting secrets as they work, with a few hallelujahs mixed in."

He loved watching the trapeze artists practicing their act. They made him think of freshly washed clothes, warm from drying in the sun. On the hot summer days of his childhood, as he waited for the circus to arrive, he would play the man on the flying trapeze on a rope swing in the backyard while his mother hung their clothes on the clothesline to dry. The role of ringmaster, though, he would only play when he was certain he was alone. Lofty ambitions, he knew, could get him in trouble.

Ann Marie and Sam were particular favorites of Marvin's, and the clowns riding unicycles in circles, honking their horns, always made him smile.

The stories that Spade and I invented about the wild animals, especially Emily, inspired Marvin to dream of faraway places. "Donatella," he'd say to me as we swung in his hammock, "one day I'm going to take you to India and Africa. We'll see elephants on the streets, tigers in the wild, and shamans whose spirits run as deep as the waters." Then he'd give me his patented ringmaster grin. But his favorite place of all, besides with me, was anywhere near the horses. Their beauty and power cast a spell on him, just as they had our Lillya, Bella, her mother, and now Ann Marie. Their effortless grace on a galloping rosinback sent shivers up and down his spine every time.

Everything about the circus humbled Marvin, and he humbled me. "How lucky are we," he'd say in the morning over his cup of tea. "Always different! What a life we lead."

He seemed so sunny and open, always the optimist, yet I sensed a darkness in him, a pain he was hiding. I could see it in the creases of his eyes and read it in the small cracks in his hands. I wondered if he would ever tell me what had really brought him here.

What happened to you when you were young? I wanted to ask, but I didn't; he would tell me one day in his own time, I was sure. I only had to wait.

But so much revolved around Marvin, more every day. He held more than the circus in his hands.

CHAPTER 28

EVERY WEEK WHEN THE circus moved to a new town, Diamond Claire would find a way to disappear. But I couldn't help noticing that she often chose places near the lions, where Roman might find her. And although she was much younger, and Roman's heart belonged to Spade, I suspected that she wanted Roman to save her.

❊ ❊ ❊

ONE DAY, WHEN DIAMOND was ten, she and her sisters were playing Olly, Olly, Oxen Free. It was Spade's turn, and when she got close to Diamond's hiding place, Diamond took three steps back and fell into a pit. "I ran to find Roman," said Spade. "I told him, 'Come quick or Diamond might die!' He flew as if one of the circus lions were chasing him and when we got to Diamond, he jumped into the pit, made a ladder from some vines, and lifted Diamond out."

I was sure that Roman had wanted to prove himself to Spade, and it looked as if he had.

Bella sent Boris to fetch me the moment Roman brought Diamond to their tent. Diamond had hit her head, and her back was covered in blood. She drifted in and out of consciousness for several days, a look of contentment on her face, occasionally calling out her savior's name. And when she wasn't shouting for Roman, she was asking for her favorite Arabian horse, whose name was Ali Baba.

We held a vigil around her bed, never leaving her alone. We didn't know if her condition would improve or get worse; we could only watch her and hope. Diamond's spine had been badly bruised. We took turns wiping the sweat off her forehead and swatting the mosquitos that got in the way.

I waited for the swelling to go down to see what damage had been done. I looked for signs that Diamond's spine was healing. The dancer in me prayed for Diamond's legs. I called on every god I could think of, used every homeopathic remedy Irina had taught me.

"Donatella knows everything about medicine and herbs," Bella tried to reassure Vladimir. "Diamond couldn't be in better hands."

Ann Marie, Spade, and Lucky visited every day. Marvin stopped by whenever he could, watching as I laid amethysts and crystals around her bed.

"Why is there an amethyst also around your neck?" he asked, and I told him it was there to help me focus. I wrapped Diamond in herbal compresses and gave her arnica for pain.

Finally, the swelling began to go down. I'd never been so happy as the day I saw her wiggle her toes and sit up.

Diamond never doubted she'd be fine, and she put up a fight when I insisted she stay in bed. "It was just a little hit on the head and a scraped back, Aunt Donatella." But I didn't yield.

Eventually we returned to our routines. Diamond spent many hours by herself and she discovered that she liked the solitude. By the time she was healed, her affinity for all things unexplainable had grown even deeper.

Lucky didn't understand where her sensible sister had gone. Finally having to accept Diamond wasn't going to change, she switched her allegiance to Ann Marie.

I proceeded by pointing out every talent Lucky possessed, but nothing seemed to work. It appeared, for the moment, that she wanted to be anyone except herself.

As far as Lucky was concerned, Ann Marie could do no wrong. Ann Marie couldn't help but be charmed by Lucky's adulation. She did her best to give her little sister the companionship she craved, even tying a scarlet bow in Lucky's hair. But sadly for Lucky, she couldn't stop time, and there was an ocean between being a girl and a teenager.

❈ ❈ ❈

WHEN ANN MARIE AND Spade turned thirteen, their bodies weren't all that began to change. Like many girls their age, they became focused on whatever was popular. They begged the older acrobats, and Sam, to teach them the latest dances and the newest lingo.

On one of our walks to visit the elephants—outings during which I often learned a lot—Spade told me that she and Ann Marie wanted to know what was going on in the world. "Sometimes we feel isolated," she confided, which puzzled me; surely the girls had seen more than most people do in a lifetime. "Isn't that right, Emily." Spade would look at Emily for agreement, then pout at me expecting approval, then continue with the assumption that I would go along with her. "We want to feel the beat of what's happening around us. We talk to all the children about the circus after the matinees, and that's real easy—but when one of the kids asks what we like to do or who we listen to when the show's over, we don't have an answer. So we've asked some of the older girls to help us out. Don't you think that's smart, Aunt Donatella?" I was at a loss for words.

The equestrians showed the girls how to shimmy and dance the Charleston and taught them the newest words. One night at dinner, I thought Bella and Vladimir were going to spit up their soup when Diamond started to sing, and Ann Marie, looking at Spade, said, "Well, ain't she a sweet canary?"

Spade paused, then came back: "That broad can really sing!"

I wanted to laugh out loud, but I knew Bella and Vladimir wouldn't appreciate my encouragement.

The older twins became rebellious, abandoning their royal etiquette. But people of court never have been held to commoners' rules. Occasionally they'd tell me about one of their escapades, so vividly I could imagine I was there. Like the time they eavesdropped on a nearby revival meeting...

※ ※ ※

"SPADE, YOU'RE MAKING TOO much noise," whispered Ann Marie.

"You'd be lost if I wasn't able to see for two," Spade snapped. "Besides, no one can hear us over the racket these crickets are making." She looked over at Jimmy, the older brother of one of the equestrians. "You're sure you know where this cabin is?"

"Of course," Jimmy replied. "I was there last night." Just then, they all heard the faint sound of singing somewhere ahead. "That's them," Jimmy said confidently, and they picked up their speed, weaving between saplings and ducking below branches.

They moved forward, lured by the soulful voices echoing across the valley. Hiding behind rocks and trees, the three of them crept stealthily into the clearing around a little white wood-frame church. Through the warmly lit windows, they could see hands raised, bodies swaying back and forth. At the end of each line of the preacher's sermon, the people roared out their approval: "Hallelujah!" A deep-throated woman began to sing "Amazing Grace," and everyone joined in—even a horned owl in the woods. The fireflies seemed to be blinking in time, and coyotes howled along at the end of each verse from the rocks down by the creek. Ann Marie, Spade, and Jimmy were riveted, drawn like moths to the flame. As cautious as a fox, they stalked closer through the tall grass, then climbed onto a rock outside a window to get a better view. A man inside was taking out a guitar from its case, and another held something the girls had never seen. "That's what they call a washtub bass," Jimmy said, eager to sound like an expert. Spade and Ann Marie looked at each other when the man began to pluck the strings. It was as if they had just witnessed the most incredible circus trick.

Then the man with the guitar started to play and all of the people joined in singing. Their voices got higher and louder, and soon all of the bodies in the cabin, no matter what their age, were moving to the music, hands and legs bouncing in whatever direction the beat took them. They lifted their voices and sang as if God had chosen to speak directly through them, harmonics tumbling like a waterfall into half and quarter tones, poured out from their souls and then slipping off their tongues. Hypnotized by the dancing and singing, Ann Marie and Spade felt their own spirits soar.

"Do you think God will visit us like that one day?" asked Ann Marie when at last they turned back toward home.

"I think he just did," answered Spade. "But right now we better pray that Mama's not still up. Good night, Jimmy, this was the best!"

"Yes, Jimmy. The very best!" Ann Marie smiled. Spade could see by the look in Jimmy's eyes that he'd done all this for that smile.

Bella was in their room when they returned. They didn't need to tell me this part; when she swore in Italian, Bella's voice easily carried all the way to my tent. I could hear her giving them a royal verbal lashing for taking off by themselves and getting back so late.

Later, Spade asked me if I knew the song "Amazing Grace." Looking at her shining eyes, I could tell that, given the choice, she'd do it all over again, no question.

However, girls that age tend to be fickle, and it wasn't long before Spade and Ann Marie had abandoned religion for fashion. Ann Marie even dared to wear olive as she listened to a Bessie Smith record on the phonograph.

The trapeze artist had another brother who lived up north. When he came to visit, they'd listen to records by Duke Ellington, Fats Waller, and the Dorsey Brothers while he told them stories of the Cotton Club and Harlem.

Lucky felt left out. "Aunt Donatella, I think their brains have gone missing. We should put up a Lost Minds notice and see if anyone will bring them back."

Poor Lucky, I thought. This was just the beginning of growing up. If she'd had an inkling of what lay ahead, she'd really have thrown a fit.

CHAPTER 29

MARVIN PUT A PILLOW under my head. He had found a little private spot with two large maple trees surrounded by blackberry bushes from which to hang his hammock. The moon was full. It reminded me of how my parents used to cradle me and make me feel safe entering the night. But this was not St. Petersburg, nor was I with my parents. I was with the circus outside of Asheville, North Carolina, enjoying the comfort of the soft breeze and how it made me tingle, or was it the man whose arms I was in, the one who had been winning my heart?

Our bodies melted together as if we were one and I could feel Marvin's strong hands lightly gripping my shoulders, completing the circle around me.

I sniffed the back of his neck. It smelled like sweat. Then I nuzzled my nose in to smell him again but reminded myself I needed to stay focused. Marvin had asked me to come over. He said he had something he wanted to tell me. It had taken a long time for Marvin to believe in me and longer still for his heart to feel free, and I had a premonition he was finally going to tell me what I had been waiting to hear.

We had become close, but still it was not going to be easy for him to trust me with his past. His childhood had become the mountain he couldn't find his way across. Every time he got close to sharing the things that made him who he was, he'd suddenly find himself busy, and I wouldn't see him for days. Then, when he did return, the mountain would still be there, and we wouldn't be much farther along than we were when we began. Tonight, though, he inferred that he had made up his mind and would reveal what he had been afraid to say.

No one meeting Marvin would think he lacked bravado, but I knew better. However, when Vladimir made him the ringmaster, he grew stronger in himself. The hardships from the past grew weaker until they no longer had power over him.

We moved from the hammock to the fire outside his tent and huddled together with an old wool blanket wrapped around us, drinking my special cinnamon cardamom tea. The stars up above shined as brightly as I'd ever seen them. We'd been silent, listening to the wood frogs' chuckling quacks, looking up at the sky, when he seemed to make up his mind that it was time.

"See what looks like a red star, there? That's Mars," he said, pulling me closer to him. His warmth beneath the blanket was comforting. "When I was a young boy," he continued, "the circus seemed as far away as that planet. It played no part in my life."

Marvin's family lived miles from any town that the circus might come to—or anyone else, for that matter. His father and older brother were his only companions, if you didn't count all the creatures of the forest: the deer, squirrels, and wild turkeys, which he loved to watch, sitting quietly for hours on a fallen log. His younger brother at that time was only a baby. His mother was as cold as his father was warm. She used her work and chores as a way of distancing herself. She cooked and she canned and she kept the house neat, but he couldn't remember a kiss or an "I love you" from her. His father had once said that it wasn't her fault, but he gave no explanation.

However, Marvin had known no other life, so he just accepted what his father said. They were all that he needed, but his life was about to change. Soon he would yearn for a world more expansive than the one he was living in.

"When I was twelve years old," he said, "my father suddenly died, and everything I'd relied on as constant and safe was turned upside down. The doctors told our mother that our father's heart simply gave out, but I often wonder if he died because it had starved." Marvin shrugged as if he were still searching for the answer. I sat in silence, wondering if some of this loss was what had brought Marvin and me together.

"The next summer, my mother married a man who could only be described as a brute. I guess she thought he'd take care of us. But the only good thing he did, as far as I was concerned, was move our family to a bigger town, a town the circus passed through. Perhaps that was enough," he said reflectively. "No…no matter how I try, I can't make it a good thing. My mother let us down when she married him, and there was no one left to protect us.

"Then one day I saw a way out, and that's when my life changed.

"It was August. I was fifteen. Sweat was dripping off my body, and my undershirt was wet. I'd been out delivering papers for hours in the glaring sun, and all I could think about was the swimming hole my brother and I planned to go to when I got home, the dark, cool water under the overhanging trees. But when I stopped to buy a soda on Main Street, a brightly painted poster in the store window caught my eye. There were lions, tigers, and bears and a trapeze artist flying through the air." He paused, as if imagining himself standing on the hot sidewalk, holding a sweating bottle of cold soda as he looked into the storefront window that day. "The letters on the poster were so colorful and bold, I inched closer to read them. They said that the circus was coming to town the next week. I swear, Donatella, I jumped on my bicycle quicker than a grasshopper and pedaled home as fast as I could.

"I wanted to see the expression on my older brother's face when I told him the news." Again Marvin stopped for a minute, then shook his head, "Neither my brother nor I had ever been to a circus. Actually, we'd hardly been anywhere at all.

"After we moved, I didn't have a lot of friends. The ones I did have—well, with a stepfather like mine, I didn't want to bring them home.

"That man was just plain nasty. I read a lot of books as a boy, and the more I read, the more disagreeable he seemed to become. He wanted more than blood; he wanted to beat the spirit out of me, and that's the worst beating of all."

We were silent for a moment, but then Marvin's thoughts turned a corner, and a sly grin appeared on his face. "That's when things changed. From the second I learned that the circus was coming to town, life looked brighter to me. I always wonder when I see the kids in the big top, watching the show, their eyes big as saucers… How many of them feel the way I did, as if they've found a whole new world?

"Donatella, you wouldn't have believed how excited I became. My every waking thought turned around the circus. It became a ritual. I stopped by the store every afternoon to make certain that the poster hadn't disappeared, and every day I bought an orange soda and left my bottle cap as a marker somewhere close by. It became almost religious for me, like paying homage at a shrine. And each time I did, I felt a rush of blood through my veins, and I felt stronger than I had the day before.

"It had been such a long time since I felt alive. Maybe not before my papa had died." In Marvin's voice, I could hear the wonder and relief, as if he was again experiencing the lifting of the pain as he had years before. Overwhelmed, he stopped to pull himself together.

"The entire town was getting ready for 'The Big Event, Under the Big Top.'" Marvin lit his pipe, and a cloud of sweet-smelling smoke drifted over us. I nestled up closer to him and waited for him to go on.

"Every night, all my brother and I could talk about was the circus. He must have carved at least five toy horses while we waited for the circus to arrive. I'd sneak into our backyard when no one was looking, when I was certain I was alone, and tell jokes to the audience who filled the imaginary bleachers. I'd announce the imaginary performers who would steal the show, with all the drama I could muster." Marvin laughed at the memory.

"Finally, the day arrived. First, there'd be a circus parade that afternoon. Everybody in town would be there. My brother and I hurried to finish our chores. We didn't want to be late.

"I'd never heard a circus band. When we got to Main Street, the windjammers were playing a waltz, and then they switched to an up-tempo march. I wanted to grab one of the brass players' instruments and start marching with them, I was so entranced.

"We wiggled through the crowd until we found a perfect spot to watch. I remember the elephants—they seemed so kind. You would have loved them, Donatella. I doubt they were as pretty as Bess or as sweet as Emily, but they made a big impression all the same. Then the horses came prancing in all their glory—I couldn't take my eyes off them. They were the most beautiful animals I had ever seen. I was spellbound.

"It seemed as if just breathing the circus air had transformed everything, every moment in my life that came before. By the time the riders passed, I'd made a decision. It had been brewing for some time, the need to leave, though I had no idea when I awoke that today would be the day of do-or-die."

Marvin stopped, as if in his mind's eye those glossy horses were dancing past him, so close he could reach out and touch them, their shoes striking sparks on the paved street. "Go on," I said finally, when the silence had stretched too long. "Don't leave me dangling."

"When the parade had gone past, and everyone was leaving, I found a scrap of paper on the ground, a flyer announcing that the circus was in town. While my brother was talking to a few school friends he'd run into, I found a place to sit on a bench outside the hardware store, just long enough to compose a letter on its back. Then I put it in my pocket as if it were a coin of gold.

"When we got home, our mother was frying something for dinner—I think we had pork chops and black-eyed peas that day. I remember while we were eating, even with all the excitement I felt, no one spoke more than three words. I tried to tell a joke to break the silence, but I guess it wasn't funny, because no one laughed. I kept putting my hand in my pocket to make sure my note hadn't disappeared.

"My stepfather was too drunk to join us for dinner—he was lying passed out on the couch. Our mother had our younger brother to care for. I felt guilty about what I was about to do, but it was as if I had no choice. Before my older brother and I left the house for the circus, I gave my mother a squeeze, my little brother a kiss, and my stepfather not even a nod.

"When we arrived, the circus band was playing 'Yankee Doodle Dandy.' The clowns were joking with the announcer, and in the next ring, dogs were jumping through hoops of fire. Everyone was looking up, so I did too. Twenty-five feet in the air, I saw a girl walking across a wire.

"One act ended, and another seamlessly began. I couldn't get enough. After the show, we made our way through the crowd. *This might be the best day of my life,* I thought. In just two hours' time, the world had gone from miserable to sublime.

"I looked at my brother, who had no idea what I had planned. For a second I thought about not doing it. But instead I jumped in the air, threw up my arms, and welcomed my make-believe audience. When I finished playing ringmaster, my brother and I laughed so hard we fell to the ground. That's when I pulled out my note and told him I would not be going home. He looked in my eyes, Donatella, and he could see there was nothing he could do but say goodbye. It was one of the hardest moments of my life."

I took Marvin's palm and turned it over as if to read it. "See this line? This is your destiny. There was nothing else you could have done."

"Thank you, Donatella, but it wasn't easy. I handed my brother the note I had written and asked him to give it to our mother. I didn't want either of them to feel guilty. My brother and I hugged each other, and I turned around and started walking in the opposite direction. I don't know if my brother ever looked back.

"I can still recite that note. I had written it in my head many times before I set it down on the back of the circus flyer. I had practiced saying it, hoping that someday I would actually use it. In it, I told my mother that I did not know what the future would hold, but if I didn't leave home, all the dreams inside me would shrivel and die, and I would not survive. I didn't want to cause her pain. It wasn't her fault; it was just how things turned out."

By now, tears were falling down my cheeks, and Marvin wiped them away with his handkerchief. "But look where it led me," he said, and I smiled.

Marvin's first circus job was mucking out the horses' stalls—not exactly glamorous. "But when I felt discouraged, all I had to do was think about my stepfather. After him, anything was tolerable. Besides, I wanted the time to learn everything I could about the circus. I can't quite explain the feeling that I had, but it was as though the circus called to me, and I simply followed."

Handsome, with a quick wit and a good sense of humor, Marvin was a fast learner. He made up in determination what he lacked in formal circus education. He could talk his way into any job, and he took the time to learn from anyone willing to share a word or an hour. Before long, it became apparent that Marvin, like Bess, could draw a crowd, and hold its attention, too. He had a strong work ethic, and he lived by a code.

"What was it?" I asked.

"That's easy, Donatella. I just do the opposite of what my stepfather would do, and it's bound to be right."

❋ ❋ ❋

MARVIN'S STORY WAS REALLY not so different from that of any other boy who joined the circus. What made him exceptional was that he had a vision, and he loved what he did.

Given his background, his kindness, and his aspirations, it didn't surprise me when he decided to extend a helping hand to another young boy with a talent and a dream who displayed a remarkable intuitive ability when it came to elephants.

CHAPTER 30

EMILY KICKED OVER A bucket, making a tinny jangling sound. I went and picked it up. "*Frère Jacques, Frère Jacques,*" I sang, hoping this simple French song would soothe her. A storm was blowing in, and she'd begun to panic. She still associated a hose and water with the poachers who dragged her away.

"Don't be afraid," Spade told Emily, but the elephant kept pacing in her stall. I couldn't tell if she wanted to stay in it or kick her way out. "We need to keep singing, Aunt Donatella."

Emily sounded a fearful trumpet. "*Frère Jacques...*" Spade and I began to sing together. By the fourth round the soft, monotonous sound of our voices had calmed Emily down.

Emily had become more trusting as time passed. She and Bess were rarely apart, and I was happy that she had found such a good friend.

Bess reacted to water in the exact opposite way. Rain seemed to invigorate her. Bess loved to get wet. "Look how she catches the drops running down her face." In the time it took for me to say this, Bess had stuck her trunk in a bucket and splashed Spade and Emily. It was the kind of joke she liked to play on us.

Emily had begun to take jokes like these in stride. Even the nervous twitch above her right eye had disappeared. But not until Harsita arrived did she really begin to sparkle.

An Indian boy of seventeen, Harsita came from a family that lived with and for elephants. His father was a mahout, an elephant trainer, and had slept next to his elephant in India for twenty years before he died, when a boulder came crashing down a hill and hit him on the head.

A British businessman employed Harsita's aunt Lilu as a housekeeper. After the accident, Harsita's mother agreed to let Harsita work for him, too. The businessman had holdings in the States, especially New Orleans, and when he decided to move, he brought Lilu and Harsita.

The businessman had invested a small portion of his money in a circus. Unfortunately, it went belly-up, but several of his past employees found work with Vladimir, and he took note of this. When he heard that the Circus of the Queens was coming to Lafayette, he decided to see what he could do.

"I asked a few of the fellas if they would arrange an introduction for Harsita the next time you came to Louisiana," he told Vladimir. "You see, I've come to like the boy, and I feel bad for him. His aunt Lilu says that he misses his father and their way of life. I thought coming here might cheer him up. But mostly I'm hoping that with your permission, he can visit your elephants, Emily and Bess."

"Where is the boy?" Vladimir asked.

"He's over there by the fence, trying to be patient. I'm told he has an abundance of that quality when it comes to those giant creatures."

Vladimir motioned for the boy to come over. "I hear you like elephants."

"Yes, sir," Harsita said. Then Vladimir led him to Emily and Bess. He wanted to see what this boy was made of, and whether the businessman was on the up and up. Since Big Jim, Vladimir had become less trusting.

Harsita walked into the elephants' stall by himself. Vladimir expected the boy to do something, but he just stood still. "I kept checking my timepiece—three minutes, five minutes. Still he didn't move. Seven minutes, and that's a really long time to do nothing but wait," Vladimir told Bella and me that evening and I wished so much I had been there. "Emily took a step toward him, and next Bess did the same. Emily nuzzled her trunk against the boy." I would have loved to see this. "Then he pulled out a piece of fruit from his coat pocket," Vladimir continued. "I swear, Donatella, they took to this boy immediately, as if they had known him all their lives. I have never seen either of them happier, and you know how I feel about Bess."

After the visit, Vladimir took the man aside. "If it's all right, and the boy is willing, I'd like to hire him to look after these elephants."

"Where would the boy live?" the businessman asked.

"I have someone special in mind," Vladimir replied.

Two weeks later, Harsita was bathing and cleaning up after Emily and Bess, and not long thereafter, Vladimir anointed him their trainer.

Marvin took the boy under his wing, just as Vladimir had hoped. I was pleased to see Marvin's affection and concern for the boy. Marvin did not verbalize his feelings easily, but when Harsita reported his daily progress with the elephants, Marvin would gently slap the boy on his shoulder and tell him, "Good job." It seemed fitting, Marvin observed, that Harsita reinforced the elephants' good behavior using the same words. "Like Bess," he told Vladimir, "the boy has a natural talent." I must admit, Spade and I were a little jealous. Harsita had won Bess and Emily's hearts so easily. However, I knew there was much to learn from him, and he would hold a prominent place in our lives.

"Would you like this cube of sugar? If you're really good"—Harsita would make a funny face and wink at Emily and me—"I'll give you an apple." Emily was making tremendous progress. "Good job!" Harsita would say.

Harsita constructed a sturdy post to which he attached a harmonica and led Emily right up to it. Then he took her trunk in his hand and helped her cover the harmonica with it. Emily took a breath, and a sound came out. Surprised, she turned her head, but a few minutes later curiosity won out. She walked up to the post by herself, wrapped the end of her trunk around the mouth organ again, and started breathing in and out. Fascinated by the different notes, she repeated them. Pleased, Harsita pulled out a piece of fruit to reward her. Emily kept on playing.

Bess had a more artistic nature, so Harsita taught her how to paint. He would pick out the colors, dip the tip of a brush in the paint, and then wrap her trunk around the brush. Bess would delicately apply flowers all by herself, adding more color where she thought it was needed. No one was more amazed than me. An elephant that paints—what a novelty! The people applauded both Bess and Harsita generously, and it gave Vladimir one more reason to brag. However, Harsita didn't teach the elephants to paint and play music merely out of altruism; he did it because it was smart. He could still hear his father's voice: *Keep an elephant busy and engaged. Never forget this, my boy. There is nothing worse than a bored elephant.* So he took Emily and Bess on walks and played games with them, always challenging them with something new.

I watched Harsita masterfully slip into the elephants' skin. "I live inside the elephant, Donatella," he'd say. Several times I even caught him imitating their sounds. "Each elephant's trumpet has its own unique quality," he explained. He studied how Emily and Bess behaved with each other, how they quarreled and resolved their conflicts. This, I believe, is the difference between a good and a great animal trainer. It's no wonder Harsita earned everyone's respect.

Emily and Bess's favorite food was watermelon. Children found this funny. They loved watching Emily and Bess eat as much as they liked watching them do tricks. Emily's finale, after gobbling up a meal, was her satisfied trumpet. She sounded almost as sweet as one of the most popular singers of that time, Marion Harris, who sang with a soulful Southern dialect. And it didn't matter that Em's eyesight was poor, or that she might not see you clearly; she remembered those who were kind, and she never forgot a friend. And when the audience thought they couldn't adore her any more, Harsita would lead Emily to her harmonicas— by now she had several in different keys. Emily would choose which sound suited her mood and play until she was through.

Bess learned how to shake hands and put her foot in Harsita's palm. No elephant was better at playing dead than Bess. Women would shriek, and children would poke their fathers' arms and ask anxiously if she was all right. By the time she rolled on the ground and stood to take her bow, the audience was both relieved and satisfied, and so was she: Bess never tired of the attention. After the show, Harsita would take her into the crowd, and she would extend her trunk to all who would shake it. Bess was the star, another queen, folks said.

Lately, when Spade and I visited Emily and Bess, we found the tables turned; now they were the ones inspiring us.

Harsita's name meant "full of happiness," and we believed that to be true. Spade sometimes felt giddy after being around him. "Harsita and the elephants make me want to strive for something higher," she said to me on one of our walks.

❋ ❋ ❋

SPADE WAS SEVENTEEN NOW, and indeed she was burning with ambition. Awed by the Great Wallendas, a famous circus family whose skills and talents she admired, when I learned that they would be performing nearby, I asked if she'd like to go see the show. There weren't enough words to describe her thrill.

"Aunt Donatella, the Great Wallendas perform their act without a safety net. Can you imagine? Papa would just die if I were ever to try that."

Spade found it hard to contain her excitement. The Great Wallendas' superhuman abilities seemed to be all she could think of. She hardly ate. At one meal, she took out Vladimir's playing cards and began counting the spades in each deck. Then she pulled out the four queens, one of each suit—heart, diamond, club, and spade—and did a double take. The queen of spades turned her head to the right, while the other queens all faced left. "Why am I different from the rest?" she asked, and I didn't have an answer.

It was March, and it had been raining hard for days, lashing against the canvas of the tents. The *Farmers' Almanac* had predicted a sunny dry spell—but what use did a Russian girl have for that book, anyway?

We had come to Atlanta for our last vacation before the circus season opened the following week. Ann Marie and Diamond were going shopping with their mother, no matter how torrential the rain. Lucky went out with Vladimir to hunt for new decks of cards and to help keep him from thinking of his last visit to Atlanta. Vladimir had given up gambling, but he was always on the lookout for another rare deck to add to his collection. He had no interest in seeing the Great Wallendas' death-defying stunts. He thought it unwise not to use a net. "The Vronskys have been circus royalty for generations," he told us. "We don't need to prove ourselves to anyone."

However, from the day she saw their show, Spade pleaded relentlessly to be allowed to walk the wire the Wallenda way. Eventually Vladimir gave in. When Spade made up her mind, she was an irresistible force—she and Ann Marie had that in common. Bella usually took pride in Spade's strong will, but this time she was uneasy. "Just this once, I'd rather she'd been less stubborn. I can't sleep, thinking of her up there without a net."

"She's a pro," Vladimir insisted. "She's been on the rope or on a balance beam since she could stand." No matter how he pleaded her case, Bella and I were not happy, and neither were the other queens. Still, we had to admit, Spade's act was thrilling.

Tonight, it would be put to the test: she would walk the wire without a net in front of an audience, though she hadn't announced it in the program bill.

❋ ❋ ❋

SPADE CLIMBED TO THE top of the platform and opened a big parasol, the colors of the rainbow, holding it over her head as she walked along the wire. Thrilled, the crowd cheered after the first part of her act. Then they heard some commotion from below and looked down to see that men were unfastening the safety net, pushing it to the side. The crowd gasped. Spade waited for the audience to quiet down, refusing to move until nothing but the sneeze of a child broke the silence. Then she readied herself for her first step, reached for three plates, and took three steps.

The audience had settled down. Spade had their undivided attention. Rumors about the net had spread before the performance; one stagehand had seen Spade rehearsing and told another. But to actually see it—*that* was different.

Music swelled as the organist played one of Spade's favorite songs, "I'm Always Chasing Rainbows." Although the lyrics were rather dreary, the melody— adapted from Chopin's *Fantaisie-impromptu*—was divine, and Spade loved the line, "My schemes are just like all my dreams, ending in the sky."

For a second, Spade seemed to wander off. I wished I had Marvin's hand to squeeze. Then quickly she returned, took a deep breath, and prepared for her next step.

Focusing on the cutout queen of spades taped up on the other side of the tent, Spade began to juggle the plates and sing along to the song in her beautiful alto voice. At the end of each eight-bar phrase the organist played, she threw the plates higher than she had in the eight bars before. The anxious crowd below began to smile. Spade didn't miss a note.

By the time she'd got to the other side, the song had reached a crescendo, and Spade was in a trance. She dismounted, and the roar of the audience broke the spell. To a standing ovation, she took her final bow. "Queen Spade! Queen Spade!" the people yelled and stomped until the bleachers shook.

At the other end of the rope, Spade had found her pot of gold: the adoration of the crowd below.

Out of the corner of my eye, I saw Roman walk away. Clearly he didn't want to encourage Spade's newest endeavor.

❊ ❊ ❊

AFTER THAT DAY, ALL of our pleading could not change Spade's mind. She only grew more stubborn as her confidence in her skill grew. Passionate about her craft, she was determined to be the best. "I don't have to perform every trick I read about. I just have to know I can do them," she'd say when Vladimir objected to one of her crazy stunts. And when she needed to blow off steam, she'd come find me, and we'd visit Emily and Bess and talk about the adventures we'd have one day. This gave her time to collect her cool— a word she'd picked up from the older equestrians. The new words seemed to be piling up.

Sometimes Roman would join us on these walks. In his pocket, he always kept the compass Louie had given him on his last birthday. "My father says we never know when we'll need it—but when you're with me, we'll always find our way home." Like I told Louie years prior, he'd have nothing to worry about, for big, strong Roman, now almost fully grown, was the kind of boy who, instead of scaring us with talk of bobcats or hungry bandits on the outskirts of town, would point out the delights of nature, wildflowers, and herbs. I took great pleasure in seeing how he'd absorbed the wisdom of Irina and what I had taught him.

CHAPTER 31

As I WATCHED THE girls grow and change, it became impossible not to think about how much I had changed as well. I had truly become Donatella the fortune-teller.

My reputation now preceded me in every town we passed through. Many times, we'd hardly have time to set up my tent and park the carriage before a line formed in front of it. I never knew what to expect. Even the police began to seek my services.

※ ※ ※

ONE SWELTERING AUGUST NIGHT, when the circus was outside Charleston, South Carolina, I heard a voice outside my tent. I pushed aside the strings of beads that covered the entrance and saw a tall, thin policeman with a frightened couple and the boy of twelve or so huddled behind him. "Come in," I said, pushing the beads aside.

"Officer Harper, ma'am." I'd been working all day, and I was still swathed in the layers of purple I always wore for my readings. After all, people expected me to look exotic. An amethyst hung around my neck, and a black lace veil obscured my face.

I held out my own hand. "Pleased to meet you."

I could see the policeman's apprehension when he entered.

"What have we here?" I asked the police officer when he finally stepped inside, followed by the couple and a boy.

Officer Harper, looking at the family, said: "It is rumored that spirits speak through Donatella. She looks into a crystal ball and sees events that reveal themselves to no one else, and we've exhausted our other resources. Sorry, Donatella," he added, realizing he had just insulted me. "I didn't mean disrespect. If I didn't have faith, I wouldn't be here."

I nodded, telling him to go on.

"The Yorks—this is Mr. and Mrs. York, and their older boy, Riley—have moved here from Perth, Australia," Officer Harper explained. The couple smiled timidly. "I believe they're a bit nervous, but they need your help, ma'am."

I gestured for them to sit down on a pillow-lined bench. "What is your trouble?" I said gently.

It was the dark blonde wife, her face weathered by Australia's glaring sun, who answered. "We were on the train to New Orleans—it stops at Union Station in Charleston, you know. There was quite a crowd—everybody was getting on and off the train—and in all that bustle, we lost track of our seven-year-old son, Trevor. I'd given him a few coins—he was excited to have some American money." She sniffled. "I think the temptation was too much—he was dying to spend them. There was a vendor selling ice cream on the platform, and Trevor snuck off the train to buy himself some."

Officer Harper broke in. "We've interviewed the vendor, and he confirmed that he'd sold a chocolate cone to a boy who fits Trevor's description and who had an Australian accent."

Mrs. York put her face in her hands. "He hasn't been seen since."

I stood up and put my hand on her shoulder. "I can help you. But I'll need a few things from you first. Can you bring me something that belongs to Trevor? Something he loves?"

"I can bring his blanket. He's had it since he was three. I'll get it right away." She began to get up, but I stopped her. "Not right away. Come back in an hour."

Mr. York frowned. "But Trevor's been missing almost ten hours! Other police units are already conducting a search. There's no time to waste."

I held up my hand. "Every minute is precious—I know that. But right now there are too many people under the big top. The energy around us is chaotic. The voices will speak more clearly when things are calm."

An hour later, I held the blanket against my cheek, hoping Trevor's vibrations would send me a clue.

"You have to find him!" his brother burst out. It was the first time I'd heard him speak. "We—we got into a fight last night over who would sleep on the top bunk. I ended up saying stupid stuff, and we never had time this morning to make up." His lip trembled. "I think he took off to prove he's tougher than me."

"It's not your fault, Riley," said his father. "Get that out of your head."

"Well, it may not help, but I have something too. It's Trevor's favorite stuffed animal." He handed me a small kangaroo, the threadbare state of its velveteen coat witness to the fact that Trevor must have dragged it along everywhere he went.

I smiled at him as I took it. "Riley, I think that may help very much. Now, you all must be very quiet while I concentrate."

I closed my eyes. The room was absolutely silent except for a small rustling sound: Trevor's mother couldn't stop fidgeting with her skirt. I knew she couldn't help herself, but I needed to block out her agitation. I focused on my crystal ball with such intensity that the ball itself almost disappeared.

It was strange. Outside this tent, I was simply Aunt Donatella, a wrecked ballerina, helpmate to the Vronsky family. But inside it, I had authority. The responsibility weighed heavy on my shoulders, but it squared them, too.

Just as the carriage had become silent, Officer Harper began to whisper to the father. I put my finger over my lips to quiet them. Out of the corner of my eye, I could see Trevor's parents scooting to the edge of their seats, waiting to hear what the spirit would say.

I asked the spirits to guide me. *Can Donatella reach into the earth and sky and see the fate of Trevor behind the moon's eyes? Speak, crystal ball, speak.* The father nervously jingled coins in his pocket. Suddenly I felt the color drain from my face.

I began to quiver, oh so slightly, and in a voice not my own, I began to speak.

"Trevor is a special boy who was fooled by a rabbit that captured his imagination. He chased the rabbit to the end of the train station platform. The rabbit posed as Trevor's kangaroo, and then he leaped off the platform, extending his back legs to hide who he really was." My voice trembled. My shivering turned into shaking. "The kangaroo rabbit lured Trevor deep into the woods. When he was certain Trevor would be lost and confused, the rabbit burrowed a hole and disappeared into it."

I could see the doubt on the faces turned toward me.

"Shh," I said. "The spirits aren't finished yet." I took three big breaths, and when the family finally quieted down, the spirits emerged once again and spoke very clearly. I became certain I was meant to find the boy. A small gust of wind found its way in through the cracks, carrying with it a vision I needed to make sense of.

"Sorry. Please go on," said Officer Harper.

"There is a huge live oak tree. It's very, very old, and its branches are like the arms of a giant octopus, only thicker, wider, and much, much longer. It grows near water, in a clearing in the woods. Eyes stare back at me from the tree, and on the ground, a bear is showing its teeth and growling.

"Your boy is in grave danger. The spirits say we must rescue him before sunrise." I lifted my veil, took several sips of tea to compose myself, and listened for more clues.

"I hear water dripping off rocks, though the sound is nothing like the waterfalls of Greenville. Maybe a spring, hidden in the woods near the giant tree. This tree is not like the others. It is as commanding as a general in the army." I looked at Officer Harper. "Does this make any sense?"

"I think I know the place you're talking about, Donatella. The rabbit took the boy to the tree that guards the forest, towering above all the others. We call it the Guardian Tree. The way there can be dangerous during the day, and getting there in the dark will be difficult at best."

I thought about Spade and her almost superhuman vision, but I couldn't put her in this kind of danger. She could slip and fall, and then what would happen to her dreams?

Officer Harper paused. "There have been sightings of hungry bears in that area," he added. "The drought we've had the past few years has brought them out. There's been a population explosion of raccoons and snakes, as well."

❋ ❋ ❋

WHEN THE SPIRIT'S WORDS had dried up like the creeks in the drought, we began to map out a plan. I asked one of the circus workers to go get Roman and to make sure he had his compass. He was accustomed to looking for missing people—and what are a few bears to one who works with lions?

We sent Trevor's mother to the police station to wait, just in case Trevor returned on his own. Trevor's father and Riley would join the party. I would lead the search with Roman and Officer Harper's help.

We borrowed lanterns and ropes from the circus. Roman brought his dart gun, equipped with tranquilizer darts that could knock out a lion and, presumably, a bear. Then he grabbed some nuts and honey, and we piled into the police wagon, headed toward the train station and the woods nearby.

Roman and Riley were close to the same age. Though they didn't exchange many words, Roman expressed his sympathy, and Riley helped Roman carry the equipment.

The deeper we went into the woods, the words between us became fewer and fewer, though Riley and Mr. York periodically called out for Trevor. We took every step with care, remembering what the officer had said about snakes.

"We could use Spade's eyes about now," Roman whispered to me.

"That's true," I whispered back. "But I couldn't let her have an accident, or be bitten by a snake."

"Would he have gone so far from the station?" Mr. York asked, puzzled that his Trevor would travel so far on his own.

"This is no ordinary rabbit," I replied. "This rabbit is a trickster. It appears he was showing off his powers to take advantage of a boy who wanted to believe a rabbit could become a kangaroo. I think your boy is homesick."

"But the rabbit's playing with my brother's life," said Riley, his brow furrowed in anger.

We came to a fork. One way was inviting and pleasing to the eye, the other gloomy and mysterious. "We should go the way of the darkness, dried grass, and twigs," I said. In the distance I saw the gleam of eyes: two raccoons staring back at me. "Take another look at your compass and remember what it says," I went on, as if nothing were wrong.

"We're being followed," Roman said, a note of fear in his voice.

"It's all right, boy," Officer Harper added, but looking at his face, I could tell he wished he'd had this night off.

A wall of rocks rose before us. We tried to find a passage to the other side, but the only way to go was up and over.

Negotiating these tangled woods and jutting rocks would have been much easier for a child, I thought. For a moment, I feared I wouldn't make it. Then Roman took my hand, and we scrambled up the rocks together. I wondered if Spade recognized what a good young man her suitor had become.

Clearly, we were getting close to water; slippery, wet moss covered the rocks, and there wasn't much to grab on to. Mr. York caught his leg in a crevice, gouging it. Riley ripped off his shirt and tied it around his father's leg to stanch the bleeding, then helped him to his feet.

"I've heard of elves and gremlins, and of course good and bad witches, but I've never heard of a rabbit that could fool a seven-year-old into thinking it was a kangaroo," Mr. York said, his voice full of doubt.

On the other side of the rocks was a big clearing. Even at night it looked lush and green after the recent rains. To our right, a creek was running high and fast.

"We're getting close," I said. And just as I opened my mouth and lifted my leg, ready to take my next step, a cottonmouth snake flashed its gaping white mouth. I froze. I had lived in the South long enough to know not to threaten it. So, like the ballet dancer I'd once been, I kept my left leg in the air, held my position, and shifted my weight to the right. I shot a warning glance at Roman. Our tension grew. We were strung as tight as a bow before it releases its arrow. Then Roman, doing his best to stay calm, took hold of my arm and helped me take one step back, and then another. I followed his lead until the snake slid off into the brush. I'd never been so relieved.

We'd made our way through the clearing when I heard an owl hoot, then another. The owls told me we were on the right path. "The owls are a sign from the spirits," I said. "Your boy is fine, though we need to find him fast." Then we all stopped dead at a sound so frightening it would have turned Napoleon around. I wanted to turn and run, but for the sake of the others I held firm.

"Trevor!" his father called out. We thought we heard a squeak. An owl swooped down and landed on the tree in front of me. Then it flew to the next tree, and the one after that, hooting all the way. Riley and Officer Harper called out for Trevor. The owl continued to lure us on until we were just outside a ring of trees. In the middle, towering over the rest, was the most magnificent live oak.

"Pop, Pop, Pop. You found me! I'm sorry, Pop," Trevor called out from the top of the Guardian Tree. Below him was the biggest bear I had ever seen. It was growling at Trevor as though he had invaded its home—and, as we soon discovered, he had. Off to the side, we saw a mama bear and her cub. We couldn't tell if the bears were hungry or just afraid. Either way, we knew to keep our distance.

We waited, hoping the bears would go away. We were worried that Trevor might become tired and fall out of the tree, but the owl kept him awake by hooting in his ear.

Neither we nor the bear made a move. I had an eerie sensation that time was running out. Even the live oak tree seemed restless, its leaves thrashing in the breeze. We had to take action.

Riley took out the honey and hickory nuts he'd brought along, and he and his father snuck off to the left. They scattered the nuts and placed jars of honey on the ground. Roman moved to the right and prepared the circus dart gun. But just as the sun began to rise above the horizon, and Roman was about to shoot, a giant rabbit, sitting up on its hind legs to look like Trevor's stuffed kangaroo, hopped out of a hole in the middle of the clearing.

"That's my kangaroo!" Trevor cried.

"Quiet, boy, and stay put!" his father said in a loud whisper.

Leaping in circles, the trickster rabbit stretched out his back legs to hide who he really was, and he continued to hop until the big bear seemed mesmerized. We were, too.

I motioned to Roman with my hands not to fire the gun. Riley stood off to the side, ready to rescue his little brother.

Though the bear could smell the honey and the nuts, the rabbit, as even Trevor's father could see, was utterly hypnotic. None of us could take our eyes away from him. After his restless night spent guarding a tree, the big black bear couldn't resist; he lumbered after the rabbit in circles that grew larger and larger. By now his family had joined him, and all three bears were following the rabbit.

I wondered where the rabbit would take them, and whether it had set a trap. But I didn't have long to think about it. The spirits had said the boy had to be rescued before sunrise, and we only had minutes before the sun would fill the sky.

I have never seen a brother run so fast to help his sibling. Riley raced up the tree, letting its octopus branches guide him. I waited for a hoot from the owl, who had been talking all night, but none could be heard. The sun was inches from the horizon when Riley lifted his brother onto his back. Then he stealthily brought him down to safety on sweet solid ground and into his weeping father's arms.

When we returned to the police station, we found Trevor's mother asleep on a cold, hard bench. Trevor ran to her and showered her with kisses, waking her up. She pinched Trevor five or ten times to make sure she wasn't dreaming.

"Don't you ever frighten your mother like this again," she said between kisses. Then she looked over to me and silently mouthed two words: *Thank you.*

Officer Harper approached me as we said our goodbyes. "Donatella, if I had heard of our evening's tale from one of the other officers, I wouldn't have believed it was true. I can see now why your reputation precedes you. You've made a friend in Charleston. If you're ever in need of help, stop by or call and ask for me. I'll be at your service. You not only did a good deed for the family tonight but you helped this police station save a life." Then he had another policeman drive Roman and me back to the circus.

I was exhausted by the time I got back to my tent, peeled off my clothes, and crawled into bed. I shut my eyes, but immediately I heard a noise and opened them again. There, between the strings of beads that hung at the entrance to my tent, stood Trevor's kangaroo rabbit. Too tired to follow him, although indeed his charms were great, I winked at him and said, "Good night. Donatella needs her rest."

My head got heavier with each breath I took as I conjured up the night and reminisced about all that it brought: a boy safely returned to his mother, Officer Harper's kind words, and a confirmation that Louie's son Roman might after all be good enough for Spade. I started to drift. It was just as well; I couldn't hold another thought in my head.

CHAPTER 32

BELLA HOPED I COULD talk some sense into her daughter. "Spade thinks she's a cat. Maybe that's why she spends so much time with Louie's son Roman." I smiled at Bella, but her own joke went flat on her, and she continued her rant. "I know her sisters aren't too pleased, either."

I worried for Spade but believed she had a right to make her own decisions, even if I didn't agree.

"Aunt Donatella," she told me, "I know you're frightened for me, but you shouldn't be. Walking the wire, even without a safety net, is second nature to me." Still, I hoped she would change her mind.

Vladimir had caved in to Spade's strong will. Spade had threatened to walk the wire without a net someplace else if she couldn't continue to do it at the Circus of the Queens. He tried to defend his decision. "A lot of girls her age are already married," he said. "At least here, I can be certain every precaution is taken. She could be walking the wire without a net with any circus. There are plenty who'd be thrilled to have her." But I knew underneath his breath Vladimir was cursing me. I felt a little guilty too for having played into her hand.

Both sets of twins were now in their teens and Bella, Vladimir, and I had to become master jugglers to keep up with them. Nonetheless, this was what we chose. Each yes or no we'd said since the day each were born had brought us to this place.

Lucky and Diamond were fourteen, and a frustrated Lucky couldn't get the words out fast enough to tell me how her other half had snuck into town to meet a boy—a "townie," Lucky called him scornfully.

"It's late, Lucky. We can talk about this tomorrow. Diamond is safe—she waved good night to me a little while ago."

Lucky stomped her feet as if she were twelve. I didn't have much patience for her in this mood. She was at that age where she was fighting to establish her own identity and independence. Her rebellion was hard for me to understand—torn away too young from my parents and my home, put on a ship to cross an ocean by myself, I had more independence than I'd ever wanted; I never thought to fight for it.

The next morning, I found Diamond and confronted her.

"It wasn't a big deal—nothing really happened," she said. "He challenged me to a bet, and I just couldn't let him win."

I told Diamond not to be so easily taken in by boys.

"But Aunt Donatella, isn't that how true romance begins?" She gave me a translucent smile, morphed into an older version of herself, and walked back to her tent. Diamond and Lucky loved each other in the deepest way. Still, they fought as hard as they loved.

Though circus blood ran through Lucky's veins, she had another side that was hard for her family to comprehend. As insecure and childish as she could be, she was also the smartest person any of us knew. I found Lucky to be quite entertaining. She had a gift for pulling words from her head and stringing them together and there were times we passed hours doing just that.

Lucky had read *Jane Eyre* seven times, loved Dickens just like my Polly, and liked composing limericks. So, while her sisters perfected their circus acts, Lucky beat a different drum and recited poetry, both her own and classics.

❋ ❋ ❋

When Lucky moved on from limericks to Keats and Byron, Diamond began to find her sister exciting. But though she admired her twin's talent, the older Diamond got, the fewer people she needed. She inhabited a universe of ukulele, singing, acting, and trying to find God. And the farther she reached into herself, the more attuned she became to what some would call the other world.

"I sit on the ground until I feel the cold, damp grass through my cotton skirt, and my hair floating up toward the sky," she told me one summer day in Lucky's Library Carriage. "Then I imagine myself as an ancient live oak, with roots reaching into the ground. When I feel one with both the heaven and earth, I close my eyes and watch my dreams float on by."

The next day, Diamond Claire had the day off, and I asked her how she spent it. "I took my ukulele out and looked for a tunnel where I could play. I played chords and blended my voice and ukulele with the echoes from the tunnel until everything just fell into place. And when it did, my thoughts seemed to vanish, and I became perfectly still. Aunt Donatella, I think this is how I pray."

I was stunned!

Diamond Claire loved her parents and especially her sisters, but that summer she came to a conclusion. "I'm going to have to leave."

Boys found the distance she put between herself and them very alluring. Many approached her with the best of intentions. But Diamond was certain Roman was the only boy who would ever allow her to be herself.

"One day I'm going to be on stages around the world. In my dreams, I rehearse all the ways that I might leave."

But nothing could have prepared her, no matter how much she rehearsed, for the circumstances under which she would go.

CHAPTER 33

TWO SUMMERS PASSED. I watched with pride as Ann Marie and Spade blossomed into young women with numerous pursuers. Lucky and Diamond were also growing up fast, though Lucky had a hard time admitting that.

The first night Kyle Erhard came to see the Circus of the Queens, no one even noticed that he was there, not even me. Though he came to the circus every night for a week, he wore dull clothing that blended into the background. He let his beard grow until he looked like a typical farmhand and was just plain, but Kyle had a plan as I would soon discover.

He observed everything around him, wanting to get a truer sense of circus life. "What kinds of people are these queens?" he wanted to know, and he had no doubt he would find out without anyone noticing he was looking. He maneuvered in and out of the tent and even visited me early one evening in my carriage.

✳ ✳ ✳

KYLE'S HAND WAS ALMOST twice the size of my own. The creases in his palm were so deep and numerous, I hardly knew where to begin.

He had come to my carriage well before the main big-top show and stood in line like the rest, waiting to have his fortune told. He struck me as a likeable quiet young man, though with an air of inner certainty. Still, I saw many men such as him daily.

"I've been told you're very good," he said. "I have someone on my mind. Can you tell me what you see?" Kyle was just another young man with a crush, I thought.

I ran my fingers lightly up and down his arms. His hands were rough and callused, but his eyes were warm and soft. I began to think there might be something more. His hands were telling me he was a man who accomplished things. The deliberate way in which he spoke gave me the impression that when he made up his mind about something, he didn't give up, and he was loyal to a fault. But he hadn't come to see me to have his own character analyzed, so I kept it to myself.

I stretched his palm out on my table and separated his fingers as I did in all of my readings. Then I pulled his pinkie finger back so I could more clearly read his lifeline. It looked like he'd live to be a hundred and five.

"You are going to marry a woman who is impossible to hold down," I told him. "You will have two children and live a very long life. This big love will come soon. She's an unusual girl with fire in her belly strong enough to lift you up, and with her you will fly away. Though this relationship does not come without hardship, the rewards will be great. That's all the spirits that guide me have to say."

I thought I would never see him again, so I had no reason to pay him any extra attention, but as he walked out of my carriage door, I stopped him. "Observe the little things. That is what she cares about most."

※ ※ ※

THE GIRLS WERE READYING themselves for their acts, fixing their hair and changing costumes. Lucky wanted to wear a violet brooch of mine, and I had come to give it to her. For a moment, I saw my mother and myself in my parents' bedroom in St. Petersburg with all my mother's jewels spread out on top of her bed. In her hand, she held the emerald brooch Lillya had given to her. And I couldn't help but wonder where it went.

My arrival didn't interrupt the girls' lighthearted bantering as they primped. I loved listening to them speak so freely. "There's a hotshot rodeo star in the audience tonight. Rumor has it he's the champion in bareback bronc riding," I heard them say. Curious, I pretended not to remember which pocket I had put the brooch in.

"My brother says it's the most physically demanding act in the rodeo," a redheaded equestrian chimed in.

"I wonder if he's here to see Ann Marie," another said teasingly by her mirror.

"You can't miss him." The redhead winked. "He's the one wearing a scarlet shirt. He's almost as handsome as that actor—Douglas Fairbanks."

"Didn't you love him in *The Thief of Baghdad*?" said another girl. "What about *Zorro*?"

With that, the violet brooch miraculously appeared, and I pinned it on Lucky and took my leave.

Like many people from Europe and Russia, I was fascinated by cowboys. They were very American and I didn't want to miss seeing a real rodeo star.

As it turned out, without his beard, Kyle was more fair than Douglas Fairbanks but just as handsome. I never would have recognized him had it not been for the scar above his right eye. With his high cheekbones, distinctive square chin, and eyes that gleamed like gems, he was hard to ignore. It took several seconds before I realized that this was the same unassuming young man who had come to my carriage the day before.

He'd obviously taken to heart what I had said and knew how to put on a more appealing face. Ann Marie must be the girl he has his eye on, or why else would he be wearing a scarlet shirt? Now he had my full attention!

Many a young man came to our circus to see Ann Marie. But Kyle was different. Clearly he had wanted a chance to survey the land before he made a move. He wanted to hear how Ann Marie laughed when she was at ease and whether she had a sense of humor. What did she find funny? Was she kind, loyal? Stories of her beauty and talent had brought him to the Circus of the Queens, but he hadn't come all this way for just a myth and a pretty face.

"I was stunned the first time I saw her ride Ali Baba, scarlet-like flames trailed behind her," he told me months later. "*She's even better in person*, I thought. How could anyone be so perfect?"

Throngs of young men swarmed Ann Marie's tent that night after the show. Each were vying for her attention. But Kyle simply stayed in the background, caught her eye, and walked away. Subtle, I thought, and the scarlet shirt the perfect touch.

❊ ❊ ❊

"Ann Marie said her heart started to flutter when she saw this boy in the crowd," Lucky told me the following night. "She said it was his scarlet bow tie that set him apart."

Very clever, I thought. I usually wasn't this nosey, but somehow meeting him before he revealed who he really was made me all the more curious.

"She said he smiled and nodded, then vanished into the crowd. That was it. She probably doesn't like him."

❀ ❀ ❀

"HE DIDN'T COME TONIGHT!" Lucky reported the evening after that. "Ann Marie seemed a bit upset. I'm sure she'll get over it. She doesn't even know him!"

❀ ❀ ❀

"IT'S AS IF ANN Marie fell off a horse and hit her head!" Lucky said the next morning. "Last night, Ann Marie ran around our room like a first-class drama queen. 'What if I never get to hear his voice?'" Lucky imitated her older sister. "'Or see him up close!' Ugh." Lucky sighed.

❀ ❀ ❀

TWO NIGHTS LATER, AFTER most of Ann Marie's other admirers had given up, Kyle reappeared. Marvin and I had come to say good night to the girls and it was impossible to miss the bouquet of scarlet flowers—zinnias, hibiscus, and passionflowers—he held along with a scarlet kerchief that poked out of the top pocket of his jacket, embroidered with a heart and the initials AMV.

We happened to be standing close by and as manners would dictate, Ann Marie introduced the young man to her aunt Donatella and the ringmaster Marvin. Neither Kyle nor I acknowledged we had met before, for in a way we had not. It had been the characters in the carriage, not Ann Marie's aunt and her suitor.

Then Ann Marie turned to put the flowers in a vase and the kerchief in her purse, though not before dropping it on the floor for everyone to see. She coyly shook Kyle's hand, then thanked him for his gifts.

"My pleasure," the handsome bareback bronc rider replied. Then he tipped his cowboy hat and left.

"I couldn't let him know how happy I was to see him," Ann Marie confided to me. "He's different from the others." Holding her new kerchief against her cheek, she spun across the room, reminding me of myself as a young girl. For a second, I felt Vladimir's strong arms lifting me up in the air, and when I landed I felt the weight of Hervé's hand on my back leading me to the ballroom before the fall that eventually brought me here and into the lives of these four girls.

That night, I gave Ann Marie some advice: "Tuck the scarlet kerchief under your pillow. It will help you to feel close to him when you begin to dream."

✳ ✳ ✳

THE FOLLOWING EVENING, JUST as the lightning bugs began to sparkle, and everyone else, including Ann Marie, was heading toward the big top, Kyle knocked on my carriage door, hoping for a romantic forecast.

"I'm sorry if I wasn't totally forthcoming when we first met," he said. "I wanted an unbiased forecast. I hope we can be friends."

The boy had charisma. Even I found it hard to resist his charm.

"I grew up in northern Wyoming, Donatella," he told me, "where snow-topped mountains rise above white-capped rivers and moose and bald eagles roam. It's God's country. Our family has a cattle ranch. With my father's blessing, I left home at seventeen to follow the rodeo. Rodeo is a part of life where I come from—it's the circus of the West.

"You should know that the fame of this circus has made its way across the Rockies. For over a year, I heard stories about Ann Marie. Finally, I had to come see if they were true." He paused for a second. "Donatella, I think Ann Marie is destined to be my wife. I know she's young, but I believe we'd be good together. She has a spirit that rivals my own. I don't suppose you'd like to shed any light on that..." He looked at me hopefully.

As much as I wanted to tell him what I saw in his future, I replied, "You'll both have to come to your own conclusions. It's the only way your love can possibly blossom."

"Tonight, I'm going to ask her if I can court her," he said.

After her performance Kyle went to see Ann Marie. "With your permission," he said to her, "I'd like to follow the circus. I could visit with you tomorrow and perhaps the day after that, if it's all right."

✳ ✳ ✳

AS PROMISED, KYLE APPEARED at Ann Marie's door every evening, and each day he added another scarlet flower to his already swollen bouquet. Ann Marie, like her father, was an expert poker player, though, and she'd learned to hold her cards—especially the queen of hearts—close to her chest.

"I'm not sure where I stand," Kyle said, frustrated. "I swear, Donatella, Ann Marie's more difficult than a wild horse!"

I couldn't help but laugh, for what he said was true. Nonetheless, it wasn't my place to step in.

"It's not funny, Donatella. I'm falling deeper in love with her. Why, just last night a young girl came to Ann Marie's tent with her parents. When she finally got to speak with Ann Marie, she told her that when she grew up, she wanted to be exactly like her. Lucky happened to be standing behind the young girl, and Ann Marie could see that she was listening, too. We both know Lucky idolizes her older sister. So, she told the girl, 'You don't want to be like me, for if you were, the world would miss what's special about you and the stars would turn into tears of sadness.' The child understood, and so did Lucky. Then she asked the little girl what she liked to do best. She said she liked to draw. Ann Marie told her about Diamond who drew, Lucky and her poetry, and Spade, who walks the wire, and how much richer all their lives were because of their differences. I knew then she was the one for me. I don't want to live without her."

Ann Marie was very taken by Kyle, but just how serious she was, only she could answer, and I didn't think she knew.

❄ ❄ ❄

ONE EVENING, I OVERHEARD Kyle ask Ann Marie if she'd like to go for a ride with him the following afternoon. It seemed like an eternity before she answered Kyle, but finally she said, "Yes, meet me at the stables at two."

The next morning, I was up early getting some fresh air when I saw Ann Marie in her riding clothes on her way to the stables. I had decided to visit Emily and Bess—it just happened that I'd have to pass through the stables to get to them. As I approached, I saw Ann Marie tackling up the slowest old workhorse the circus owned.

"Who's going to be riding him?" I asked, curious. "Kyle," she answered matter-of-factly. I could barely keep the surprise from showing on my face. What was she thinking?

"I'm sorry—I have to go find Diamond Claire," she said when she'd finished tightening the last strap. "I have a favor to ask of her."

It was obvious Ann Marie had something up her sleeve.

❄ ❄ ❄

AROUND FIVE THIRTY, WHEN the sun was beginning its slide toward the horizon, gilding the big top with its deep, warm rays, I ran into Diamond Claire on my way to my carriage. "How did Ann Marie's ride go with Kyle today?" I asked, as casually as I could.

"Oh, it went fine…eventually. Kyle showed up right at two, but instead of Ann Marie"—she smiled impishly—"he found me."

"What?" I was a little disconcerted.

"I told Kyle that Ann Marie couldn't come—but she didn't want to deny him his ride, so she'd insisted that I take her place. I guess he didn't want to hurt my feelings, so he went along with it. I suggested that we ride in the meadow behind the horse cars—'It's very pretty there,' I said. Then I handed him the reins to our old workhorse, just like Ann Marie told me to do. 'This is Ralph,' I said. 'His back is so wide, we had to make a special saddle for him.'" Diamond Claire was obviously enjoying telling me the story with considerable dramatic flair.

"What did Kyle say?" I was flabbergasted. "How did he react?"

"He laughed, and so did I. 'Ralph seems to be a nice old boy' was all he said. "Then he scratched Ralph's nose and mounted him happily enough.

"He remained the perfect gentleman. I was truly impressed. He even asked me questions about myself—had I always wanted to be a trapeze artist? How did I like life in the circus?

"We walked away slowly from the stables. Well, seeing that he was on old Ralph, slowly was the only way we'd be going anywhere.

"He was real easy to talk to. I told him I was born to be in a circus and perform. My mother and my grandparents on both sides and all of my sisters were in the circus and several had become rather notorious. My father's mother, my grandmother Lillya, was actually quite a famous horsewoman. I found myself rambling on, telling him how I hadn't spoken until I turned three, and that 'pony' was my first word. He found that sweet. He spoke of Wyoming and the rodeo. I said that for me, just like him with the rodeo, swinging on the trapeze had been my world, but recently I'd been thinking more about acting and singing. I don't even know why I told him that, Aunt Donatella.

"Kyle was a good listener, and he seemed to be enjoying himself. Not one complaint about old Ralph, even when a steer passed him on a path because he was going too slow."

I laughed. It was an amusing picture, though I felt a little sorry for Kyle.

"We rode for a mile or so, until we passed a barrel painted blue. I didn't know what to expect, but that's where Ann Marie had asked me to rein the horses in. We were only there for a minute when Ann Marie mysteriously appeared out of a clump of brush. She was leading two horses, a beautiful mare for herself and our most spirited horse for Kyle.

"'His name is Panther,' Ann Marie said, smiling. She looked as if she was quite amused by her own joke. 'We call him that because of his shiny black coat and the way he can run.'

"Kyle seemed pretty amused himself and real happy to see Ann Marie. 'Why, you devil, you,' I heard him say, and then he laughed, dismounted old Ralph, and went to Ann Marie and gave her a kiss on the cheek. I think she turned the color of your favorite soup, beet red.

"Kyle didn't complain once," Diamond said. "He was a very good sport. He's who *I* would choose.

"As I was leaving Ann Marie was challenging Kyle. 'I'll race you to that big...' Ann Marie said when Kyle had mounted Panther. Then I watched them disappear."

❈ ❈ ❈

"AUNT DONATELLA, YOU SHOULD have seen us," Ann Marie told me later that evening, her eyes shining. "I challenged Kyle to race me to that big old oak tree, and we galloped away through the meadow, the long grass was tickling the bottom of my feet. The sun was beating down on me, but my heart was already warm."

She paused, and I could see she was back in that meadow in her mind. I smiled to myself. Kyle's patience and persistence had obviously paid off. "By the time we reached the big old live oak tree," he would confess years later, "I thought I might just be the one who wins the heart of Ann Marie."

He was right. "I learned more about Kyle in that half hour than I have since we first met," she said on the day of their first ride. "He's kind and patient, and he can take a joke. He didn't mind riding old Ralph. He's confident. In my eyes, he's a champion."

❈ ❈ ❈

TWENTY-ONE NIGHTS LATER, KYLE came to Ann Marie with a scarlet bouquet twice the size of all the others. "I want you to be my wife," he proclaimed, getting down on one knee. "I won't stop asking until you say yes." And three nights later—the third week of September—she did.

"The handsome cowboy lassoed the heart of Ann Marie," I said to Bella.

"She's his main event." Bella winked.

❋ ❋ ❋

ON THE NINETEENTH OF October, Vladimir gave away the bride. Ann Marie wore a flowing white gown. She walked to meet her groom along a path strewn with scarlet petals, all the circus people lined up along it, Spade, Diamond Claire, and Lucky by her side. After the ceremony, Kyle boosted Ann Marie up onto his own horse, Sir Charles—named after his grandfather Charlie, who was from the British Isles—and together they rode away. Vladimir, Bella, and I felt certain that Lillya and Anton were with us.

"Aunt Donatella, did you see how high she threw her scarlet bouquet? I thought it might disappear," Lucky recalled that evening, as we all sat around a fire we'd lit to keep the autumn chill at bay. "The way they were galloping, Sir Charles looked like Pegasus flying!"

"She was a beautiful bride," I said, smiling.

Several months after Kyle and Ann Marie galloped out of our lives, Bella and Vladimir received a letter. In my tent over coffee, Bella took out the thin sheet of onionskin paper and read Ann Marie's words to me:

Kyle built us a house under the tallest tree on our land, and he made me a swing and hung it from the highest branch. Now every day my feet meet the clouds, and every night they see the stars. I feel the wind touch my soul as I fly through the air. I want you to know that I'm happy in my new life.

P.S. Tell Lucky I miss her most of all, and send my love to Donatella, Spade, and Diamond Claire. My swing is waiting for her.

CHAPTER 34

IT WAS THE SPRING of 1929, and the early rains had given way to a flood tide of blossoms. The peach trees were almost in full bloom. Irina had told me once that the Chinese believe the peach tree to be the most vital tree of all because its blossoms appear before its leaves sprout, and its wood and the seed of its fruit are believed to possess a protective spirit. I found a branch that had fallen from a tree, laden with sweet-smelling pink flowers, and I put it on the table next to my bed. Marvin and I had argued the night before, and I wanted to make amends. Ancient rulers of China believed a branch from a peach tree could protect their home and keep them safe and healthy. Its sweet smell filled the tent, reminding me we had entered the season of birth and rebirth. I wondered how this renewal would reveal itself. Without Ann Marie here, we were all a bit out of sorts.

Though Vladimir was happy for Ann Marie, he felt her absence. He didn't know how to fill the gap left by the loss of her contagious laugh and free spirit. "Of course, I know Kyle is a very good husband," he'd say, "but it's been months. What would it take for them to pay us a visit? Bella and the girls miss her terribly!"

"Kyle's a good man," I found myself defending him. "He wouldn't keep Ann Marie away from you unless there was a very good reason, and remember your daughter, like her twin, has a will of her own. Patience, my friend, now you have a sense of how Bella's parents felt when you dragged their daughter across an ocean."

Everyone missed Ann Marie. Now that one of the four queens was missing, none of us was playing with a full deck. Our lives had become lopsided, even though on the surface everything seemed normal. It was as if the circus were riding on the back of a three-legged dog who was learning to make the most of his three legs but, try as he might, couldn't find his balance without the fourth.

Vladimir tried to fill the void he felt by putting all his energy into Spade's high-wire act. "She's as good as any high-wire walker," he would brag to anyone who would listen. "And prettier, too. You name a trick, and my Spade has mastered it. All she has to do is decide what suits her mood."

This enthusiasm pleased Spade, now a young woman, but it also came to feel like a burden. She visited my tent one morning, looking rather strained. "Aunt Donatella," she said, "I love that Papa is paying so much attention to me, but sometimes it's smothering. He misses Ann Marie, and he's trying to replace her with me. And Mama's no help in this matter, because she doesn't approve of my choices. Do you think you could encourage him to spend more time with Lucky and Diamond? He listens to you."

Sadly, I never got to have that conversation with Vladimir. Life can fool you into thinking you have all the time in the world, that everything will go on and on as it always has, and then things change.

❋ ❋ ❋

EVEN THE WARM GLOW that Harsita and his work with the elephants had given us lost its effect. The peach blossoms in my tent wilted, and I had a sense of foreboding I couldn't explain.

Small discords that had been seething just below the surface showed themselves more and more. Lucky was jealous of Diamond and the freedom she'd claimed for herself. Diamond envied the attention Roman showed Spade. Spade distanced herself from the problems of her younger sisters; she was focused on her high-wire act and Roman, although she still enjoyed taking walks with me and Emily and Bess. "I'm more mature," she said, justifying herself, but we all knew it was something more.

I went to visit Roman and his father when I had extra time. Marvin was exceptionally busy, and I knew that Louie appreciated it. My conversations with Louie hadn't really changed much over the years; still, there was comfort in their sameness. Louie was perplexed that his son's crush had grown.

Roman had turned into a handsome young man whom women found attractive, and this newfound attention boosted his confidence greatly. Other girls began to look at him in the same way he looked at Spade. He had a long, lean build and strikingly beautiful hazel eyes.

188 A U D R E Y   B E R G E R   W E L Z

Even Diamond's friend Katie had a secret crush on Roman. Her parents told me that she giggled and blushed whenever he came into their store.

He had no interest in Katie, but like any other young man, he wasn't immune to the charm of a compliment.

When Katie confessed her crush on Roman to Diamond, Diamond was none too happy. "She knows he loves Spade. Think how it would hurt Spade if she found out." If Diamond were honest, though, I thought, she would admit that it was she, not Spade, who was hurt.

Diamond, more than any of her sisters, asked me to predict her future. I refused. Still, with Ann Marie married and gone, Diamond knew Roman's time to tell Spade how he really felt was running out.

Finally, Roman worked up the nerve to tell me how he felt about Spade. "I don't want to play the role of her younger brother any longer. I've talked with the lions long enough. It's time to take Spade aside and tell her how I feel. It's time I asked her to be my girl." I'd been waiting years for him to speak his mind.

"I want to give Spade something really special," he said the next time he came to my carriage. "Something she can hold onto when we're old, a souvenir on which to build memories."

I thought of all the years it had taken for him to get up the courage to act; I was so happy. "I have something that might be perfect," I told him instinctively. Then I reached into my dresser drawer and handed him a hand-cut rose quartz necklace. "This stone is very powerful. It has the ability to soothe and open hearts to the possibility that you are both worthy of love. Take it. Let this be my gift to you."

Roman shook my hand long and hard. "Donatella, tonight's the night. Thank you." Then he left to ready himself for his special evening.

❋ ❋ ❋

THAT EVENING, I CAME to the big top early. When Roman entered the tent, I immediately caught him out of the corner of my eye but made a point not to stare too long. He had put on his favorite olive shirt, which brought out the hazel in his eyes. The necklace I had given him, I assumed, was in his pocket, and I could see him checking his reflection in a mirror. He ran his hand through his unruly hair as if waving goodbye to the boy that he'd been and made certain his shirt was neatly tucked in. A change in weather brought me back into the moment.

The wind began to whistle, then howl. Then a lightning bolt lit up the sky. Caught up in his own storm of emotions, I wondered if he even heard the rain and thunder brewing outside.

I hadn't expected it to get so heavy. The raindrops drummed against the big top's canvas sides harder and harder, I tried to put it out of my mind.

I was certain Roman wouldn't let a little bad weather get in his way.

I smiled, thinking of these young lovers who had grown up together. It had been twelve years since Roman first laid eyes on Spade.

Spade was on the rope. She looked so beautiful and graceful. Juggling her plates, she began to sing her favorite song. Unlike Roman, who only had room for thoughts of Spade, I couldn't help but notice this storm was heating up.

Diamond was with the other trapeze artists waiting in the wings; she would be the next act. I saw her glance at Roman curiously. The rose quartz was working its magic, and he was gazing up at Spade with an unshakable sense of certainty, and a big grin.

As if to break this trance, a blinding flash of lightning illuminated the tent, and the lights began to flicker on and off. Then suddenly everything went dark.

Tension filled the room like a string tied too tight, about to break. All eyes focused on Spade. In the dim light, she was only a shadow above. I squinted to see her. She took two steps forward and one step back, not knowing which way to go. I was sure it took all of her concentration to maintain her composure. I could hear the conversation she was having with herself: *I've done this all my life. I could do this with my eyes closed. I could do this in the dark.* And I knew that she could, but still I was afraid for her.

I could faintly hear Spade singing, "My dreams are just like," when an explosive clap of thunder so violent it shook the entire tent, caused everyone in the audience to gasp. The sound like a physical blow broke Spade's concentration. For a fraction of a second, all hearts seemed to stop. A beat later, they resumed. Like an outsider looking in, Spade's life flashed before me as I watched her lose her balance and slip; her very first performance, our visits with Emily, Roman! Roman's mouth was open, his face rigid with panic.

Gravity ruled, and speed took over Spade's body. I saw her grab one last big breath and fill her lungs with life. She looked like an angel as she fell.

Silence filled the big top and no one dared to shout "Queen Spade."

CHAPTER 35

IT ALL HAPPENED SO fast. Diamond slapped herself on the face, wanting it to be an illusion, and then ran to her sister.

As Diamond took her sister in her arms, I could see the limpness of Spade's body. She was already gone. Diamond gently closed Spade's eyes and began to howl like a wounded coyote. It seemed like forever before anyone could pry Spade's body from Diamond or coax her from her sister's side. "Don't you touch her!" she screamed even at me. "Stay away!" No one could get near her.

Roman didn't move or make a sound. He just stood and stared as Diamond held her sister in her arms.

Vladimir cursed and paced and punched himself in the chest. Someone had to find Bella and Lucky before they learned of Spade's death from a stranger. But it was too late.

My eyes were adjusting to the lack of light. It wasn't the darkness that had caused Spade to fall; it was the startling violent crack of thunder, like a mountain being split in half, the monster that had been hiding underneath it for centuries making his way out. I could see Marvin instructing the clowns close by to run and get torches. By now, several had been illuminated, casting an eerie flickering orange light as they moved through the audience.

Then I heard Bella. I will never be able to forget the raw animal-like wail that escaped her as she ran into the tent. "Tell me it's not true! Tell me it's not true!" She took over the beating of Vladimir's chest. Vladimir grabbed Bella and held onto her until she collapsed in his arms. In the background, Emily and Bess began trumpeting mournful cries. They didn't have to see Spade to sense what had happened, and once they started, the rest of the animals joined in until it became a cacophony of sadness.

The audience, in shock, was unable to move. They couldn't comprehend what had happened or the instructions being given. Marvin was trying to keep everyone calm and get the audience safely out of the tent, but he was having a hard time getting their attention.

I heard a man cursing, "*Canard! Merde!*" Children were crying. Mothers and fathers covered the faces of their young ones, trying to console them as the crowd emptied out.

I hadn't taken a step. The nightmarish glare of the torches, the unearthly trumpeting of the elephants, the horrified faces of the audience—it seemed all to spin around me, making me dizzy, and my sweet lovely Spade was lying on the ground in front of me, dead.

Lucky, who had been in another tent with the windjammer band, stormed in and went directly to Diamond. Usually the most emotional of the Vronskys, she revealed another side of herself as she talked Diamond down. She quickly assessed that she would have to grieve for Spade later. A corner of me was proud of Lucky, even as I was overwhelmed with sadness and guilt.

Diamond clutched Lucky. Bella slowly walked over toward her daughters. I could see Diamond nod, giving Bella permission to enter the ring. Bella hugged Diamond and Lucky so tightly I thought they might die from lack of air. Then Bella gently moved some strands of hair that had fallen over Spade's eye. As she pushed them back, we all noticed the scarlet barrette that Spade was wearing, with its faceted hand-sewn beads. Ann Marie had given it to Spade on their birthday this past year.

I moved in closer but didn't interfere. Bella began to sob again, barely able to catch her breath. "How am I going to tell Ann Marie?" I heard her say. Vladimir's women held Spade's body and each other, and they wept and wept.

Vladimir stood on the sidelines, watching his queens grieve. He walked over to me, his face white. "It's my fault, Donatella. I was too confident of her talent." He grimaced as though he had been stabbed and his heart was lying on the circus tent floor, completely exposed. The pain he felt must have been almost unbearable.

The tent had emptied by now; we were alone with Spade's body. Vladimir gave his wife and daughters time before he walked over to his family. He kissed Spade on her forehead, and then lifted her in his arms and carried her out of the tent. A small procession made up of me, Diamond, Lucky, and Bella followed

Vladimir. We didn't know where he was leading us, but it soon became clear he was headed for my tent. Marvin had prepared a special bed there, and very carefully, as if he were afraid that he might hurt the dead, Vladimir laid her down on it. That's where she would rest until we buried her.

※ ※ ※

MARVIN SPENT HOURS MAKING arrangements with the bookers and advance men, canceling the circus's performances for the following week. After a week of mourning, we would pick up the tour in the next city on our junket, which happened to be Charleston.

It was two days before Bella could bring herself to write Ann Marie. I helped Bella with the wording, feeding her the details that I knew Ann Marie would want to know. Sadly, given the distance, Spade would be in the ground before Ann Marie ever received the news. Bella felt it best that she find out about her sister in the form of a letter rather than a telegram or call. She wanted Ann Marie to have something tangible that she could read over and over, until it sank in that her twin sister was dead.

I offered Vladimir and Bella a patch of earth in the small family graveyard in Savannah. I didn't think the colonel or Irina would mind. Spade would have a peaceful place to lie, and we could all continue to be by her side in the coming years. She was familiar with the farm, and I wanted to think of her in a place that she had once told me reminded her of heaven on earth, and where she had appeared to me as an angel.

Only our immediate family would be at the funeral. I asked Roman to join us, but he wasn't yet able to face Spade's death.

※ ※ ※

MY GARDEN IN SAVANNAH was already in bloom when I arrived, a day earlier than the rest, so I could talk to Polly and the others and help them prepare. They all expressed their sympathy.

"In some ways, she reminded me of you with Irina when you first arrived," Polly said. "The way she could repeat the names of all the herbs and flowers, and which ones needed shade and which ones sunlight. How she sat in the middle of your garden and waited for the hummingbirds. Yes, there was a big piece of you in that girl."

When everyone else arrived, Diamond and Lucky asked me questions about Spade's visit, and I'd find them with chairs sitting in the middle of my garden, the sun beating down on them, trying to soak up the memory of their sister. They were happy to have a place where they could privately mourn.

We buried Spade in a spot that I had set aside for myself, near a patch of Jasmine between the wildflowers of the meadow and the woods. As we laid her in the ground, we each said a prayer and then threw a handful of dirt into the grave.

Just when I was turning to leave, three hummingbirds appeared, circled Spade's grave, and flew away.

❋ ❋ ❋

MARVIN ARRANGED A TRIBUTE to Spade, an hour before we would reopen the circus gates in Charleston, so all of the circus people and their friends could pay their respects. He had accepted the privilege of organizing this sad affair as the rest of us were all rather numb. I was not looking forward to yet again having to confront the reality of Spade's death. Deep down, we all wanted to get back to our routines, to help keep our minds occupied and pretend this never happened.

Marvin rented a 1929 Packard limousine and a driver to take us from the farm in Savannah to Charleston. Built to hold seven, it had an intercom in the back so that we could have our privacy but still communicate with the chauffeur.

On our way to the circus grounds, the streets were unusually busy. "I wonder what's going on." I said. "There was probably some sort of accident."

The closer we got to our final destination, the slower the traffic moved. Then we noticed cars parked along the side of the road and policemen directing a throng of people making their way along the street. We were utterly perplexed as to what the commotion was about.

"Everyone seems to be going the same way we are," Lucky pointed out. "And they're all dressed in black." Right then, a police car with flashing lights appeared behind us. We pulled over to the side. When I saw Officer Harper jump out of his car, I understood.

I smiled at Officer Harper—the first smile that had touched my face in days—and asked him what he was doing. He looked at me kindly and said, "I thought you might need some help."

Word had spread of Spade's tragedy, and the many adults and children who had come to the circus over the years to see her perform, ask questions after a matinee show, and felt a personal connection with her and her family all wanted to pay their respects. Others came because they sympathized with our loss. Overwhelmed, I felt my eyes brimming with tears of gratitude.

We arrived at the circus grounds to a crowd of hundreds singing "Amazing Grace" in harmony. Vladimir and our family climbed the podium Marvin had had erected, Officer Harper and his men took off their caps, and the crowd stopped their singing, followed suit, and bowed their heads in silence.

Vladimir swallowed the lump in his throat and began to speak. He talked about Spade as a little girl and her dedication to her craft and her family. He mentioned her twin Ann Marie and their love of the circus, and how all of the queens loved everyone who was here in attendance. Vladimir spoke of Spade's kindness and of her extraordinary eyesight—how she would focus on a cutout of the queen of spades that she had taped on the other side of the tent. And when he heard a mournful trumpet outside, he mentioned the special relationship she had with an elephant named Emily.

"The Lord has taken our dear Spade to be his messenger in the sky, for she was always chasing rainbows on the ground. He needed someone as sweet as the nectar of a flower is to a hummingbird to sing him her favorite song. Now neither our Lord nor our dear Spade will ever be alone. How sweet the sound." When Vladimir had finished speaking, he bowed his head, and there was a minute of silence.

During the minute of meditation, I quietly stepped off the podium. Before the ceremony, I had asked Marvin to bring the calliope in and place it close by. It had been years since I had played anything that resembled a piano, but I knew the notes in my sleep. I had not planned on doing this, but I felt inspired, and I silently let our organist know that I would be taking his place.

I sat down on the bench. My hands skirted the top of a few notes, getting familiar with the keys. The minute of silence had ended. At first, the sound that came from my fingers when I pressed down on the notes frightened me. I almost left the bench. Then I felt Mme Strachkov's hand lightly slapping my back. *A one and two and three and four...* I began to play, and the entire crowd joined in singing once again, "Through many dangers, toils and snares...grace will lead me home."

After the ceremony, Marvin hung a black wreath outside the big top with a placard underneath: "To our Queen of Spades, whose dreams ended in the sky."

In the middle of the wreath was a picture of Spade that had been taken for her proud father Vladimir the day before she died.

❋ ❋ ❋

THAT NIGHT, THE CIRCUS was free of charge in honor of the deceased. Every half hour the audience would file out, making way for those waiting their turn patiently outside. Officer Harper's men stayed to direct the flow of the crowd. At the end of the performance, the windjammer band, with me accompanying it on the calliope, played Spade's favorite song, "I'm Always Chasing Rainbows." Everyone on the circus grounds inside and out stopped what they were doing, stood up, and sang along. Chopin, whose melody they sang, would have approved.

❋ ❋ ❋

ONE WEEK AFTER THE ceremony, Roman came to see me in my carriage.

"I took the rose quartz necklace out of my pocket today," he told me. "I buried it in the ground, along with my dreams. I made a small cross with some twigs, and I told Spade everything that was in my heart. I think she heard me. I could feel her essence in the air. Donatella, she hasn't completely disappeared."

❋ ❋ ❋

VLADIMIR, PARALYZED WITH GRIEF, wandered the circus grounds, his mood so dark that friends, including me, were wary to approach him. I often found him praying by the wreath that Marvin had placed outside the big top. Several times, I heard him apologizing to Spade.

And on a night when the moon was especially bright and Vladimir could not close his eyes, he began to count the tears on the pillow of his wife. "Like counting sheep, Donatella—nothing could help me fall asleep. Then, as I watched Bella's tears flowing like a river, mine began to flow too. In that flood of emotions, I made a promise never again to walk the rope or watch this part of the show. The Russian high-wire walker that you have known all your life is gone. What I have loved is dead to me, just as my daughter is dead."

❋ ❋ ❋

I KNEW I NEEDED to be strong, but still I felt weak. It was if a boulder had been placed on my body, causing it to break in two. In this state, how could I be helpful to anyone?

Exhausted, I made my way back to the tent. Every muscle and joint in my body ached in a way it had not since I was a girl at the Imperial School in St. Petersburg. I got into bed and threw the covers over my head, burying myself in my own grief. I thought about Sasha my pony and wondered what happened to him, my good friend Broni and her brother, Catherine, Archie and the Bradleys, Irina, Mme Stachkov, my mother, and especially my father. So many goodbyes.

I thought about Spade, my sweet Spade always chasing rainbows, her passion and bravery. A part of me wanted to run back to Savannah unearth the dirt where she was buried and hold her in my arms.

A momentary calmness overcame me and I found myself reaching for my deck of cards on the night table. I knew what I'd see; still, I laid down the four queens. All but one, the queen of spades, were facing in the same direction. "Why am I different from the other three?" I remembered Spade asking.

I had no answer then, and still, I had no answer now.

I heard the distinct sound of Marvin's shoes approaching and the scent of his pipe tobacco in the air.

"You dropped something my dear," he said as he entered the tent. "It must have fallen out of your box. I'm glad to see you're playing cards again, even if it's solitaire." He handed me a playing card of a woman with long auburn curls riding a horse dressed in green. Trying to hide my astonishment, I nonchalantly put the card into my silver hammered box that held my mother's hairbrush, but not before getting another look. I had seen this card before and I couldn't quite believe it had showed up this evening purely coincidentally. How did it get here? Who left it and what did it mean?

My eyelids were getting heavier. They felt like fifty-pound weights were strapped to them. I knew the mystery would not be solved tonight. I had done all that I could for the day, so I wrapped my leftover thoughts, my mysteries and sadness, all my worries and fears, and I put them in an imaginary suitcase and closed it for the night.

❋ ❋ ❋

Smokey Mountains, North Carolina, 1929

WORD OF SPADE'S DEATH spread. "That family deserves some misery," Big Jim Baldwin told his new friend when he found out the news. Louie, our lion tamer, happened to be picking up supplies in Spruce Pine and found himself coincidentally eating lunch at the table next to Big Jim.

Under normal circumstances, he would be fretting about Roman. How would his son find his way without his very best friend and the girl since boyhood he had planned to marry?

"Actually," Louie told me later, "focusing on something else, even something as everyday as picking up supplies, seemed to help alleviate my own grief. But then I had to run into that big oaf! I recognized him on the spot. And when I did, I quickly pulled my cowboy hat down so he wouldn't recognize me."

As devastated as I was, I couldn't help but see humor, a Russian lion tamer wearing a cowboy hat. I still couldn't get over the fascination men around the world had with the Wild West.

"Donatella, I don't think they even noticed me. Besides, there was nothing I could do. If I had made a fuss, all the attention in the room would have turned to me.

"When I sat down it, so happens, they were talking about Spade. It took everything in me to stay seated. I wanted to punch Big Jim. But then they started to speak about Vladimir and I decided I should sit still and listen. It's been my experience, Donatella, that a cheater will always remain a cheat. Big Jim continued to say the Circus of the Queens has had a dishonest advantage for years! Can you believe he had the nerve to say we were dishonest when he was the one caught with cards up his sleeve?

"The waitress came around for orders. It was early in the day. Big Jim ordered 'the usual.' For him it was ham and eggs. He was sitting with a man he referred to as his new partner Larry and that scrawny younger cousin three or four times removed, Billy, who seemed to be in conversation with himself. But when Big Jim mentioned Vladimir's name again, both Billy and this Larry fellow's eyes lit up!

"Right then, the boy behind the counter started making a chocolate shake, and he was real loud," Louie said. "This is where I got a little lost." He went on.

"It was noisier, and I could only lean in so close without being suspicious. Big Jim told Larry that he knew why they had come together. 'He makes your skin crawl, too,' he said to this fella Larry, referring to Vladimir. But this Larry guy kept a straight face.

"Big Jim inched in closer as if Larry was a puzzle he was trying to solve. 'What I can't figure out yet is what did he ever do to you?' And Larry just shrugged his shoulders, acting like Big Jim bored him, and he probably did.

"He's a mean man, Donatella!" Louie stressed once more. "Beware, Donatella, and tell Vladimir, too, this man will use whatever he can against Vladimir and the Circus of the Queens."

CHAPTER 36

S PADE'S DEATH WAS LIKE the San Francisco quake of 1906; the aftershocks sometimes felt as jarring as the event itself. No place was safe. There was no escape. Our attempts to put our lives back together were constantly being undermined by a pain that never let up.

I didn't know what to do with my grief. *Why did our Queen Spade have to look the other way and do things differently? Why?* I asked myself.

I began to rely more on Marvin. He was proving to be solid and dependable. The barriers I had for so long previously erected around the fortress of my heart quit making sense. Life had become too precious.

Every day, just as Spade and I used to do, I went and visited Emily and Bess. Sometimes, during their rehearsal, Emily would go and stand at the exact place where Spade fell and sigh a mournful trumpet. I felt certain it must have matched the one made by Emily and her mother the day the poachers took her away. Then Bess would look back at us with her sweet soulful eyes and remind me we weren't the only ones in mourning.

Being around Emily and Bess became almost selfish. The elephants gave me a joy during those first months I found nowhere else, and I realized I could learn something about loss from these gigantic, kind creatures. For they'd been torn from their families and those that they loved, and they had discovered a way to move on.

❃ ❃ ❃

SPADE HAD BEEN LIKE a daughter to me, and in this one instance I wished I had been less encouraging. I became conflicted by my own beliefs. My ability to see into the future seemed cruel and useless as Spade would now forever be a part of my past.

I tried to reconcile my confusion by adopting an Eastern philosophy, but no matter how many spiritual books I read, I finally had to accept that I was still attached to the living and the dead.

❀ ❀ ❀

Lafayette, Louisiana 1929

I STOMPED MY FOOT to the beat until my toes were coated in a thin layer of dust, but I paid it no mind. Whenever I was in Harsita's presence, a little piece of his happiness rubbed off on me. In a world that wasn't fair, I found it reassuring to be in the presence of someone who radiated such joy.

Harsita was in an especially good mood. His aunt Lilu had come from Baton Rouge to visit and brought with her a tin full of chapati, samosa, and gulab jamun.

"Donatella, wait till you try one of Aunt Lilu's samosas; but right now I have a surprise for you, Aunt Lilu." Harsita pulled out and played for her what he had secretly taught himself.

"The boy practices scales every night. No wonder I'm here so often," Marvin smiled. He was soaping his face, preparing for his morning shave. I loved watching how he always held his razor close to his skin and finished with an upstroke. Aunt Lilu should be gone by now. The coast is clear for both of us." He left me with a kiss and words I wanted to hear. "Don't feel bad about a smile."

That afternoon, when I went and visited Emily and Bess, I was greeted by Harsita and his big announcement: "Donatella, I decided if Emily can do it, surely I can, too. Do you know the song 'Sweet Georgia Brown'? I've been practicing it in private or in the company of Emily and Bess for weeks. Of course, Marvin has heard me, too. Will you sing with me? Even Aunt Lilu tried last night."

I protested, but by the third request, Harsita became impossible to turn down, and soon I was singing not only "Sweet Georgia Brown" but "Ain't Misbehavin'" and Hoagy Carmichael's "Stardust." The sight of a young Indian man and a Russian woman playing and singing such quintessential American songs on a harmonica for two Asian elephants was a little comical, but inspiring, too.

After Spade's death, I seemed to get clear. I stripped myself of inhibitions, rules, and boundaries that made no sense and threw them into the grave with her, and I thanked Spade for the gift of waking me up to life. Marvin began more frequently to slip in and out of the quarters he shared with Harsita and find his way under my covers, where I sought the fulfillment of my desires. Deeper and deeper I traveled with him until I felt completely swallowed.

❋ ❋ ❋

WITH MARVIN AT MY side, I could summon up the fortitude necessary to face those that I loved who now more than ever needed me. "Poor Diamond," I revealed to Marvin. "Every night she relives the memory of holding her sister in her arms and how it felt to close her eyes. It's been really rough on Diamond. But today she did something she hasn't done since Spade's passing—she came to visit me."

Diamond began to stop by my carriage more frequently. One day she walked in clearly agitated, then blurted out, "Life is just a bunch of noise."

"What? Do you mind explaining that?" I asked.

"Ever since that night, I've known my time to leave has come," Diamond said in, almost a whisper.

The softness of her voice told me she wasn't ready to act.

"Diamond's horse, Ali Baba, has become her closest confidant. She talks to him more than anyone else," I shared with Marvin. "I needed to drop off papers at the stables this morning and I accidently walked in on Diamond having a heart-to-heart with her horse about Spade. I left as quietly as I could, and Diamond went on and on telling Ali Baba all her truths. I'm worried about her. She seems to be drifting further and further away. Even her interest in Roman appears to have vanished."

❋ ❋ ❋

STEEPED IN SORROW, LUCKY turned out to be the strong one among us. She opened Spade's drawers, a task none of us had been able to do, and she pulled out all of Spade's belongings and sorted them into baskets.

"Somebody had to do this," she told me and Bella. "In the big baskets are the things I believe Spade would want us to donate. On the left are pictures and letters and posters and other things personal, and in the middle are the items I think she would want passed on to Ann Marie, Diamond, or me." Then, very matter-of-factly, she commanded, "Please have Marvin arrange for someone to remove Spade's bed." Then Lucky pulled out a rolled-up piece of paper she said she found inside of Spade's closet. "This is the poster from her very first performance. I was only a little girl, but I remember it clearly, just as I remember the morning you two dragged us out of bed to see the circus's new banner."

Bella and I stood there in awe. Lucky had done the hardest thing of all: she had gone through Spade's life and made the tough decisions, and she expected us to abide by them. And we did.

CHAPTER 37

THE COUNTRY WAS NOT doing much better than the circus. Hardship and sorrow could be felt both inside and outside the circus grounds. Vladimir barely had enough money to pay the bills. "If Big Jim tried to steal our circus today," Vladimir half joked with Marvin one afternoon when he thought I was asleep in the hammock, "I just might let him."

The days were unusually cloudy. One gloomy day followed another. Finally, a large storm passed through and broke things up. It rained for hours, and right before sunset the sky offered up a little sprinkling of sunlight. "Did the rain come to wash away our sorrow?" I asked myself; then I looked up, wanting to bask in that small ray of light, and instead I was rewarded with a rainbow.

"Is this a sign from God?" I asked Marvin the next day when the rainbow returned.

It came and went as the rain and sun politely took turns. On the fourth morning, the rain disappeared and Marvin and I were awakened by bright skies and the sound of Lucky shrieking. Needing to see what the commotion was about, I threw on a robe and stuck my head outside.

Walking toward me was a woman carrying a baby. Both were dressed in scarlet, and to their right was Kyle.

"Ann Marie! Kyle!" I ran toward them, trying to keep my robe in place. "A little one is just what this circus needs," I said, smiling.

"Ann Marie wanted to surprise you all with the baby," said Kyle as he patted their little one on his back. "I can't wait to see your parents' faces when they lay eyes on their grandson."

Marvin joined the conversation while I went to throw on a dress. After so much grief and sorrow, I wasn't about to miss out on a happy occasion.

Ann Marie, I could see, was trying to hold herself together. "It's very strange to be here, knowing I'll never see my sister again," she said to Marvin. "How can there be a Circus of the Queens without her?" No one present could answer her question. Marvin excused himself.

When the rest of us got to Vladimir and Bella's sleeping car, Lucky's shriek of joy turned to a low hum. "Shhh," she told everyone. "We don't want to wake the baby."

Bella showered Ann Marie and Kyle Jr. with kisses until Vladimir's patience had run its limit. "When's Papa going to be able to hold his grandson in his arms?" Just then, Kyle entered.

"Sit down," Kyle instructed. Then he lifted Kyle Jr. and put him on Vladimir's lap. "Meet your grandson. His name is Kyle Vronsky Erhard Jr."

Vladimir counted Kyle Jr.'s fingers and toes. "They're all there." He laughed. "Spade would have loved him so." And with that, Ann Marie went over and kissed her father. "How could you have kept this baby a secret?" Vladimir asked, and he reached out to his oldest daughter and held onto her as though his life depended on it. The baby between them cooing and smiling, Vladimir and Ann Marie broke down sobbing.

Just then, an almost unrecognizable, jubilant Diamond Claire came running into the room. Like a hard, faceted diamond, her entrance broke up the intensity until it dissipated and turned to joy. "How long will you stay?" she asked, then looked at Vladimir in his chair. "Oh my God, who do we have here? I heard you were back, and that you brought a surprise." Diamond swooped up her nephew in the most natural of movements and started giving the baby big smooches on his belly.

"This is Kyle Vronsky Erhard Jr." Ann Marie smiled. For a second, I thought I could see the translucent sparkle I had always associated with Diamond return to her cheeks.

Kyle Jr. didn't know anything about sadness, mourning, or death, and soon his big grin and funny gestures began to rub off on everyone. We had been in darkness too long. We reveled in the baby's goofy antics, and when Vladimir saw him lift his foot and reach it behind his head, he puffed up with pride. "Now that's the mark of a true Vronsky," he said smiling from ear to ear.

❊ ❊ ❊

Every day, Harsita took Kyle Jr. for rides on Bess and had Emily play the harmonica for him. Together they put on quite a show, and everyone who could made up an excuse to be there and watch, especially me.

"It's no wonder he's a happy baby. Look at all the attention he's getting," Marvin laughed as he squeezed my hand.

"Look at the twinkle in that little boy's eyes. Don't you love to hear him gurgle?"

I lit up whenever I saw Kyle Jr., and when I saw him with Emily and Bess, he became doubly irresistible.

Unable to bear the thought of the baby leaving us, we all did what we could to prolong Ann Marie and Kyle's visit.

"I could use a little help with the books," Bella told her daughter Ann Marie.

"Harsita would love your opinion about a new trick he wants to teach Emily, Kyle," said Vladimir. But just wanting them to stay wasn't enough for Kyle. He was a professional and he was proud.

Eventually, Kyle came to me to ask for advice. "We love our ranch, but right now we believe Ann Marie's place is here with the circus and her family. Still, I have a family to support. Do you think Vladimir would consider letting a rodeo boy join his circus? I'd put together a fine act!"

With young boys dreaming of becoming cowboys, Spade dead and buried, Vladimir refusing to walk the rope, Diamond uncertain what direction her own life should take, a fresh act like Kyle's was just what the Circus of the Queens needed. I set my mind to make this work.

"I know exactly what to do," I told him.

Later that same night, before Marvin and I went to sleep, I made certain he was in a good mood, and then I gently nudged him.

"Kyle dropped by this afternoon. We got to talking about the rodeo. He helped me understand its artistry and tradition. He reminded me that the rodeo is the circus of the West, and it got me thinking how foolish we are to be sitting on one of the best Western circus acts in the country and doing nothing with it. When I looked at it that way, I thought, wouldn't it be great to add Kyle to our lineup?"

"Funny you should say that," Marvin replied. "Why just today I put out the word that the Circus of the Queens is looking for a new act, and who better than Kyle? But Donatella, don't get your hopes up. I know Vladimir wants Ann Marie and baby Kyle close, but I'm not certain how he'll react to adding rodeo to his show."

"We've all had to readjust our dreams," I replied, a little snappish.

The following night, Marvin and Vladimir sat by the fire while Kyle, Ann Marie, Bella, and I anxiously waited in my carriage. It could go either way, we all knew that; still, it didn't stop Bella from praying Vladimir would see the beauty of the plan. However, we knew there was always a chance that he would not.

We sent Lucky to do one of the things she did best: eavesdrop. When she heard her father ask for Kyle, then the cork from a champagne bottle go flying, she shrieked so loud it would have been annoying if we hadn't been so grateful!

"We all deserve a treat tonight," Vladimir said to Lucky, aware that she had been in the bushes. "Go fetch your mother, Donatella, Ann Marie, and Diamond."

In the time it took for Lucky to get us and return, she had composed a limerick to honor Ann Marie, Kyle, and the baby. Impressed, I later asked her to write it down. It was clear she was finding her way back with words.

> Ann Marie left us for cowboy Kyle.
> They rode Sir Charles for many a mile.
> He built her a home
> So she wouldn't roam,
> This queen, like a bee, oh so fer-tile.

Despite the new infusion of life that had come in the form of Kyle Jr., Roman continued to visibly look lost. Not even a baby could lift his spirits. And if any of Spade's loved ones had a smile on their face when they passed him, he would give us a look as if to say we were betraying Spade's memory.

One day, he stopped me as I waved hello and almost immediately he began to sport a self-righteous attitude. "Donatella, I can't get her out of my head. Sometimes I think Diamond and I are the only ones still missing her."

With that, I lost my temper. I had had enough. "Don't you ever say that!" I said, so sharply he pulled back from me as if I had slapped him. It was the first time I had ever been truly angry with Roman. "Don't you ever assume you are the only one still suffering. Have you seen Vladimir? Have you not heard Bella weeping every night? Don't you understand the sadness and the guilt we all feel? How dare you!" I glared at him until he shivered and then I turned around and left.

I had never been so harsh. Much of my anger had nothing to do with Roman; I too had needed to lash out. What was the answer to the puzzle I was trying to solve? Could Hervé be near? And if he was, what did he want from me and why would he come back to haunt me after all these years? No, I decided it had to be someone else. Still, until I could make sense of the cards that had been left and the shadow I sometimes felt following me, I would keep it to myself.

Yes, I felt badly about how I had behaved in regard to Roman, but he wasn't the only one trying to move on—and anyway, I felt as if he'd deserved it.

"It's okay, Donatella," said Marvin when I told him about it later that same night. "Roman loves you, and once he's recovered from the shock of losing Spade, he'll understand. Who knows? Maybe you knocked some sense into his head."

Marvin made me feel a little better, though my encounter with Roman showed me how close to the surface my anger and sorrow were residing.

We are all a mess! I thought before I gently laid my head on my pillow for the night.

Similarly, Lucky put up with Diamond's morose mood until she couldn't. "All of us are sad, Diamond," she finally said, "Spade would never want this for you and I can't stand to see you like this." When Lucky told me about this encounter with Diamond, she confessed her own dream of moving to New Orleans to study literature. "I'm going to have to convince my parents. Do you think that I can?" Lucky asked.

Not long thereafter, Lucky and Bella took a short trip to New Orleans and Lucky returned with a new stack of books. Had Lucky told her mother about the dreams she'd shared with me?

CHAPTER 38

ANN MARIE, KYLE, AND the baby returned to their ranch to pack up their belongings. It was a sentimental time. Ann Marie had mixed emotions but knew she was doing the only thing she could do. And like with everyone else, I became the keeper of the truth even though I kept my own secret worry hidden:

"Kyle's hired a caretaker to keep an eye on the property and to make certain no poachers move in while we're gone," Anne Marie explained. "He's packed up the barn and his favorite saddles and brushes, and I've bundled up only what we will need and things of great sentimental value."

When the waves of sadness wash over me like a tsunami, I get on my swing and go as high as I can. Then I close my eyes and talk to Spade. I ask for her forgiveness for having been so far away.

While Ann Marie and Kyle packed up their lives, we at the circus awaited their return. Darkness had fallen over us like a heavy morning fog, but we'd witnessed a glimmer of light and had learned to bask in small gifts. We had had no idea, before Spade fell, how death can bury the living in guilt.

❊ ❊ ❊

AFTER SPADE'S DEATH, BOTH Diamond and I began to share an innate need to dive deeper into our souls, then see if we could go even further. Most people would find this frightening and uncomfortable, but Diamond and I found it exhilarating, and it helped to build a quiet understanding between us. Vladimir and Bella counted on me more and more to help make sense of their daughter's actions. But sometimes even I was at a loss.

Ann Marie and Kyle were still back at their ranch when Diamond stopped me one afternoon on my way to visit Emily and Bess.

"Lucky's right," she confessed. "Spade wouldn't want me wasting my time spending my days being so sad. She'd want me grabbing onto life, doing what I think I should do, even if it's different. I've made up my mind. I'm going to leave, and I think it would be easier for everyone if I made my move before Ann Marie and Kyle get settled in and we start to get attached to one another again. If I don't do it now, I'm afraid I never will."

Diamond didn't say when she intended to leave, what she planned to do, or where she would go. But several days later a written invitation appeared on my pillow:

> *Please join me by the fire*
> *For song and cheer*
> *Rainbows and dreams*
> *Ten o'clock sharp tonight*
> *Stories, verse, spirit, truth*
> *—Diamond Claire*

When I mentioned the invitation to Bella, she said that she and Vladimir and Lucky had gotten one, too.

❋ ❋ ❋

THE NIGHT WAS CRISP. It was early September and the touch of chill was reminding us that winter was just around the corner. As Diamond had asked, we all gathered by the fire outside of Bella and Vladimir's sleeping car at 10:00 p.m. She had laid out Bella's favorite biscotti, my special citrus and bergamot tea, and Nat Sherman cigars for Vladimir. She played her harp—no mean feat with cold fingers—and sang Vladimir a beautiful rendition of "Danny Boy." To this day, I can't understand how this could be a Russian man's favorite song.

Then Diamond sang Hoagy Carmichael's "Stardust," which Mitchell Parish had just written lyrics for, and she sang it a cappella. She knew Bella had fallen in love with the song—which I had learned from Harsita, of all people—after hearing her practice it. Diamond was being very calculating. That's when I became certain Diamond was about to drop something big.

A touch of mischief suited Diamond; the sparkle had returned to her eyes. But she hadn't counted on just how well her family knew her. Even Vladimir could see the diversion she was creating when out of her lovely mouth came the most crystalline of notes.

She was about to start another song when Bella stopped her. "My sweet Diamond, we know why we're here. Remember, when you were a child, we learned to read your body before you uttered a word. Tonight, my darling, you are perfectly transparent, especially to your mother and father."

Diamond bit her lip and gathered her nerve. "Mama and Papa, and Donatella..." She took a second to swallow her fear, and then blurted out, "Ann Marie's returning soon with Kyle and the baby, Spade's no longer with us, and Papa's turning many of his duties over to Marvin; everything's changing and I feel it's time for me to change, too. I'm wasting my talent. I'm not inspired. Please understand I'm not saying this to hurt you, but I've come to the conclusion it's time for me to leave."

Diamond didn't have to wait long for a reaction. "Who do you think you are, young lady?" Vladimir immediately railed. "You're only seventeen, much too young to go gallivanting off. I'm not going to stand by and watch my family fall apart." With that, he got up and started to leave.

"Sit!" Bella snapped, for the first time in their marriage. Vladimir, shocked by her tone of voice, could see that there would be trouble if he didn't comply. Sheepishly, he went back to his seat. "Go on, Diamond," Bella urged her daughter, giving Vladimir such a look that he didn't even think of opening his mouth. That night, it was clear that Bella ruled.

"I've been thinking this over for a while, since long before Spade died," Diamond began. "I want to be onstage and act and sing. Spade's death, and seeing how brief her life was, has pushed me to follow my dreams."

"Where do you plan to go—New York?" Vladimir's voice dripped with sarcasm. He just couldn't help himself. He needed to make his presence felt.

"Yes," Diamond replied calmly, with surprising confidence. "That's exactly where I plan to go."

"We don't know anyone there!" Vladimir shouted, starting to rise from his seat, but Bella's eyes put him back in his place.

Very quietly, almost in a whisper, I spoke up. "I do."

"What?" Vladimir's jaw dropped.

"Yes. Catherine. She's Russian, the sister of an old family friend. Catherine's the woman I stayed with when I first arrived in America. She'll be quite old by now. We only exchange letters once a year or so, but I wouldn't be surprised if she said yes.

I think she could probably use some help. She owns a brownstone in Greenwich Village that's quite large."

Diamond looked at me and silently thanked me. "You would ask?" Before answering, I looked at Bella, avoiding Vladimir's eyes. When Bella nodded, I said, "Of course I will."

"Please understand, it's not that I want to leave my family. It's just that Spade's death has made everything clear," Diamond went on. "I need to see if I can catch my own rainbow. Not yours or hers, but mine. I promise I'll make you proud!"

Lucky, who had been silent, chimed in, "She's my twin. Of course she will."

"Please"—Diamond looked pleadingly at her parents—"Spade would want this for me." And even though using Spade's name was not quite fair, we knew it was true.

I understood, and so did Bella, but poor Vladimir looked as if he had been run over by an eight-man team driving a circus wagon.

❋ ❋ ❋

TWO WEEKS LATER, AFTER several telegrams to New York, Diamond Claire was packed and ready to go. She didn't want to make a big deal of her leaving and asked that we keep it a secret. She didn't even tell Roman, but she did stop by for one last visit with her horse, Ali Baba.

"I gave Ali Baba some sugar and an apple and explained my plans." Diamond laughed, sharing her story with me as she laid out more new hay. I had joined her in the stable as she had asked if I would stop by and visit Ali Baba each day on my way to see Emily and Bess. "He was so sweet, Donatella. He nuzzled his nose into my chest. I'm not certain if he understood me, though I think he did. Kind of the way you know when Emily understands you." Yes, I understood.

Vladimir, Bella, Lucky, and I went to the train station with Diamond. Bella cried the entire way, but Vladimir had already shed too many tears and had none left.

"Say goodbye to Roman for me," Diamond said to Lucky as they hugged, "and tell Ann Marie that I will miss her and that baby of hers." Those were Diamond's last words, but I could see she was thinking of the one who was missing as she climbed the steps to the train. Spade's ghost hung over all of our farewells.

The porter shouted, "Last call for the train to New York," the whistle blew, and Diamond smiled, turned her head, and walked inside, on her way to a new life.

CHAPTER 39

"**Y**OUR FATHER IS HAVING to extend his definition of circus," I wrote Diamond. "Kyle's equestrian act is different from any we've seen inside the Circus of the Queens' big top. I think you'll really like it!" Ann Marie and Kyle had returned. "He hangs upside down on Sir Charles while attached to a strap. Then he exits the ring by jumping off Sir Charles's back while the horse is galloping. The audiences find his performance daring and exciting, which makes Ann Marie happy. Still, she sorely misses you and Spade, and the way forward seems difficult for her to find." But soon that became true of everyone in the country. By the time I laid down my pen on my writing table and dated the letter October 29, the day would forever be known as Black Tuesday.

As if there hadn't been heartache enough, October 29, 1929, the stock market lost its footing, and everything came crashing down. The circus, which for so many years had given me a family and so much delight, within months began to feel as if it were inhabited by ghosts. In the papers, there were stories of wealthy men who seemed to have it all, and they were jumping out of buildings and off of rooftops. Misery or fear, usually both, were etched onto the faces we saw as we continued our travels from town to town, trying to keep up appearances.

Empty and exhausted, I either plunged into Marvin's arms or withdrew from him completely. The only time I let my guard down was when I visited Emily and Bess. Sometimes I found myself envying them. They completed each other in ways that best friends and couples of the human kind rarely seem to manage; they never expressed anger, only love and humor. Watching them, I discovered I felt better about myself; they inspired me.

Strangely, for a while, the circus business seemed to surge. At first it gave Vladimir, Bella, and I a false sense of security. We thought we had been spared.

We were so caught up in ourselves that we didn't recognize our patrons were spending the little money they had left on entertainment and what we were experiencing couldn't last. The world—myself included—was trying to ignore the cataclysm. Little did any of us know it was just the beginning. Even John Ringling, who the September before the crash had bought the entire American Circus Corporation, would soon find himself down from six circuses to four.

Still, during those initial months, our ticket sales were on the rise. "I don't know why they continue coming to the circus when they lack so many necessities," Bella said. We were in my tent darning socks, preparing for the upcoming winter and trying to be frugal. Knowing there would be little money for extras, we applauded ourselves for thinking ahead. We shuddered to think about all the people who continued to spend what they didn't have on entertainment.

"It's not just us," I reminded Bella. "Don't forget our newest competitor, Hollywood. People are enthralled with Al Jolson's singing and the movies he's in."

That made us think of Diamond Claire, who was trying to get her own show business career started.

"I feel better knowing she's with Catherine. She's clever. She'll get by."

I missed a stitch and looked down to fix it. With that Bella, switched the conversation to Vladimir. "He's lost himself in Kyle Jr."

"There is nothing like a baby to help you hold onto life," I said.

"Vladimir reads to him as often as he can," Bella chimed in. "Right now, he is reading Kyle Jr. Smoky the Cowhorse. Kyle loves watching the expressions on Vladimir's face, and it keeps Vladimir occupied."

However, soon even bedtime stories couldn't distract Vladimir from the circus's problems. I had wanted to talk to him about the mysterious cards that had been left for me to find, but he had so much more on his mind, and every time I was about to begin, another trouble would surface; I was afraid if I added to the weight, he might just break.

The families who had always come to the Circus of the Queens finally drew the line when they started struggling just to feed their children. Some had lost their homes and were begging on the streets. Many small circuses were being sold, others just abandoned.

Every once in a while, I noticed that a horse had been sold or a gilded wagon had gone missing. Marvin's beautiful dark brown hair began to show streaks of gray from worry, but he was still my rock when I would let him be. However, no one could deny that audiences were shrinking.

The Gentry Brothers, Christy, Cole, Robbins, Robinson, Sparks, 101 Ranch, and Sells Floto—they were all folding their tents. Every night I said my prayers, hoping that God would somehow spare our circus and my farm in Savannah and watch over Diamond in New York. Vladimir and Marvin insisted they continue parading down Main Street in the towns we visited. With our high-stepping horses pulling brightly painted wagons, we brought a little festivity and color into lives that had grown pinched and gray. However, during every parade when I saw Ali Baba without a rider, I missed Diamond even more.

Catherine had literally died of disappointment a few months after the crash when she found out that her bank account was empty. Her accountant had cheated her, and she had nothing left. Catherine just lay down, quit eating, and said she was ready to die, Diamond said; and then she did.

Diamond found work in a pub in exchange for a bed and food. Though she appeared strong, we knew it was hard and scary. I read somewhere that 233 plays were staged in New York in the 1929–30 season, and only 187 were planned for 1930–31. "I'm auditioning for roles," Diamond wrote to us, ever optimistic, "and I feel sure one will come through." She had just had a callback for the musical *The Band Wagon.* We were just happy to know that she had food and shelter.

The farm in Savannah was managing to make ends meet. With so much land, my managers and I had focused on us staying diversified. We grew cotton, peanuts, tobacco, and soybeans. Even so, times were tough. "Don't expect a large crop," Joseph, the caretaker, had recently written, warning me that the plants had begun to suffer from the lack of rain and it had just gotten worse and worse.

"How could God be so cruel to hit us with a drought on top of everything else?" I lamented to Marvin. "It's as if we're cursed!"

"You more than most should know that life isn't fair," was his response.

Savannah's role as an important southern seaport, its pulp industry, and its large sugar refinery helped it weather the storm. However, my accountant wrote to tell me that inside the city walls, many people were getting sick, and jobs were getting more difficult to come by.

I began to feel torn between my two homes. They both needed my attention, but the day finally came when I had no choice. I received a letter with unsettling news from Joseph:

Dear Miss D,

We tried our best, but it doesn't seem to have been enough. Between the boll weevil and the devastating drought, I don't know which destroyed the cotton fastest. If you want to hold onto the farm, you need to come quick. I'm sorry to be the bearer of such news.

Your loyal caretaker,

Joseph

Worried about me going to Savannah by myself, Marvin asked Harsita to accompany me. As Harsita was very light-skinned, we took the risk of Harsita sitting with me, but he would have it no other way. So I decided we would ride first class so as to invite fewer questions. It was the 1930s, but it was still the South; and away from the circus, where more things were segregated, we had to travel with attitude, a sense of belonging, and not leave ourselves open to questions from strangers. If necessary, I had decided that I was a well-traveled French Russian whose best friend had married a British aristocrat and now lived in India, and Harsita was her son, Harry. No one would dare to doubt so exotic a story for fear of sounding foolish themselves.

※ ※ ※

THE TRAIN PASSED SLEEPY little towns, parched plantations, and shacks. The rocking back and forth of the train car put me to sleep and I drifted into dreams. When I awoke, Harsita and I spoke of Emily and Bess and how much we would miss them. We spoke of the joy they brought and all their funny antics until we arrived in Savannah.

Ben picked us up at the station. He was uncharacteristically silent on the drive to the farm. When we arrived, I understood why. The Spanish moss that usually festooned the trees around the mansion so luxuriously was dry and brown. The soil was bare and cracked beneath the yellowing crops. Even the paint on the porch columns was beginning to peel. I knew I had arrived just in time. The farm needed more than love and attention; it was going to come down to hard work.

After all their years in Savannah, Joseph and his family were closing up shop to join relatives in the Midwest, hoping to build a better life in Chicago. Polly stayed on because the farm in Savannah had become her home and there was nowhere else she wanted to go. Besides she was clever and her skills would come in handy. Polly could prepare a meal out of anything, even weeds, and make it taste good.

Ben, my jack-of-all-trades, surprised everyone by also proving to be a decent farmhand. Apparently, he could do anything and morph into whatever kind of worker we needed.

Everyone understood that if they wanted a roof over their head and food on the table, they had to pitch in; our survival depended on it.

I took off the purple dresses and the scarves around my neck, everything but my amethyst necklace. I cleaned out the first floor of the mansion, set up rooms with four cots in each, and put up signs: "Wanted: Single Young Men Who Are Hungry and Want to Work."

Harsita took care of the animals that were left, which weren't many. We had no choice but to return to primitive farming methods, as there was little money for gasoline. Parts that broke were scarce, impossible to replace. The horses pulled the plows. Several cows and goats were kept for their milk, and a few pigs were fattened for slaughter.

That first year, I grew muscles in places I never knew I could and calluses I never wanted to see. I developed a commanding voice with which to bark orders and a brain for business I never suspected I possessed. Luckily, Irina's colonel had always farmed in a way that respected the earth, and although times were rough, our topsoil was still good. I had planted soybeans and peanuts as well as cotton and several acres of tobacco, so I was blessed with some money to fall back on, which I managed carefully.

Determined that somehow we would not only survive but eventually flourish, during these tough times, I used the gifts Irina had nurtured in me and shared what I knew with my workers and neighbors. Malnutrition was rampant, and malaria had become common, so my knowledge of medicine and herbs became invaluable. I lost count of the lives I saved.

Harsita and I slept on the second floor in opposite wings. I made one of the guest rooms my parlor and another an office. The workers and vendors believed that Harsita was my nephew. And at night, when I finally laid my head down to rest, I held court with the spirit world.

Harsita and I shared the letters we received from Marvin. Lucky sent me poetry and limericks, and in the middle of the doom and gloom, Diamond penned some hopeful news: "I got a bit part (that means small, in show business) singing in the chorus of a play called *Of Thee I Sing*. It's a political satire by someone named Gershwin."

Ann Marie wrote as well, balancing Diamond's good news with bad: "The Circus of the Queens is in decline. Papa is slowly facing the truth: we might still be the most famous Russian circus, but that doesn't mean we are the most prosperous. As necessity has dictated, he has sold many of our animals." She made no mention of Emily and Bess, and we were too afraid to ask.

CHAPTER 40

IT WAS THAT MAGIC hour, the one where daylight invisibly turns to dusk, the sky shifting from gold to red and then to an iridescent blue. The blue reminded me of my mother's abalone hairbrush. *One, two, three, a hundred times.* I closed my eyes for a moment and let the memory of her wash over me.

Harsita and I were sitting on the porch with glasses of mint tea, gazing out over the green fields, which were finally beginning to look fertile and productive again. This is where we convened at the end of each day, on a porch swing, one day facing east and the next day west. We had been gone a little over a year, and up to this point the farm needed nothing less than my undivided attention and likewise the circus had needed Marvin's. I couldn't believe how swiftly time had passed. Only now could I begin to think about slowing down and how much I missed everyone.

"It's been too long," I said to Harsita.

He knew exactly what I was talking about. We both felt a strong urge to see everyone and make certain the elephants were all right. And I missed Marvin more than I cared to admit, and letters weren't enough.

"There's something special about a circus, and circus people," I said, almost to myself. "There's no reason to wait. It's never a good time for a farmer to leave." I wiped a drop of sweat off my brow.

The soybeans and peanuts had been harvested. Ben could handle the tobacco…I mentally ran down my list. When I got to "water the garden," I took a sip of my tea, then smiled at Harsita. "We'll surprise them!"

✻ ✻ ✻

LUCKY WARNED ME IN a letter that rumors of the Circus of the Queens were spreading. "They're saying Papa gambled away our family jewels, or we wouldn't be in the fix we're in." I'd received her letter earlier in the day and was just now reading it to Harsita. It made me angry. It was true that Vladimir's family had once had a large collection of jewels—but didn't these people understand that they were probably being worn by the wives and lovers of Stalin or Lenin? "*Grrrrrr!*" I felt like a mama bear defending her cub.

"They're also saying Papa sold his collection of playing cards to a French gentleman," Lucky went on. When I read this, alarms started going off in my head. "Sadly, I believe that is true," Lucky ended.

Harsita and I tried to prepare ourselves for what we might find when we arrived. We'd meet the circus in Charleston. I hadn't been there since Spade's memorial.

"We'll have to call Officer Harper and thank him once again," I said. "What a wonderful friend I made, and all because of that trickster of a rabbit."

❋ ❋ ❋

I CLIMBED DOWN FROM the train. The smell of wild beach roses and jasmine was a heady mix with the salt-sea air. The excitement I felt knowing I was only hours away from seeing the people I loved and Emily and Bess had already added a healthy glow to my face.

It felt good to be free of my daily routine. Even though Savannah has a seaport, I hadn't taken the time to walk by the water in months. We'd been too busy working to save the farm. "Look, there's Fort Sumter in the distance," I told Harsita. "That's where the first shot rang out in the war between North and South."

We took a stroll down King Street and followed Broad Street to the water. On this walk, I remembered the way Charleston looked before 1929, when porches of homes were filled with families, children frolicking, lovers kissing, and phonographs playing tunes, many of them by Louis Armstrong and Duke Ellington.

Harsita and I took our time. We were in a hurry, but yet we were not. We had put our things in a locker at the train station, and I hired a driver for several hours to follow us so we could enjoy the sights and unwind. It had been such a long time since we had done anything frivolous.

After we'd had enough fresh air, our driver took us to get our things, and then we made our way to the show. No one knew that we were coming, so there was no one anxiously awaiting us.

❋ ❋ ❋

I LOOKED UP AT the circus banner that had always been so sharp and crisp, stretched above the entrance. For the first time, I thought it looked dingy and gray. With a twinge of sadness, I hoped it wasn't a foreshadowing of what was yet to come as I handed over the money for two seats, like anyone else. I wanted to see our circus through the public's eye. A stranger greeted us and collected our tickets, and we immediately made our way into the big top and sat among the sparse audience. The bleachers were emptier than I'd ever seen them.

"I don't think anyone saw us." I winked at Harsita, trying to keep things cheerful. "Our surprise is safe."

Inside the big top, the setup for the show was much the same, but somehow it too had lost its shine. Everything looked old and tarnished. I was afraid my instincts were going to be correct.

Three clowns rode their unicycles, but there were no dogs jumping through hoops on fire. When Marvin came out, I could feel the blood rising to the surface of my skin, and I knew exactly how much I missed him. Roman's father Louie did his act with the lions and was brilliant as always, but the only equestrian act was Kyle's rodeo show. "That Kyle appeals to everyone," I whispered to Harsita.

"Where are Emily and Bess?" he whispered back. I didn't know. We'd both been on the edge of our seats, waiting for them to enter with the boy Marvin had hired temporarily to show off what Harsita had taught them.

When Lucky came out with the band, playing the bass drum, I about jumped out of my seat, wanting run and hug her. I kept looking for Vladimir, but I didn't see him anywhere.

Marvin was as marvelous as he could be under the circumstances. But by now, neither Harsita nor I could wait for the show to be over. I couldn't believe how much had changed in just one year.

After the tent emptied out, we hurried to find Vladimir and Marvin. A new security guard tried to stop us, but out of the corner of my eye I saw them and started to yell and wave. At first the security guard thought I was nuts, but a few seconds later he saw his boss and the ringmaster weeping as they ran to greet us.

"I've missed you so much," Marvin said, reaching out to kiss me, but when he did, my body went rigid. Instead of telling him how thrilled I was to see him, the first words out of my mouth were, "Where are Emily and Bess?"

I could tell by the look on both men's faces that I was not going to like what I heard.

Marvin finally spoke up. "They're gone."

Vladimir lowered his eyes. "It was feed them or us," he said, trying to rescue Marvin. I could feel my blood rushing through my veins. My cheeks had passed rosy and gone to bright red. "We were all very sad, but with these hard times come hard choices." The pain on Vladimir's face said all I needed to know.

"Where are they?" I asked. "Together, I presume?"

Vladimir looked down without answering and bit his lip.

My tears were welling up. "Oh, no. What happened, and how long have they been gone?"

Harsita started to tremble. He looked as if he might collapse. Marvin got him a chair.

"Remember Jim Baldwin?" Vladimir asked.

My heart sank. "No! Not Big Jim!" *Anybody but Big Jim*, I thought and remembered what Louie had told me.

"Well, he tricked me again. He sent an agent from Thailand who said that Bess's previous owners would buy her back, and she could go home. I was so desperate, I believed him. He always wanted a queen; now he has one." Vladimir was barely holding himself together.

Somehow I managed to find a breath. I still had to find out who had taken Emily. Vladimir knew where I was going next.

"She's in a small zoo in Mississippi. The only elephant they had up and died."

"She's alone?"

"Yes."

"We have to do something," I said in a whisper. But I don't think anyone heard me.

CHAPTER 41

"**I**'M LUCKY SPADE WASN'T here," Vladimir said, looking at his feet. "It wasn't easy, but I did what I felt had to be done. I didn't know I was being tricked." Then he turned and walked away.

Ann Marie and the two Kyles came running to greet us. Kyle Sr. had always been particularly fond of Harsita, and he immediately began with a lively anecdote about Sir Charles and his adjustment to circus life, giving Ann Marie and me a chance to catch up for a few minutes. When Kyle had finished his story, Harsita lifted Kyle Jr. onto his shoulders and asked if the two of them could visit Roman together.

"You can see Papa is still fighting for his life," Ann Marie said sadly after the boys had left. "Every morning he puts on his guilt with his undershirt. He feels responsible for Spade's death. The only thing that keeps him from jumping off the ledge is Kyle Jr. When they're together, he's like another person, joking and laughing like the father I grew up with."

"How is Bella coping?"

"You know Mama; she's Italian, not Russian. It's her nature to appreciate what she still has. She puts on a good face and tries to make Papa smile by cooking good food. She's been trying to convince him to drink more wine and less vodka—it's a more cheerful drink.

"Papa and Marvin have had to sell off so much of the circus, but even if we're a little wobbly, we're still standing. Marvin's missed you terribly, Donatella. Not a day goes by that he doesn't mention your name. He's been torn between his responsibility to the circus and wanting to hop on the next train to Savannah."

There was a pause as I looked at my own feet, wondering if it would have changed anything if I hadn't gone away. Just as I was opening my mouth to reply, I was saved by an unmistakable shriek.

"Donatella!" Lucky practically broke me in half, hugging me.

"Look at you! I can see that you haven't forgotten how to laugh," I said.

"Yes, Lucky is the keeper of humor," said Ann Marie. "I don't know what any of us would do without her. When this horror is over, I'm going to push her out the door toward New Orleans so she can write all day and read all night. I know playing the bass drum in the windjammer band is not her life's ambition."

I had to agree.

❋ ❋ ❋

OUR VISIT WAS NOT turning out the way Harsita or I had hoped. I was trying to emulate Bella—let go of the past and be grateful for what we have—but poor Harsita felt lost. There were hardly any animals left for him to visit and none to train, though he gave Ali Baba some of the attention he would have given the elephants. "You're the only one who needs me," he confessed.

"Don't worry," I reassured him. "We'll get Emily and Bess back somehow, and I'll need you more than ever. But for now we have to push their memory away and focus on our friends while we are here. They've done their best."

❋ ❋ ❋

THE NEXT MORNING, LUCKY came and asked me to come with her to visit Ali Baba. "I've taken it upon myself to look after him for Diamond." As we entered the area where Ali Baba was kept, dust motes gleamed in the slanting rays of early sun, and the air smelled sweetly of hay. "I won't let Papa sell him, at least."

"How is Diamond?" I asked as Lucky began to brush Ali Baba down.

"She's well. I think she's almost too busy to even realize what's happened to us. Sometimes I envy her—she got away before the beginning of the end. But I guess it's good to be with family when the world collapses." She paused. "I know you're angry at Marvin for not telling you about the elephants. Please don't be. He loves you, Donatella."

"I feel bad about how I behaved last night," I said, offering Ali Baba an apple. He took it delicately and concentrated on chewing it up, juice dripping from his mouth, as Lucky lifted the saddle onto his back and tightened the girth. "I was so upset I could barely look at Marvin, and I know I made your father feel like a failure. It wasn't fair of me—he was only trying to protect the circus.

The elephants became a luxury he couldn't afford, and then that ogre Big Jim tricked him. My intellect understands, but my heart still can't accept it."

Lucky bridled Ali Baba and handed me the reins. "Take a morning ride. It will clear your head," she said. "When you return, I'll make us some hot coffee."

＊ ＊ ＊

ALI BABA AND I headed away from the circus grounds, across a field still sparkling with morning dew. The sound of Ali Baba's hooves brushing through the tall grass was soothing. I leaned closer to his neck and nudged him into an easy canter, my hands on his neck, feeling his muscles moving under his warm, silky coat. When we reached the tree line, I brought him back to an easy walk on a loose rein along the edge of the woods. In the cool shade, my head felt clearer.

We'll get Emily and Bess back somehow... When I'd said those words to Harsita earlier, they'd been an empty promise. But now I said them out loud and knew they had to be true.

＊ ＊ ＊

BELLA WASN'T TOO PLEASED with the way I'd treated Vladimir and Marvin, and she let me know it. "I understand how much Emily means to you and what she meant to Spade. She and Bess meant that much to Vladimir too, but selling them was the kindest thing to do," she said as soon as I entered her kitchen. "Vladimir did the only thing he could, no matter how hard it was for him." She bit her lip and turned back to the counter where she was chopping onions.

"I'm sorry," I said and touched her shoulder. And with those two words she laid down the knife and turned around. The iceberg that had come between us melted, and we fell into each other's arms.

"I've missed my good friend," I said. "Life is not the same without you. I know the circus is your home, but remember, Spade isn't the only one welcome in Savannah. Irina left me the gift of land, and it's beginning to give us new crops. Whatever I have, I will share with you—never forget that."

"It's good to know we'll never be homeless, but the Circus of the Queens means everything to Vladimir." She turned back to throw the onions into a saucepan, where they sizzled in melted butter. "As long as there's a chance it can survive, I have to support him here." She hesitated. "Please try to forgive Marvin. I don't know what we would have done without him. He helps hold us together."

Bella was right. I owed Marvin an apology. I hugged her again, left her to her cooking, and headed out to find him.

❄ ❄ ❄

I COULD HEAR HIM calling out orders as workers dragged pieces of scenery into place in the big top. He looked at me with his big eyes when I walked in, clearly disappointed in me.

"If you've come to tell me I was wrong, Donatella," he said, "walk out the way you came in. I just can't hear it."

This wasn't the reunion he'd imagined; I knew I would have to find a way to make amends. Oblivious to the circus workers standing around, I went and kissed him on the lips. Then I unclasped my amethyst necklace and put it in his front pocket—it was my way of saying he possessed my heart.

To my surprise, Marvin kissed me back as if we were alone. Then he grabbed my hand and led me to his tent, where he laid me on his bed and showed me, in no uncertain terms, that I was his.

❄ ❄ ❄

OUR TIME IN CHARLESTON passed too quickly. Marvin and I talked every night until our heads were so heavy we couldn't hold them up, and every morning I had to push him out of bed.

One night, just as I was about to close my eyes, Marvin propped himself up on his elbow and gazed steadily at me, his eyes catching the light of the lantern he hadn't yet extinguished. "Donatella, have you ever thought of becoming my bride?"

I didn't hesitate, though my answer was a surprise to both of us. "When the soybeans and peanuts flourish on the farm, and Emily and Bess are reunited once again, then I might say yes."

CHAPTER 42

ELLA'S DINNERS SEEMED TO have gotten bigger and richer even than I remembered, as if she were trying to stuff herself and everyone else until there was no room for grief. I often found myself talking with her as she cooked, sometimes chopping vegetables for her, though she usually poured me a glass of wine and told me to sit down with it while she did the work. I'd hardly spoken to Vladimir since I confronted him about the elephants, but Bella filled me in.

"Vladimir's become both Marvin's mentor and his friend," she said. "Every day he works with Marvin, he seems happier than the day before. He's a good teacher, and he enjoys sharing his years of experience."

Knowing I would enjoy hearing it, she told me how Vladimir bragged about Marvin. "He's always talking about how much the audiences adore him," she said. "You should hear him going on—'Marvin's like a brother to me,' he says. 'He loves this circus almost as much as we do.' Though with you in Savannah, we both know Marvin's torn.

"Vladimir sometimes says that if times weren't so difficult, he might turn the entire circus over to Marvin. 'You and I could take long strolls and sit on the beach playing in the sand with our grandson,' he'll say. Of course you and I both know Vladimir would be lost without the circus. It's what defines him."

I smiled. Bella was right—we both understood that though Vladimir liked to fantasize about other lives, he was too attached to this one to make a move.

"Still," she said wistfully, "that doesn't stop me from imagining the sound of the waves breaking and the warm sand between my toes. And if I had to choose, Marvin would be the guy I'd choose to take over the circus. I love our Kyle, but he has too much to learn."

Just as I was about to leave, Vladimir walked in. "Sorry I'm late," he said, kissing Bella. "There was a small problem."

"Is Marvin okay?" I asked, worried.

"Yes, yes. He's fine. A zebra broke loose during the show. His trainer slipped and dropped the zebra's reins. I was about to step into the ring, but the problem got settled without me, thanks to your Marvin."

Vladimir sat down across from me at the table, and Bella handed him a glass of wine and then poured one for herself and sat down, too.

Vladimir was in a genial mood and had apparently forgotten all about the tension between us. He was in his element as he launched into another story, smiling faintly as he looked into the ruby liquid in his glass. "When I was about ten years old," he said, "my father had a ringmaster-in-training, like Marvin. He hadn't been with us long. Anyway, I was off to the side of the ring one afternoon when I saw one of the circus dogs nip the leg of a dancing bear. The bear didn't take to this annoying small creature very well, and he swooped up the little dog with his big paw and held him in the air. Just as he was about to bat him out into the crowd like a ball, my father jumped into the ring with a jar of honey and a stick. As you can imagine, my father was used to dealing with these things in the circus, and he was quick on his feet, like me.

"My father took several steps toward the bear. The honey was dripping off the end of the stick he was carrying. The bear immediately forgot anything else existed. He dropped the dog, walked over to the honey-dipped stick, and started licking it. The little dog ran to its trainer, who scooped him up and took him away."

Vladimir laughed. "It just took the finesse of a man with a little more experience. That's what my father said to me, and that's why I always stay close by. My years of experience have averted many a mishap, but Marvin is quick, and he thinks ahead. For example, Marvin knows that a zebra spends sixty percent of his day eating or looking for food. He also knows that the animal does not have the disposition of a horse and needs to stay calm; so the performers are instructed to never charge after the zebra. At the end of each day's performance, the roustabouts lay out a bale of hay and oats for the zebra, and when he is finished eating, Roman feeds the zebra a bag of carrots for a treat. So what did the zebra do with its freedom? He followed his daily routine, and Roman was able to get ahold of the reins while the zebra happily chomped on its carrots. Yes, nine out of ten times Marvin is right, and because of it today, once again, an accident was avoided."

❀ ❀ ❀

MARVIN HAD TO STAY sharp in every sense of the word. He had to be aware of everything and everyone under the big top, and as ringmaster, he also had to look sharp. Image was everything, and the ringmaster was the embodiment of the circus. Though in recent years Marvin might have been forced to comb through thrift shops for his suits rather than buying them new, he still did his best to keep up with the latest in European fashions. As he put it, "The circus has to maintain its veneer."

He knew he was lucky to have a job at all. Everywhere we turned, hard times were reflected back at us. "When I look around at what others are suffering through, Donatella," he said, "sometimes I'm uncomfortable. We have so much. I try to stay grateful."

Vladimir liked the dark side of Marvin, which followed him like a shadow. "He'll protect what he loves, Donatella, and that means the circus and you. Don't ever forget that."

I could tell Marvin was burdened by his thoughts. I knew what questions he was asking himself—*What do I do with my love for Donatella and my love for the circus? Who am I without one or the other?*—but I did not tell him that. I could not be the one to wade through the river of his feelings. All his answers had to come from him.

Still, I hoped he'd find them himself…and soon.

❀ ❀ ❀

MARVIN WASN'T THE ONLY one at the circus struggling with matters of the heart. Trying to come to grips with Spade's death, Roman had begun dating one after another of the circus's trick riders. He clearly lusted after the girls, but I'm not certain that he liked them. Still, every night after the show, when we gathered to share our stories by the fire, he'd take the hand of his most recent flame and make a point of displaying his affection. It fell flat on me. We had very little to say to each other. I think I reminded Roman of Spade, and he didn't want to feel the pain.

❀ ❀ ❀

LIKE MANY OF US at the Circus of the Queens, Marvin lost himself in cards. He loved playing poker almost as much as his mentor. He believed in fate, and recently he had become interested in astrology. "Didn't fate lead me to Vladimir and the Circus of the Queens?" Marvin told Bella, who in turn told me. "Maybe it's fate that delivered this dilemma to me, too."

It wasn't easy for Bella to be objective. She knew what a void Marvin would leave behind for Vladimir, who had already lost too much. Bella was a lover of love, though. For her, love trumped all.

In the past, Marvin had occasionally sought council from Ouija boards, tarot cards, and even me. This time, though, he couldn't ask me to use my gifts—I was the subject he wanted to discuss. Instead, he found a different route.

✷ ✷ ✷

THE NIGHT BEFORE HARSITA and I were to return to the farm, Indian summer had set in. The leaves were waiting for permission to start changing color, but the heat wave was giving their branches a different set of instructions. It was too hot to sit by a fire with the others, so Marvin and I excused ourselves. I could tell he was working up the courage to tell me something.

"Like Roman," he began, when we were on our own in his tent, trying to cool ourselves down with iced tea, "I tried talking to the lions. When that didn't work, I went to Ali Baba. Poor Ali Baba, Donatella—I rode him so long, I was afraid for his back. My question is simple, but the answer is far from it. Should I stay with the circus, where I'm desperately needed, or catch the next train to Savannah to be with you? I think I'm needed there, too.

"None of the animals could tell me what to do. So I began talking with Roman. I must be in trouble, I thought, if I'm asking Roman, of all people, about my love life! Surprisingly, though, I learned more from him than I thought was possible. Donatella, my stomach ached each time we spoke of love. I could feel his pain, the pain from losing Spade. She left a big hole in his heart. I don't know if it will ever fully heal."

The words sizzled, and Marvin's desire grew from a spark to a flame.

When we were through, Marvin took a deep breath to regain his composure. Then he took my hand. "I've had a lot of time to think about my world and what's truly important to me. And more than being ringmaster, when it comes to my deepest desire, who and what I want in my life, I always return to you." He kissed my hands and held them to his face. "I want you, my beautiful Russian ballerina fortune-teller. You and your impeccable manners and the three languages you speak. I want to be with the soul who has the ability to see what is special in everyone, even me. Donatella, I'd like to go with you to Savannah. Will you take this devoted old fool?"

CHAPTER 43

T HAT NIGHT I DREAMED of the Russian women in my life, and their men. I gathered bouquets of lilacs with my mother and watched my father kiss her when she sent me into the kitchen and they thought I wasn't looking. I saw Irina's eyes shine like sapphires when she said yes to Colonel Butler's proposal of marriage. And I watched Lillya galloping through a forest in the Loire Valley, standing tall on her saddle, Laurent seeing her from afar but not yet knowing who she was. *Love wears so many faces.* The thought floated through my dreams. I turned onto my stomach and continued to drift until streaks of morning sun shone through the canvas of Marvin's tent, and I gently woke him up.

Harsita and I said our goodbyes. Marvin would join us in two months, when he'd had time to put all of his management work in order. "Vladimir is doing his best to be happy for us," he wrote a few days later, "but he feels as if he's watching his circus be disassembled piece by piece. Keeping it together is becoming harder and harder for him, but he believes it's his duty to continue his family's legacy. He feels a deep responsibility to his mother and his father, who entrusted him with their life's work. He does it for them, for Bella, and for the queens."

Bella, Lucky, and Ann Marie also sent letters, with news about Diamond Claire, who was beginning to make a name for herself. "Reading Diamond Claire's letters is a great escape," Lucky wrote.

When we heard from her, we traveled to worlds unknown, and for a few moments we lived a life inhabited by famous people and movie stars. Was this what it was like for Vladimir when he was young?

That Gershwin fellow she had mentioned before seemed to be gaining a reputation. That association was good for Diamond.

Harsita and I tried to find out more about Emily and Bess. After my first letter to him, Big Jim had refused to accept any others. "A deal is a deal," he scrawled on the back of a postcard bearing a hand-tinted photograph of his circus's big top, "and this one is done. Little Bess seems sad and lonely, but she still knows how to put on a good show. Say goodbye, Donatella, for this is the last letter from you that I'll open. If you have anything more to say, contact my manager Larry, but I don't think he will go out of his way to help you."

I read the card to Harsita. He turned away from me, claiming a gnat had flown into his eye, and left the room. My heart ached for him.

"Don't give up," I told him as we sat on the porch that evening. "I won't. You never know what time will bring. Remember, Big Jim's a gambler and gamblers make mistakes, and when he does we'll be waiting in the wings. It may take years, but I can be patient when it concerns matters of the heart."

Emily was alone in a Mississippi zoo. Happily, the trainer didn't seem to be a bad man, and he took the time to answer my letter. "She'll be fed and cleaned, and I promise she won't be abused," he wrote.

I'm certain our Emily was confined to what was the equivalent of a jail cell. When I thought about it, I got so angry. Why hadn't Vladimir told me what he planned to do? I might have been able to help, but how? Eventually I came up with what seemed to me like a pretty good solution. I hoped one day I could use it, but for now, restoring the farm to its former glory was the task at hand. And alongside Marvin and Harsita, that's what I'd set myself to do.

Harsita and I worked hard every day, as did all the men who'd come in response to our signs. By the end of that first year, we had constructed a dorm-style sleeping area with a large kitchen in an old barn on the property. The men preferred it. I put in an outdoor shower and gave them access to the indoor plumbing on the big house's first floor. Polly kept her old room. It was home to her. No one received much in the way of money, though the workers had all the food they could eat. We all labored hard to keep a roof over our heads and food in our stomachs, grateful for what we had and what we had achieved.

I deeded each of my three managers—who'd had almost nothing when they arrived—five acres of land, with the stipulation that they continue to work for me. All three built homes where their wives toiled in their private gardens and their children played. On one of the five acres of each manager, we pooled our resources of labor and farmed together so we could make the most out of what we had and each manager could make a little extra profit on top of their wages. Given a sense of ownership, the men worked with pride.

Harsita and I had put all this in place before Marvin joined us in Savannah. I realized that I was more resourceful than I had ever given myself credit for.

❋ ❋ ❋

WHEN MARVIN ARRIVED, ALMOST to the day he had predicted, he brought a surprise—Roman.

Roman had broken up with the last in his line of equestrians, and his talks with Marvin had made it obvious that his feelings for Spade were still unresolved. He needed to come to the place where Spade was buried, to be in her presence. This made me happy; until he dealt with the hole that Spade's loss had left, he would always be restless, never finding true contentment.

"Donatella," he said, "I'm sorry if I was distant the last time I saw you, but I just couldn't look you in the face."

I gave Marvin and Roman a tour of the mansion. Seeing their transparent surprise at how grand it was, I realized that they'd suspected me of romantic embellishment when I described the place.

Polly brought them each a plate of ham and potatoes, and later one of her famous desserts, sweet potato pie. After the meal, Harsita took Marvin out into the fields and introduced him to the workers. At first I don't think they knew quite what to make of him, but he was a tall, strapping man with large hands that might prove useful, so they accepted him happily.

Roman and I walked in the opposite direction; I'd told Marvin I wanted a little private time with the boy. "Let's go see Spade," I said, taking Roman by the hand. "I think you'll like where she's buried."

Leaving the glare of the fields of soybeans and peanuts behind, we walked in the cool shade of live oak trees, ghostly Spanish moss dripping from their limbs. Beneath us, chicory and the last of the wild daisies danced in the sunlight along a path that lead to a black wrought-iron gate, with a big *B*, for Butler, at the center of the scrolled arch above it. Here was where generations of the Butler family were buried, including my dear Irina.

At a clearing on the other side, a few white and purple irises grew wild, and the honeysuckle I had planted scrambled over a small fence that separated Spade's burial place from the others. It's not that I wanted her to be alone—I thought I might be buried here too—but since she wasn't a Butler, it seemed more respectful.

Behind Spade's headstone, I'd set a pole with a piece of wood attached to the top on which Diamond had painted a rainbow. On the headstone, Vladimir had carved the words, "To the one who believed in chasing rainbows, may you rest in peace."

Roman stood looking at the grave silently for a few minutes. "Donatella," he said finally, turning to me, "you might have wondered what happened to the planter box and flowers you gave to Spade all those years ago. Every year she bought new seeds of the flowers she'd chosen to fill it with and tended them with care. It was one of her most prized possessions. The day after she died, I took the box. She loved the flowers so, and I knew I would care for them the way she would. I couldn't bear the thought of them shriveling and dying, too. I hope you'll give me your permission to keep the box. This spring I planted the leftover seeds. They're in full bloom again. I think the zinnias are my favorite."

Seeing that Roman's eyes had begun to well up, I took that as my sign to leave. "Just follow the path back to the house when you are finished," I said. "Take your time. And, of course, the box is yours."

❋ ❋ ❋

ROMAN FOUND ME THAT evening just after sunset as I sat on the porch, gazing out over the darkening fields and listening to a distant whip-poor-will. His hazel eyes reflecting the light of the lanterns that hung from the porch columns; he looked newly invigorated, as if a great weight had been lifted from his heart. "Donatella, it was so strange," he said. "I was ready to declare my love to Spade, as I had planned on doing the night she died, and I asked God if he could tell me if Spade already knew what was in my heart.

"Just as I laid out this question, I saw something shiny on the ground. I bent down to look for it, but it was gone. I thought my eyes were playing tricks on me, so I stood up. And there, only several feet in front of me, were a mama deer and her little fawn, so young her legs were still a little wobbly. She saw me staring and froze, but before she ran away, she looked at me the same way Spade used to do. Life goes on, Donatella, and so does love, though both are fragile. I've been so angry with God and the world that I couldn't see what was in front of me. Spade knew my heart long before she died, and I believe her heart was already one with mine. I can't begin to tell you the peace that knowing this gives me."

The front screen door creaked, and Marvin and Harsita came out onto the porch, carrying tall glasses and a pitcher of mint juleps. "This is some place you inherited, Donatella," Marvin said, a gleam in his eye. "My imagination is running wild with ideas for it. I know there's a lot of hard work to be done, but maybe we can all write down our thoughts and decide which dreams we want to realize first when better times return."

"Count me in," said Harsita.

"I've got some ideas of my own. I hope I'll be here, too." Roman raised his glass. "To Donatella's beautiful farm, and to dreams."

Me, I just smiled. I already knew the dream I wanted one day to bring to life.

CHAPTER 44

January 1, 1932
Jackson, Mississippi

Dear Donatella,
Happy New Year! I start off the year sharing good news, Ann Marie is pregnant again. We spent Christmas here in Jackson. Kyle dressed up like Santa Claus after the show, and we gave candy to all of the children. This depression we are in seems as if it will never end, but happy moments like these, when I get to share joy instead of sorrow, are like spoonfuls of sugar, sweetening what has been so difficult to swallow, and help me to hold onto promise. Our dear Spade has been gone three years, and I can't say that I miss her any less.
    I embrace you, my friend, and wish you and Marvin the very best.
    Always,
    Bella

January 8, 1932
Butler Farm, porch swing facing east

Dear Bella,
Congratulate Ann Marie for me! I wonder what gifts the newest member of our unconventional clan will bring to this world. Babies always astonish me. They're born with a power they are unaware of—innocence—and they have the capacity to take us back to a time when life was so hopeful and fresh.
    Marvin, Harsita, and I rang in the new year with a lot of quiet resolutions, and one that will remain left unspoken.
    Yours truly,
    Donatella

March 1, 1932
Tampa, Fla.

Dear Donatella,

Kyle wakes up by six every morning. He says it's to catch a little quiet time. Following in Marvin's footsteps, he acquired a hammock too. "Rocking for five minutes is like a twenty-minute nap," he says. When he's done, he begins his paperwork before the circus starts waking up. It gives him time to play catch with Kyle Jr. He adores that boy! It also gives him the opportunity to sneak off for fifteen minutes of alone time with Ann Marie while I watch Kyle Jr. in the afternoon.

He has taken on many of Marvin's past responsibilities. He helps Vladimir prepare his books and figures out the workers' weekly schedules. He hands out the checks, which has made him even more popular. And when Ann Marie goes to make the beds, she finds them already done. Kyle insists it's Sir Charles who does it. He thinks the world of that horse.

He's taught Kyle Jr. all about horses and put him up on a pony. The boy can barely run without falling, but he can ride.

It's getting late, so I'll save what's left for another time.

Your devoted friend,

Bella

March 12, 1932
Butler Farm, porch swing facing east

Dear Kyle,

Bella tells me what a wonderful job you are doing. Marvin and I are so appreciative to know a good man is there to help Vladimir.

I am thrilled for you and Ann Marie, but still, during times like these, I'm certain the good news comes with its own set of worries. Every father in this country shares your fear, especially when no one knows what the next day will bring.

I'm here to tell you, don't worry. As long as I have this farm, you and your family will always have shelter and food, a stable for Sir Charles, and a yard for your children.

You listen to me. No worries!

Always,

Donatella

June 24, 1932
Orlando, Fla.

Dear Donatella,

I'm enjoying the audiences, though they have become much smaller. I had forgotten what it is like to be the ringmaster, but it feels so natural, like a gift that I was born with. After all, generations of circus people inhabit me. I still have to leave the tent when "The Amazing Renaud Brothers" enter the ring. I can't think of any act replacing my dear Spade, but every once in a while when no one is around I climb the platform and take a few steps to help me clear my head. Not a word, Donatella.

Bella misses you, and so do the girls.

Your friend,

Vladimir

July 24, 1932
Memphis, Tenn.

Dear Donatella,

After a night of labor, Ann Marie gave birth to a healthy little girl at 7:23 in the morning on July 23, with eyes as deep and dark as her namesake's. We have named her Scarlett Spade Vronsky Erhard. Ann Marie was quick to remind me that with only three queens, we've been a little lopsided. Now a fourth is back in play, and so is my Vladimir, who once again had a reason to pass out playing cards to all his friends. I am hopeful that this is a new beginning.

Bella

September 2, 1932
Winston-Salem, NC

Dear Donatella,

I worry about Ann Marie. Though she is happy in her marriage and thrilled with Kyle Jr. and that new baby of hers, she still has difficulty getting through the day. I try to help, and I babysit. But sometimes I wonder when my own life will begin.

Diamond's another case. I love her and miss her, but she makes me angry. She just up and left us. I know I played a part in instigating her departure, and I look forward to her letters, but I can't stand that I've begun to live vicariously through her.

I must sound like the most horrible sister. I hope you won't think ill of me.
Your favorite queen,
Lucky

March 4, 1933
Butler Farm, porch swing facing west

Dear Bella and my queens,
I write to you facing west, in the hope that this upcoming season is full of new opportunities for you.
This winter we had buckets of rain, and soon our gardens should be dancing with bright spring blossoms, so beautiful and fresh, reminding me that anything is possible.
Roman says his father needs him in this, his final season. It's hard to think we are all separate.
My fortune-telling has been in hibernation with the bears, yet I get premonitions. Some I'd rather I didn't. Marvin, Harsita, and I are doing well and are happy, but still I anxiously await your letters. There is nothing sweeter to my ears than Ben saying, "I got one for you, Miss Donatella."
Donatella

April 3, 1933
Jacksonville, Fla.

Dear Donatella,
I'm sorry, but the truth is, I am writing you for selfish reasons. With you away for so long, I have befriended our German trapeze artist, Greta. She is very smart and has read much about psychology, which we talk about often. It gives me something else to think about, but Greta always brings it back to me. There's no escape with that girl.
She says I must tell the person closest to me what is on my mind—and that is you. She says it will help me to be a better wife, mother, and grandma. So here I go.
I fear for my Vladimir. Our circus is held together by a thread, and Vladimir has started drinking heavily again. That makes me worry. I watch over him like a bird. We both know he can get reckless when he drinks.
Greta says I also must share something good. Yesterday Kyle Jr. rode with me on Ali Baba, and like our Diamond, he did a somersault in the saddle and shouted, "Pony!" I laughed so hard, I thought we would both fall off.

Oh, how I wish my father could have gotten to know our little boy, who brings us all so much joy.

When I was a little girl, we had horses and ponies everywhere. My father owned the finest in all of Italy. Oh, the regrets we have in life. I should have brought the girls to see my parents, but at the time it seemed like too much trouble. As you know, Mama and Papa only met the girls the one time they came for a visit. Diamond and Lucky were still just babies, and it felt as if we had forever to do it again.

How foolish of me. I see now how mean I was not to give them more happy moments. Poor Vladimir's parents, Anton and Lillya, never got to see them once. Oh, they must have longed for their grandchildren, the queens of their family circus. Sad the girls never had the comfort of knowing they came from good Italian blood, not just Russian blood that mixed with the aristocracy.

Your loving friend,

Bella

April 7, 1933
Butler Farm, porch swing facing west

Dear Bella,

I love your letters, and I don't care if you're writing them for yourself. I miss all of you terribly.

Marvin has become my rock in even bigger ways. I needed a strong man, a leader, a ringmaster to orchestrate the workers. With him here to do all these things, life on the farm is getting better, and my bank account is getting stronger every month. The soybeans and peanut fields are finally yielding a profit. The pigs, we keep for ourselves. I hate killing them, but our workers have to eat, and I make certain they are slaughtered in a humane way, though, as you can imagine, ending their lives makes my heart ache. Do you remember how I used to catch crickets by hand to remove them from my carriage? I know you think me silly.

But on to sweeter things—let me tell you about Marvin. His relationship with Harsita has deepened. Harsita's become like the son Marvin never had, and it's good for both of them. He's such a good boy—or, I should say, young man—and you know how grateful I am to him for having stayed with me to help when times were really bad. I feel a little guilty that you are still struggling at the circus, although I know most of the country is struggling as well. I am lucky that Irina left me land, and that the crops are turning into money. A small check is in this envelope, to make up for what you and Vladimir have given up by loaning me my two men. You must cash it, Bella, before you mention it to Vladimir. Tell him it would be impolite to turn down a present. This isn't charity. It's what sisters do for one another.

Will write again soon. There's much to do, much to plan. Who knows what is around the corner? Our new president Roosevelt seems to be a good man, and he has ties to Georgia.

Yours always,
Donatella

April 21, 1933
Greenville, SC

Dear Donatella,

I don't know what to do. I try and try, but I think you Russians are even more stubborn than us Italians.

I deposited the money as you asked me to, and when I told Vladimir, he got very angry. It's as if he has become two people. One man I adore, the one who gave me four children, and the other is a man who has not found a home for his grief and tries not to let anyone see. He needs a man who can tell him what his wife can't, a man like Marvin.

I would be grateful to you if Marvin could be spared for a short visit to come to the circus and help his brother Vladimir remember who he is.

Bella

May 4, 1933
Butler Farm, porch swing facing east

Dear Bella,
By the time you get this, it will be old news. Marvin is on his way. When I read him your letter, his mind began to race, figuring out everything he would need to do before he went and everything he might need to do once he arrived. Seeing his turmoil, in a voice as tranquil as an ocean sunset, I told him, "Go, our friend needs you."

Marvin and I continue to be very happy. I waited a long time for this kind of love. He knows what I think and what I carry in my heart. Sometimes I wonder if he's the one with the visions. I spend so much time in my garden, he says I must be waiting for more then a bloom to sprout and grace us with its presence, and he is right.

Did Marvin tell you that he ran into old Moses, who used to shoe the horses while he was out buying hay? It turns out that Moses has a buddy who works construction for Big Jim's circus, and he said Bess may not be happy, but she is well. Big Jim, as we know, has a new manager named Larry. I'm told he's educated and may not be the kindest of persons when it comes to people, but Moses says its clear the man likes animals. Moses has promised to notify us if anything changes. Marvin slipped Moses a little money on the side to help keep the lines of communication open. You know, Bella, every night I ask God to watch over Emily and Bess and let no harm come to them. Don't worry. I pray for you too.

Your friend who loves you,
Donatella

May 15, 1933
Raleigh, NC

To my love,

I understand Bella's concern. Our dear friend is going from bad to worse by drowning himself in alcohol and grief. Roman, Vladimir, and I were sharing a bottle of whiskey and some hearty beef stew that Bella had made, and although Vladimir does not have the temperament that my stepfather had, I couldn't help but think of him when Vladimir passed out by the fire. Then he started mumbling incoherently, and when he opened his eyes, he yelled at us for interrupting a dream he was having about Spade. Then he took a bite of stew and fell back asleep.

Minutes later, he awoke for real when a piece of beef got stuck in his windpipe. He grabbed the whiskey bottle right out of my hand and took a swig. I thought he was going to have another swallow, but instead he turned his head the other way, and suddenly tears began to fall down his cheeks. I told him, snap out of it— you have a wife and family who need you. Seeing him in that state was more than Roman could take, so he said good night.

After Roman left, Vladimir asked, "How does a father ever get over such a thing?" What could I say, Donatella? It felt as if he wanted permission to fall apart, and I wasn't about to give it to him. I just told him that first he'd have to let go of the bottle.

Did you know he is walking the rope when no one is around or looking? Bella has Greta and her psychology and Vladimir walks across a wire high above the ground to find peace below him.

I send you kisses.

Your love,

Marvin

June 17, 1933
Asheville, N.C.

To my love,

Today was bright and sunny. It amazes me how the weather leads my mind to places I have not thought about in a long time. I was taking a walk, and I saw one of our posters on a pole. I was reminded of the day I first saw that circus sign and the way I bicycled home as fast as I could to tell my brother. I know I don't talk of my family much, but I do think of them and wonder what kind of men my brothers have grown up to become. All the same, I'm so grateful that I found the courage to run. I just wanted to tell you that I'm happier with you than I've ever been.

Ann Marie is enjoying being a mother. Diamond is building a good life in New York City, or so her letters report. Bella shared a few of them with me. Lucky reminds me of a bird waiting for the opportunity to fly away, wondering why she clipped her own wings. Kyle is as solid and helpful as ever. I think our Bella wishes she could return to Italy, though she knows it's not an option. And me, I wait to be back in your arms.

Marvin

July 24, 1933
Chattanooga, Tenn.

My love,

Yesterday was Scarlett Spade's first birthday. I'm sorry you weren't here. The blaze of fire that had always been our Ann Marie is slowly returning. She can see herself in her young daughter, and she remembers the way she used to fly through the air on Napoleon's back and the passion that she felt. Even Vladimir seems to be doing better. Every now and then I come across him laughing, and on several occasions he has shown some restraint with the vodka. I hope to make my way home to you soon.

Funny, for some reason I keep thinking of my older brother, and the excitement we felt watching the circus parade that day becomes real again. When I take a deep breath, the smell of sweet popcorn in the air makes it feel like yesterday. I see the clowns and the dogs and remember how the windjammer band drowned out all the sounds of the town. But what I remember most is the look on my brother's face when I handed him my letter. Neither of us ever looked back. Perhaps it's time? So many things could have brought about a different fate. We wake up every morning thinking we know what the day will bring, but really we have no idea. The only thing I know for certain is that I love you.

Marvin

August 17, 1933
Butler Farm, porch swing facing east

Dear Marvin,

Your dream seems to have come true. Harsita answered the door, but when I got there, staring back at me was a slightly older version of you. Yes, it was your brother Tyler, who sells spices from port to port, I learned, and is a quiet, kind, and respectful man.

I invited him in and fixed us both some mint tea. For years, he said, he'd kept an eye out for you. When he traveled, he'd visit any circus that happened to be close by and strike up conversations with the carnies, trying to find you. Eventually he gave up. Then recently, while in Atlanta, he was invited to play cards with an old acquaintance. His friend said that a nasty circus owner would be there, who was always ranting on about his competitors, and if Tyler led him on with questions and complaints, he might find something out. It turned out to be—you guessed it—Big Jim.

Your brother said he took a seat directly behind this man. Hoping to bait him, he raised his voice as he began telling the story of a run-in he'd had with a six-foot-four man who worked for a circus and thought he was smarter than anyone else. Your brother all but said you were a rather cocky kid. I found it sweet.

He told the men that this know-it-all gave him a wicked tongue-lashing, just because he beat him in poker. Right on cue, Tyler said, this Big Jim fellow turned around and said, "Sounds to me like you met the not-so-marvelous Marvin."

Then he went on to tell your brother what an arrogant ass you were. You'd learned all that you knew, he said, from a self-righteous circus owner named Vladimir who passed himself off as Russian aristocracy. Big Jim also mentioned that he thought Marvin was living in sin with a woman named Donatella on the old Butler farm in Savannah.

Once he—your brother, that is—had what he wanted, he disentangled himself, but not before Big Jim threw in his last words. He said something to the effect that he wasn't the only one with a grudge toward this Vladimir fellow. "There are a few of us who wish him bad luck!" From there, your brother said it wasn't hard to track us down.

Tyler and I talked for several hours, until he had to catch his train to New Orleans. We took a walk and picked some flowers, and Polly put them in my favorite purple vase by the phonograph. Then she added some jasmine to fill out the bouquet, knowing that I love its sweet fragrance. Tyler said he'd be passing through again in three weeks. After that, he'd be moving to California. He left a note in case he misses you. I put it in my top dresser drawer.

My love, the time has come for you to return and for Vladimir to be strong.

Yours,

Donatella

CHAPTER 45

"WHAT DO YOU THINK the letter says?" asked Marvin.

"You're the psychic."

"You're his brother. I only spoke with him for several hours."

Marvin shook the envelope, hoping to hear answers to the questions that had been haunting him for years. He'd returned to Savannah immediately after he received my letter with news of his brother. He had been home a day but had not gathered the fortitude to read Tyler's words.

"You know, Donatella, I tried contacting them once. Two months later, my letter was back in my circus mailbox, marked 'Return to Sender, Address Unknown.' I thought I was dead to them."

Marvin stared at the sealed envelope, as if he might in that way divine what he'd find tucked inside. Finally, unable to bear it any longer, he handed it to me.

"Will you?"

"Are you certain?"

Marvin nodded.

I went and got a sharp knife to use as a letter opener. Then, carefully, keeping the letter and the envelope in pristine condition, I unsealed it.

"Are you ready?" I asked Marvin. He nodded, and the words began to lift off the paper and out of my lips:

Dear brother—or should I address you as Marvin the Marvelous? You always did have a spirit, and yes, you were a marvelous brother. That may be why I have searched for you these many years, but it is not the reason I write. I wanted to tell you that I'm happy you left us, though angry too, for after you departed, our stepfather took most of his rage out on me. He broke my leg and burned my back once, when he threw me to the floor and pushed me into our fire. Better me, though, than our little brother Jimmy. Mama felt some of it, too.

But one night, when he started beating up on Mama something fierce, I couldn't take it anymore. I had the sense to get little Jimmy out of the room, and then I rushed back. He looked like he was going to kill Mama. Out of the corner of my eye, I saw the hammer I'd been using earlier that afternoon. I don't know what overcame me. It was as if my body were following someone else's orders. But I ran and grabbed the hammer off the counter, and I hit him three times on the head, each time a little harder, and I watched him fall to the floor.

I stood over him in disbelief. He still had some breath left in him, and he gave me a look. Actually, his lips turned up oh so slightly, and a small smile appeared. It was as if he was telling me that all this time he had been waiting for me to have the courage to hurt him back. He'd wanted to be beaten. It felt so perverse.

I sent little Jimmy next door to get help, but there was nothing to be done. Both Mama and I were shaking. Undoubtedly we were in shock. Little Jimmy didn't fully understand the gravity of the situation.

Our stepfather suffered for three days until he died. They said it was probably from a blood clot in his head. I was arrested, and I had to stand trial, but I was acquitted of any wrongdoing. I'd clearly been defending myself and our mother. Sadly, Mama died soon after this—from sorrow, I think. Her heart had shriveled up from the drought of love for so many years. She had no more forgiveness left in her, for herself or anyone else. I was sad for Mama, but I celebrated the death of our stepfather, and I don't think that God blamed me—Lord have mercy on me.

The court made me little Jimmy's legal guardian. Luckily, he was young and doesn't remember much. With me, he grew up safe. Little Jimmy has a good nature, and I think he was happy in the home we made together. He lives up north in Buffalo now and has a wife and daughter, so you are an uncle.

There have been times I have cursed your name, though now I'm glad one of us was spared some of the pain. It took a lot of courage for you to leave. I want you to know I don't hold any bad feelings now, and if possible, I'd like my brother back in my life. I'm not certain if you'll see me before I go to California. If not, I will hold you in my thoughts, just as you looked the day the windjammer band carried you away. No matter what, I promise to stay in touch.

Your brother who loves you,

Tyler

On another slip of paper he left a short note to me:

Donatella,

When Big Jim was bragging, he mentioned an elephant. He said that he tricked her owner because the owner deserved it, and because he could. He said the owners, a Russian nobody named Vladimir, and "the not-so-marvelous Marvin," think they are big shots. Keep an eye out for him. He's nothing but trouble for you and I think his manager is, too.

But if this elephant means anything to you, which I think she must, I get the impression—that if the price is right—he might consider selling.

I hope this is helpful. Be well, and take good care of my brother.

Tyler

After I'd read the letter, I told Marvin not to expect Tyler; his emotions were too overpowering. I think Marvin didn't want to face his brother in person either; he was afraid of the pain that could rise to the surface. But he was happy, Marvin told me. He finally knew his family story, and that both Tyler and his little brother Jimmy were well. "For years," Marvin said, "I wished horrible things on my stepfather, but little did I know he was already dead." He laughed at the irony. "How absurd it was to harbor so much anger for so long. It's time to let it go."

❊ ❊ ❊

DAY IN AND DAY OUT, month by month, the team of workers I assembled worked alongside Marvin and Harsita, turning over the rich earth. The more they planted and sowed, the more the farm became a part of me. Despite all the manpower we had, by 1934 we were beginning to prosper once again and needed to expand our workforce. This happened to coincide with Vladimir's tightening of the reins, which displaced even Roman. Vladimir by now had sold most of the animals except for a few horses, Ali Baba among them, and Roman's father had retired to New Orleans after donating his lions to the zoo. Without a lion to care for, I cleared out another bedroom so that Roman could join us for as long as he needed or wanted. Poor Colonel Butler would have been appalled to see the motley assortment—myself, Marvin, Harsita, Roman, and Polly—that had taken over his once grand home.

❀ ❀ ❀

DIAMOND WROTE WITH SOME exciting news about a circus musical that she had won a part in. She said it was called *Jumbo* and was sure to be a hit. "It's as if the play was written for me. There's a man in it named Jimmy Durante, who is so funny. Oh, how I wish you could see it! Some fellas called Rodgers and Hart wrote it."

Diamond's letter left my brain spinning, and before long an idea had been woven.

CHAPTER 46

I**T** WAS EARLY APRIL, and Easter was just around the corner. The shop windows were draped in pinks and lavenders, among which cavorted rabbits dressed as country gentlemen. It was hard to walk by the candy store displays of fat chocolate hens, marzipan chicks, and colorful foil-wrapped candy eggs without purchasing a bag or a box. I even tried my hand at making some candies myself. It's a good thing Polly was around, or by evening I might have burned the house down. As it was, my fudge boiled over and clogged the gas pipe on the stove.

We had all struggled through such trying times, I felt we deserved a little fun. The farm had almost completely recovered, and it had been too long since any of us took time out just to enjoy life and make new memories. We'd all wanted to see Diamond on Broadway. Now was the time!

Ann Marie, with young Scarlett, needed to stay behind, and Bella of course would not leave her side. But Lucky joined us at the farm, and our little family—me, the honorary matriarch, Marvin, Roman, Harsita, and Lucky—had Ben drive us to the station.

I'll carry forever the thrill of excitement that appeared on their faces as the train we were about to board to take us to New York City pulled into the station. I thought their eyes would pop out of their sockets!

The train was painted in brilliant citrus-hued stripes, yellow, orange, and green. They recognized it immediately. This was not just any train; I'd booked three sleeper compartments on the Orange Blossom Special! It was an extravagance, but considering how much I had been given, I joyfully passed on what good fortune I could.

"Donatella, you shouldn't have!" both Lucky and Marvin exclaimed. Once they were on the train, though, it would have taken a Strong Man and three bodybuilders to pull them off.

The Orange Blossom Special was a luxury passenger train known also for its speed. It only ran in what was considered the winter season, and, was first class in every way. Cakes and pies were baked on board under strict supervision. Cut flowers and fish were brought in fresh at intervals along the route, and the best wines and champagne were stocked, all at pre-Prohibition prices.

As the train pulled out of the station, I thought of my father and Russia. I wondered what he would have thought about the farm, and America. Out the train window, one Georgia shack after another flew past. Ragged clothes were strung on lines, and barefoot children played in red-dirt yards. The European paintings and Oriental rugs on the train made the shacks outside seem all the bleaker, and once again I was reminded how fortunate I was, and I had to admit I felt a little guilty.

Lucky looked out the window too, but I think she saw the rosy visions floating in her head, dreams that were planted in childhood, stories her sisters had told her. "I hear the Cotton Club is fabulous," she said. "We can listen to the blues and then travel to Greenwich Village for a poetry reading. I think I'm going to love it!" Most of all, I could see she wanted to see Diamond's world for herself. Perhaps then she'd be able to move on and find the realm she could call her own.

We each had our own vision of what New York would be like. I, of course, had been there before, but not since I was a girl. How young and naive I had been! I had to admit I was most excited to take the tunnel under the Hudson River and see Penn Station. Neither had existed when I first arrived in 1905.

Lucky and Roman were excited to see Diamond. I warned them, though, that she might seem to have changed, at first. "A city does that to a person. Eventually everyone does their part to blend into the look and feel of where they live, but underneath the exterior will be the Diamond we've always known: glittering, beautiful, and as ethereal as ever."

As the train bowled along, moving us closer and closer to the big city, I ate chicken cordon bleu in the dining car while Lucky and the boys had rib eye steaks and potatoes. Our waiter was a young man from Oklahoma. He'd always been fascinated by trains, he told us, and loved traveling across our big country as he worked. "This train is just about the finest of them all," he said, and suggested we try either New York cheesecake or a French dessert with chocolate called profiteroles. Once again the odd one out, I ordered profiteroles; everyone else had cheesecake. Our waiter brought us a box of white and dark chocolate Easter eggs that we could take back to our rooms. "Like our desserts," he said, "the candies are made in our own kitchen."

The dining car helped us pass the time. "Can we have a round of coffees with a shot of Canadian Club in each?" I asked our waiter, and we got into a discussion as to whether the whiskey was better when it was made in Michigan or across the Detroit River in Windsor, Ontario, where it had been given a new home and a new name after Prohibition took effect.

Some of the fellas sitting close by joined in.

"Of course it was better when it was known as Club Whisky," said a stylish man in a fine wool suit.

"That mobster Capone didn't care which name it had or which one tasted better," another said. "The one he liked best was the one that turned the biggest profit."

Strangers became curious when they realized who we were. Many had come to our circus and heard stories about us, and they thought this a perfect time to set the record straight. "Yes, I am Russian," I told them. "Yes, Vladimir and I once danced at the Winter Palace. No, I was not a queen, just an honorary aunt, but Lucky is the Queen of Clubs."

With that, Lucky pulled out a deck of Chas Goodall & Son playing cards and we played countless hands of poker with our new friends before returning to our sleepers.

The following afternoon, we would arrive in New York City.

CHAPTER 47

I HELD MY BREATH and pinched my nose as the train went under the Hudson River and pulled into New York's Penn Station. When we emerged into the station's grand Beaux Arts concourse, we stopped as one to gaze up, speechless, at the soaring steel-and-glass vaulted ceiling 150 feet overhead. Seemingly oblivious to this grandeur, a throng of busy commuters flowed around us with an air of importance; they all seemed to feel that the world revolved around them. I had forgotten about the city's delightful confusion, people bustling about, each headed in a different direction, each with something to do or someplace to go.

Soon we were walking out through the regal colonnade at the station's entrance, the columns bearing the weight of the building and greeting the people at the same time. The late afternoon sun beating down against the pink marble almost blinded us, but soon we spotted Diamond in the crowd, standing on tiptoe to look for us. Now an official New Yorker, she'd commandeered a porter at rush hour, an impressive feat. He lugged our bags toward a waiting limousine.

"Where did you get such a car?" I asked as we squeezed in. It turned out that the theater had given it to her for the day. It was the happiest I had seen any of us in more than five years. Roman, Marvin, and I had recently taken to playing that new board game, Monopoly, in the evenings, and I felt as if we'd just all pulled a card that read, "Go! You will be happy for the next five days."

Lucky, usually a bit insecure, didn't shrink at the sight of Diamond's beautifully styled blond curls but happily said, "Your hair looks very pretty, Diamond."

"I saw it in my favorite fashion magazine, *Vogue*," Diamond said, looking pleased. "I can show it to you later."

Through the theater owners, Diamond had arranged accommodations for us at the Waldorf, not far from Central Park Zoo, where Harsita and Roman were planning to spend much of their free time. The hotel was as grand as Penn Station but more intimate, with its soft lights, dark paneled wood, tapestries, rugs, and crystal chandeliers. In the middle of the main lobby, commanding everyone's attention, towered my favorite piece of all: the gilded Waldorf Astoria Clock, its bronze base decorated with pastoral scenes and portraits of Queen Victoria, Benjamin Franklin, and six American presidents, topped by a miniature Statue of Liberty. I couldn't decide if I loved it or hated it, but for some reason it spoke to me every time I entered the lobby, and I ended up feeling that it became a friend, similar to the grandfather clock on the *Amerika*.

Sitting in the grand lobby, you would never have imagined the hardship outside. Still, wealth was no guarantee that tragedy and heartache would pass by your door. Look at Jacob Astor IV, once a partner in this stately hotel; his money didn't stop the *Titanic* from sinking and he along with it.

✻ ✻ ✻

EARLY THE NEXT MORNING, Marvin climbed out of bed, kissed me, and waved goodbye.

"Where are you going?" I asked.

"Saks Fifth Avenue. My wardrobe is a little out-of-date." He smiled.

Marvin had always taken such pride in his clothes. "Harsita and Roman are going with me, too. We'll be back in about two or three hours."

I lounged around our room, then I went downstairs to the restaurant. "I'm here to see my niece Diamond on Broadway," I told the waiter who brought me my tea. Diamond had just come to say goodbye on her way to the theater. I was both excited and nervous about seeing her in this play, but I was also a little concerned about the glint in her eyes every time she looked at Roman. I hoped she'd outgrown the urge to stage an accident just to see whether Roman would rescue her.

Then, like Marvin and the boys, Lucky and I headed out to Fifth Avenue. Recently soybeans had been fetching a good price, and the farm had turned quite a profit. Before we left, I'd given a present of cash to everyone, with the stipulation that each of us would buy something that would normally feel out of our reach. Then we would wear our new finery when we went to see Diamond on Broadway. After years of frugality, we all felt a little uncomfortable about this one little extravagance, but I thought it important that we reward ourselves for all our hard work.

I bought a sequined lavender dress at a store on Fifth Avenue. It lent a certain glamour to the silver streaks now showing in my hair. Marvin, Harsita, and Roman each purchased brand-new Italian suits. Lucky, who had borrowed an elegant seafoam-green dress from Ann Marie, splurged on a set of gold chains for her neck. They made her skin glow—she truly looked like royalty. In the short time since we arrived, Lucky seemed to have transformed into the person she had been waiting years to let out. This was her chance to be more than a queen and she knew it. I couldn't have been more pleased. She stood taller, radiated a new confidence, and sparkled with wit when she spoke. She left the jealousy that had stifled her behind at the farm. New York was a big city; and she could see, there was room enough here for both her and Diamond to shine.

Still, there was no doubt in any of our minds as to who would be the queen that night. The theater vibrated with the excitement of all the people waiting to see the performance. It was hard to stay seated. Marvin pointed out Diamond's name in the program, and we each turned to the same page with pride.

The play *Jumbo*—a story about a financially strapped circus family—hit a little too close to home. Even more bizarrely, woven into the tale was the story of an irresistible elephant named Jumbo who ended each performance by resting his foot on Jimmy Durante's head.

For most of the audience this was a fantasy, with beautiful music and songs like "My Romance." But for us it was a piece of reality. Our Diamond didn't need to play a part; she needed only to be herself. Still, it was exciting to see her on a stage in New York City, surrounded by some of the greatest actors alive. Besides showing off a few tricks on the trapeze during the show, she did some singing and dancing.

Diamond had developed a wonderful poise. When we accompanied her out the backstage door, people lined up, holding out programs that she autographed graciously and asking questions about the play: "What's it like to be in *Jumbo*? Does the elephant scare you?"

"Absolutely not," Diamond answered serenely. "I grew up with elephants." Diamond's background had gotten her a lot of publicity, and the producers took it straight to the bank.

❋ ❋ ❋

IF I'D WORRIED ABOUT the ghosts that this trip to New York would stir up, the anxiety didn't last long. The last time I walked down Broadway, I'd been a distraught young dancer with a board tied to my leg, a lonely girl who didn't know what to do with herself. Today I was a mature, confident, accomplished woman with Marvin and my circus family at my side.

When the rest were eager to go to the top of the Empire State Building, I didn't let on that I was afraid of heights for fear the others might change their minds. At first I pinned myself against the inside wall of the observation deck, afraid to move, but the enthusiasm of the others became contagious. I asked Marvin to take my hand and gingerly stepped across to look out at the cityscape spread all around, and then at the people down below on the streets, with a distinct sense of magnificence. To see how small I really was and what a minute amount of space I took up in the universe put my world into perspective but left it no less meaningful to me.

After dropping Marvin and me back at the hotel, Diamond took Lucky, Roman, and Harsita to a poetry reading in Greenwich Village. Along the way, she pointed out Catherine's brownstone and told them that Catherine had relayed that my favorite little dog, Woof Woof, was buried in her backyard, and I asked them to tip their hats when they passed in remembrance.

The boys didn't quite know what to make of Lucky's transformation, but Diamond told me the next morning how impressed everyone one was with her. "She struck up a conversation with a doctoral student of poetry from Columbia University. I had no idea Lucky was so well versed," Diamond said. "This young man, Thomas, seems really taken by her. He's almost as tall as Marvin, and as handsome, too—only he has a mustache, and his glasses give him an intellectual look. Tomorrow he's invited us all to Harlem for dinner, and afterward he said he'd take us to the Cotton Club."

When I heard that, I was certain Lucky had finally met her match—and it sounded as if Thomas might have met his.

※ ※ ※

ON THE THIRD DAY, Marvin, Harsita, and I took a carriage ride around Central Park. I made special note of the flowers planted. Lucky had requested we visit the Shakespeare Garden. I particularly enjoyed seeing a white mulberry tree surrounded by rosemary and pansies. The garden, we learned, had originally been called the Garden of the Heart but was renamed in 1916 in honor of the three hundredth anniversary of Shakespeare's death.

Our carriage driver told us that the new mayor, Fiorello LaGuardia, had taken on the job of cleaning up Central Park as a part of his platform and appointed a good man named Robert Moses as commissioner. "Why, just a few years ago you would have seen more weeds than flowers," he said.

Lucky and Thomas were in a separate carriage close behind us, close enough so that when I turned back to wave at them, I could see Thomas take Lucky's hand.

❀ ❀ ❀

THERE WAS A REASON that Diamond and Roman hadn't come along on our carriage ride; in fact, I'd engineered it myself.

I felt so much unspoken tension between them that I arranged an afternoon for just the two of them. Before we left the Waldorf, I tipped the maître d' and asked that he procure a small corner table for Roman and Diamond. They had barely spoken since Spade's death. Diamond and Roman had a wall between them that needed to come down, and it was spelled S-p-a-d-e.

Neither objected. Roman, who'd made a point of being out of town whenever Diamond came south for a family visit, had marveled at how much she'd grown, and he delighted in her shine. I had no idea what their lunch would bring, but I hoped they'd both find a little clarity.

At dinner, I could see that some sort of intimacy had grown between them. One would brush up against the other as if it were an accident. They made conversation but avoided each other's eyes. Between our main course and dessert, I saw them by the restroom. It was obvious that Roman had slipped Diamond a kiss or said something sweet.

Later Roman said to me, "She's such a beauty and has so much style. Has she always been so talented and pretty?"

I nodded, smiling inwardly. *The only queen you were able to see when you were growing up was Spade*, I thought.

❀ ❀ ❀

LUCKY AND DIAMOND HAD become closer on this visit in a way I hadn't seen since they were girls. Besides blood, now they both had love. Thomas and Lucky had become inseparable, and our party had grown by one.

Thomas seemed to be serious about Lucky, and he loved every limerick she composed. He thought her poetic: she was Russian and Italian, after all, and had grown up in a circus. You didn't need to be a fortune-teller to see that Lucky was the answer to Thomas's dreams and that he was the answer to hers.

Thomas impressed me, too. I took notice of his Southern accent and discovered that he'd recently accepted a teaching position at Tulane in New Orleans and had been studying French. "*Je parle français*," I told him, and we began to freely converse in French.

He knew little about circus life. His family lived in Charleston, and he had come from a long line of educators, just as Lucky came from a long line of circus folk and equestrians. I imagined that one day he might write a novel about Lucky and her family. Perhaps he would title it *The Circus of the Queens*.

❀ ❀ ❀

THE NEXT MORNING, DIAMOND took me aside. "Roman kissed me last night. My entire life I've been in love with him, and now that he is free to love me, and I think he might, I don't know if it is right."

"What do you mean?" I asked, though I was pretty sure I understood.

"It's so hard, Donatella. If ever I had a soul mate, I believe it would be Roman, but in these past several years our lives have gone different ways. I don't think I could leave the New York stage and be happy."

"You don't have to know everything at once," I told her. "See what you still have in common, and how you feel when you're around him. Later you can consider the rest." Diamond had spent a lifetime waiting for Roman to come to her, and she found it impossible not to explore her feelings.

Marvin had been talking to Roman about his relationship with Diamond, too. Could he find a way to live in New York if she wouldn't leave?

"What would I do here?" Roman considered the question. "My life has been about animals, nature, and farming, and there isn't much of that in New York City." Marvin nodded; that much was obvious. "Wall Street is not full of the kind of beasts I'm used to taming. I guess I could work at the Bronx Zoo."

Despite their doubts, Roman and Diamond spent every possible minute together. It was as if they had been starved. Their coming together had been difficult, and I suspected their parting would be, too. They were working their way through Spade's death, and they could only find their way through that together. And neither knew what would happen when they said goodbye.

❀ ❀ ❀

HARSITA SEEMED TO BE the only one of us without an agenda or plan. He simply wanted to breathe in the city and enjoy his time away with friends, but now he felt a little left out. Marvin took him to Nat Sherman's, the famous cigar store on Fifth Avenue, to introduce him to the finest tobacco in the world. "The shop was filled with well-dressed men," Harsita told me that evening, "and the air in the room smelled pleasant, but nothing is better than the scent of the fresh tobacco we grow on our land. We'll replant some next spring and send the boll weevil up north on vacation." We both laughed, realizing that here we were, an Indian boy and a Russian girl, talking like Southerners about Southern concerns.

※ ※ ※

GOODBYE WAS THE HARD word we each had to say. It wasn't easy for any of us. Back on the Orange Blossom Special, as we pulled out of Penn Station, headed south, I marveled once again at how so much had changed.

Thomas and Lucky had made their own way to the train station, unwilling to give up any time they could spend together. On the train, Lucky sat next to me. "I think Thomas and I are a match made in heaven," she said, and I had to agree. They had some planning to do, Lucky said. First he would come to the circus so she could introduce him to her parents, Ann Marie, Kyle, and the kids. Then he would take her to Charleston, if Vladimir and Bella approved of him.

A more contented bunch I had rarely seen. Our fortunes, though, were about to change with just three words.

CHAPTER 48

LUCKY STAYED ON FOR several days in Savannah before taking the train back to the circus. Every other sentence that left her lips began or ended with "Thomas." Roman wasn't much different, only his word was "Diamond," over and over, and when he was in a serious mood, he'd add her middle name, Claire.

Harsita returned to the farm a happy young man. He had waited a long time to gain a father's love. He and Marvin had that in common. The special moments they'd shared in New York were ones he could draw upon for the rest of his life, and they gave him a sense of security.

Harsita and Roman had become like brothers on our trip, especially after the two of them went to the zoo. Both had an extraordinary fondness for animals, and besides the lions and elephants, they were enthralled by the gorillas. "We must have watched them play for at least half an hour. Did you know the average gorilla's brain weighs twenty ounces?" Roman asked.

Before Lucky departed, I decided the time was right to share my little plan—the one Marvin predicted wouldn't stay little for long. I asked Polly to help me make a special meal I had in mind. Minutes later she returned, wearing the apron I had just given to her, the one with the pictures on the pockets. The pocket on the right had a picture of the Statue of Liberty and the pocket on the left a picture of the Empire State Building. Before we departed I had raided a souvenir shop, bringing back as many souvenirs for Polly as I could fit in my bag.

I put on my favorite apron with the big yellow roses, placed a record on the phonograph by that new gypsy guitarist Django Reinhardt and French violinist Stéphane Grappelli, and Polly and I began cooking an amazing meal of crabs and potatoes. She insisted, though, that she be the one to make the peach cobbler, which made the house smell like a home.

Everyone was gathered on the porch, swinging east and west, with fresh mint juleps in their hands, when I made an announcement. "I don't know the next time we'll all be together. Supper will be ready in ten minutes, but before we have our dessert, there is something I'd like to discuss with you." And in the dining room, our bellies full but reawakened by the aroma of Polly's cobbler, I shared my idea for the first time.

Everyone gathered around. Without skipping a beat, I started right in. "Before Lucky leaves and we get back to our routines, I'd like to share with you the grand scheme that's been on my mind." I coughed several times to be certain I had everyone's attention.

"The boll weevil destroyed the cotton on a large piece of my land. I know you've wondered why I haven't replanted there. How I could let that rich soil lie fallow? It's because all along I've had something else in mind for it, and if I have my way, one day soon that land is going to be put to good use."

"What are you talking about?" Harsita asked.

"Patience, my boy." Marvin smiled. "You'll like what Donatella is about to say, at least if it's what I think it is."

I glanced over at Marvin, smiled back, dusted the crumbs off my apron, and kept on talking. "The land that we've planted is beginning to turn a nice profit, and it looks like our harvest will improve this coming year. What I'm saying is, I believe our farm, as it is, is bringing in enough money for us to live comfortably, and that there is something else we can do with this other piece of land.

"I want to plant something there, but something of a very different nature, something I think will bring us all a great sense of satisfaction. I'm beginning to feel I've already waited too long."

Everyone inched in closer.

"With your help, I'd like us to rebuild the old barn that sits on this land and sow grass for a pasture." I paused, looking at the confused, expectant faces turned toward me. "Then we'll bring home Emily and Bess, and this will be their home."

Their stomachs full, my audience was slow to react. "I'm not certain how we'll accomplish this, but we will. Emily and Bess are more than circus animals. They have been the heart and soul of the Circus of the Queens. They represent us, especially Spade, and I know of no better way to honor her. I've decided to do what I can to make it happen."

You could have heard a lightning bug singing, it was so quiet in the room. Like a fire-and-brimstone preacher, I'd gotten so worked up that I needed to stop and catch my breath.

"It's not going to happen overnight, but I've been planting the seeds of this dream for some time and I suspected you wouldn't want to be left out."

"Donatella, Donatella!" Harsita cheered.

Marvin went and got a bottle of champagne and offered up a toast. "To Emily and Bess, and Donatella!"

Everyone started jabbering at once, plotting and throwing out ideas. Grabbing a spoon off the table, I banged a large glass pitcher like a judge calling my court to order. "This is what I know." I waited for them to quiet down. "Being inside the city limits, we need permits. I have, hypothetically, discussed something of the likes of this with our city planners, and because I own so much land and pay such high taxes, it seems likely that they will issue them.

"The zoo that bought Emily is almost bankrupt, and I believe her time there is limited at best. We all know Big Jim is greedy above anything else. I can't bear the thought of abandoning Bess to such a scoundrel. I hear his new manager, Larry, is not much better. Vladimir was desperate, or he never would have let this happen."

"Going up against Big Jim is going to be our greatest challenge," Roman said thoughtfully.

I smiled. "But it will be our greatest satisfaction, too. Marvin has a contact on the inside at Big Jim's circus and we've been paying him to feed us information. While we wait, we can prepare the land and pasture—quietly, of course. When the timing is right, we will be ready."

Again, we toasted Emily and Bess. I silently expressed my gratitude to Irina. I had already gone to Spade's grave and shared my plan with her. "Don't worry," I told her. "I won't let Emily's story end like this."

Harsita grinned. "I can't wait to hear Emily play the harmonica and see what Bess decides to paint next. You can definitely count me in!"

We stayed up late, listening to the phonograph, and Marvin insisted I play the piano, which had been left covered far too long. I had been learning some of the songs from *Jumbo*, so I played "The Circus Is On Parade" and "My Romance." Having seen the play, everyone joined in and sang along. It made us all feel as if Diamond were with us again.

❉ ❉ ❉

I HAD DREAMED OF this kind of happiness. As a child, I thought this was the way life was supposed to be. But then the messenger of death came to our front door and told my father about my mother, and later he appeared with a revolution thrown over his shoulder. I'd become afraid of happiness, worried that once it was within my reach, it would disappear. Then how could it show its face again to someone who didn't believe?

As I laid my head on my pillow that night, I asked the fear to go away. Happiness had entered my home, and I had come to understand that life dishes out happiness in moments, months, even sometimes years. These past days, with or without belief, I had been blessed with true happiness.

❉ ❉ ❉

THE NEXT MORNING, I woke up early to take Lucky to the train station.

"Thank you, Donatella," Lucky said when we were alone during our ride, "for everything. You've always been more than an aunt to me. I think I found the direction of my life on this trip, and it never would have happened without you. I believe I'm going to marry Thomas and move to New Orleans."

I smiled. I thought so too. Still, for some reason, I found myself distracted the entire way to the station, as if I were a little tipsy, or I had let something important slip. I'd broken out in a sweat. Lucky noticed and asked me if I felt all right.

"I think maybe I've caught a cold," I said. "Be certain to put on your sweater when you get on the train."

I tried to tell myself this was a new beginning, but neither of us wanted to say goodbye. Lucky grabbed me and held me close before she let me go. "I promise to send everyone's love," she said before she boarded the train. Once inside, she waved goodbye and put her cheek against the window. I thought I could see a tear.

The whistle blew its mournful note, and the train pulled out slowly, as if it were almost too heavy to move.

❉ ❉ ❉

IN THE CAR, DRIVING back to the farm, I began to shiver. I had to be sick. Why else would I be so restless from the outside in?

When Marvin saw me, he told me to calm down and put me to bed. I tossed and turned, unable to lie still even in my dream. Marvin told me later I looked frightened. I could vaguely see a steep mountain and a bridge, but clouds kept passing in front of me, obscuring my view. It was a puzzle that I couldn't solve.

I awoke frustrated, but I went through the motions of getting up and getting to work, even though nothing felt right no matter what I did.

❊ ❊ ❊

THE NEXT DAY, A man with a telegram arrived at our front door. I should have known not to answer it.

Three words—that's all I needed to read. Numbly, I handed the telegram to Marvin. Then my legs collapsed and I fell to the floor.

The sound of my fall brought Harsita and Roman running to the door. They looked at me, and then at Marvin, who was standing like a statue, the blood drained from his face, gripping the telegram. They picked me up and carried me to the nearest couch. The young boy who delivered the telegram didn't know what to do, but he patiently waited for someone to give him a tip. When Marvin regained his wits, he stuck his hand into his pocket and pulled out some change. The boy left, and Marvin came to my aid. I kept mumbling three words. Harsita and Roman couldn't understand what I was saying, so Marvin translated.

❊ ❊ ❊

LUCKY WAS ALREADY ON the train to West Virginia when the telegram addressed to her, Marvin, and myself arrived at the farm. She'd planned to meet up with the circus in Davis, a small town in the mountains of West Virginia, near the famous Blackwater Falls.

Later she shared, "The entire way there, all I could think about was Thomas and how wonderful it would be to introduce him to Mama and Papa." She'd begun to cry and spoke through her tears. "My thoughts were of no one other than myself. Well, that's not completely true. Every once in a while, I did think about Roman and Diamond. I thought how odd that Diamond and I, twins, should find love at the same time." Then Lucky completely broke down. "I feel so guilty now, for being so happy."

"That you were thinking of Thomas was entirely natural," I said. "At the time, you had no reason to think of anything else. You didn't make this happen. I'm sorry, darling. Cry as much as you need to."

The circus had been crossing the treacherous Blue Ridge Mountains. The scenery was some of the most beautiful in the country, so even though the roads were grueling, no one seemed to be particularly bothered. Davis was a regular stop on the tour. Until recently, the circus had traveled entirely by train, but during these hard economic times, only the animals and heaviest equipment had that luxury. Vladimir had bartered ten of the rail cars for a small fleet of trucks and passenger cars, along with a little cash to keep the circus afloat.

Ann Marie, Kyle, and Scarlett were in one car, Vladimir and Bella in another. Kyle Jr. had begged his parents to let him travel with his new best friend, whose mother joined the equestrians after I left. Ann Marie would tell me later how excited the children were at the idea of seeing a waterfall, whose drop was five stories tall.

After I spoke with Lucky, she put Ann Marie on the telephone, and as difficult as it was for her, she explained in detail what had occurred that fateful day.

"We were driving the winding roads on our way to Davis. Well, you know what they're like. You've seen them from the train windows. They're treacherous and dangerous at best, let alone driving with packed carts and trucks. Everyone was being extremely cautious.

"We climbed and climbed until we reached the top of a large hill that looks down at the river. Kyle Jr. was waving to us the entire way up." Ann Marie broke down in tears. "There's a small bridge that crosses the river gorge. The view is spectacular; still I hold my breath every time we have to go over it."

"Beauty can be deceiving," I chimed in.

"There's only one lane, and the bridge doesn't hold much weight. Being cautious, we crossed one car or truck at a time. The children were both excited and frightened as they waited for their turn. The rest of us just wanted this part of the journey to be over.

"Two-thirds of the circus had made it to the other side, and Kyle Jr. was the next in line." Ann Marie's voice started to break with emotion. She could barely get out her words.

"Okay," I told her. "We can talk about this later. You don't have to tell me now."

"No, but I do," she replied. "I just need to stop for a second." I could hear her breathing and imagined she was nervously playing with the cloth of her dress. Then she took a deep breath. "All right, I can go on.

"Papa and the construction boys were helping each vehicle prepare for their turn. It could get pretty windy, Papa said, and he wanted to be certain anything loose had been tied down.

"The bridge was louder and creakier, older, and narrower than I remembered it being. Kyle Jr. waved, and then he blew me a kiss as their vehicle rolled onto the bridge. They were about midway across when the wind began to wail, and the bridge began to sway. The driver stopped and waited for the gust to pass. Though I was a bundle of nerves, Kyle didn't want our son to see that we were afraid.

"When nature settled down, the driver inched forward. And just as he made his move, a giant gust of wind shook the bridge like an angry mother grabbing her child by the collar. Then the bridge began to crackle. Fearful, the driver pressed on the gas and drove as quick as he could. It was a race between safety and death, and I didn't know which would win.

"They almost made it to safety. I thought that they had. But then I saw that two-thirds of the car was on land while the other third was hanging off the cliff and the partially collapsed bridge. I thought I would die as I watched the car swing back and forth until finally both the bridge and the car steadied themselves. Kyle Jr. was too scared to scream. I handed Scarlett over to one of the trapeze artists, who was standing next to us—I felt so weak with fear, I was afraid I might drop her.

"Kyle shouted to our son, 'Shut your eyes and promise me you won't move. If you do what I say, we'll let you stay up extra late, and we'll have a sleepover tonight.'

"'I promise, Daddy,' Kyle Jr. said, and he didn't move one hair.

"I was beside myself. Boris was on the other side of the bridge and was able to get everyone out of the car but Kyle Jr. If they grabbed him, the car would surely fall, he said. It was going to take a miracle to save our Kyle. I wanted to break down and sob, but I had to be strong for my son.

"Kyle Sr., a few of the men, and Papa were all trying to hatch a plan. From their sudden silence, it seemed they had something in mind. I didn't ask. I just let them get to work.

"Did you know, Aunt Donatella, that Jimmy, the tall man, used to be a javelin thrower? Suddenly I saw Jimmy, with the help of Kyle, pounding a spear he got out of his truck into the ground. The men tested it three times before he threw a second spear across the bridge, with a cable attached to it. Boris took it upon himself to hammer the spear into the hills and rock. That's when I realized the cable would become a makeshift high wire.

"It would be a delicate maneuver. The wire had to be positioned exactly right, within arm's reach of the swaying vehicle. The men on the ground moved fast. Time was running out, and they knew we had only one chance, if that. I prayed to any god who would listen.

"Kyle was determined to be the one to save his son. And you know what he's like when he gets stubborn. He was not going to let his son die, and definitely not in front of me. Did you know that he learned to walk the rope after we met? Still, this was going to take much more skill than my Kyle possessed.

"Then suddenly I saw Papa take Kyle to the side. Later that night, Kyle told me what Papa said, and he reminded me there wasn't time to argue. Papa ordered Kyle to step aside.

"He said that there was only one person good enough to save Kyle Jr. He hadn't performed on the rope since the night Spade died, but he admitted that he'd been practicing, as a way to clear his head. More importantly, he was the only man who stood a chance of saving our son. Kyle knew that Papa was right, and there was no time to let his ego get in the way. Papa had been waiting to do something extraordinary all his life, he told Kyle, something bigger than the circus—he just didn't know it until that moment. His last words to Kyle were, 'If I can save my grandson and spare my daughter any more grief, I will consider my life complete.'"

Ann Marie started sobbing uncontrollably. "Papa didn't even stop to kiss Mama. He just shook Kyle's hand, gave him a hug, and headed straight to the cable.

"His first step was a little wobbly, and he almost slipped. But he soon proved to be the master he had always been. I believe it was his proudest moment. Excuse me…" Ann Marie paused to find the words.

"My Kyle yelled to Kyle Jr., 'Keep your eyes closed and don't move. Grandpa's coming. Everything is going to be okay. Listen to every word your grandpa says. Stay calm, boy, and we'll be laughing about this at supper.'

"On his fifth step, Papa started singing Spade's song. Everyone began to nervously sing along, and the camaraderie helped us stay calm and focus.

"Papa was almost at the finish line. Kyle Jr. was just a few feet away from safety when I heard the bridge make a noise like firecrackers. It was too old and tired to take the stress any longer—everyone gasped, then put their hands to their mouths, muttering 'No!' It must have been just like that, when Spade fell, I thought.

"Kyle Jr. started to yell, 'Mama! Mama!' Papa was amazing. He stayed focused.

"Kyle Sr. yelled out to our son, 'Your grandpa's almost there. You're going to be okay.'

"Clearly, things were not fine. This is the moment when what happened becomes a blur. Everything occurred so fast.

"Papa took two big steps, scooped Kyle Jr., and quickly passed him to Boris. But just as he released Kyle Jr. into Boris's big hands, the bridge collapsed, taking Papa and the rope with it. There was nothing anyone could do.

"For a second I thought he might survive. He's always been my hero, and I thought he was invincible. He held on to the end of the cable, but then a dark cloud that had been building finally burst, and rain came pouring down. His wet hands slipped on the cable, and he fell to his death.

"In my heart, I have only one consolation. I believe Spade came and took Papa's hand and let him know he was about to enter God's heaven, where a special seat of honor would be waiting for him, and that night he would rest with the angels.

"Donatella, I pinched myself. My son was safe, and on the other side was big ole Boris cradling Kyle Jr. like a baby, but my father had disappeared. Mama, next to me, was frozen in disbelief. Kyle Sr. squeezed my hand."

"Three words," I said. "Three words, and our world will never be the same."

Vladimir is dead.

CHAPTER 49

ALL THAT WAS LEFT of my Russia was buried in the valley and river on the day Vladimir fell to his death. Without him, I was cut in half. He was the only one who shared my past. Bella and Marvin tried to understand the life we'd lived, but it was impossible to explain. How could they comprehend the romance of that royal Russia from the eyes of a young person growing up in the midst of it? As a boy, Vladimir had been treated like a prince. In Russia, being invited to the Vronskys' for dinner was like being invited to high court. Oh, I was going to miss Vladimir.

I knew that my self-pity wasn't attractive. I needed to be strong for Vladimir's family, but I was tired.

Bella had been pacing like a ghost, Ann Marie told me, day and night since Vladimir slipped away. Lucky had spoken to Thomas, and he was waiting to hear from her about Vladimir's memorial. He wanted to support her any way he could, even from a distance. Lucky had spent most of her life envying her sisters. Now, in the blink of an eye, she'd grown into her name, the luckiest of them all.

"I called Diamond," Lucky told me. "It was the hardest call I hope I ever have to make."

Bella was in no condition to talk to anyone, even her daughter, and Ann Marie just couldn't do it. So, as she had at Spade's death, Lucky had to be the strong one.

When I next spoke to Ann Marie, I could see that she was carrying guilt for what had been beyond her control. I tried to comfort her with what I believed to be true: "I knew your father very well," I told her. "And given a choice as to who would die, hands down he would have chosen himself. Know that and remember it. My heart is with you."

I spoke to Lucky next; she needed to talk about her phone call to Diamond. "I picked up the receiver," she said, "and my heart started pounding and my hands began to shake. I could barely keep them steady enough to dial her number. Then, when I got her on the phone, I didn't know what to say. We'd just had this fabulous visit—she was probably still thinking of Roman—and I had to tell her that our father had fallen to his death, saving Kyle Jr."

"Lucky," I reminded her, "it wouldn't matter who it was—your father would have done the same. He could never have stood on the sidelines if he knew he could help."

❋ ❋ ❋

THE STORY OF VLADIMIR'S death traveled from one mountaintop to another. First it made the news in West Virginia, especially in the towns surrounding Blackwater Falls and Davis. It broke the townsfolks' hearts. Everyone wanted to help. All the able-bodied men who lived nearby, organized by the sheriff, formed a search party to find Vladimir's body. They were determined to return this hero to his family. "We know the river, woods, and mountains well," they told us. "You've suffered enough. We'll find him."

While the townsmen looked for Vladimir, the queens and Bella were left to deal with their grief and other circus affairs. The women in Davis and the surrounding area welcomed Bella and her family into their homes and insisted on cooking and doing their laundry. But poor Ann Marie could not leave the house with Kyle Jr. to take advantage of their generosity. Though kind and helpful, everyone wanted to catch a glimpse of the little boy who was rescued and see the queen who was his mother.

On the fourth day of searching, the men found Vladimir's body washed ashore five miles from the bridge where he'd fallen. I was happy Kyle Sr. was there to identify Vladimir and arrange for him to be transported to a mortuary.

Vladimir would be buried next to Spade, we decided. The service would be for immediate family, myself, Marvin, Harsita, and Roman, with a memorial celebration later the same day for anyone who wanted to come and pay their respects.

Kyle and Marvin paid the circus workers two months' wages, though not before asking if they would help move what was left of the circus to Savannah. For the first time in generations, there would be no Vronsky circus. We were temporarily closed.

Marvin cleared out a barn and had the men put up some extra fencing. The Circus of the Queens—including Ali Baba, who was getting quite old—would live in my back pasture.

Bella, Ann Marie, and her family, along with Lucky, arrived in Savannah before Diamond. The circus folks, according to Marvin, would make their entrance at around three o'clock the afternoon of the funeral. We would bury Vladimir at eleven o'clock that same morning.

Marvin stepped in as the ringmaster, arranging both the memorial and the funeral. Polly took command in the kitchen. Kyle lent his support by getting the family to the farm. Diamond took the train from New York; she would only be able to stay five days, though, before she had to return to the theater.

Polly and I searched all our gardens and cut only the most beautiful flowers. "If it isn't perfect," I said, "leave it." Ben, whom I usually would have called on for a task such as this, was helping Marvin. So Polly and I, armed with our sharpest pruning shears, cut roses, lilies, iris, and dahlias and put them in vases, filling them out with baby's breath and greenery. When we were through, we planted them around the gravesite where Vladimir would be laid to rest.

The service was simple, personal, and heartfelt. Marvin spoke of his friendship with Vladimir. Lucky read a poem that she had found in a magazine and clipped out, Mary Elizabeth Frye's "Do Not Stand at My Grave and Weep":

> *Do not stand at my grave and weep,*
> *I am not there, I do not sleep.*
> *I am a thousand winds that blow.*
> *I am the diamond glint on snow.*
> *I am the sunlight on ripened grain.*
> *I am the gentle autumn rain.*
> *When you wake in the morning hush,*
> *I am the swift, uplifting rush*
> *Of quiet birds in circling flight.*
> *I am the soft starlight at night.*
> *Do not stand at my grave and weep.*
> *I am not there, I do not sleep.*
> *Do not stand at my grave and cry.*
> *I am not there, I did not die!*

Diamond sang "Amazing Grace," and I read what I described simply as a song lyric in Russian about two dancers who, thrown together by circumstance, became best friends. Remembering that Vladimir had been brought up in a religious family, I hired a Russian Orthodox priest to say the final blessing in the Trisagion service. The priest asked God to grant our departed "rest in the bosom of Abraham, Isaac, and Jacob" and then closed with a final exclamation: "Grant eternal rest, O Lord, to the soul of Thy departed servant Vladimir, and make his memory be eternal," to which we faithfully sang along with the priest, "Memory Eternal."

Kyle Jr. had insisted on coming to the end of the service so he could say goodbye to his grandpapa. He blew Vladimir a kiss, laid a flower on his casket, and, following his mother's instructions, picked up a handful of dirt and threw it on his grandpapa's grave. Bella stood to the side, weeping, as everyone else followed Kyle Jr.'s lead, saying their goodbyes with handfuls of dirt.

When the ceremony was over, Diamond and Roman laid yellow roses on Spade's headstone. Afterward, we all went inside for the lunch Polly had fixed for us and waited for the circus to arrive. Thomas, who was unable to attend, called and expressed his condolences.

At three o'clock, we heard bagpipers playing "Danny Boy," and then the windjammer band marched up to the farm playing "Auld Lang Syne" to remind us of the friendships we had formed throughout the years. All of Savannah by now knew that the Circus of the Queens was moving onto old Colonel Butler's pastures. The boys and girls from the local high school sang along with the band and carried black-and-white flags to show their sympathy.

The equestrian, whose car Kyle Jr. had been in on the bridge, arrived with Roman's father Louie, who'd come up from New Orleans, and the fire-eater performed Vladimir's favorite trick—after all his years in the circus, Vladimir had still been in awe of a man who could swallow a flame. The clowns and jugglers wore tuxedos. The beautiful female equestrians who had been with the circus returned dressed in lavish costumes, wearing hats with plumes of every color, black lace veils that covered their faces, and black ribbons attached to their jackets to show that they were in mourning. Riding sidesaddle, they made their way to the farm, each horse lifting its hooves in time with the others. At the end of the line was our sweet Ali Baba, moving as slow as he pleased, confident nothing would start without him.

I found Marvin scouring the crowd, looking for me. I wasn't easy to find, as I was wearing black like almost everybody else there. I signaled to him, but he still didn't see me, tucked between the giant, the man with the longest beard in the world, and Diamond Claire, who was sharing confidences with Ali Baba, the one male to whom she could fully give her heart. Ann Marie was holding onto a letter from her old mentor and friend Samantha Divine that had arrived that day. She didn't share it with anyone, even me, but put it into a pocket in her dress so Sam could attend the memorial, too.

It was amazing how festive the pasture looked. I had erected a tent for the occasion, ornate carriages were scattered about, and there were masses of people. A stranger passing by would never have guessed a funeral had just taken place. This was Vladimir's last party, a celebration of an amazing life. The girls asked Marvin if he would introduce Bella, and then she would say a little something to all of Vladimir's new and old friends.

Marvin folded Bella's small hand into his to calm her and led her to the podium he had erected.

"Thank you, Marvin, for helping me up the stairs and for all you have done for my family. Vladimir was right to choose you as his brother." Bella played with a crumpled piece of paper, unrolled it, then rolled it back up and, throwing it on the ground, began to speak. "My daughters helped me put words on paper, but I would rather tell you what my heart wants to say. For more than thirty years I loved this man, and he only brought me honor. Well…honor, a circus, and four lovely queens who are my daughters. All four are here, but sadly one is buried next to Vladimir.

"Vladimir loved the circus. He was breathing circus air in his mother's womb. From the moment he was born, there was no question who he would become or what he would do. But he was also a generous and loving husband, and oh, how he loved his daughters, when everyone wished him a son.

"Most of you here know his favorite game was cards, poker in particular. You wonder why I bring that up.

"When our daughters were born, each was named after a queen in the deck of cards. At each birth, my Vladimir passed out Chas Goodall & Son playing cards instead of cigars. This morning, I took those two decks of cards Vladimir cherished, and before my sweet Vladimir's casket was closed, I snuck into the room where he had been laid." Bella looked down at Ann Marie, Diamond, and Lucky, who all looked surprised; this was the first they had heard of this.

Bella gave the girls a mischievous grin. "A wife must do what she has to do," she said, and then continued with her story, "and from those decks of cards minted the years of our daughters' births, I took two queens. From the first deck, I removed the queen of hearts and queen of spades, and from the second, I removed the queen of diamonds and queen of clubs. Then I put the four queens under Vladimir's shirt and laid them on his chest, over his heart. I wanted my husband, my love, to never be without his daughters. Even buried in the ground, he would always have his queens to keep him company. And just in case they don't have a deck where he has gone, I left the rest of the playing cards in his right hand.

"This makes many of you smile who played a hand with my Vladimir, especially his good friend Boris. But a woman must know her man and what makes him happy." Then she paused, and tears welled up in her eyes. "I don't know how to live without him. He was my everything. He was my passion, my life. And you, the circus and all of you who are here, and our family, you were his everything. He was my hero. I am honored to be the wife of such a man. Thank you for sharing your love with us today. Thank you for paying your respects."

※ ※ ※

THAT NIGHT I SHARED my bedroom with Bella. As I was drifting into sleep, I could hear her weeping and tossing and turning, as if her bed were too big for her. Then I began to weep, too.

When I woke in the morning, Bella had just finished washing her face. She looked at me and said, "I had the strangest dream last night. I was visited by a rather messy man with a towel wrapped around his head. He told me something was missing, and that I, or the queens, needed to find it. He sounded spiritual, but I got the impression that it was material." Then she said firmly, "I'm going to Italy," as if that were the most obvious course.

"What?" I said, taken aback.

"I'm going to Italy," she repeated. "It's time for me to redefine who I am. I was so young when I met Vladimir and came to this country. I had no idea what I was getting into. All I knew was that I was in love, and that this charismatic, funny, intriguing foreigner was doing everything he could to sweep me off my feet. Within a short time, his dreams became mine."

"But Bella, what about the girls and the circus?"

"Ann Marie, Kyle, and the kids will be fine. If they want to start the circus again, I'll leave it in Kyle's hands. That Kyle is solid. He'll know the right thing to do. Lucky is going to put that brain of hers and all her energy to good use, and her talent is working for her. And although I have not met him yet in person, I believe I'm going to like this Thomas fella."

I had never heard Bella speak so frankly before. "But what about me?" I couldn't stop myself from saying. "I want what's best for my sister, but I'll miss you terribly."

"Oh, Donatella, you should go back to being Donatalia. I started calling you Donatella because I was homesick. It's become clear these past days—" Bella paused. "Now, I'm not trying to take your place as a fortune-teller, but it's become clear what your Russia has always meant to you.

"With Vladimir dead, the only concrete thing that binds you to your past is your name, the name your mother and father wanted for you. You would wear it well. You should try it on again."

"Donatalia," I said. I looked in the mirror. "Donatalia," I said once more, glancing at my reflection in the window. "It feels strange to say it after so long a time, but I think I like it."

"Good." Bella smiled.

A stranger looking on at this moment would never have guessed that these were the same women who'd spent the night weeping after burying the dead. I wondered how our tears had made Bella so strong.

"Maybe you and Marvin can call me Donatalia," I said.

✳ ✳ ✳

BELLA DIDN'T WASTE ANY time. Once she'd made up her mind, she was ready to cross the Atlantic. She traveled with Diamond back to New York City, where she was able to see Diamond's show before she boarded the ship to Italy. I was a little nervous about how she'd get back and worried for her safety. I read in the newspapers that matters all over Europe were getting more and more precarious. Mussolini had invaded Ethiopia, and he seemed to be as power-hungry as that German madman Hitler. But nothing would stop her. She was going home, for however long it took.

On the other hand, Lucky and Thomas, having known each other for little more than a month, were ready to settle down. As soon as school ended, Thomas had made his way south. I liked him quite a bit. He seemed to bring out the best in Lucky. He found endearing the very eccentricities that had sometimes annoyed us. The way Lucky shrieked sometimes when she got excited used to drive us crazy, but with Thomas around, we began smiling at that habit rather than gritting our teeth. And when she composed one too many limericks and wanted us to listen to every last rhyme, we were amused rather than irritated.

The first several months after Vladimir passed, I visited his grave every day. I talked to him about his family, Marvin, and the circus. I could feel he was particularly concerned for Ann Marie; he needed to know she was fine before his soul could float away and become one with the heavens. But what can one do for a dead man but help him get to God, knowing it's okay to leave?

Two other souls still needed my help. I worked hard and watched over the farm, but whatever extra time I had I put into learning as much as I could about Big Jim and a little zoo in Mississippi.

CHAPTER 50

EVEN WITH BELLA AND Diamond gone, we were a full house, with Ann Marie, Kyle and the kids, Lucky, Harsita, Roman, Marvin, and me.

Kyle Jr. had started school. Scarlett was walking and getting into anything she could open or climb into. I'm not certain if I had ever met a child more curious. "Don't forget to shut that bottom drawer," I constantly reminded everyone. "More than once I have found our dear Scarlett napping with the linens."

One morning over coffee, Anne Marie asked, "Would it be okay for us to stay longer than we had expected? Kyle Jr. has been through so much, and he's happy here."

"You know the answer, Ann Marie. The farm would seem empty now without you and the children. I've been thinking about that pasture near where Kyle keeps the horses. The shack next to it is falling apart, but its foundation is surprisingly well built. I was thinking we could tear it down and replace it with a house. What kind of house do you think would look nice there?"

Ann Marie's face lit up. "Oh, that would be wonderful, Donatella. I'm sure Kyle will have some ideas." We'd just started to talk happily about porches, how many windows and bedrooms for the children, when there was a knock on the door. A few minutes later, Ben said some of my favorite words: "Got one for you, Miss Donatella." It was a letter from Diamond, so I read it out loud to Ann Marie.

"Neither of us wants to let go of what we have," Diamond wrote. Though she and Roman talked every week on the phone, things between them were still unsettled. "I'm not sure what to do. There's no question that I love him, and I'm certain he loves me, but we love our lives, too. Roman said that perhaps he would apply for a job at the zoo, but he's not sure if it's the right move. You said time would tell what we are meant to be, but no matter what the outcome, I will always be grateful knowing we have loved each other freely."

"It looks like what's good for one—right now, at least—isn't the right life for the other," Ann Marie said.

I had to agree, sadly. "Roman's told me that as much he loves Diamond, he's always been a lion tamer's son, and he wonders what more might be waiting for him. I think he's finally ready to explore more of the world and himself. But Diamond, I believe, is exactly where she belongs. It's hard to admit there might be no happy ending."

Diamond had relied on Roman during the difficult time after Vladimir's death. I'd seen them sneaking off at night, unaware of anyone but themselves, but I couldn't see how their two very different worlds could meet. I was afraid they might have to learn the lesson no young person quite understands: that sometimes love isn't enough.

※ ※ ※

THAT AFTERNOON, I FOUND Marvin sitting at his big oak desk, sifting through some papers Kyle had just handed him, looking very much the prosperous man of affairs. It made me smile. "Getting on top of things?" I asked.

He grimaced. "Vladimir left us a mountain of work."

Vladimir's death had left us with a lot of loose ends to tie up, and I wondered what surprises we might have in store. The circus as a business was in disarray, and no one knew much about his personal affairs.

"I know he had no intention of dying that day, but I do wish he'd been more organized. From now on, I'll try to keep my own affairs in order in case anything happens to me," I replied.

Sometimes I felt that Bella had abandoned us, although she had more than earned her right to leave. Vladimir's will had named Kyle as executor but asked that Marvin be consulted on anything related to the circus. Without Bella's guidance, the task of deciding how to distribute Vladimir's possessions, many of which were purely sentimental in value, was not always easy.

※ ※ ※

KYLE AND MARVIN WENT through the stacks of papers a little at a time. Months after Vladimir died, they came to me with something quite mysterious.

"We found this buried at the bottom of one of Vladimir's trunks full of circus memorabilia. What do you make of it?" Kyle asked.

Wrapped in an embroidered Russian shawl was a beautiful black-lacquered box. I immediately recognized the hand-painted scene on it; it was from a Russian folktale, the story of Alyonushka and Ivanushka. The box showed the sister carrying her brother across a river. Inside the box, under a silk kerchief, I found a key and a sealed envelope. I knew the contents had to be something special. Why else would they have gone to all this trouble? These boxes were painted in only a small handful of Russian villages; this one, I believed, came from Fedoskino.

I looked up at Kyle and Marvin. "This key makes the sealed envelope inside even more mysterious." They waited, but for a while I was silent. I was lost in a memory of a day many years before. "Vladimir received a package along with a letter from his parents," I said finally. "At the time, he was frustrated because he couldn't convince them to leave Russia, even though they were in grave danger. Receiving anything from Russia was highly unusual. He told me he didn't want to open the envelope—he'd wait until he was in a better mood. 'Be certain you put this someplace safe,' I told him.

"But why did he open the box and not the envelope?" Marvin asked.

"I think he thought it might be their final farewell, and he didn't want to face it. So instead he put the box and envelope in a safe place and told himself he would open it later. Over time, it just became easier to let it sit."

I stared at the envelope. "Okay, Vladimir, here we go." Very carefully I broke the seal, as if the envelope had come from the czar himself.

I pulled out the note inside, gently unfolded the thin, yellowed paper, and read it to myself. Kyle and Marvin sat next to me, anxiously waiting. When I was through, I gave them a translation:

Dearest Vladimir,

We have come to believe that our Russia, the Russia you were raised in and taught to hold in high esteem, will soon be no longer.

We hired at a considerable sum a man—who, for obvious reasons, will remain nameless—to make a delivery to a bank in Charleston, South Carolina. The bank is located at the corner of Broad and State Streets. This key will unlock a box that's registered in your name, and inside it you will find our gift. In case something happens to us, this should secure your future and that of the circus.

Presently, Russia is dangerous, and travel is out of the question. When this upheaval comes to a peaceful end, we will reunite, if possible. Be safe, son, and give our love to your wife and family. You are in our hearts.

Your loving parents

The letter was dated October 23, 1916. "Whatever is in the box is probably worthless at this point," Ann Marie said when I read the letter at dinnertime.

"But we have to find out," I countered. "Whatever is, or was, in the bank is your heritage, and your grandparents wanted you to have it."

The next day, Kyle and Marvin called the bank manager in Charleston. He would need us to come in person, he said, with a death certificate, identification, supporting evidence, and, of course, the key.

***

TWO DAYS LATER, ON a crisp autumn morning, Ann Marie, Lucky, Kyle, Marvin, and I all went to Charleston. Roman and Harsita stayed at the farm to take care of the children and chores that needed to be completed.

Before leaving, I decided to give Officer Harper a call. I knew getting through this web of papers and officials was not going to be easy, and we might need someone to vouch for our character and confirm that we were who we said we were. Who would be better than a police officer?

When I called the station, I was told that no Officer Harper worked there, but if I wanted to speak with Captain Harper, they would give me the number.

The bank was exactly as I imagined: a big ornate granite building, very airy, with fourteen-foot ceilings. I thought that Charleston had the most elegant architecture in the South—with the exception of Savannah, of course.

The manager who approached us looked as if he belonged on Wall Street. He wore a neatly pressed gray suit, an impeccable light blue shirt, and a tie that looked very expensive. Not one hair was out of place.

Framed pictures on the wall showed that the building had been remodeled. We were told the safe deposit boxes had been, too, and the locks to those boxes had new keys that matched these more modern times. But wax imprints of the old locks and keys had been made, and if our key matched their wax-cast mold, we would be given a new key and be taken downstairs where the boxes were kept.

We were all nervous, the queens especially. Whatever was inside the safe deposit box would soon belong to them. I looked at my watch. "I hope he didn't get called someplace else," I fretted.

The manager introduced himself as Mr. Charles Milton. "We spoke on the phone the other day," he said. "Do you have the papers I asked you to bring, and of course the key? I need to gather a little more information." Then he took what we'd brought and went back into his office and closed the door. Behind the glass, we could see him walking back and forth as he made several calls. We were left wondering what was being said.

When I looked up and saw Captain Harper walk through the front door, I breathed a sigh of relief. I was certain that with his help, everything would get settled.

Captain Harper walked straight into the manager's office, leaving the door open, and proclaimed, "These people are my friends." Captain Harper then turned back to me. "Hello, Donatella, it's good to see all of you again. Don't worry about a thing. I'll make certain you are shown the best of Charleston hospitality. Mr. Milton happens to be an old school buddy of mine. Isn't that right, Charles? Donatella is not just my friend but a friend of my entire department, and you know what that means."

Immediately following Captain Harper's speech, the secretary came in carrying a shiny new key, and handed it to the manager. Captain Harper winked at me and then nodded to Mr. Milton. "If Donatella runs into any trouble or needs anything, she knows where to find me.

"By the way I was very sad to hear about Vladimir," he said to Lucky and Ann Marie. "Your father was a hero and will be missed."

I thanked Captain Harper and congratulated him again on his promotion. Almost out the door, he turned to me. "It's because of that trickster rabbit we became friends. Funny." And he tipped his cap to us and left.

We walked down the stairs to where the boxes were kept. Mr. Milton handed me back our old key. Once so light, it now felt like a ten-pound weight, but I held onto it for good luck. I thought about Vladimir's parents and wondered what we would find.

"I can only let two people in at a time," the manager said. Then he unlocked two steel doors. Kyle and I were the first to enter. We had all decided Kyle would be the most sensible, and more than likely we would need a Russian translator.

Mr. Milton put the key in our box, turned it to the right, and pulled it out. Leaving the box closed, he laid it on a table and handed Kyle another key. "I'll be right outside the door when you are through. If you want to change places, let me know. But remember, there can only be two of you at one time."

Kyle and I looked at each other as if we'd been offered the first spoonful of a hot fudge sundae but were uncertain if it would make us sick. We had no idea what we'd find, but it had to be something important for Vladimir's family to have gone through so much trouble. Kyle handed me the key. "I think you should do the honors."

I took the key and, in Russian, said a blessing to our saint of missing things, Saint Feofil of Kiev. He was known for having worn a boot on one foot and a slipper on the other and a towel wrapped around his head. The image made me smile. I thanked him for bringing us to this box, and then suddenly I remembered Bella's dream, though I kept it to myself.

I closed my eyes, and as I unlocked the box, I thought about Bella's dream. Was this what the girls were supposed to find?

When I lifted the lid, Kyle cried out, "Oh my God!" I opened my eyes but had to squint, the contents of the box were so dazzling. Necklaces, brooches, and rings—set with diamonds, rubies, emeralds, sapphires—lay in a pile, reflecting the overhead bulb in brilliant shards of light. "So this is where the Vronsky family jewels have been! And it must be how the rumor got started that Vladimir sold the family jewels. The man his parents hired must not have been able to keep the secret, and the person he told must have told someone else, while all along we had not a clue. The jewels given to Lillya, Vladimir's mother, had rarely been seen, and were part of the myth that made her notorious." I stopped for a second and smiled at the irony, then said to Kyle, "I think the girls and Bella just became very rich!"

We walked out into the hall so that Ann Marie and Lucky could enter. Though we said nothing, we couldn't wipe the smiles off our faces. When Lucky and Ann Marie returned, they teased Marvin. "You're going to be greatly disappointed," said Ann Marie.

"Just a bunch of old money, like I thought," said Lucky. By now Marvin was beside himself.

"Well, Donatella, is it my turn yet? Or did I just come to take care of you all?" Marvin took my hand, and we entered together.

After everyone had had a look, Kyle and I closed the box and told Mr. Milton we'd be back soon.

Still holding our breath, we walked out of the bank, keeping our poker faces in place. We went one block north, turned a corner, and started jumping and screaming. When we quieted down, Ann Marie and Lucky asked, "Did Papa know, and if so, why did he let us all suffer so?"

"At the time," I mused, "I believe this envelope represented all of your father's fears, and he couldn't bear to confront them. I feel quite certain that he put the box someplace he thought would be safe and eventually forgot about it. Or perhaps he decided it was best to leave the past in the past and pretended it wasn't there."

"We need to find an honest appraiser," Marvin said. "One who knows how to keep a secret. These jewels are priceless. You girls are going to have to decide what you want to keep, what you want to sell, and what you want to do with the money. I would say, by the looks of it, your mother's future is now secure."

"She could use her portion as principal and live off the interest," I added.

That afternoon, we visited as many jewelers as we could and asked a lot of questions. Lucky asked to see sapphires. "Can you tell me the difference between these two? What cut best shows off a sapphire, and which do you prefer?"

The first jeweler answered, "I prefer the cut that makes the gem most valuable." The second jeweler answered, "I prefer the one that best displays the color while enhancing the gem's luster."

Ann Marie asked about rubies. "I hear they are made of the same mineral as a sapphire; can you tell me what makes them different?"

"Their scarlet color, of course," the second jeweler answered. And on the basis of these two answers, and because the jeweler described the red as scarlet, we decided to go with him. As Ann Marie said later, "I believe his answer set this gentleman apart."

Marvin asked about security and insurance. He wanted to be sure that our box of jewels would be safe and that the jeweler understood the meaning of discretion.

Early the next morning, we headed back to the bank, where we told Charles Milton again that we'd be in touch soon. This time he was the one left wondering what would happen next. Then we returned to Savannah with the key to our treasure chest.

When we got home, Polly said Diamond had called three or four times, and before we could unpack our suitcases, the telephone rang again.

Ann Marie picked it up.

"So?" Diamond asked.

Ann Marie coughed several times, code for "We should talk about this in private"; our phone was a party line. When her coughing fit ended, she simply said, "It went well. Now that I know New York City is not so far away," she added, "perhaps Lucky and I will pay you a visit."

"Come soon," Diamond Claire responded. "You know I'm not very patient."

❋ ❋ ❋

DESPITE ALL OUR EFFORTS to keep it quiet, between the bank, jewelry stores, insurance men, and long-distance calls, an ambitious reporter uncovered the reason for the queens' mysterious trips. Like everything else that involved the family, the story of the Vronskys' jewels became news. When Larry read about it in the papers, he erupted like a volcano. "How can that man continue to haunt me in death?" he was reported to say, while Marvin pictured Big Jim snorting like a bull, wondering how he would take his revenge.

Bella, still in Italy, sent a letter to Ann Marie and Lucky. "Go see Diamond. Have your meeting and do as you choose. Your grandparents always meant them to be for you. They're your legacy."

Diamond, Lucky, and Ann Marie each kept several pieces and put aside several they thought Bella would appreciate. Diamond's favorite piece was a butterfly brooch tastefully filled with gems of all colors. Ann Marie kept a beautiful platinum necklace in the shape of a heart filled with teardrop diamonds and a larger teardrop at its center. It matched how she felt, Ann Marie said.

One-fifth of the spoils they left in the safety deposit box for safekeeping. All the rest they sold, except for one piece, a delicate filigree band of ten inverted hearts in which ten small but perfect rubies were set in the middle of each heart, which Lillya had wrapped separately with an attached slip of paper on which was written, "my mother's wedding band." Diamond and Ann Marie gave that piece to Lucky, simply saying they thought she should have it.

When they finished with their calculations, one portion was left: the one that would have gone to Spade. That, they deposited with Marvin's help into my bank account, with a note to me saying, "This is for you and Spade, to help you facilitate your dream." I didn't know how to thank them, but I promised it would be put to good use.

❋ ❋ ❋

THINGS BEGAN TO SETTLE down. We were falling into a rhythm. However, a big wave could arrive at any minute, and I wanted to be certain we were ready.

Kyle and Ann Marie always had either a child or a hammer in their hands as they built their new home. "I want to be able to say to my son, 'Look what we did. We built the place where you, I, Scarlett, and Mommy live,'" Kyle said.

Lucky and Thomas traveled back and forth between Savannah and New Orleans so frequently I thought they'd probably beaten down their own trail. "Aunt Donatella," she confided, "I found an engagement ring in Thomas's suit pocket right before the family jewels were discovered, but since then he hasn't said anything. I think he's afraid to propose to me in case I think he wants to marry me for my money. Do you think he's waiting for me to ask him?" I started laughing, but upon reflection I thought that she was right and told her so.

On Lucky's next visit to New Orleans, that's exactly what she did. She told me all about it on her triumphant return.

"Thomas said yes, Donatella. 'I'll marry you, Lucia Akinsya Club—' And then he stopped. I was afraid he'd changed his mind, but then he smiled and added 'tonight.' And we married that same night!" Lucky was about to shriek, but instead she proudly displayed her hand. On it she wore a beautiful engagement ring Thomas had bought for her, next to Lillya's mother's wedding band. It was a perfect match; each shone brighter because of the other. "I hope you're not mad, but we couldn't wait another hour."

Then Lucky hugged me and let out a shriek, and we both laughed.

"Vladimir would have been proud," I said, "and I know your mother will be so happy for you. She's quite fond of Thomas, as we all are."

Lucky spent two days packing up her belongings and moved to New Orleans. Everything seemed so much quieter without her.

Until it didn't.

CHAPTER 51

Big Jim thought he would win. But every man—even ones like Big Jim—has a weak spot. I believed our turn would come, though we might need a little help. So, I hired a private detective to learn about Big Jim's comings and goings and from that I mapped out a plan. I tried to find out a little about Larry, but his trail seemed to go nowhere. All I learned was that he had a fondness for horses but no longer rode.

Big Jim had already committed so many wrongdoings, he should have been in jail long ago, but somehow he always found a way to make his charges disappear.

"Big Jim is a cheat and a gangster," the detective said. "His only interest is in putting money into his own pocket. He's doing business with several shady construction companies, and he hires incompetent workers instead of skilled, seasoned men.

"It's whispered he started a moonshine business on the side this season. It's got to bring in some pretty good extra cash because he recently moved into a big log home in the Smokey Mountains not far from Spruce Pine, North Carolina, where he used to live. His stills, I'm told, are up by Loafers Glory to keep out the competition from Johnson City. And that Larry fellow, I think he just ignores Big Jim's side business."

Unfortunately, Marvin's informant got sloppy and it became too dangerous for him to keep working. I couldn't let retrieving Bess come at the cost of someone's life.

I hated to think of Bess being stuck with a man like Big Jim. The authorities looked the other way; they were making too much money skimming his profits to do anything unless they were pushed.

I needed to see that Bess was okay. With Marvin's man no longer in place, it took some coercing on my part, but finally Marvin gave in to my scheme.

❋ ❋ ❋

STANDING BEHIND A COTTON candy truck, we were able to sneak a peek at Bess. She wore a crown on top of her head and a mask around her eyes with diamond-shaped cutouts running down her trunk. A large, ornate red, yellow, and green blanket inlaid with little mirrors covered her back. A long line had formed of children waiting to ride her. With Harsita's help, I'd dressed Marvin as a Sikh, complete with a turban. I myself wore an Indian sari and an ankle bracelet, with a scarf wrapped around my head.

"We can't enter the tent," Marvin had warned me. "Too many workers know who we are, and we can't afford to be recognized. We've got to move fast and learn as much as we can."

Holding a big pink cloud of cotton candy in front of me to obscure my face, I peeked out at Bess again. I thought I detected some sores behind her ears. "If they've hit her with a hook," I told Marvin, "I'm going to want to kill Big Jim myself."

I wondered if Bess could sense that I was close by. Did she know I was staring at her? When it comes to elephants, I believe they have feelings much like humans. If she knew that I was near but didn't stop to say hello, it would break her heart and mine.

Suddenly, I heard someone call out for Larry. Both Marvin and I looked in the direction of the man who turned around and answered. I only got a quick glance. But there was something familiar to me. Knowing my instinct to stay, Marvin grabbed my arm and pulled me back behind the concession truck before I could get a second look.

Bess was the star of Big Jim's show. She was billed as Queen Bess, an elephant who came from a long line of Russian aristocrats. "Her lineage speaks for itself," the barker called out.

In the background, I could see a snake enchantress doing a tribal dance as she weaved her magic to an exotic theme of organ music. I became distracted. "Donatella, remember why we are here," Marvin whispered.

"This is not just any elephant," the barker went on. "This elephant has lived among queens and other royalty. Her mother performed for the czar of Russia.

She is known throughout the world." Bess played the part, helping to raise Big Jim's status, but I couldn't help but notice how sad she looked.

"Patience, Donatella, you don't want to spoil our chance of bringing her back home."

Marvin was right. I had to control my emotions and bide my time.

❃ ❃ ❃

OUR CHANCE TO WIN Bess back would come sooner than we expected. Big Jim and his moonshine boys had become too greedy and began to cut more and more corners. By August, their rash pursuit of riches had caused a highly publicized accident, leaving three men dead, including one drunk but beloved clown, as well as his circus dog, for whom everyone mourned.

Big Jim's moonshine men had started to travel behind his circus, carrying a still made of big plastic buckets. Everyone in the South knew how dangerous that was; it put hundreds of innocent people in danger. But with the circus close by, they had a built-in customer base. They hired a wrangler to bring in townspeople who were looking for some shine. They could make a lot of money—especially in dry counties, of which, at the time, there were many—and that was all that mattered.

Then some wet-behind-the-ears kid that they'd hired on the cheap snuck off for a smoke, leaving the still unattended. He'd been gone five minutes when the still exploded.

"I'm told it sounded like the world was coming to an end," Marvin said, telling me the story as we sat in the kitchen. He was peeling shrimp while I chopped up peppers, onion, and celery to make a roux. Thomas had introduced Lucky to the pleasures of New Orleans cooking, and she'd passed those techniques on to me.

"For a few, sadly, it *was* the end."

"But the point is, Donatalia, Big Jim is in jail now, and his legal bills are going to hit the roof. I also hear that he and Larry have been fighting. Rumor has it he warned Big Jim that the still would cause more problems than it was worth and if anything happened he would leave and so would Bess. Maybe it's time to do some dealing."

I couldn't stop thinking about that poor clown and circus dog, but I had to admit that Marvin was right. A chance had opened, and we needed to act. And to act, we needed to know our adversary and use that knowledge.

It was clear Big Jim hated Vladimir, alive or dead, and he loathed the Circus of the Queens, open or closed, more than he detested being in jail. He'd always been jealous of Vladimir and resented Vladimir even more for getting the upper hand all those years ago in Atlanta, disgracing him. He couldn't stand the thought that Vladimir, even on his worst day, had what Big Jim didn't—respect and class—and he let everyone know how he felt.

What Marvin and I couldn't understand was why this Larry fellow, who no one seemed to know, felt much the same. I tried to relive our day at the circus and focus on the face that I saw and figure out why it was familiar, or was it nothing at all?

Initially, Big Jim, and maybe now this Larry too, had bought Bess as an act of revenge, but now they viewed her as a touchstone, the benchmark of their success. It was as if they would lose every other animal—the entire circus—before either would let Bess go. But Big Jim remained the greediest man most had ever known. Even when he put up a good front, everyone knew, especially Larry, that it was money that kept his heart beating. And though Big Jim swore he would never, ever knowingly return Bess to the Circus of the Queens, every once in a while, when he thought Larry wasn't looking, he'd let someone make an offer just to see what she was worth.

Given this information, I asked myself, how could we make this happen? Our enemy was weak, but he was mean, and he surrounded himself with criminals and thieves, and the partnership that in our eyes had once made him strong now made him vulnerable.

"What about Emily?" Marvin asked as he dumped the shrimp shells into a pot with some onion and the ends I'd cut off the peppers, to make stock for the étouffée. He'd been taking cooking classes from Thomas himself, it seemed, though we differed in how thick we wanted the stock to be.

"I haven't abandoned her, if that's what you're thinking. I just think that Big Jim is the thornier problem and we don't know as much about this Larry as I would like to. I've had my eye on Emily's zoo. It won't be long before they're ready to sell—she's an expense they can't afford. Besides, an unhappy elephant isn't much of a crowd-pleaser."

Just then the phone rang in the hall, and Marvin went to answer it. When he came back, he was grinning wickedly. "I just got news," he said. "Big Jim made bail. It must have cost him a bundle."

"Do we know what he used for collateral?"

"The rumor is he had to put up his house and a portion of his circus. Now that there's only one month left on the tour, I've heard his animals are being neglected except for Bess and the horses. He seems to blame the rest instead of himself for his predicament."

"He's tried to wiggle his way out of every mess he's created by flashing his money around, and so far it's worked." Finding myself stirring the roux a little too vigorously, I lowered the flame and turned to face Marvin. "But with Spade's inheritance, we have resources, too. More importantly, we're smarter than he is, and we want to do something good."

"If we're going to make a move, now's the time to do it. Big Jim is being buried in lawyers' fees and circus debt, his stills are closed so there's no side cash coming in, he's facing twenty years in prison, and Larry is keeping his distance and doesn't seem too pleased. He's probably calculating what he should do. I feel horrible"—Marvin smiled—"but I have an idea that's going to make Big Jim even more miserable!"

❋ ❋ ❋

MARVIN CONTACTED THE THREE other circus owners who'd been there in Atlanta at the infamous card game, and seen Big Jim's underhandedness firsthand, and told them about our plan to bring the elephants home. Though they didn't quite understand why we would go to all this bother, they respected Vladimir and wanted to honor his memory, and they disliked Big Jim, so they were happy to join in.

The month of October, each of them sent a handful of workers to local churches near where Big Jim and his circus would be performing. They mingled with the congregation and complained every chance they got about the wickedness of this man and the drunken company he kept. "He's been recruiting our boys to drink his liquor and work his stills. Boycott Big Jim!"

Once the word got out, it didn't take much for the townsfolk to take up the cause. They picketed Big Jim's circus and home until I heard he had to confine himself to his house.

The protests in every town Big Jim's circus traveled to grew larger, and by early November, just before the end of circus season, he was forced to close completely.

We had to find a way to continue to pressure him; however, the citizens had created a momentum, and they went up Grandfather's Mountain and found where Big Jim lived and continued their shouting. When Big Jim tried to sneak out to discuss business at the Old English Inn, they followed him, and they didn't stop this harassment until 1938.

"We don't want no clown and dog killer in our town!" they shouted. "His drunken men want your daughters!" "He's a fake, and so is his circus!"

I bet that last insult bothered him more than any other.

At Marvin's request, Henri, the circus owner from Baton Rouge who'd exposed the dealer and helped Vladimir in Atlanta so many years before, sent his son-in-law, Juliette's husband Patrice, to assess the situation and help broker a deal. Patrice would attempt to buy what was left of Big Jim's circus with some of my money from the jewels. If he put together a solid deal, and it went through, we would then sell the circus back to Patrice and Henri at a bargain-basement price. This way, they could expand, and we could bring home Bess.

"Big Jim's not going to need an elephant where he's going," Henri told Marvin and me. "Besides, he needs the money to pay for his defense, but this Larry is a wild card!"

Big Jim's pending jail sentence hadn't made him any less arrogant, though, and he turned down the first offer Patrice made.

"He's pretending he's not the skunk everyone knows him to be. But I think reality is just around the corner," Henri told us the next time he called. "Our Patrice is keeping a very close watch."

❋ ❋ ❋

FOR WEEKS WE HEARD nothing, and poor Marvin had to listen to me fret.

"What if Patrice can't broker the deal, and something happens to Bess?" I sat up in bed, unable to sleep. "What if he's willing to sell everything off except her? What if he catches on that we're the ones who want to buy him out?"

"Calm down, Donatalia," Marvin said, yawning. "Henri and Patrice are on top of this. Besides, they have an extra incentive—they are not doing this for you or me or Bess, they are doing this for Vladimir."

"Let's hope it works."

"O ye of little faith," said Marvin. "When did that happen?"

When he said that, I felt ashamed. But I still tossed and turned.

The next morning, Henri telephoned to let us know that Patrice had made another offer, at a very fair price. But Big Jim, greedy as ever, and with an exaggerated sense of his own importance, turned him down again. "I'm sorry," Henri said. "We'll approach him again soon. Don't give up."

I thanked him, though I felt crushed.

"It's just the beginning," Henri said, trying to cheer me up.

Not for me, I thought. *I've been plotting this for years.* Then something else struck me for the first time. What if Emily and Bess didn't remember me? Or worse yet, what if in my memory I'd romanticized them and what they meant to Spade and me, let alone each other?

I shared my fears with Marvin, as I did everything else.

"Since when did you quit trusting your instincts?" he asked. "I've never known another person who's more perceptive than you. Stop it, Donatalia!" he said, quite sharply. "You know what you're doing!"

❋ ❋ ❋

APRIL SHOWERS BROUGHT AN abundance of May flowers, and my garden was beginning to look like a rainbow of colors, almost as beautiful as my mother's once was. I kept a small path open down the middle and placed a chair there, where I'd think about whatever came to the surface. Sometimes it would be Marvin, another day the queens, Kyle Jr. or Scarlett, Emily or Bess. But lately my thoughts kept turning to Bella and sometimes even to Hervé. Europe was sounding more and more like a teapot about to blow its top, and it worried me.

On fronts other than nailing down Big Jim, things were moving along. Harsita and Roman had finished building the elephant barn, which also had room to store the gilded carriages and other circus paraphernalia that we'd been keeping in the back pasture. And the zoo that owned Emily had started negotiations with Marvin. I was a nervous wreck, fearing that if the word got out, it could sabotage our plan. Big Jim, I assumed, would be on high alert and waiting for a trap. I tried to keep busy, letting Marvin, who was a bit more detached, pound on the doors of city hall and work to get our permits. "Soon, Donatalia, soon," Marvin would say when he returned, but my patience was wearing thin.

Just when my spirits were at their lowest, the phone rang. Patrice was on the other end, speaking rapidly in French. "*Je pense que je l'ai fait*, Donatalia," he said. "I think I've done it!"

"Larry's agreed, too?" I asked.

"It appears so," he answered. And we both hooted and hollered, as Americans do. Usually we would both be too refined, but in this case our excitement won out over manners.

"I should know by noon tomorrow if Henri is the new owner of Big Jim's circus. If he is, we would be honored to bestow upon you your old friend Bess in honor of Henri's friend Vladimir." I could feel his smile across the phone wires. "Make sure you're ready to take her. If this happens, it's going to happen fast."

I immediately shouted out to Marvin, "It's happening!" In turn, he shouted out to Harsita, who shouted out to Roman.

"Let's double-check our work," Roman said. "No, triple-check it!" And they all ran out to the elephant stable with me close behind.

It had been eight years since I'd seen either Emily or Bess up close. So much had happened since then—death, new love, a depression to dig ourselves out of, dreams both realized and lost. I had held onto this dream for so long, and now it might come true. But just as I felt this surge of happiness, a fear just as strong rushed in. Everything I had worked for might get washed away.

"Donatalia," I said out loud, "calm down."

Then, out of nowhere, I felt the spirit of Irina envelop me, and I regained my focus and became still. She told me to look closer. At first I didn't understand what she meant, but then I saw the face of the man at Big Jim's circus, the man they called Larry, and I remembered his eyes, but mostly his grin. It had been years, but I would never forget those eyes from the bottom of the staircase staring back at me as I turned white in pain. I started to shake and felt certain he had laid a trap. But why? And after so many years it didn't make sense. But then it did make sense to me. All the cards, it had to be him! I was as frightened as I had ever been.

"Donatalia," I said out loud again. "Calm down!"

I took a long, deep breath, savoring the smells of Savannah, the grass, the rich soil, a hint of tobacco. I didn't know what kind of sick trick this man wanted to play on me or why, but as I looked out at the magnificence of my land, I realized that all I had was because of what he had done. I felt an unshakable peace and my fear subsided.

I wondered how long it would take to get reacquainted with Emily and Bess. Harsita and Marvin would retrieve them by train, and I'd be waiting at the farm to greet them. I told them to be especially careful, that I had placed Larry as someone I believed might be looking to get revenge. I reminded myself I was doing the right thing. "They won't be cooped up, they'll have fresh air and exercise, Harsita and each other," I reassured myself.

The next morning, we all hovered near the phone. Every time it rang, whether it was my party line ring or my neighbors, my heart pounded like a jackhammer. So I'd take a deep breath, then I'd pick up the receiver just in case the operator had been mistaken, but Marvin could tell by the look of disappointment on my face that it wasn't Henri or Patrice.

Tick, tick, tick… It was twenty past twelve. "Where are they?" I asked.

"Something might have come up," said Marvin.

Tick, tick, tick. It was ten to one, and I was beginning to give up hope.

"Maybe you should do something to keep your mind occupied," Marvin said. "They'll let us know when they have news."

"What if they call and I don't hear them?"

"I know you well enough to know you won't be out of the phone's reach."

"No," I said. "I'm not going anywhere, though I will make us both sandwiches."

Doing something with my hands and mind helped to pass ten minutes at most, eating the sandwich another five.

Tick, tick, tick. It was two twenty, and I was giving up.

"If not today, perhaps tomorrow," Marvin said—and just then the phone rang, and it was *my* party line ring. I stood frozen, afraid to answer it.

Marvin looked at me. "Pick it up, Donatalia."

On the other end of the party line, Charlotte Lou Ellen Barton, whose family owned the farm next to ours, Madgerie Smith, whose husband owned a trucking company, and Winifred Cornelius Martin, one of Savannah's socialites, were all listening in. "*Tu es pret?*" Henri asked. None of the other women—well, except for Winifred, perhaps—understood what he'd said, but when I answered, "*Oui! Oui! Oui!* Yes, I've been ready for years!" They all comprehended that answer immediately.

Marvin got me a tissue—I'd started to cry—and picked up the phone. "How can we ever thank you?"

"You and Bella thanked me many years ago with the gift of a horse, and that sweet horse recently died of old age. I heard Kyle has a mare for sale that I believe would be perfect for our granddaughter. Maybe you would ask him not to sell her to anyone but us?"

"Please consider Fiona, our dapple gray, our present to you. An elephant for a horse and a circus—I think we both have gotten a good deal." Then Marvin put the phone to my ear so we could share the receiver.

"I'm sorry I'm calling so late," Henri continued. "But negotiations didn't start on time, Patrice said, and once they got going, he couldn't take a break. It would have weakened our position. So as grueling as it was, he kept pushing on until we had what we wanted."

At that moment, Patrice joined the conversation, having just walked into the room Henri was calling from. "You know Big Jim had no intention of selling Bess with the circus," he said. "He planned on keeping her for himself. But I told him our deal had to include her, or all bets were off. Even then, he was ready to let the deal fall apart. We were at a standstill. I was actually headed for the door when, without Big Jim's permission, his partner Larry shouted for me to stop. He asked if I minded taking a fifteen-minute break so he could talk to his partner.

"Those fifteen minutes felt like they lasted forever, and I found myself in the middle of a storm. They were screaming and yelling at each other, Larry saying, 'You're willing to lose money when it's not your own,' and Big Jim answered him by throwing the vase in the office on the floor, and I heared it break into a hundred pieces.

"This Larry guy seemed to understand the absurdity of it all. Although it was clear they both had wanted to seek revenge on Vladimir, he finally slapped Big Jim, then shook him saying, 'Don't you see that you won? Vladimir is dead and his poor mother Lillya probably doesn't even know! It's over!' And with that he walked back in, sat down, and said, 'You got a deal.' Big Jim followed and nodded 'yes,' clearly disappointed as if he had misjudged his partner's hatred of Vladimir.

"You can imagine how relieved I felt, but I didn't want to show it. I stayed businesslike and detached until I left the office. I'd hoped I could come through for you and my father-in-law. I'm so happy I did.

"Bess will be ready by Friday. Can you make that work?"

"Donatalia would move a mountain to bring Bess home," Marvin said.

Patrice laughed. "I think she did."

CHAPTER 52

FRIDAY COULDN'T COME SOON enough—but all of a sudden, it seemed like it was coming on like a runaway train. Bess would be here in the blink of an eye, and we still had to secure Emily. I had another mountain to move, and fast.

The zoo that had Emily was headed into bankruptcy and the city was seeking donations. The upkeep of an elephant wasn't cheap. Emily's daily diet could make a rich man go broke. But I had a Russian treasure chest, and for Emily, I was willing to use it.

Marvin, handling the negotiations, offered an additional 15 percent if the zoo would have Emily ready by Saturday. The board of directors agreed that it was in their best interest to push the deal forward. They even offered to help with transportation to ensure Emily's safety. Jonas, who'd tended to Emily these past few years, would be there to hand her over to Harsita.

But first we needed to bring Bess home. Harsita and Marvin accompanied Henri and Patrice to Big Jim's circus. Now that the papers were signed, nothing Jim could do would stop the sale.

❋ ❋ ❋

MARVIN CALLED ME FROM the train station to tell me, "Everything's fine. I'm bringing Bess home." He'd arranged for a police officer to meet him at the station in Savannah and walk with them to the farm while directing traffic. Needless to say, the closer they got to the farm, the more attention they got and the more curious I became to hear about the details of their day.

When Ben saw the men and Bess approach the farm, he had Polly pull me away from the kitchen, where I'd been nervously chopping watermelon and bananas to keep myself busy. I ran out to greet her. She was still the prettiest elephant I had ever seen. A crowd of children and a few of their parents were following her on either side, unable to resist her charm. Even after all she'd been through and the events of the day, Bess was patient, understanding, and gentle.

When I gave her some of the fruit I'd cut up, she wrapped her trunk through my arm and got watermelon seeds all over my chest. Everyone burst out laughing, including myself.

Like his father in India, the mahout who'd slept with his elephant, Harsita didn't want to leave Bess's side. After taking her for a walk around the grassy pastures of her new home, we sent the children on their way, saying Bess was very tired. Then Harsita gave her a bath and let Bess throw some water on him. It almost felt as if all of us had never been apart. At around ten or so, Marvin came out. We said our good nights, and I finally reluctantly let him drag me back into the house. Harsita planned to stay with Bess until morning, but we convinced him to come in for a celebratory toast. I wanted to hear how it had gone at Big Jim's, so we all sat down in Marvin's study, with its club chairs and art deco floor lamps with amber glass shades. Henri and Patrice joined us; they'd decided that they wanted to stay another day, to be there when Emily came home. Marvin lit a pipe, the rich aroma of the tobacco mingling with the smell of leather and old books, settled back in his chair, and launched into his tale.

❋ ❋ ❋

"I DIDN'T WANT TO upset you Donatalia. I wanted you to enjoy your victory, your reward, but things turned out to be a little more difficult than what I've let on. Walking down the midway to where Big Jim's animals are now kept, I had to look straight ahead. Many are just chained to stakes, but knowing that they will soon be with Henri made me feel a little better.

"Big Jim was waiting for us and we suddenly found ourselves face-to-face with him. He planted himself about ten feet in front of us, stopping us cold with an icy glare and gritted teeth. Jail time and bankruptcy doesn't seem to have made a dent in his inflated image of himself; he was dressed to the nines and puffed up like a tom turkey.

"'Well, well, if it isn't Mr. Marvelous, and the boy who talks to the animals! Your Bess isn't going to be worth much soon.' Big Jim smirked and began to strut away.

"Henri, never one to stop, went after Big Jim and got right under his nose. 'If she's even one pound lighter, I'll make sure you regret this day.'

"Marvin raised his glass to Henri, who looked a little abashed. 'I have to admit, you're a lot tougher than I would have guessed, Henri, from your man-about-town looks.'

"It's a good thing you weren't there, Donatalia. Big Jim didn't give two figs for the deal he and his partner had made. If he wasn't going to have Bess, neither would anybody else.

"Harsita was the sharp one, though. While Big Jim was busy trying to sidetrack us, he didn't bother listening, but just hurried to find Bess. When he got to her stall, he found Big Jim's partner Larry struggling with a young man almost half his age who was holding a giant syringe in his hand."

"I broke in," Harsita said. "I lost all sense of self. I grabbed this man's arm and told him to tell me what he was doing and to put down the syringe. He refused and started to struggle with me. Larry, who's pretty old, caught his breath, then took hold of the man's leg.

"'I'm a vet,' the young man said.

"'Like heck you are!' I shouted.

"'I'm just following Big Jim's orders,' the imposter stated. 'This here is a disturbed rogue elephant. She's real dangerous! A menace, and she needs to be put down.'

"'Show me the papers,' I demanded."

If the story hadn't been so horrifying, I would have laughed at Harsita's imitation of the man's Southern drawl.

"'I plan to do my job with or without some interfering pipsqueak or a disloyal partner seeking redemption.' At that, Donatella, I got so angry, I punched him," Harsita confessed. "I'm much stronger than I realized—all this farming has made a fit man out of me. Then, seeing he had been thrown off balance, Larry knocked him over, and I kicked him for good measure. Just hard enough that he'd stay down awhile. Larry grabbed the syringe out of the roughneck's hand and emptied it.

"'Take Bess and get out of here as fast as you can. Big Jim is not rational and there's no telling what he'll do!' Larry yelled. So I grabbed Bess's lead and ran as fast as I could until we'd put a little distance between us and the circus. Bess must have sensed the danger she'd been in—for she didn't hesitate a moment."

"A good thing, too," Marvin said. "If we'd gotten to the circus ten minutes later, Bess might have been dead."

"Big Jim's partner, Larry—well he's probably not his partner now—is really the one that saved her. I don't know what his motive was, but I'm glad he was there," Harsita interjected.

"When Henri, Patrice, and I got to her stall," Marvin went on, "she was gone, and so was Harsita. We didn't know what had happened, but we knew something was wrong when we saw that man knocked out on the straw and Larry checking for a pulse.

"'He's going to be okay,' Larry looked up to say. 'Your boy has Bess. He ran off in that direction. I told him to get out of here as fast as he could, and you should, too.'

"I don't know why, Donatalia, but I knew he was telling the truth. We were following Harsita and Bess's trail, when we heard a cluster of rifle shots."

Harsita took up the story again. "I didn't know whether to turn around or keep running. I'd left a watermelon under a big tree a ways down the road from the circus, so that's where we headed. Bess was scared and I thought that would be the quickest way to assure her of my good intentions.

"I was shaking, but I gave her the watermelon anyway to calm us both down. Just as she finished the watermelon, Marvin, Henri, and Patrice came running toward us and I felt we'd be safe, but we needed to keep moving, for Big Jim was on the loose and he was gunning for us."

"When we got to the train station, I alerted the authorities to Big Jim's last-ditch attempt at revenge and told them about Larry and the vet," Marvin continued.

"Do you know what happened to Larry? Was he shot? Is he alive?" I asked.

"We'll find out tomorrow, Donatalia. For now, there is nothing we can do but celebrate that Bess is safe and back where she'll be well taken care of, and soon she'll be reunited with Emily," said Marvin.

I bit my tongue. It was hard to banish the image of Larry possibly lying bleeding on the ground with that giant syringe, which was as dramatic as anything I had seen in life or on stage.

✳ ✳ ✳

Saturday morning, we woke to an overcast sky. I got out of bed and threw open the window. The sun was trying to find its way out from the clouds and I was more nervous than anything else. Marvin and Harsita would meet the train. Roman and I would stay with Bess. Ann Marie and Kyle, who'd finished building

their new house on the farm and had just returned with Kyle Jr. and Scarlett from
a short rodeo tour, would make certain we hadn't forgotten anything. Henri and
Patrice would enjoy a bit of Savannah and be back at the farm by two.

I had Marvin call the authorities before they left, but they only asked him
questions and wouldn't say what happened after we left.

I was pretty sure Bess had recognized me. Even more importantly, I believed
she'd recognized Harsita. As I went about my business that morning, I found myself
conversing with the dead. With Vladimir and Spade, I was free to say anything.
I recounted the story that Spade and I had woven together many years ago about
Emily's capture and journey, and I began to imagine, in my head, the new twist it
might end with. Later, I tried it out on Kyle Jr. He was utterly engaged. "I'll be the
only one at school with an elephant—no, *two* elephants!—in my backyard."

Bess didn't appear to be too disoriented. I prayed I was doing a good thing
by reuniting her with Emily. Poor Emily had been confined for eight long years
and hadn't seen another elephant in all that time. I had no idea how either would
react when they saw the other.

Lucky called from New Orleans to say that she and Thomas wished us well.
Then, unable to contain herself, she let out a short but high-pitched shriek.
Diamond Claire sent a telegram announcing that tonight's performance of *Jumbo*
was being dedicated to Emily and Bess and that Jimmy Durante sent his regards.

The sun had found its place in the sky by that time and was shining down on
our lush green pasture. The land I'd set aside for the elephants was about the size
of three football stadiums, and we had plenty of hay to supplement the grass. We
stocked up on fruits and vegetables and the stalls had running water. Actually, their
living quarters would be more luxurious than those of most poor Southern farmers.

We put Bess in the pasture while we waited for Emily's arrival. We wanted to
be sure Emily would have time to get her footing before we brought them together.

I was calming my nerves by washing some dishes in the kitchen sink when
a young boy on a bicycle drove up and started pounding at our front door.
"Come quick!" he yelled. "Marvin the Marvelous sent me to tell you Emily's
almost here!" The children in our part of town couldn't believe their good luck
at having circus people for neighbors. Some of their parents agreed with the
children and some did not.

I threw my apron on the mantel and followed the boy outside. Walking up our long and narrow drive, I could see two men and an elephant and, once again, a lot of children.

Emily had no idea how to comprehend where she was going. I felt for her. Marvin kept the children at a distance, giving Emily some space. She wasn't as comfortable with crowds as Bess and I noticed that she had a bit of a limp, probably from having been chained.

Once Marvin and Harsita had Emily settled in her new stall, I came in and scratched her trunk and gave her a gentle hug and kiss, for I didn't want to scare her. It was hard to hold back my emotions, but then a veterinary doctor stepped in to check her out.

"Other than the fact that she's had very little exercise and looks a bit depressed and weary," he said, "she seems physically okay. I would wait another day and let her familiarize herself with her new surroundings before bringing the elephants together, though."

Henri and Patrice decided they could wait another day, too. "This is a special occasion," Henri told Marvin. "A reunion like this doesn't happen more than once in a lifetime. Plus, we're enjoying ourselves and we'd much rather stay than go."

That night, we decided Harsita would remain with Emily until morning and Roman with Bess, to keep them company and give them an extra sense of security. Kyle would fill in when either needed breaks. Me, I'd wander from one stall facing one side of the pasture to the other stall facing the opposite way, making certain all was right.

HARSITA HAD GONE IN for supper. This was the first quiet moment I was having with Emily. A narrow beam of late-afternoon sun slanted into the high-roofed barn, making it feel almost like a place of worship, and everything seemed hushed. I sat quietly on a bale of hay, Emily's trunk draped over my shoulder as she stood near me. Suddenly, in the distance, we heard a great crash—a big tree must have fallen. It scared us both half to death. And just as Spade and I had done so long ago, whenever Emily was afraid, I began to sing the same old Welsh folk song:

Sleep my child and peace attend thee
All through the night.
Guardian angels God will send thee
All through the night.
Soft the drowsy hours are creeping,
Hill and dale in slumber sleeping,
I my loved ones' watch am keeping,
All through the night.

Amazingly, as if no time had passed, Emily calmed down.

❋ ❋ ❋

IN THE HOUSE, MARVIN and our guests had been telling circus stories while they played poker in honor of Vladimir. Trying not to think too much about Big Jim, I returned in time for Polly's dessert. As she was putting it on the table, there was a knock on the front door.

It was rather late, but I went to the door anyway, rather anxiously expecting it to be the authorities. What bad news might they bring? I took a deep breath and opened the door.

On the porch stood Bella. I screamed with delight and kissed her three times on both cheeks. In her hand, she held a small package. "I found it in front of your door." Bella heard my question before I had a chance to ask it. "There's a card on top with the initials HLF." The blood left my face and I turned white. "What is it?" she asked.

"I don't know," I answered. "But please don't say anything until I have a chance to open it."

❋ ❋ ❋

A MOMENT LATER, MARVIN, Ann Marie, and Kyle Jr. ran to the door to see what had set me off. Then they started screaming, and I used that time to pull myself together. Soon Henri and Patrice followed.

"I should have known you wouldn't miss this," I said.

"Miss what?" Bella replied.

"Let Marvin take your suitcase. Sit down and eat some food, have some wine, and I'll tell you what's going on. We have some catching up to do."

After admiring Kyle Jr. and Scarlett Spade and playing a few hands of cards with them, Bella followed me to the pasture and the barns. I gave both the elephants some fresh hay and watermelon and caressed their trunks as a welcoming gesture. Tonight, they could have anything they wanted. "You're going to spoil them rotten," said Bella. "This would have made Vladimir very happy." She smiled.

❋ ❋ ❋

As we walked back into the house, we continued a conversation about Italy that we had begun in the barn. These days, you couldn't speak of Europe and Italy without talking of the threat of war. "The world is going crazy," she said. "Men are hungry for power and land. This Hitler and our Mussolini are not good. They're getting us all into trouble. It's getting harder and harder to travel anywhere. I was afraid if I stayed in Italy much longer, I wouldn't be able get back at all. You know my grandfather was a Jew, even though I was raised Roman Catholic. My dear Italy, which I love with all of my heart, is being led down the wrong path and she might find herself upside down, along with Henri's dear France."

Remembering we were together in celebration, Bella stopped herself. When we entered the house through the back dining room door, she picked up an unopened bottle of Henri's Châteauneuf-du-Pape, removed the cork, and poured everyone a small glass.

"I'd like to make a toast. To Emily and Bess, to family, and to the closest friend I've ever had, Donatalia."

❋ ❋ ❋

I waited until I was certain Bella was asleep. I hated keeping this from Marvin, but this was something I had to do on my own. It was a small box, about four by four inches and had been wrapped in a cotton hankie, once again with the initials HLF. The first and the last letter made sense, but the middle initial made me think it could be someone else. However, I knew that was only me trying to fool myself.

My heart started beating so fast and hard I thought it would bounce right out of my body and across the floor. My hands started to shake to the point where I thought I would never be able to control them, but eventually all I had left to open was the box. I went into the bathroom, turned on the light, and locked the door. Inside the box was a folded-up piece of paper, and when I picked it up, underneath it was the small circular emerald brooch Lillya had given my mother, who gave it to me; the one I last saw on the ship coming to America, the one I last saw with Hervé.

The walls of my body came crashing in, and I thought my lungs and ribs would collapse, thinking of the ramification. Slowly, I unraveled his note and began reading it:

Dear Donatalia, or is it Donatella now? My full name is Hervé Laurent Fluery.

Was I reading this right? Did it mean what I think it did? By the next sentence, I knew it was true:

I bought this for whom I thought would be the love of my life, Lillya. I gave it to her the day we took vows in the forest. I'm sorry, Donatalia, that I was not forthcoming as we got to know each other better.

When I saw you on the ship's deck, I had no idea who you were; I only knew you lit a spark and the man I once was seemed to light up in your presence, and all that I felt otherwise became mixed with sprinklings of smitten with you.

I never meant to cause you harm; nonetheless, when I met you, I was tangled up in bitterness and anger from a love past I had not let go of.

I won't share details of the pain I've lived with, the curse that I made, the guilt that I have carried every day praying it wasn't I who was responsible for so much sorrow. I made so many bad decisions. Foolishly, I gave away what I liked and respected most in myself. I once was a good and honorable man.

I was truly charmed by you and I wanted to make amends when I returned to the United States. I watched you from afar as you were already with Marvin. I didn't know what to say or do, so I said and did nothing. Then I met Big Jim, and being in his presence made it so easy to let my bitterness boil over again, and it did. But when he was away and my feelings like the water had a chance to simmer then settle, I realized that the hatred and jealousy I had wrapped around my body like a poisonous serpent had left its venom in me, and if I were to make anything out of the life I had left to live, it was time to release what was destroying me, but I didn't know how and I waited for some sort of sign. Then I overheard a conversation that Big Jim was having with this so-called vet, and something snapped.

Maybe I wanted to impress you, or I was seeking redemption. Either way, I became determined to protect what you love. And when I did something good for good's sake, for the first time in years I thought I still might have a chance, not with you, not with Lillya, but with myself. After I knew Bess was safe, I got up on our best horse and I rode until I made myself sick. When I got off the horse, I began to heave. I threw up everything inside of me, even the venom and the hatred that were stuck to the walls of my belly.

On my way home, I found a creek. Its waters were almost as blue as your eyes and I jumped in it and I soaked until all the bile in my body was washed clean.

I'm not certain what is next. I will return to France and see if any pieces of me are left in the bushes or under the trees. Perhaps what is good in me is waiting for me to come home.

I wanted you to hear the truth. I only hope you can find forgiveness in your heart. I am sorry!

Sincerely,

Hervé Laurent Fluery

EPILOGUE

THIS WAS THE SHOWDOWN, the day I had been waiting for. Bess and Emily were about to get reacquainted. I chewed nervously on my fingertips like a little girl, half waiting for Mme Strachkov to reprimand me. Still, after last night I felt fresh and clear. No more mysteries to be solved except the one today. I touched the emerald brooch I'd put on before I left my room. I could hear my mother's distinctive laugh and feel Lillya's joyful spirit when I looked down at the brooch. "They are here with us today," I said, and I touched the brooch again, hoping they could feel me, too.

Bess had slept well, Roman reported, but Harsita had been up with Emily most of the night.

I glanced out into my garden, looking for a sign that all would go well. Then I went to the cemetery to talk to Spade and Vladimir. I saw that Bella had beaten me there.

"You've made quite the life for yourself, Donatalia," she said. "You should be proud. You came with nothing and now look at all you have. I'm not just talking about money or jewels."

"Yes, I have Marvin, you, your daughters, our extended family, and even Polly. For all my trials, God has blessed me with good fortune." We both smiled. "I can't stay long. I have to visit the animals again to make certain everyone is ready."

"What do you want from this day?" Bella asked as I was about to leave.

"For everyone to have peace and for these animals that I love to rediscover friendship and to live out their days in happiness, without fear or pressure. Today, the elephants, nature, and God will have their way and it will be what it is. I've done all that I can." I could almost hear Irina in my words.

"Thank you. It's good to know," Bella replied. I left to tend to business at hand.

I brought each of the elephants some bananas and apples and explained to them, as best I could, what was going to happen.

Emily was the wild card. No one knew how she would react. "Being cooped up, chained, and confined to a very small space had to affect her psychologically," I reminded Harsita and Marvin and later Kyle and Roman. But Bess had healed Emily once before, and if I had been a gambler—which, in a way, I was—I would bet that she could do it again. I believed that Bess would help Emily and together they would find happiness. But still in the pit of my stomach the aching question remained: *What if I am wrong?*

We all stood by the side of the fence. "Well, you did it, and if it doesn't work out today, there's always tomorrow," Henri said, trying to display an optimistic attitude, though it sounded a little dark to me. "You have the stall on the other side of the pasture, just in case they aren't simpatico immediately. Some things happen in their own time." I knew what he was saying and that he had the best of intentions. I hoped he was mistaken, though, and we wouldn't need the other stall.

At eleven o'clock sharp, Roman put Bess out into the pasture. She ambled out and immediately tucked in cheerfully to some newly grown grass. "She hasn't had a day off in years," I said, smiling at Henri. "This must seem like a vacation to her—only instead of lazing around drinking martinis, she's lazing around being fed fruits and berries."

"We're as ready as we're going to be," Harsita said when I checked in with him, and I walked back to where the others were standing.

I felt like an anxious gambler at a horse race, only here we had two elephants, leaving from two different gates, taking an undefined course to an unknown finish line. On the other side of the fence, Harsita walked Emily out with a harness to guide her first moves. Then he gently removed it. The hair on my arms stood at attention.

In the distance, Emily heard an elephant call. I couldn't tell if she knew it was Bess, but she perked up her big ears. Then Bess came into view. Emily let out a loud, primal cry and charged at Bess and Bess in turn charged at her.

I grabbed Marvin's hand so hard he flinched. I couldn't take my eyes off the elephants. Their tusks were in the air as they charged toward each other. They were moving so fast, it looked as if they'd trample or kill anything in their path. There was nothing I could do to stop them.

Almost to their marks, I closed one eye and squeezed Marvin's hand even tighter. I could have broken it and I wouldn't have known. "Please, God!" I said under my breath. I didn't want to watch my dream turn to dust, blood, and hide. With my one eye barely open, I saw Emily and Bess plant their combined eight legs firmly. Like two giant trucks slamming on their brakes, they came to a screeching halt. No one said a word.

Slowly I opened both eyes. Serenity filled the air and dissipated the fear. Everyone present was aware that we had witnessed a scene worth every day, hour, minute, diamond, ruby, sapphire, and emerald that it had cost and I silently thanked Hervé too for regaining his humanity when it really counted.

Each elephant had her trunk and tail wrapped around the other's, and they were nuzzling and making noises. It seemed like they would never let go. *I will make certain you are never separated again,* I said silently to myself. *Till death do you part.*

Then I remembered the promise I had made to Marvin. *When the soybeans and peanuts flourish on the farm and Emily and Bess are reunited once again, then I might say, "Yes."*

Marvin had been waiting for years, patient with me in every way. He shouldn't have to wait any longer. I turned to look at him and asked, "Marvin, will you marry me?"

Oh, the look of shock on his face! But after all these years, he smiled and said, "If we can find a priest who will marry us with these two elephants and all our friends."

"What are you saying?"

Bella looked at me before Marvin had a chance to answer. "He's saying, let's do it today. He wants to marry you this afternoon."

Just at that moment, Harsita and Roman came running to us.

"Could you believe it?" Harsita said, trying to catch his breath.

"Have you ever witnessed anything more beautiful?" Roman chimed in.

"Do you boys have plans for later today?" Marvin asked.

"Of course not," they said almost in unison.

"Well, you do now. Harsita, will you be my best man?"

Harsita answered by giving Marvin a giant hug; me, a big kiss on the cheek.

"Henri, Patrice, we would be honored if you'd stay."

"We wouldn't miss a second of this day," Henri said.

"It's all been so exciting," Patrice chimed in.

Then I looked at Bella and I took her hand. "You've been my dearest friend all these years. Perhaps this is why you returned to us when you did. Will you be my matron of honor?

"I'm marrying Marvin," I said out loud, as if to make it more real. Then I looked out at the pasture and admired Emily and Bess. I was quite content.

"Scarlett, will you be my flower girl?" Bella explained to her what a flower girl actually did.

"Kyle Jr., will you do us the honor of holding the rings?"

Before leaving to get ready for what had already been an incredibly big day, I went once more to see the elephants. "I'm going to have to tell Spade the new ending to our story," I said to Emily. "Vladimir will be so happy to know you are back with us. I'm sorry he had to let you go, but you're safe now and I won't let anyone ever hurt you again. But now I have to go get ready for my wedding."

I asked Polly and Ben if they would join us. It had been more than twenty-five years since we first met. They represented a part of me that few had ever seen or known: the insecure Russian girl who had lost her life, her family, and home, the one Irina had breathed life into until she found her truest self, the one Mary Bradley had comforted as a child.

❋ ❋ ❋

AT FIVE, WE MET outside next to my garden. Bella had picked out a flowing lavender dress for me and she wore navy blue. Scarlett had on a purple dress and she insisted on wearing a scarlet ribbon in her hair. Kyle Jr. wore a gray suit that made him look like a miniature of his father. Marvin, in deep charcoal gray, looked extremely dapper. Harsita, never one to dress up, wore the suit he'd bought in New York. Ben wore his old chauffeur tuxedo, and Polly, in the middle of fixing our dinner, had on her favorite flowered apron and a simple but pretty yellow dress.

Kyle and Ann Marie had been very busy in the hours since the reunion of Emily and Bess. They immediately called a judge we knew from our circus days and asked him to officiate. Marvin took out the ring that he had been saving in his sock drawer for years, and Bella gave us a most generous gift.

"I think Vladimir would want Marvin and you to have this. We had many happy years of marriage and I know that's what he would want for you. Besides, you don't have time to shop and I had this tucked away in my closet." Then she placed Vladimir's grandfather's wedding band in the palm of my hand. "He was a larger man than my Vladimir and he had big, thick hands, I was told, so I think it should fit your taller, thinner Marvin."

Ann Marie approached me with a fresh bouquet of yellow daylilies, two white trumpet lilies that she accented with purple iris, and dark purplish-red blanket flowers tipped with bright golden yellow. She filled it out with baby's breath and a little honeysuckle draping from the sides. "I feel like a real June bride-to-be," I said.

"You are," she answered.

Bella, Kyle—who would give me away; Scarlett and Kyle Jr. were so excited, they couldn't stand still—Ann Marie, Roman, Henri, Patrice, Polly, Ben, and the judge all waited for instructions. Kyle and I stepped out of the house together and started walking toward what had become our little family plot. The others followed. I had decided that I wanted the spirit of Irina, Spade, and Vladimir to be close by.

As we got closer, I noticed that Harsita was missing. He must have forgotten something, I thought. But when we got to the cemetery, I understood where he had gone. Standing next to him, in the spot where we would marry, were Emily and Bess.

We all took our places. Scarlett swam down the makeshift wedding aisle with Ann Marie holding her hand, strewing petals everywhere. Kyle Jr. walked with pride, knowing he was the one responsible for the rings. Then Kyle left me at Marvin's side, with Bella next to me. The judge said only what he deemed necessary to make our union legal and prompted us when it was time to speak what was in our hearts.

I took out a piece of paper on which I had written my vows. "You have supported me and stayed by my side when many a man would have walked away. You are the greatest gift God has given me and it is my one desire now and in the years to come, that I remain worthy of the love you so generously have bestowed upon me. We have witnessed and shared joy and pain, hardship and sorrow, good times and happiness. Today, in front of our extended family and close friends, I vow that I will honor and nurture this love we have been given. I promise to never take it for granted, for you are my partner, my love, and my best friend."

Emily trumpeted as if to shout hallelujah, making the judge smile. "Thank you, Donatalia. Marvin, what say ye?"

"Donatalia, my Donatella, you know I have loved you for years. You started out as my confidante and then I realized that my life would have so much less meaning if you were not a part of it. Your psychic intuitions, the way you still dance when no one is looking—you are my exotic flower who fertilizes my passion and dreams, the one ingredient that means more to me than any other.

"I too will strive to continue to earn the love you so freely give me and promise always to respect our union and all that happens between us. Consider me your humble servant in this life and the next, knowing I will love you always."

We were just about to kiss when three hummingbirds appeared and circled above our heads, as if there were a pot of honeysuckle. Then, as quickly as they came, they flew away.

Marvin and I kissed, and everyone cheered and shouted congratulations. Emily and Bess intertwined their trunks, as if they'd taken vows too. Before we went back to the house for the lavish dinner Polly had so quickly put together, I asked Marvin if we could make a detour. "I need to visit Irina."

"Thank you for asking me to come along," Marvin said.

"Of course, husband. Who else would go with me to ask her for her blessing?"

In truth, I knew I already had it, but I did need to pay my respects.

Dear Irina, I silently said,

Today I married my Colonel Butler and I think we will be as happy as you were. I know I've said this before, but once again, I am so grateful. You saved my life when I thought that it was over. You showed me how to believe in myself, and I will never be able to say a big enough thank you for giving me the gift of me.

We brought Emily and Bess home. Maybe tomorrow I'll bring them for a visit so you can officially meet them. Well, maybe not tomorrow—Marvin and I might have other plans—but soon. I asked my friends to go into Savannah and buy caviar so that tonight we could honor you, my father, and mother, Colonel Butler, and even Mme Strachkov, my friend Vladimir, and his parents. What a journey I am on! Well, I can see Marvin's ready to go up to the house, so we'll be on our way. I'll be back with Emily and Bess very soon.

"Are you ready, Marvin?" I asked.

"Yes, my queen," Marvin replied.

Just before we departed, I closed my eyes and I saw Bella and me as young women again, with her daughters at our side. Flying high above the big top was a banner much larger than the one that it replaced. Where the *Vronsky Family*

Circus had flown for generations, now—with a heart and spade on one side of it and a diamond and club on the other—it proclaimed *Circus of the Queens.*

I saw our lives, the legacy, the legends and myths, all intertwined and woven into those four words. My heart full of love and life, I smiled at Marvin. "Let's go back to the house," I said. "We have a celebration to attend."

THE END

A special thank you to Donatella,
for telling me her story
so I could share it with you.

Acknowledgments

MANY THANKS TO TYSON Cornell, Julia Callahan and all the people at Rare Bird; my early champion Miranda Ottewell and her husband Krister Swartz; book cover designer Alice Marsh-Elmer; and author photographer Marianna Newman. Thanks to Dianne Athey, Theresa Renaud, Gail Currey, Michelle Dennis, Patrice Kavanaugh, Lillian Neiman, Martine Bellen, Sandra Sokoloff, and Merle Saferstein for their input and love; to generous souls such as Daniel Nayeri, Suzie Hollander, Scott Ross, Neil Young, Pegi Young, Rhonda Novick, Stan Greene, my sister Laura Berger Crossland, and my brother in law, Danny. My angels: Julie Harris, Dove, and Zviki Govrin; the entire Welz family especially Peggy; my inspirations: Jonathan, Kaya, Sky and Solaura; Rachel, Isaac, and Max; Becky and Lennon; my husband Gary Welz who loves *The Circus of The Queens: The Fortune-Teller's Fate* as much as I do and is my biggest fan. In memory of my old friend Lew Fein who predicted this novel before I ever saw it, the always smiling Richard Harris, my cousin Alan Flatt who will promote my book in heaven, my mother Beatrice Berger who taught me how to love, my father Louis Berger who taught me how to live and who together gave me the strength and courage to fall and the confidence to get back up again.